HORSE OF THE YEAR

LINDA SHANTZ

HORSE OF THE YEAR

Cover Artwork by Linda Shantz

www.lindashantz.com

eBook edition ISBN: 978-1-990436-21-5

Paperback ISBN: 978-1-990436-20-8

Hardcover ISBN: 978-1-990436-22-2

ALSO BY LINDA SHANTZ

The Good Things Come Series:

Bright, Broken Things (*a prequel*)

Good Things Come (Book 1)

All The Little Things (Book 2)

All Good Things (Book 3)

This Good Thing (Book 4)

Merry Little Things (Book 5)

All The Best Things (Book 6)

Horse of the Year (Book 7)

Good Things Come Series: Books 1-3 Box Set

Good Things Come Collection: Books 1-5 Box set

Good Things Come Series: Books 4-6 Box Set

Buy direct from the author:

https://bit.ly/LindaShantzDirect

For updates and bonus chapters, sign up for Linda's newsletter at

https://www.lindashantz.com/writes

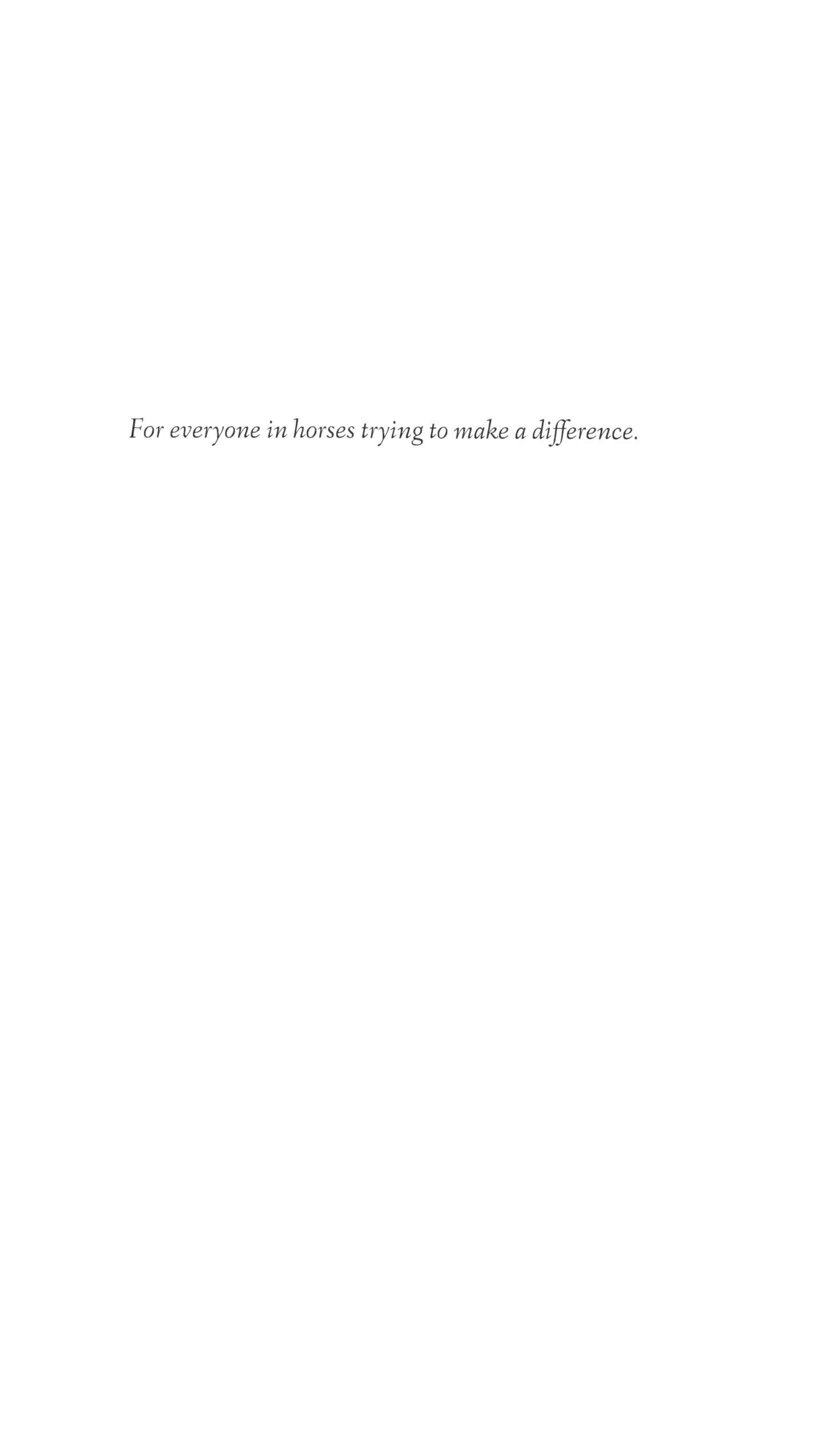

For everyone in horses trying to make a difference.

A NOTE TO THE READER

Horse Of The Year takes place immediately after the body of *All The Best Things,* but before its epilogue.

The Good Things Come Series is set in the world of North American Thoroughbred racing, which has its own vocabulary. If you're unfamiliar with this world, there's a glossary of terms at the end of the book. Feel free to point out any that I'm missing!

In 2023, following the death of Queen Elizabeth II in September 2022, the Queen's Plate returned to being called the King's Plate to reflect the new British Monarch, King Charles III, but this story takes place before the change came into cffcct.

CHAPTER ONE

It was as if she were part of a Munnings painting — a landscape of pale blues and greens, the horses various earth tones — except everything moved and breathed, nothing was static. Marshmallow clouds drifted, manes and tails flowed, riders' caps and jackets infused vibrant strokes of hue.

Coming up to the gallop, Liv's horse was eager like he'd never been before — his ears pricked, a solid weight on the bit with a serious case of the fear of missing out. As the first flight of horses took off before him, she adjusted her reins. *Don't you worry, Big Horse, you'll get yours too.*

Waiting for one more horse to go, she let him barge ahead, locked into her crossed lines, her weight balanced against his strength. It would be no contest if he decided to blow off her tenacious hold, but he contained the beast he was growing into because he was still, in his heart, a gentleman. Lucky for her.

The big chestnut beneath her fit in despite his North American background, and she, too, felt she'd found the place she was supposed to be. Like until now, her life had been good, but not quite right. Here, it all aligned — the supple stretching and contracting of her mount's powerful muscles resonating with their surroundings. This was where the Thoroughbred had originated, after all: Newmarket, England.

When she pulled Just Jay up at the end of the gallop, endorphins flooded her, every cell in her body alive from the thrill. She realized she was smiling, aware the slight ache in her face mimicked the one in her arms and core and legs. A good feeling. She probably had bugs in her teeth.

Her peace was short-lived.

"He looks brilliant, but he's not going to beat the horses over here," the man on the horse next to her said with a grin that dominated his face.

Gone were the days of feeling justified in ignoring such assaults on her solitude. Though, as assaults went, she could do — and had done — much worse than Rory Anderson.

It still took a second, like the click of a call being connected overseas, for her brain to adjust to his accent. She didn't have to concentrate as carefully as she had when she'd first encountered the Scottish head lad, but it had only been a few days. Liv had been tempted to let herself revert to her own native French Canadian accent — one she'd carefully schooled herself away from when she'd first attended high school in Ontario — just for the fun of it. It might have made for more of a fair fight when it came to comprehension, or lack thereof.

Liv controlled her mouth, relaxing her facial muscles so just the edges of her lips tipped upward. "You think I brought him across the pond to play tourist?"

"Why not?" Rory said, cheekiness lighting up his face. "It is beautiful here."

It certainly was, but she rolled her eyes. She hadn't decided if this was just his natural state, or if he was flirting and she was still too oblivious to see it. She was painfully slow picking up on such cues. Did it matter? He could flirt all he wanted, but nothing was going to come of it.

If Liv let herself overthink it — something she did far too well — she'd convince herself it was too much. Too ambitious. But every day Jay dragged her up the gallops, Liv's body taxed to its limit, he fed her confidence. *We belong. We're up for this challenge. We're here to prove them wrong.*

Walking back to the yard, she rode Jay with a light fist on the knot, the thick twist of leather filling her hand as the other rested on her thigh. Jay's head pulsed in time with his purposeful stride, the fiery lick of his mane lifting and falling with it. She pulled out her phone and took a short video, then posted it with only hashtags for a caption:

#Newmarket #JustJay #justdoit

Tuning out the conversation around her, lads and lasses tossing banter back and forth, she let herself blend into the landscape again.

Jay had no issue with the things most North American horses would find challenging about Newmarket: the undulating terrain, the long uphills. Liv had her sister Emilie to thank for that. This time last year Emilie had pulled Jay out of the paddock he'd been decorating since recuperating from an injury the previous winter. Em had thrown a saddle on him and started hacking him about the rolling hills of the farm at home in Canada. After weeks turned to months — those long walks becoming trot and gallop sets — Jay had emerged sounder and stronger than ever, convincing them he deserved another shot at racing.

Running him in the Dubai World Cup in March had been a lofty choice — and maybe a little insane — but the horses she conditioned were becoming known for thriving on crazy. Chique, the first to have Liv Lachance's name listed as trainer in the program, had brought her own crazy to the table. Just Jay

— a sane, gentle, giant — needed Liv to invite the madness of putting him on a plane to the Middle East after only two come-back races: one a small-time marathon stakes event in Ontario, the other not even a win, though the prize on the line had been significant. That madness had exposed his greatness, so why not come here? Newmarket, the land of his forebears, where the racehorses that would become known as the Thoroughbred had been bred, honed, and refined. Local stock crossed with the magic conjured in Dubai. Desert secrets breathed into the blood and bone of the Arabian stallions credited with being the founders of the breed.

Now, on this hallowed ground, they'd chase the next honour. She'd thought Dubai was the pinnacle, but while the experience and massive purse had been humbling, their target here was all about prestige.

Ascot, where royalty presided.

After putting Jay back in his box, Liv rode out on some of the other horses in the yard to help. In return, she received a mix of gratitude and suspicion. The lads and lasses didn't quite know what to think of her, this reserved North American trainer who worked alongside them. Maybe trainers in the UK only watched the gallops in their Land Rovers, like in Dick Francis novels.

Rory seemed the only one who rolled with it, regularly poking her with his questions. He stood outside the door of the box as she picked Jay's feet once all the horses had been trained, his arms crossed. Why wasn't he doing his own work? Maybe her willingness to help gave him too much free time.

"Do you think you're doing this horse justice, putting a rider on him who doesn't know the course? Someone who hasn't a clue how things are done over here?"

She met Rory's eyes briefly before asking for the next foot. "I think given the choice of a mediocre British jock versus one of the top riders in North America, it's only logical to go with the latter."

His lips twisted, eyes alight. "I think you might find you'd have the option of some of the less mediocre riders. Wouldn't have anything to do with your rider being married to you, would it?"

It didn't, actually. Hadn't she given Nate Miller the mount on the horse she'd dreamed would win her the Queen's Plate because it was the right thing to do? She wasn't sure they'd even been friends back when Chique had started her career. Cautious allies, maybe, pointedly avoiding the threat of feelings. Their status may have changed — significantly — but her pragmatism had not.

"Nate's been on the horse for every start. Gallops him daily at home," she responded. "If I'm not riding myself, there's no one I trust more."

"Ah, but there's what should really happen. It should be you."

Liv tried to keep her smile benign when his comment brought out that latent longing in her heart. She loved the animals regardless of her role, and enjoyed training, but never would it call to her like riding races — and now and then she let her mind play with that idea. Imagine it. Run off with it.

Who she was — who she had been — was not a secret. The injury that had interrupted her vocation as a jockey had not been career-ending, but circumstances had stepped in to divert her focus. She'd never intended for it to be forever. But as tempting as it would be to step in, to say she'd ridden at Ascot — because what would make this adventure even more amazing than getting to ride over that course — she couldn't do that to Nate. He'd won with Jay in Dubai. He deserved to be up on Saturday.

"Maybe next year," was all she said.

Maybe by next year Roger, the trainer for whom she'd taken over last fall, would decide it was time to come back.

Or maybe by next year they'd find a new trainer, someone more qualified than her.

Next year, Léa, the filly waiting in the wings on whom Liv's future dreams rested, would be two. And Liv would ride Léa. That was just how it had to be.

"They could invite me to ride in the Shergar Cup," she offered. Had she watched the international jockey challenge wondering if one day she could be there, a Canadian representative on the women's team? Of course she had. "Next year."

Thankfully, Rory wandered away to do something more important than interrupt her time with Jay. Because while galloping was the rush, grooming the big horse and catering to his legs afterward was the counterpoise. It soothed her. The old-time books called it "ministering," but she felt it benefited her as much as the horse, this quiet communing.

Today's Just Jay was transformed from the horse who had won the big race in Dubai, that version of the chestnut soft in comparison. Running her hands over every inch of him, she could feel his fitness as well as see it, the final dusting with her rub rag bringing out the rich copper sheen of his coat. He was lean, his body cut to perfection. She understood now, that before this, she'd been easy on him, too cautious. Afraid to break him.

They're babied these days.

The voice of her mentor, Geai Doucet, flowed clearly into her mind. He'd been gone four years, but in moments like this she felt him as close as the delicate medallion he'd once given her — always tucked safely under her shirt, her hand automatically touching it through the fabric. It came with the pang of loss, but more often these days it bolstered her, making her want to be a trainer he'd be proud of.

Was the way they trained horses in North America really responsible for so many of them falling apart, and not how they were bred, as Geai had suggested? Liv didn't think it was that simple — there were too many variables — but if there was a way to do things better, she owed the horses, and the horse-woman Geai had molded her to be, to consider that piece of the puzzle.

She left the stall reluctantly, Jay poking his head over the half-door like a kid's pony, hoping for one last treat. Obligingly, Liv dug into her pocket for the roll of candy. Polo mints, of course. They were in England, after all. She'd read her pony books. Liv tapped Jay lightly between the nostrils as he inhaled the mint, softer than the candies they bought at the bulk store in Canada. English mints, to be exact, which made her wonder why the pony girls didn't feed those.

"Maybe tonight you'll let me buy you a drink to thank you for your help."

Liv was so wrapped up in her horse, she jumped at the sound of Rory's voice. He wore that usual grin, sparked with mischief.

She turned from Jay and held up her left hand to give Rory a royal wave — which was more of an obvious gesture to show him that she still wore the same white-gold band she'd had on each day — no longer hidden under riding gloves, its accompanying diamond sparkling in the sun. Liv had balked about wearing a ring after Nate had proposed, worried, because riding horses, broken fingers were a real possibility and it might have to be cut off if that happened. But here especially, it was an asset. Not that a wedding ring put off every man.

"Or, maybe not," she said, grinning back before walking away, tossing a light, "See you later!" over her shoulder.

Another great thing about this place? The commute, a short walk to her accommodations in the centuries-old town. It gave her time to think — as if she didn't have enough of that right now.

Since Jay's win in Dubai, it had been on her mind to come here, but it hadn't been a snap decision. They could have stayed on their home continent, popped into tracks across North America for the big purses; taken him back to California, where he'd been injured, like there was redemption to be had.

But Roger Cloutier, who had trained her father's horses before Liv had taken over late last year, had left her with words that continuously replayed in her head. *This horse will take you places.*

She might never have a horse like this again, so if Jay was up to it, so was she. Seize the day. Go big or go home. Insert cliché of choice here. *If you don't take risks, you don't drink champagne.*

And Jay seemed to love the adventure as much as Liv did. Nothing ruffled him. It was easy to feed off his confidence. Doubt might creep in when she was back in the flat she'd rented for the duration of her stay, its quiet corners calling her out, but as soon as she was on the big chestnut again, they fled like so many birds scattered by a playful dog.

She already asked herself the question: what next? But she had less choice in that than she'd like. Because after winning in Dubai, negotiations had begun with a stud farm in Kentucky, and any syndicate was going to demand he run in the Breeders' Cup Classic to cement his appeal as a stallion. Not exactly a hardship — how could she complain about finally having a horse for the Breeders' Cup? But there would be no chasing other whims, like the Prix de l'Arc de Triomphe in France. She'd have to save that one for another superstar, should she be favoured with such a horse again. All the more reason to cherish this experience.

It hadn't really been a surprise she'd fallen in love with this place, had it? She'd felt as if she'd been born with the innate predisposition, nurtured by reading too many of those Dick Francis novels as a teen. Dubai had been fun, but when it was over, she'd been ready to leave. Newmarket? She'd stay here forever.

Liv loved how they did things here. She'd never be able to train horses this way at home. And after this race, the syndication — a lucrative deal that would see Just Jay stand as a stallion at a fancy Kentucky farm next year — would fall into place. And with that, even before Jay retired, she would lose a portion of her control. She had to accept that, but couldn't deny it concerned her.

As she unlocked the flat's door, the ring of her phone interrupted her rumination, and she pulled the device from her pocket to check the caller. Her father. Liv's heart catapulted out of its steady rhythm.

"Papa?" she answered, vocal cords tight.

"Everything is fine," he said quickly, tone soothing, clearly catching her worry. "How are you doing?"

"Great," she said, dropping onto the couch now that he'd assuaged her fears. "Jay's training brilliantly."

She gushed briefly about her experience so far. Her father wasn't concerned with social media, so wouldn't see the photos and video she shared on Instagram. Then she paused, waiting for him to get to the reason for his call. Probably just to share travel plans for the race — Liv hoped he wasn't going to tell her he and her mother couldn't make it.

"I've been talking with Triumph," he began. *The farm heading the syndicate for Jay.* "They're pushing to finalize the agreement before the weekend."

"Of course they are," she said. "Because if he wins, they'll have to fork out that much more, won't they?"

"There's something else, Olivia."

No one but her parents used her full given name — except Nate when he dropped it into a song — and it made Liv sit up.

"After the King George IV and Queen Elizabeth, they're pushing to send Jay to an American trainer."

Someone may as well have slammed her in the chest.

"To take him to the Breeders' Cup." Her voice was flat. Because she was good enough to get the horse this far, but too inexperienced to win the Classic? Except she was sure it wasn't her inexperience they were afraid of. It was her fascination with less conventional ways of doing things, running off on little side trips when there were perfectly fine races on home soil.

"I'm not prepared to close the deal before Saturday," her father stated.

Liv exhaled, but it only relieved some of the strain. Because his *but,* however unspoken, rang loud and clear.

Her father had never verbalized pressure. He knew horses, knew racing. *Anything can happen.* But this news shifted the stakes.

Winning on Saturday would go miles toward improving the argument that Jay should stay with her. If he came up short, it was completely possible that if her father refused this condition, they might lose the deal.

No one could ever accuse Claude Lachance of being only about money. He legitimately cared about the horses and what was best for them. But they were talking millions here, funds they could invest back into the farm that would make an enormous difference for a small operation like her father's Triple Stripe Stables.

"I know you'll do whatever you feel is right," she said into the silence that had stretched over the ocean.

"Let's wait until Saturday and see what happens."

"Thanks for calling, Papa."

Liv disconnected, a heaviness replacing the levity she'd felt earlier. She was grateful her father had never been one to keep things from her, but she wasn't telling Nate. He needed to go into the race expecting to be successful, not *needing* to be because something huge depended on it.

The real world had caught up with her. She'd feared losing control, but she hadn't thought it might mean losing Jay completely.

CHAPTER TWO

Nate showed up at five AM, because that's when he and Liv always arrived at the track. She was that kind of trainer; or maybe it was more that she'd never really accepted she was the trainer at all and still acted like that horse-girl owner's daughter he'd first gotten to know five years ago, back when she'd just finished her third year of vet school.

That spring, they'd both galloped for Triple Stripe's private trainer, Roger Cloutier, once her father's horses were back from wintering in Florida. But she'd been there as early as the grooms, insisting on being the one to care for her favourite, Claire — just like she'd insisted on starting the filly the previous September, when that was the job she'd hired Nate to do. Like a normal exercise rider, in those days Nate rarely got there before five-thirty, ready for his first mount to go out when the track opened at six. So now, like then, he could have stayed in bed another forty-five minutes, if bed was a place he wanted to be. Which it was not, at the moment.

Jo, the assistant trainer, had been here since four-thirty, as had the two grooms, Michel and Sue, so even coming at five

Nate felt like a slacker. He called the ritual *'Morning'* to Jo as he walked past the first two stalls, which housed the horses she cared for on top of her other duties. Michel and his girlfriend, Sue, had four each, while the swing groom picked up the stable pony.

Or that's how it was supposed to go. Sue had the baby now, and there was no daycare on the Woodbine backstretch, so the kid was parked in a carrier in the tack room, Sue half-distracted — or mostly distracted — running around with a baby monitor receiver on her hip. Marie, the swing groom, was the godsend in the middle of this, filling in the cracks, doing whatever needed to be done. Sue should've been taking time off because the backstretch was no place to raise a baby, but she'd asked to stay. This was their dysfunctional track family now.

Before Nate reached the tack room, he heard the baby fussing, so he waved Sue off, ducking in and scooping the kid up.

"What's up Leo?"

He grinned at the baby's expression as he held Leo at arms' length, open-mouthed wonder replacing the scrunched-up face that had greeted him, then shifted the baby to his hip. The kid had Michel's dark hair and brown eyes, and Nate wondered whether he'd take after his father on the personality side too — though Michel had mellowed considerably with his new responsibility. Nate hadn't much liked the guy when they'd first met, but now Michel was a little less brash, a little more serious. Came with the territory, probably. Nate didn't expect to find that out himself. Liv was non-negotiable on having kids.

The same, ancient radio hung in the tack room's doorway, blaring the same, terrible pop music it always had. Jo's domain, Jo's music.

"Sorry, kid," Nate apologized, then began to sing along to a top-forty hit that had somehow infiltrated his brain. It would be stuck in his head for the rest of the morning until he purged it on the drive home.

Sue dashed in, the blonde ponytail that had surely started out tight slipping so strands fell loose around her face. She tossed the rub rag she was carrying over her shoulder and reached for the baby.

"Thanks, Nate. Michel has Cam ready to go for you. Marie's putting the bridle on Reba. Nicole's already up on Kiss."

"Great," he said, pressing on his helmet and grabbing his stick from the corner. He stepped onto the shed.

Can't Catch Me stalked around the corner next to Michel, and just the sight of the big bay colt made Nate tired. If there had been a choice in the matter, this would not be the horse he'd select for his first mount of the day.

He glanced at Michel when the groom brought the colt to a halt in front of him, the shadows created by the dim overhead lights accentuating Michel's sharp features and the darkness under his eyes. Nate checked over the tack, even though there was never anything wrong with it, because he wasn't about to give up the habit. By the look of him, Michel had been up half the night with the kid. There wouldn't be enough caffeine in the world to make up for that, so it wasn't impossible the groom might have missed some loose stitching on a stirrup leather or billet strap. Cam was enough of an adventure to gallop without a tack malfunction.

"Don't skimp on the leg up, Mike," he said once he gathered the lines and psyched himself for the launch.

Nate didn't wait for Marie and Nicole once he was on. Cam couldn't be trusted around the fillies, so the big colt trained alone. Somewhere to the east the sun was rising, but it struggled to do more than make the grey sky slightly less dull — the haze in the atmosphere unsettling, smoke from out west migrating to Ontario. With the poor air quality, a concern for horses and humans, he was glad they weren't racing today. Thankfully, the wildfires ravaging Alberta weren't anywhere close to his parents in Calgary, but it made him hurt for his home province, and reminded him of his fears that something was not quite right with his mom and dad.

Cam was an excellent distraction. The three-year-old required Nate's full attention both to keep him out of trouble and to hold him back from going too fast. Coming up to a race, Nate didn't want to be the one everyone blamed for messing up the colt's training schedule. In his last start, Cam had dead-heated for second in the Queen's Plate — the country's most famous race — and the first jewel of the Canadian Triple Crown. On Tuesday, Cam had a rematch with the Plate winner, Big Sensation, in the second jewel — the Prince of Wales Stakes. Nate knew Cam had it in him to beat that horse, he just hadn't figured out how to drag that ability out consistently.

On the walk back from the main track, he tried to nail down the mood even Cam hadn't been able to dislodge. *Admit it, Miller. It's resentment.*

He resented Michel and Sue bringing the kid to the backstretch, and it wasn't because of the logical argument that this was no place for a baby. He didn't want to admit how much he loved having Leo around, or be reminded almost daily of the one thing he'd given up by being with Liv.

He resented his brother Tim finally getting both his hockey career and his feelings for Liv's younger sister, Emilie, sorted out — because when Nate went back home at the end of the morning, it was to all that *happy,* making Liv's absence more obvious.

He resented Liv being in England with Jay, without him. Which wasn't fair, because it had to be this way. It was probably a good sign he missed her, counted the minutes until he'd see her again, but it didn't mean he was pleased about the arrangement.

Before he left the barn to get on the horses his agent had lined up for him to breeze, Nate took a moment, because without fail Cam sapped him and there was no energy drink potent enough to top him up. Nicole and Marie would get the rest of the Triple Stripe string out, while he did his job working horses for other trainers. Horses that, in most cases, he'd ride in races in the afternoons. Only sheer mind over matter got him to the next place, up on his next mount. Right now it all felt like going through the motions, but he'd been doing it long enough he hoped no one could tell.

At the end of the morning, he collapsed on the couch in the office and called overseas. Long distance charges were a business expense when Jo left him to update Liv on how the horses had trained.

"Where are you?" he asked, indistinct sounds on the other end of the line.

"Just got back to the flat after feeding," she said.

"What are you wearing?"

Her laugh was low — and very far away. "No, Miller."

"Fine," he grumbled, then asked instead, "How's the Big Horse?"

"Even better than yesterday." There was satisfaction in her tone, the assurance that this had been a good idea; her cheer directly proportional to his grumpiness. "How'd training go today?"

He updated her on the Woodbine string, one by one — from Cam giving him the usual hard time, to Trop, whose castration a couple of weeks ago seemed to be having the desired effect. The new gelding was more serious about his job and not trying to eat the hotwalker daily. Then Nate passed on reports on the ones Marie and Nicole rode. There was rarely anything new, but he was glad he had this excuse to speak with her. Liv probably could have gone days without conversing with him otherwise.

"How are the kids?" she asked.

Obviously, she meant Emilie and Tim. "Nauseating."

Liv laughed. "That's your fault."

"Is it really, though? I think this setup was a group effort."

"You might be right."

"It's like now that they're on the same page, you'd think they've been together all along. It took us years to figure it out."

"It did not," she protested.

He snorted. "I'm sorry? Three years anyway."

"But who's looking backwards?"

"That's my girl." He grinned at the phone. "Going to the pub tonight?"

"No," she said. "Much to Rory's chagrin."

He wondered if she realized how grateful he was that she didn't even try to toy with him, make him jealous. "We'll go when I'm there, just to say we did. I want to meet this Rory guy."

"You will. What's that book you love say? He's mostly harmless."

Ah, *The Hitchhiker's Guide to the Galaxy,* which also reminded Nate not to panic. This separation was temporary, and Liv was not tempted by the guy with the Scottish accent that would take most women out at the knees. "Like you know what harmless looks like."

"Hey!" She sounded mildly affronted. "Though you may be right, because that's probably what I thought of you."

"And look what happened."

"I knew you were high danger from the start."

He forgot he was in the office at the track, closing his eyes as his breath caught, because she'd done that subtle thing with her voice that once he would have thought she was totally unaware of — a rare raw note to her words. Given she was on the other side of the Atlantic at the moment, it was almost cruel. Could he head to the airport right now? *See you in eight hours.*

"Miller?" she said, pulling him back to reality.

He gave his head a shake, refocusing. "So what will you do tonight instead?"

"Read. It's been nice not to have distractions."

"I interfere with your reading, do I?"

"Often."

There it was again, with one simple statement. He had to force himself to stand, reach for the door. "Okay. I'd better go. I miss you."

"Miss you too, Miller. It won't be long."

She hung up first, and he listened to dead air for a beat before pulling the phone from his ear. She was eager to get back to her reading. He, on the other hand, faced the part of the day he hated: the part where he went back to the farm alone. Emilie and Tim didn't count. Their existence now as a couple nullified his ability to rely on either of them for companionship.

He needed to do what he could to prolong his departure, so he went looking for Jo.

"How's Liv?" Jo asked when he found her in the feed room, preparing the horses' lunch.

"Good. Here, let me do that." He picked up the bucket of feed and accepted the scoop Jo handed him. "What's our plan for Prince of Wales day?"

"You're bringing down the truck and trailer?" Jo asked, hands on hips, looking slightly as if she didn't know what to do next because Nate had disrupted her routine.

He nodded. "I'll bring it in the morning and catch a ride

down with Em and Tim. Are there silks down there, or do we have to take them?"

"I'll call today and check," she said.

The horses were rumbling, wondering what the holdup was. Nate called, "I'm coming!"

Michel flipped the feed tub hanging on the door as Nate approached with a full scoop at the ready; Cam's head popping over the gate then disappearing, as Michel unsnapped the screen to hang the tub in the corner of the stall. Nate wished the groom would go clean his halters or something instead of being helpful so this task would last a while longer — even if the horses appreciated the more efficient service. Michel followed him all the way down the line.

Once he returned the bucket to the feed room — *sure, now go clean your halters, Mike* — Nate picked up a rake. The grooms kept the area in front of their stalls neat because both Liv and Jo were insistent on it, but now that no horses were walking around, the sandy aisle needed its daily maintenance. If the job of levelling the dirt wasn't done each day, it became a rutted nightmare and fixing it was backbreaking. Michel hated the task, because nine times out of ten, it landed on him. Nate didn't mind doing it, maybe because he hardly ever got to anymore.

"Nice work, Miller," Michel quipped, rag in hand as he buffed a brass halter plate. "I don't see why you can't do this every day before you go to the jock's room."

"Where's the laser level, Mike?" Nate joked. "It's perfection."

Grabbing the fan rake, he strode to the far end to start the final back-and-forth touch of a herringbone pattern. When he finished, it really was a thing of beauty. He didn't want to ruin it, so he slipped outside and walked to the office across the lawn instead. Let someone else bear the guilt of being the first to leave footprints on the pristine surface.

Even climbing into the Porsche wasn't the same without Liv there to argue over who was going to drive home. Nate sat there trying to figure out what music he wanted and opted instead for the randomness of the local alternative station, afraid his own music would contribute to his funk.

When he was almost home, he stopped at Triple Shot Café. Faye Taylor's eyebrows, always threaded to perfection, lifted as she caught his arrival over the shoulder of a customer. As the man left, Nate nodded in passing.

"You look like you're feeling sorry for yourself," Faye said, the way one side of her lips crimped giving away her complete lack of sympathy. "What can I get you for that?"

If they hadn't once had a relationship that had ended in flames, Nate would have thought the comment suggestive. Now, though, Faye — Liv's best friend — was happily ensconced in a relationship with his best friend Will. Funny how things worked out.

"Surprise me," he suggested.

"Hmmm. We'll start with a cappuccino, that goes without saying." She began setting up the espresso machine. "What's it been, two days since Liv left? You already look like shit. How are you going to be by the end of the week?"

He smirked. "I can always count on you to give it to me straight."

She placed the white cup and saucer on the counter and picked out a butter tart, taking the time to microwave it briefly. "Better stick with the trusted and true in times like this."

He lifted the cappuccino and wandered to a nearby table — another tactic to *Not Go Home* — and she followed with the tart when it was ready, pulling out a chair to sit with him.

"To what do I owe this honour?" Two years after the fact,

the two of them were long past the antagonism of a fresh breakup, but the lack of a to-go cup and the extra care of heating the tart were gestures above and beyond.

"I can be nice," Faye said. "Liv's loving it over there, obviously. The photos she's posting are fabulous. You know, if you're into the whole international racehorse scene."

Liv toned down her excitement when she spoke to him, Nate was aware of that, but she hadn't felt the need to suppress her social media presence to spare him. He'd seen the images she shared on Instagram. Of course, it might be partly his fault. Way back when he'd just been an exercise rider and she'd been an apprentice jockey in the first few months of her career, he'd suggested she use the platform to maintain her visibility when she was laid up with a broken arm. She'd taken the advice — and kept the account active, even though her job description had changed.

"I don't know what your problem is," Faye continued. "It's not as if you're not going too."

"Used up my quota of sympathy, have I?" Nate tried not to inhale the butter tart, biting it in half, then tempered the bath of sweetness with a swallow of the cappuccino.

"It's best not to mope," Faye said. "Not a good look."

"You're right." He finished the pastry and drained the last of the drink, pushing back his chair. He needed to find something productive to keep him occupied. "You and Will coming to the Prince of Wales?"

Faye shook her head. "Tuesdays are always too busy here."

"Remind Will then for me I won't be at his place in the afternoon?" The trip to Fort Erie meant he'd miss their usual band get-together. He pulled a twenty from his pocket and tossed it onto the table.

"You don't have to —" Faye started.

"Save the free coffee for the time when I might need it."

Those eyebrows peaked again, this time with wryness. "You expect to be broke one day?"

"I ride racehorses for a living. It could happen." He grinned and headed for the door.

The effect of Faye's kick in the butt — along with the combined sugar and caffeine surge — didn't last long enough, Nate's spirits faltering before he made it to the house. This time of year was filled with too many bad memories. It really shouldn't surprise him that Liv being away was affecting him more than he'd expected. Layering on what had happened last summer triggered all the old memories. He'd thought they'd be facing it together this time, but couldn't blame Liv for not feeling it as acutely — because she was, after all, thousands of miles away.

CHAPTER THREE

Not every day was an oil painting. This one gave Liv a taste of the England everyone expected, though it had been the exception rather than the rule on her visit — grey, cool, and damp, the steady drizzle that beaded on the repellant surface of her Gore-Tex jacket soaking through in the parts where the weather-proofing had worn off. Today, the crew seemed more grateful for her help, though an air of gloominess pervaded. They'd all be anxious to get back to their homes — or the pub.

The weather was appropriate for her mood, the magic sadly absent that morning when she took Jay up the gallops. He still felt incredible, but it wasn't enough to loosen the extra weight Liv brought along. She should hang onto every moment, rain or not, knowing these could be the final days of her relationship with this horse, but Liv didn't have it in her today.

Jay tugged at his haynet as she rubbed in liniment, quick hands working from his knee to his ankle, the sharp smell of it stinging her nostrils. Once the alcohol evaporated off, Liv rolled on thick cottons then wound wide white flannel over them to trap the warmth. The bandages were as much about protecting those precious limbs as anything therapeutic. His legs remained flawless, cool and tight once the heat escaped when she removed the wraps each morning.

Liv straightened, a hand braced against Jay's shoulder for support, legs half-numb from kneeling in the bedding. Jay craned his neck, ducking his head to her torso, and she dug the Polo roll from the pocket of her jeans and pushed a candy to his muzzle. His whiskers tickled her skin as he whuffed it up.

After a quick once-over with a soft brush and a rub rag, she dressed him in a light sheet — or was it a rug? Was that term reserved for heavier blankets? Liv had caught on to most of the differences in vocabulary, but sometimes she still felt like a neophyte, afraid to get words wrong in case the locals laughed at her, as if she were speaking a foreign language.

"That's you done for the day, sir," she said, though she'd see him at feed time. *Evening stables,* they called it here, though they didn't serve the horses dinner until around six.

At least with the all-weather gallops, the tack wouldn't be hard to clean. She sorted through the equipment and attacked it with soap, water, and sponge.

"Let me take you to lunch."

Rory. His tenacity probably wasn't wrong. A friendly gesture. But today, she just wasn't in the mood to play this game. How many times could she say no without it becoming an insult?

"You have to eat, don't you?" he persisted.

That always sounded like a line to her, and she consciously tempered her hackles, releasing a long breath. Her first instinct was to say no, but maybe the best plan wasn't to sequester herself at the flat where she'd just dwell on what would happen, should Jay lose Saturday's race.

"Tell you what," she countered. "I'll take you. For showing my horse and me such hospitality." Her tongue wasn't really implanted in her cheek, and her tone shouldn't have been so wry, but she couldn't help it. It was a warning; a drawing of boundaries.

Rory's eyebrows rose before he shrugged, not without his cheeky grin. "If you insist."

Mostly harmless, she'd told Nate. But Liv wasn't letting her guard down, because it was too easy to give someone the wrong impression, even when in her mind that person should know better. She wanted to avoid the possibility, however remote, of finding herself in an awkward position having an awkward conversation. Liv had been there with Dean, Faye's brother. If Rory thought she was being too careful, that was fine. She wanted to be. No mixed signals. Would she ever be able to distinguish friendly from a come-on?

Lunch in a British pub probably fleshed out the authentic English experience, though it wasn't all that different from the pubs back home. Not that Liv frequented them, but the one in the small town near their farm was a pleasant spot to grab a bite to eat on those rare occasions she and Nate went out. She didn't think Nate would be too upset she was doing this without him. At least, no more upset than he already was about not being here with her from the start.

Dubai had been different. It had happened before the racing season at Woodbine began, so he'd been free to come along. Now he had commitments. Races to ride. A riding title to chase. He couldn't just disappear for a week like she had. Guilt crept into her conscience, not for the first time, that she was the one who got to have a working holiday in horse heaven.

"What'll you have to eat?" Rory asked. He'd seemed almost affronted when she said *no thanks* to a pint.

She scanned the menu quickly, sure she'd disappoint him again. "Just a salad, I think."

"We've already established you aren't riding in the race this weekend," he said wryly. "No need to be cautious. The fish and chips are excellent."

"It is tempting," Liv said, and it would be another tick mark for the authentic experience. "But my stomach's always unsettled after long flights. Maybe I'll have that a little later in the week."

Rory grinned like he'd won something. "We'll come back, then?"

She set the menu down and reached for her water, squeezing a lemon wedge into it. "When Nate's here, we'll have to. He'll have a pint with you." The corner of her lips twitched.

"Are you homesick?"

Liv tilted her head slightly, caught off guard by such a direct question. She didn't think that she was, but no harm in letting Rory believe that's what had her down today. It wasn't as if she was going to tell him the horse she'd come here with might not be hers to train for much longer. She didn't know Rory well enough to be sure he wouldn't share it. The potential for that tidbit to spread like wildfire was just a few taps of a phone keyboard away. Despite the ocean between the United Kingdom and North America, people here knew people there. The internet made the small world of horse racing even smaller.

"A little, maybe," she said. "It's wonderful here, but I wish Nate could've come for the whole time." No harm in keeping her relationship front and centre.

"I know what would cheer you up."

"Oh?" Liv said cautiously.

"A pal of mine has National Hunt Horses. Do you know how to jump?"

"Well, yeah," she said. "I practically grew up on the backs of show ponies, and I evented as a teenager. Would he let me ride something? School over hurdles? Whatever you call it."

She took a breath, aware she'd been rambling. "Is that possible?"

"You're a bit of an adrenaline junkie, aren't you?"

"You've obviously figured that out if you made the suggestion." Liv grinned. "This would be another one for the bucket list." Canada only had flat racing, so the only opportunity she'd ever had to go fast over fences had been the cross-country portion of a horse trial.

"I think I can arrange it." Rory had already polished off his burger, chasing it with a slug of his pint. "Though you know, most people go visit the Tower of London or Windsor Castle."

"I've never been most people," she replied, a straight response to his teasing. She wasn't trying to be funny. It was true.

"You were a decent jockey. Do you really want to go back to it?"

Liv quirked an eyebrow. What did he care?

He was probably just making conversation, and it was better than being hit on. Rory couldn't know the question niggled at her. She didn't need to be doing any soul searching right now. Or maybe she should be doing exactly that, when in a week her training career might look very different.

"I was respectable, I suppose," she said, then admitted, "I miss it."

"But the only time jockeys have power is the race, and you like to be in control."

This guy didn't even know her. Was she that transparent? It was still true, as much as she thought she'd learned to be less of a freak about it. "That's what I loved about riding. It's the ultimate control. I hate the moment I throw the jock up and all I can do is watch." She probably wasn't alone in that as a trainer, but few were physically capable of race riding like she was. They had to rely on others.

"Is it better or worse when the jockey is your husband?"

"I guess it's better. And I try not to be too hard on him." Her lips twisted.

Rory matched her wry grin. "It probably makes you the worst boss."

"It can. But he's good at reminding me I should know better."

There was no one else Liv would rather have on a horse, but she constantly had to suppress the conflict that crawled through her each time Nate went out there. When he was on the track, he went somewhere she couldn't follow. A place where he had to make decisions alone, because they could discuss strategy all they wanted, but never perfectly predict what might happen on the racetrack. Part of her felt it gave him something over her. They would never be equals.

Then there was the constant she both couldn't think about, and couldn't ignore: he was putting his neck on the line, the looming one-year anniversary of the accident that could have killed him a stark reminder.

She was glad when Rory redirected the conversation, quizzing her about North America — something with more straightforward answers. There were plenty of people in racing in Canada who had originally come from the UK.

"You don't know how good you've got it," she said. "Not galloping horses in circles every day."

"You don't know how good *you've* got it," Rory countered. "Better money, shorter hours."

That's what drew people like Rory to her continent. Liv was aware money wasn't something she'd ever had to worry about, though she liked to think she'd paid her own way with her father's horses, even with dropping out of vet school. Jay alone made up for it financially, though Liv wasn't sure her mother would ever completely let go of the disappointment of that abandoned university degree.

"I just wish we could train more like this at home," she said.

"And that's why you'll keep training, even though you love to ride. Because as a trainer, you can make those changes."

Could she, though? She and Nate had talked about it briefly after the Dubai World Cup, but once they'd returned to Woodbine, they'd carried on as they always had. It was easier to go with the flow than believe she could make a difference in a business so firmly entrenched in its ways.

Rory didn't waste time setting her up at his friend's yard, and the next day she found herself on a wiry grey horse, sleek and leggy, built to go for miles, taking hurdles in stride. What she'd told Rory about her experience over fences felt boastful now. The only jumping she'd done in years had been at a just for fun short course event a few weeks ago. She hoped her obsession with exercise gave her enough fitness to not look like a complete fool.

Doubt soon fell away, replaced by the rush; a sensation of flying as her mount soared over the schooling fences. Tomorrow she'd ache from the physical effort, despite the ibuprofen she swallowed when she was back at the flat, but it was worth it to forget her uneasiness for a few hours.

Sinking into the couch after a shower that had drained the tankless water heater, Liv closed her eyes, the calm of a thorough workout taking over her whole body. Life here felt like a fantasy, and part of her wanted to run away from reality, live in this story instead of her own. She was better cast as a side character, mucking and riding out in the background, instead of centre stage with a horse like Just Jay.

Maybe the syndicate manager was right. Why had anyone thought she was qualified for that job? Except, it had been expected of her — her whole life. She'd taken a detour, quitting school to become a jockey, but the course had veered back to her fated path of its own accord. Was there any point in trying to escape again?

She reached for her paperback, needing to get her head out of this traitorous line of thinking. How lucky was she to have these opportunities? Even if Jay went to someone else after this, she should be grateful to have had the experience at all.

And Rory was right. If she were only ever a jockey, she wouldn't be able to change a thing.

CHAPTER FOUR

Nate ran. Even though he'd worked a full morning's worth of horses. Even though he'd ridden every damn race on the card in the afternoon. Maybe if he could sleep, he'd be able to get his head sorted out. Running was supposed to help with that. So far, it hadn't, but he had hope for tonight.

The sun dipped below the horizon, muting the surrounding colours like someone had dropped a filter on a photo. It was dimmer in the trees, and he dashed through like something was chasing him. Something was — the mosquitoes, though they weren't as bad as they'd been a month ago.

It was getting too dark to see the horses clearly, but he thought he could make out Claire and her filly, Léa, thanks to the flashy white that decorated both mare and foal. He wouldn't bother them tonight, leaving them to their silent grazing with the others.

He didn't slow until he got to Chique's paddock near the front of the farm, next to the barn where she'd been born. He slipped through the boards and sauntered toward her. She left her companion to meet him, her low murmur matching his.

"I hate to be the one to tell you this, sweetheart, but you're getting fat."

She didn't care, bumping his hip with her strong upper lip to remind him where the peppermints were.

"This won't help, you know," he said, reaching into the pocket of his nylon shorts and handing her the white disc, soon demolished by her molars. She tipped her head up to blow a hot minty breath on his face, and he kissed her between the nostrils. When he retreated, she didn't follow, dropping her muzzle to the grass. She knew the routine. It wasn't as if she could come into the house with him to keep him company, though if invited, he'd bet she'd try.

He remembered coming to this farm — it would be six years, the end of next month — when Chique had been the dream in utero. The excitement had been palpable in Liv and Emilie, but Nate hadn't shared it, even if he'd understood it. The anticipation wasn't his to have. Chique soon stole his heart though, once she was on this side, starting with her dramatic entrance into the world. Still, he'd never imagined he'd become such a key player in her story, a tale that had taken them to Canada's most prestigious races. Now, she carried the next hopeful, and this time he was fully aware of entertaining the dream of it all. Not because he owned any part of that foal, but he expected to have a stake in its future.

The barn he left behind held a lot of memories. Until fairly recently he'd lived in the overhead apartment, which is why he'd been around the morning Chique's mom, Sotisse, had gone unexpectedly into labour — and why he'd been the one to help Liv when things had gone wrong.

When he'd proposed to Liv last fall it hadn't been a planned thing, where they'd live the last thing on his mind. They hadn't even figured it out when her parents announced they were moving back to Montreal, and offered him and Liv the house to share with her sister Emilie. Generous, but intimidating. Nate had grown up in a small, suburban bungalow, lived for a few months in a tack room on a farm outside Calgary, then moved to the one-bedroom apartment that came with the job here at Triple Stripe. Graduating to the big, modern house made him uneasy because he hadn't earned it. He felt like a squatter.

He reached the house, kicked off his shoes and peeled off his socks, then walked straight through the sunken living room to the patio doors, dragging his fingers through his damp hair. Emilie and his younger brother, Tim, were by the pool and their presence kept him from stripping off his sweaty running clothes. He wouldn't do that to Em, so he just peeled his drenched t-shirt over his head before he dove. He swam to the other end and back again, then pulled himself out, the water pouring off of him into a puddle at his feet. That was his energy, done.

Damn. A towel would have been good to grab first. He ruffled his hair half-heartedly and sat himself in a chair, dripping.

Tim lived in that apartment over the barn now. His brother had stayed at the house when he'd first come to visit because he'd been on crutches after knee surgery, so stairs hadn't been practical. Now that he'd officially relocated from their hometown, Calgary, to Toronto, he'd moved up there. It was temporary, Tim insisting he planned to get something in the city. Nate wasn't convinced it would happen, because Emilie was pretty tied to her life up here, but it wasn't Nate's job to figure out how they'd juggle their schedules if Tim followed through with that plan.

They weren't uncomfortable to be around, his brother and

Liv's sister; it was already like they'd been together for years instead of a few weeks. Affectionate, sure, but whatever they were or weren't doing physically, they did when no one was around — likely because Em was sympathetic to Tim's aversion to public displays of affection. Nate showed no such restraint with Liv anymore. Watching Tim reminded him of how Liv had been in the earliest days of their relationship, and he wondered if he recalled them accurately, or if his own history kept him from seeing it clearly. Honest answer was they'd both had issues to overcome. He, at least, might still be dealing with insecurity; worrying some slick guy with an accent was trying to pick her up over there. Not that Liv couldn't handle herself. Or that she'd give in. So what was his problem?

Emilie turned her head toward him, breaking off whatever she'd been saying to Tim, then rose and disappeared through the patio doors.

"Something I said?" Nate grinned at Tim. He hadn't noticed Holly, Emilie's black Lab, but the dog came over and plunked her head on his knee. The Labrador, at least, did not care that he was wet. Wet was one of Holly's favourite states. She was a Labrador, after all.

One corner of Tim's mouth crimped, the arch of his eyebrows a giveaway he wasn't sure he should find humour in this moment. "You okay?"

All Nate could do was laugh. Apparently he was not.

Emilie reappeared and dropped a dry towel into his lap, setting a bottle of beer on the small glass table next to him before going back to her lounger.

Great. Now he'd be drinking alone, too. Tim didn't drink and Nate wasn't going to question it, but Emilie had largely curtailed her own alcohol consumption since getting together with his brother. Again, it wasn't something Nate was going to judge, just so long as they didn't start judging him.

"Thanks, Em," he said, patting what was left of the water from his arms and legs before towel-drying his hair. He stood to drape the towel over the chair and finally reached for the beer when he was seated again. "You two coming to the Prince of Wales Tuesday?"

"Duh," Emilie said. "I booked the night off weeks ago."

"I'm glad I'll have you cheering for me again." Nate tipped the bottle to his lips.

"Too bad you weren't back on Reba for the Wonder Where," she said, speaking of the three-year-old filly, officially named She Sings. Emilie's favourite of the racehorses — except for maybe Just Jay.

Nate wasn't sure he'd been given a choice which of the two Triple Stripe starters he got to ride in the Queen's Plate. He'd been on Reba when she won the Canadian Oaks, but when his nemesis, Cam — Can't Catch Me — finished such a good second in the Plate Trial, it only made sense to run them both in the prestigious classic. It would have been fun if Liv had ridden one of them, and he didn't think it was exactly impossible that the stewards wouldn't let her at least ride horses she conditioned. But she was embracing her role as trainer, so she'd given apprentice Cory MacDonald the call on the filly after strongly suggesting Nate should be the one to ride the often rank colt. It made sense for Nate to stay with the one who would benefit the most from someone familiar. Neither horse had won, so with no possibility of a Triple Crown to be had for their barn this year, Reba had returned to all-female competition on Saturday, finding her way back to the winner's circle.

"It wouldn't have been fair to take Cory off the filly," Nate said. Though no one would have questioned it, him being married to the trainer and all. He'd watched the Wonder Where Stakes from the jock's room, because his relationship with Liv also prevented him from riding anyone else in the race. Rules were rules. He drained the bottle, which had probably gone down a little too quickly. "Time for bed." And maybe if he was lucky, for sleep.

"Good night, Nate," Emilie called as he yanked open the sliding glass door.

The main bedroom in this house was huge, and it seemed bigger still with Liv gone. He should have at least stolen Emilie's dog. After rinsing off the salt water in the shower, he decided to call his mom. It would delay climbing into that empty bed a little while longer.

When Connie Miller answered, she sounded breathless, as if she'd just run through the door, so his timing was right. She was just getting home from the ballroom dancing class she taught at church. Though his mother had a cell phone, she never used it. His parents still had the same old landline. The same old rotary phone. It was probably a collector's item.

"Nate! What a nice surprise."

Was she really ever surprised to talk to him, though? They talked regularly. "Just calling to say hi."

"I just got in. The ladies still always ask about you, you know."

Nate chuckled. His mom had regularly dragged him with her to those classes to be a partner because her students were almost always women. "Well, give them my best next time."

"How are Tim and Emilie? I'm so glad everything worked out for them."

"So am I."

"Did you talk to Liv today?"

"Yeah, of course."

"Is she having a good time? You must be excited about going."

It hit him now, why he'd never suspected there was

anything wrong between his parents — his mother had a way of directing the conversation, and by the time Nate asked how things were with her, she'd answer with a simple *everything's fine* and *I should let you go*. When Tim had been around he'd picked up on subtleties that raised suspicion, but now that Tim was here and not there, both he and Nate were in the dark.

"Oh, there's news!" she exclaimed. "Julie's pregnant."

"That's exciting," he said, sounding anything but. He wasn't sure how he was supposed to muster cheer for the pronouncement. Julie was his ex-girlfriend's older sister. The ex-girlfriend who'd dropped Nate to marry his brother. The ex-girlfriend who'd died last year in a car crash along with his brother. His feelings about all that would forever be complicated. "How's that going to work, then? With the twins?" Twins Cindy and Phil had left behind after their fatal accident. They were three now, and probably enough to manage on their own without a new baby to consider.

"I'll help when the baby comes. She's not due until February. We'll figure it out."

She sounded confident, but it still seemed like a lot.

Sure enough, before he could start digging any deeper, there it was:

"Well, I'm sure you're tired. I should let you go. Talk soon."

And they would. And it would be the same thing all over again.

He was tired, but the conversation with his mom wouldn't help him sleep. He wished he could call Liv, not to talk about his mom's news, because it would only make Liv uncomfortable, but just to hear her voice. She'd be in bed, though. He hoped she was sleeping better than he was.

Next to the car he drove — a Porsche 911 Carrera — the baby grand gracing the room they normally shared was the most extravagant thing he owned; Liv's wedding gift to him. It wasn't the best company, but it was better than no company at all, and not the first time in his life a piano felt like his only friend. He slid onto the glossy black bench.

For a moment, he only sat there, hands resting on his thighs. His eyes traveled around the too-big room, tastefully decorated with its reading corner, a walk-in closet and ensuite, sliding doors out to a balcony off the side of the house. An old song came to him — a flashback to one of his first nights in Toronto when he and his buddy, Will, had gone to a club for his birthday. Nate hadn't stayed long, leaving Will there while he bolted, Talking Heads' "Once In A Lifetime" chasing him out the door.

He'd had nothing then, and though at least now he had money in the bank, his beautiful wife was on the other side of the ocean, and this wasn't his house.

Same as it ever was.

Not really. This was pitiful. He'd have to stop by and see Faye again so she could slap him upside the head, knock some sense into him. His life was great.

He played nothing with lyrics because words only conjured up everything he was feeling, making it all worse. The guy who thought there was a song for everything, could not find a single one that would smooth over his mood. But not every song had words. Who knew one day he'd be grateful his piano teacher had made him do the Royal Conservatory grades?

He played until his fingers stumbled, doltish and clumsy on the smooth keys, the neurons in his brain no longer firing fast enough to elicit the notes in proper sequence. With a final discordant jolt he gave up, hands falling flat, the jarring tones fading away as he pushed himself around on the bench and stared balefully at a bed that had given him nothing but insomnia these last few nights.

Its queen-sized mattress and comfy pillows taunted him. Four more days till his flight to England. Maybe he'd be able to sleep on the plane.

CHAPTER FIVE

Liv set it aside. It wasn't as if she could do anything more than she was already doing to improve Jay's chances this weekend. Which meant accepting that if he didn't win, some other trainer's name would likely be next to his for the Breeders' Cup Classic.

She would not kick and scream, she would step aside with grace. The fantasy — the one where she hid out here in Newmarket and worked as a stable lass — needed to be set aside too. Regardless of what happened with Jay, she was still responsible for the rest of her father's small string in Canada.

Which was doing fine without her.

She'd watched the Woodbine livestream of Reba's race Sunday, pleased with the filly's winning effort, and especially happy for Cory MacDonald getting the first stake win of her career. The victory reminded Liv she had other nice horses besides Jay, though none of them were so good someone might want to take them away from her.

Can't Catch Me, however, was a horse she might not miss.

An ocean away, on the screen of her laptop, Liv watched Jo

put the tack on the big three-year-old in the saddling enclosure at Fort Erie Racetrack. The colt had so far been on the fringes this year. He frustrated her. There was no question Cam had talent, but he had yet to show his full potential. Cam always trained like he had something to prove, but the chip on his shoulder got in the way of doing just that. Or maybe he actually wasn't as good as Liv wanted to think. Just Jay had taught her not to make rash judgements, though, especially as Cam was by the same stallion. He was still maturing. Jay hadn't even made a start at the same point in his life.

The Prince of Wales was the second jewel in the Canadian Triple Crown. Fort Erie, on the US-Canadian border, was an hour and a half jaunt from Woodbine. Cam had never shipped to run, so that was the first question he had to answer. Could his baby brain deal with it?

Jo had agreed sending along Paz, their stable pony, was a wise move, though it had the potential to backfire because Paz wasn't always the most positive of influences. Liv still laughed when she remembered the time Nate had used him to accompany her and Claire to the post one winter at Gulfstream, and the older gelding had somehow caught sight of the gargantuan Pegasus statue in the track's parking lot. He'd had a mini-meltdown, gawking and nearly slamming into Claire. Liv had never seen a racehorse even notice it. It was just one more thing in the concrete jungle that was Gulfstream Park. Claire had rolled her wall eyes at her frazzled escort and huffed in disgust when the starter's assistant finally relieved her of the older gelding's embarrassing presence.

Assessing Cam from only glimpses in the paddock was difficult. The post parade gave a slightly longer vantage, her charge number one in a ten-horse field. Cam looked keen. Confident. He wasn't giving Paz a hard time. So far, so good.

The camera cut briefly to him in the warmup before moving on to one of the other starters. Still behaving.

The gate was set in shadow — she could visualize it from past Prince of Wales editions more than see it on screen. Post position one meant Cam went in first and had to wait for the others to be loaded. Liv couldn't make out anything but dark shapes against the lighter framework of the metal barrier, but Cam was still in there, so she'd take that as a positive sign. She imagined Nate controlling his own energy, having Cam ready for the break but not exploding, with nowhere to go before the doors opened. Thinking about it, she forced herself to take a deep breath.

The camera view shifted to the front of the barrier. Liv leaned forward, straining her tired eyes, focusing on the inside stall. What was taking so long? The announcer's prolonged pause worsened the clench of her stomach. The wait was too long. Someone was acting up, but it was impossible to tell who. She turned the volume up, hoping somehow she'd hear what she couldn't see. No such luck.

Then finally, movement, the announcer's droning *They're off* as the horses leapt from the gate. All of them were just small dark forms in a monochromatic scene, but Liv trained her vision to the one on the rail she knew was Cam.

Nobody seemed to want the lead. It had been her biggest concern when she and Nate talked strategy. There wasn't an obvious pacesetter in the group, and Cam came from behind. He needed speed to run at for things to go his way.

Once the field skipped out of the chute, the picture was clearer, but she frowned when she realized it was Cam leading the way. *Not you, Miller.* There had to have been someone else who would set the fractions, didn't there? But Nate was an excellent judge of pace. The man had a clock in his head. She told herself not to worry.

When they hit the first quarter in a pedestrian time, Liv relaxed. They were letting him away with it, and Cam galloped, ears pricked as if he'd never imagined the joy of leading the pack. Maybe this was the key to unlocking the colt's best self, and tonight would be the breakout win he needed.

Nate kept him just a length on top, holding him there, turning in a turtle-pace half-mile time. She didn't like that it looked as if he was way off the rail, leaving all that room to his inside, but riding Cam, there was a balance between giving him direction and accepting you didn't always get what you wanted. She wasn't allowed to judge when she wasn't on the horse herself, as Nate liked to remind her. Especially not from the other side of the ocean, watching an already dim scene on a small laptop screen.

When Cam rounded the final turn, she could see exactly how far wide he was — and that the Plate-winning favourite, Big Sensation, rolled freely along the rail, saving valuable ground. No worries — because Nate saw it, too. He angled Cam in, and Liv just prayed it didn't go awry. With their colt, you never knew.

At first, Cam wasn't impressed. His head went up and he gave a lash with his generous tail. His attitude changed as Big Sensation slipped stealthily up, sneaking past, stealing the lead. Cam flattened, sights set on his moving target. Nate had switched his stick to his left hand in what might become a valiant but vain attempt to control the colt's trajectory. Did it really surprise her when Cam ended up so close to his foe it sent her heart into her throat? *Get him off, Miller, get him off!*

He did. It probably cost him the race, but both horses crossed the wire safely, Big Sensation the winner by a neck, one triumph away from becoming the next Canadian Triple Crown winner.

Liv watched them gallop out, then waited for the replays. It was becoming increasingly difficult to keep her eyes open. She'd watch them again tomorrow when she was more awake, but she knew Nate would call. She closed the laptop after studying the head-on view, which showed just how scary that near-incident had been. Really, if Nate had pushed to win that one he'd have seriously risked a spill. It had been close enough as it was.

Staying seated she was sure she'd drift off, so she wandered around the flat as she waited. It was modest but clean, and it made her think of Saratoga; how locals moved out of their homes for the duration of the meet, to rent to the backstretch community and tourists. Newmarket was an hour and a half from Ascot, but Rory wasn't wrong, it would be a wonderful vacation. To take in the horses and history, traveling to the races, using this as base camp for other excursions.

They'd stayed in a four-star hotel in Dubai, and the atmosphere had been quite different there, but it was so far removed from their usual routine it had seemed like a holiday. Maybe she should write a memoir: *Seeing the World with the Big Horse.* The Arc would fit so nicely with that story. Instead, it would be Del Mar for Breeders' Cup — all going according to schedule, of course. For Jay anyway.

The phone vibrated in her hand, startling her even though she'd been expecting it. "Hey Miller. That was a little harrowing."

His laugh was energetic, still riding the wave of adrenaline. "A little."

"Glad you're okay. How's the horse?" she asked, tucking a leg underneath herself as she dropped to the couch.

He snorted. "Fine. Oblivious. Bouncing off the walls of the test barn right now, I bet. Maybe we should cut him, too."

She hesitated. "Maybe we should."

"You're serious."

"It's worth thinking about, isn't it? That could have gone badly out there tonight."

"We should probably sleep on it," he backtracked.

"Good idea," she agreed. "Drive carefully, okay? You sound tired." She could hear it in his voice, despite his post-race high.

"I'm going back to Woodbine with Jo in the truck. She'll drive. Letting Em and Tim take the Porsche and meet us there."

Liv laughed. "Ooh, who's driving? Did they have their first fight?"

She felt his chuckle, warm against her ear. "The true test of young love. Talk to you tomorrow."

After his voice was gone, she put the laptop away, crawling drowsily under the covers. His presence in the same bed was such a normal thing now it was easy to imagine him near, his arms around her.

She tried to think of the good things. Nate joining her on Friday, Ascot on Saturday. The honour and prestige of having a horse worthy of bringing here.

Thoughts of those who doubted her competence festered in her mind. Of course they were men, the members of the prospective syndicate, and of course they'd shared their concerns with her father instead of dealing directly with her. She'd struggled with her fair share of imposter syndrome in her life when she'd made the snap decision to quit vet school to ride, and when Geai's death had spiralled her into a debilitating slump. But this slight smothered the negative voices in her head, stoking her indignation, fuelling her determination.

The only problem was, on race day none of it would help her.

CHAPTER SIX

IN THE PICKUP, as they traveled with Cam from Fort Erie to their Toronto home base, Nate rehashed the race with Jo, then played it over and over in his head once they lapsed into silence. Oh well. It was Cam, he could only expect so much cooperation. But something whispered in his ear that he'd held back, that his nerve wasn't what it once had been. *Before.*

But the spill last summer at Saratoga hadn't been due to his or another rider's recklessness. His horse had literally died underneath him. No one truly ever got over that, did they? He'd put enough rides in between that event and the present to be over it, hadn't he? If he didn't believe that, he might as well give it up.

Once Cam was settled back into his stall at Woodbine, Nate crawled behind the seats of his Porsche, content to let Tim keep driving it — until they got back to the farm, at least. It was uncomfortable as hell in such cramped quarters, but the sound of the car's engine, the soft music from the stereo, and Tim and Emilie's muted conversation — touching, then receding from his consciousness — had a soothing effect.

"We're home." Tim's voice woke him.

Nate squinted at his brother with one eye, shielding his sight from the interior light, which seemed altogether too bright. "Home?" he croaked.

"Sleep in your car if you want," Tim said, his face disappearing, followed by a subtle jangle. "Keys are on the driver's seat."

I could just stay here. He had actually fallen asleep. Probably not the best idea, though. Nate shoved his way upright and retrieved the keys.

Emilie was in the kitchen, the kettle steaming on the counter top, a mug next to it. At her feet, Holly lay, tail thumping. When Nate slumped onto the bench of the breakfast nook, Holly jumped up, the steady wag of her tail making her body sway.

"Since when do you like tea, Em?" She was a cappuccino drinker. As were all of them, it seemed, since Faye had taken over the café.

"I don't," she said, unplugging the kettle then pouring water over the bag, holding the attached string to keep the tab from being dragged into the liquid. She poked the bag with a spoon before setting the cup in front of him.

"What is it?" he asked, staring into its depth suspiciously.

"Chamomile."

"Does that actually work?"

"I don't know. It's the thought that counts, maybe?"

"Placebo effect?"

"Report back to me tomorrow, okay?"

"Sure, Em."

"Sleep well," she called over her shoulder, Holly deserting him to follow her.

He peered into the mug again. *Here's hoping.*

Giving the tea a few minutes to brew, he flipped over his

phone. It was late, but it was two hours earlier in Calgary. Nate hit the dial icon in his contacts.

"Nate! Is everything okay?"

It was a fair reaction. They spoke regularly, but two nights in a row was out of the ordinary.

"Yeah, fine, Mom. Sorry. I just got back from Fort Erie. Late race. Too amped up to sleep yet, so thought I'd give you a call." It wasn't the kind of lie his mother would catch. Not that he thought he'd fall asleep as soon as his head hit the pillow.

"Oh, it was the..." She paused. "Prince of Wales race!" She sounded proud of herself for remembering. "How did it go?"

"Okay. We were second, only beaten a hair." He left out the details she wouldn't care to hear, like the near-wreck.

"Are you all right?"

He should have known better. His mother caught everything. Nate sighed, then admitted it. "Just — I don't know. Having trouble sleeping."

It surprised him when she laughed. He didn't find it funny.

"Me too. But I'm of an age where I'm told that's normal. When do you leave for England?"

She wasn't changing the topic on him, exactly. She was letting him know she understood, though he was also aware she'd steered their talk away from herself. Again.

"Thursday afternoon. I'll get into Heathrow around ten-thirty, their time."

He was too exhausted to have any influence on the conversation, so he let her carry it from there, content to hear the voice of someone he thought might be lonely, too — if his suspicions were right.

"I should let you go. You must be tired," his mom said, following the script. "I hope you can sleep tonight."

He was beyond tired, but his mind wouldn't shut down. If he wanted to have any hope of finding out what was happening in Calgary, the answer was obvious. He was going to have to go out there and corner each parent, one at a time.

But he was in no state to do that right now. He'd figure that out later. Like next week, after Jay's big race, when he and Liv were back here, and she was beside him instead of just a voice over too many miles.

Caffeine and adrenaline, that was what fueled him right now.

The verdict was still out on the tea. Nate had tried it again, like maybe it needed to accumulate in his system, but had yet to log a solid eight hours. Yeah, last night hadn't been the one. He was really banking on the flight over the Atlantic being the thing that finally knocked him out. *Just a few more hours.*

With time to kill after a busy morning before Tim took him to the airport, Nate slipped in with the mares and foals, immediately attracting the attention of the babies. Their mothers ignored him. The youngsters strode toward him with purpose, Claire's filly, Léa, leading the way.

The filly commanded respect from her peers much the way her mother did, without overt displays of aggression to assert her position. Even though at six months she was a gangly, hairy tufts springing from her ears, Léa was still a standout, her bold white markings a contrast to the dark bay base of her coat, even though it was bleached at the moment.

The foals demanded nothing but affection from him, because treats were meaningless at this age, so he scratched withers and laughed as they nuzzled his face with whiskery muzzles. When he wandered over to visit with the mares, they followed him in a line. Léa, of course, leading the way.

Claire accepted the peppermints he offered, and even allowed him to sneak some candies to her companions. It wouldn't be long before weaning began, the farm shifting to its next phase for late summer. The foals would learn to live without their mothers' comfort. The yearlings would start their training under saddle.

Dutifully escorting him back to the fence, the fillies peered after Nate as he crossed the alleyway between fields to look in on the colts. He didn't go in with them like he had with the girls. The boys weren't as polite.

Next on the tour were the yearlings, and like the foals, as soon as Nate ducked between the rails he was swarmed, poked by curious noses, wild manes sticking every which way over necks dotted with lumpy fly bites. He scratched itches and ran his eyes over legs, looking for injuries, but they all appeared clean-limbed. Then his eyes drifted to the loner, keeping her distance.

Fleur was a full sister to Chique and Feste — the promising colt they'd lost unexpectedly last summer. That recollection still tightened like a fist around Nate's heart. He wasn't disappointed they weren't planning to go to Saratoga this year. That's where it had happened — the colt's tragic death, the scary injury Nate had suffered in the spill. Events that had nearly torn him and Liv apart. He shook his head, clearing the memories from his mind. *Who's looking backwards?*

Breaking away from the hive of yearlings, he ambled toward the murky-coloured filly, trying to detach himself as he studied her. No chance. A layer of emotion was fused to this one, yet it was as if she wasn't connected to anyone.

Chique had been Nate's. For whatever reason, they had attached themselves to each other like siblings. They didn't always agree on everything, but there was a bond there that would never be broken.

Feste had been Liv's. She'd loved that colt with the same ferocity she loved Claire. Fleur had arrived amid the overriding turmoil of their lives. Nate didn't want to think the filly had been forgotten, but neither he nor Liv had claimed her.

It was time to make up for all that.

Except Fleur didn't seem to like him. Fair enough. She didn't know him yet. He could change that. Today, with Liv away and him feeling the void, seemed a good time to start.

Fleur stood her ground. She wasn't afraid of humans. That wasn't the issue. And the fillies, after following for a few steps, fell off as they realized his intent, like they were leery of Fleur. An interesting dynamic in the small herd. At the same age, Chique's companions had been wary of her, despite the fact she'd been the smallest of them. Chique had always been in the thick of it; in his face, warning the others to back off. Nate was hers. At the time, he'd been grateful to her for that possessiveness, because no one else had seemed to want him.

The solitary Fleur pressed her muzzle to his palm, scenting him in short huffs before leaving his hands to explore his arms. By the time Chique was this age, he'd had her eating peppermints. But he'd been around all the time in those days. Galloping at the track in the mornings, sure, but free in the afternoons to indulge his favourite yearling. He'd started when she'd been just a foal and Liv had asked him to keep an eye on her when Chique was still at her mother's side. With Liv and a two-year-old Claire off to Belmont Park, he'd readily agreed. Truth was, he'd already been paying the cheeky brat daily visits.

He pulled his eyes from Fleur's traveling nose, performing the same scan he'd done on the others. Her coat, the same smudgy-dark as both Chique and Feste, had a yellow tint from the sun, bringing out dapples along her barrel. She had her share of tiny bumps from the incessant flies. His gaze was drawn next by the two white hinds that looked as if she'd stepped in white paint halfway to her hocks — their mother,

Sotisse, had decorated this one with the most bling so far. Finally his gaze rested on the fronts, from her blue-grey feet to the long, sturdy black pistons.

Nate craned his neck around to see the inside of the leg closest to him and stopped. A scrape a couple of inches long with a slow drip of blood coming from the origin. It didn't look serious, but merited closer examination which required an extra set of hands. He snapped a photo of the laceration and sent their farm manager, Kerrie, a text with the image.

Fleur wasn't the least bit disturbed by his departure, or his reappearance with a lead. She came with him willingly, if not eagerly, parting the other fillies who scattered at her approach. She gave off respect vibes that left him feeling inferior in her presence.

Kerrie was ready with a bucket of warm water and some disinfectant soap in the barn. The farm manager had at least four inches and probably fifty pounds on Nate. As fit, he imagined, as the days when she'd played goal for Canada's women's hockey team. Her snowy-white hair, ready smile, and the freckles scattered over her model-perfect nose and cheeks put everyone at ease, but he was always careful around her; more so after he'd learned that nugget about her past. He'd bet she could take him, so he wanted to stay on her good side.

"Superficial," she confirmed after sluicing the soapy water over the wound, Fleur's only protest to stomp her foot at the trickle dribbling to the mat beneath her. Nate had visions of Chique at the same age, in the same position, leaping to the rafters. Kerrie stood and reached for the shank. "See for yourself, so you can report back to the boss."

Nate mirrored her grin before he peered at the wound, snapping another photo, the flash activating in the dim light of the aisle. "Hardly newsworthy," he agreed.

"This feels more like you looking for things to do," Kerrie

said. "In which case, you can throw some Vetrap on it. The one end is a little deeper than the rest of it. Won't hurt to keep it covered."

Or, try to keep it covered. The forearm of a yearling wasn't the easiest location to keep a dressing in place. If the filly didn't tear it off herself, a curious pasture mate might, should Fleur let them get close enough to try.

Kerrie had set out the small equine first aid kit in the tack room and he selected what he needed from it. He tucked a tube of antiseptic gel in his back pocket. Fleur rolled the eye closest to him, giving him a glimpse of the normally hidden white sclera, as he crouched at her off fore. As make-work projects went, it was a short one. A quick dab with a gauze sponge to remove the serous fluid that had accumulated in the interim, a smear of the gel, gauze roll to hold the non-stick pad in place, all of it topped with a self-adhesive bandage.

"Purple," Kerrie nodded. "Nice touch."

"Who bought that?" Nate asked. Not Liv. At the track they had white for rundown bandages, and black for hoof dressings.

Kerrie laughed. "Just guess."

That meant Emilie. Of course. Nate could hear her. *Would it kill us to have some colour around here?*

"We're going for a walk," he said, taking the lead rope from Kerrie. "Don't worry, I'll bring her back."

Kerrie shrugged. "Your farm. Your horse."

He raised an eyebrow, but didn't respond. It wasn't his farm. Sure, he called this place home, but he didn't own any of it. And he definitely did not own this, or any horse.

Fleur strode next to him, unperturbed. She wasn't afraid of anything. Didn't spook at the squirrels that took off, chattering, into the trees. Didn't blink at the motorcycle rumbling slowly away from the training barn. Didn't hesitate when he walked her in, finding Emilie attaching Excursion — who she now called Curtis — to the crossties halfway down the aisle. Nate stopped, holding the filly loosely. Fleur stood, waiting, her expression one of, he had to say, boredom.

"Who's that?" Emilie straightened from her crouch at the gelding's front end, neoprene brushing boots in her hands. She might recognize Nate's silhouette, but the filly likely looked like a nondescript yearling, dark against the bright frame of the doorway.

"Fleur," he said.

Emilie laughed. "Why?" Her eyes dropped to the bandage as she came over. "Did she hurt herself?"

"It's superficial," he said.

Letting Fleur explore her palms, the filly nuzzling reservedly, Emilie slid Nate a look. "So... what are you doing?"

"Hanging out. How was your lesson?"

He listened while she recounted what seemed like every stept. He'd never actually had a formal riding lesson himself. Back in Calgary he'd gone from being the kid who climbed on his buddy Will's grandfather's old drafties and stock horses, snatching pointers here and there as they were tossed his way, to getting a leg up on racehorse trainer Al Wilson's stable pony and learning how to gallop. Around the same time, Al had taught him how to start yearlings, claiming the best way to really learn how to ride racehorses was to begin with the babies. Grow up with them, so to speak. Nate couldn't say Al was wrong; it was the only thing Nate had known, and he'd turned out all right. He didn't know if Liv had an advantage, having received proper instruction from a coach who'd once been considered for the Canadian Olympic equestrian team.

"You didn't really answer me," Emilie said, circling back. "What are you doing? With Fleur?"

"I feel as if she's been a victim of everything that's

happened in the last year. She hasn't gotten the attention Chique or Feste did."

Emilie's smile was coy. "Maybe she doesn't want the attention."

Was that it? It was now, probably. Nate still believed Fleur's aloofness resulted from that lack. It wasn't negligence by any means — she'd received regular vet and farrier care, been properly fed and handled. It was just, compared with her two siblings, she'd never been fussed over. Not that young Thoroughbreds normally were.

Liv hadn't ignored the filly, exactly; it was more like she avoided Fleur. Sure, she checked on the yearling from time to time to see how she was developing, but the excitement that should have been there was not. Because Fleur was as perfect physically as Feste had been, and the colt had been beyond talented. He'd been more promising than Chique, which is what made his death all the more devastating.

All of which was the reason, Nate suspected, for Liv's withdrawal when it came to Fleur. She'd given her heart to that colt, and she'd been crushed when Feste's own heart had, literally, let them all down.

Nate was just as guilty. He'd been so shattered by the accident, he hadn't made time for anything like this. So he was making time. Because he had time. If he hadn't been so self-absorbed last summer after the spill, he could have gotten to know Fleur then. Instead, here he was, thinking, *you will like me.*

"Let's go play in the round pen," he said, turning her around.

He was sure if Fleur could have shrugged, she would have, following as he walked her to the circular ring next to the barn.

There was comfort in this. It felt like returning to his roots. This is what he'd been hired to do, back when he'd gotten the job on this farm. Starting yearlings. Though he'd helped with the routine farm chores too, because they'd also been looking for a general worker. That job came with the apartment, something he'd desperately needed. He hadn't wanted to become too comfortable on Will's couch.

If someone had told him the first day he'd come here that he would be where he was today, they would have had to pick him up off the ground because he would have fallen down laughing. That the reticent young woman who'd interviewed him would be his wife? He'd have asked them exactly what drugs they were smoking. Never in his wildest of dreams. He hadn't even truly believed he'd ever become a jockey back then. All he knew was that it was a nice farm, and the job was one he could do, if only they gave him a chance. True to form he'd almost screwed it all up. *Young and stupid.* He couldn't remember what had kept him from that. Probably his mother. *There but for grace.*

He didn't do much with Fleur. Just a little circle around him each way, familiarizing her with basic commands, getting her to move her feet. Walk on. Whoa. Stepping in to scratch her on the withers, which she tried not to admit she liked. She didn't offer resistance to anything he asked, but she sure didn't expend any more energy than she had to, either. Sotisse had obviously given the most spunk to her firstborn. Was there any correlation between horses with a higher percentage of white on their bodies being calmer than those with less? That was just the pattern he was seeing with this family. Weird coincidence, no doubt.

When he was finished, he stood in the middle of the round pen with the filly, reaching into his pocket for a peppermint. Fleur pressed her nose to his palm again, pushing the candy into it, then lipped it before raising her head and standing quietly, like she was hoping to be dismissed. Oh well. She didn't have to be as gregarious as Chique to be a racehorse. It was strange, though. Give it time. He'd draw her out.

"You're like a perfect little school kid," he said, tucking the mint back into his pocket and running a hand over her neck. "Candy's okay once in a while, you know."

Lifting his phone from his back pocket, he stretched his arm as far and high as he could to frame himself, the filly, and the wrapped leg, and snapped a picture for Liv.

"C'mon miss. Back to your minions."

He'd successfully killed an hour.

When he returned Fleur to her companions, he watched as she laced her ears to her head, splitting the small bunch in two. Fleur's pasture mates snorted and eyed the oddly decorated limb, because — yearling fillies, right? It was new. It was different. They were bored.

He watched their silliness as Fleur drifted away from them and started nibbling at the grass, then texted the photo to Liv, smiling because he'd see her for real, soon. *Think Fleur is looking for attention? Don't worry, it's a long way from her heart.*

The thing was, he was completely sure, as Emilie had pointed out, Fleur felt she could do without any attention at all.

CHAPTER SEVEN

Liv parked the car and raced for the terminal, knowing she was completely early. The flight information on the display screen inside matched her phone — on schedule, not magically ahead — but she didn't know London well enough to predict what kind of traffic she'd be dealing with, and hadn't wanted to be late. Better for her to have to wait than to keep Nate waiting. No one enjoyed standing around an airport wondering if something had gone sideways to keep their ride from showing up.

Noting the gate number, she searched for it, butterflies darting around her abdomen. Only a few other people loitered, as eager as she was to meet the passengers who likely wouldn't emerge for another hour. She found a spot to sit nearby and perched on the edge of her seat, unable to concentrate on reading the book she'd opened on her phone app, her gaze flitting up to the information monitor in case there had been a change.

It was in the down time she'd felt his absence. He'd ruined her. She used to love being on her own. Now, without him, there was a hole, an emptiness. A vacancy. Part of her hated it

— the old part, harbouring those remnants of mistrust and doubt that things could not possibly be as perfect as they were. She worked hard on the other part, the new part. After an unexpected road trip back to her native Montreal last fall, which had forced her to face everything about a past she'd so desperately buried, she'd chosen to believe this thing between them was right and as forever as anything in this life could be.

Finally her phone pinged, a notification flashing on the screen and she bounced up, double-checking the monitor. The flight had landed, and though she still had a wait because Nate would have to go through customs, she weaved her way close to the front of the growing crowd. She calculated when she could expect him to appear, pushing down the anxiety threatening to surface and standing her ground amid the press of bodies.

He was one of the first out, eyes locking onto hers immediately, a single carry-on bag slung over his shoulder. He looked weary, but what did she expect after a long flight across several time zones? A twinge of concern wormed into her head. He had to ride in a race tomorrow that had become important to win for more than the associated prestige.

Liv shook it off. Nate was a professional. It was part of his job description to work through pain and fatigue. Balanced on the balls of her feet with one eye on security, she forced herself to remain where she was until he was on her side of the barrier — when she'd envisioned hurdling over it.

Finally, there was nothing between them, the miles melting away, and the flood of completeness she felt made her realize just how much she'd missed him — and she didn't hate that fact. She molded herself against him, their lips fused, reclaiming what they were.

"Are you sure it was just a week?" he murmured. "It felt like months."

"It did." She grinned, pulling back with reluctance. "We've

become those embarrassing people making out in an airport. Let's get out of here."

Nate reset the strap that had slipped to his elbow and grabbed her hand, letting her lead the way, and Liv thought he seemed revived, more energy in his step, some of the exhaustion in his features smoothed away. Or was she just being hopeful?

When they reached the tiny rental, he looked surprised, and maybe a bit impressed. "You're safe in that thing? Wrong side of the road and all that?"

"I'm very adaptable, Miller."

"Well, I appreciate you doing this."

"Did you think I'd make you take a bus?" She opened the passenger door for him before skipping around to slip behind the wheel.

She had to focus more than she would have at home — driving on the left-hand side of the road was a major adjustment — but Nate remained silent, and her worry resurfaced. Was it only jet lag?

"What's up?" she asked, risking a glance his way.

He drew himself back from wherever he'd been. "Nothing. Just... it's surreal, right? Being here. In England. On the way to Newmarket. Getting ready to run Jay at *Ascot*." The emphasis he put on the name highlighted a reverence Liv understood. Nate gave a subtle shake of his head. "I'm trying to get my head around it."

"I'm still not sure I have, so don't use up too much energy trying." Her lips twisted, but it didn't budge his solemnity, his gaze once again locked on the city outside the passenger window. It made her wonder if he was keeping something from her. What could she do, though? She was guilty of the same.

"Six years ago right now, I'd never been out of Alberta. You know that?" he said. "Do people get used to this? How is it not always incredible?"

She loved that this wasn't ordinary to him, either. This year had been one wonder after another, and she hated withholding from him that it all might come to a premature end — just when, for once in her life, she'd been enjoying the ride. Today she'd let herself almost — but not quite — forget it, because Nate was coming; and now he was here, with her, sharing this thing. Except she'd expected him to be excited instead of... whatever this was.

"We're doing this wrong, you know," Nate said, his gaze finally settling on her.

Liv glanced at him quickly before returning her eyes to the road, the local laws still at odds with her brain. "What are you talking about?"

"Here we are, in London, and not making the best of it. We might never be over here again."

"We've already established that I fail as a tourist, if that's what you mean."

He gave her a crooked smile. "You did okay in Dubai."

"So what are you saying? Should we take a couple off days after the race?"

"Would you?" He looked skeptical.

His expression didn't surprise her. Was she missing out, letting the horses absorb her? Keeping her world small by limiting it so much to her work with them? It wasn't as if she couldn't be away, it just never occurred to her. Maybe now was the time, when the uncertainty of her future with the horse who had brought them here was up in the air. It was a reminder that her relationship with the animals in her care was tenuous, but the one with this man could not be if she wanted it to last.

Liv didn't like being idle, and she'd hated the two times she'd been injured, forced away from her job. But last year when she and Jo had discussed how they would handle Roger's absence, when the trainer who had always managed the Triple Stripe string had needed to take time away because of his wife's illness, they'd promised each other they'd be more balanced — something they both struggled with.

You have to protect this, Jo had said.

Even though the very foundation of her relationship with Nate was that they understood the demands of their careers, it was because of him Liv wanted to try.

"Let's see how the race goes, okay?" she hedged. "I'm sure they'd survive another couple days without us."

His eyebrows took on a higher than normal curve, humour teasing his lips — like he'd believe it when he saw it. What could she say? She hadn't totally made the transformation to believing in *and* executing work-life balance.

Once they were free of the city, Liv relaxed her hands on the wheel. A fresh anticipation washed over her with the thought of showing this new happy place to him, somewhere she'd immediately felt she belonged. Conversation lapsed again, his eyes glued to the landscape rushing past the car's window, just as hers had been on the same journey last week. *This is normal.* They were never about endless chatter. They were about presence. Sharing space. Sharing experience. She was his intermittent tour guide, words coming out only in short streams along the road... but his lack of enthusiasm was getting to her.

"I thought I was having a good time here," she said, her voice soft, almost as if she was talking to herself. "But now that you're here, it's so much better."

Liv felt his gaze and would have reached a hand out had she been confident enough she didn't need both to drive. His eyes drew her focus from the road — tired, sure, but more relaxed that they'd been earlier in the journey.

"Now I have to convince you we should relocate," she added with a grin, sounding more like herself.

Nate laughed. "Just like that? You'd leave home behind?"

"Home is wherever we're together, right?"

He flashed the smile that had always toyed with her heart and her head. "Who knew you could be so sentimental."

"Not me," she said. They were close to Newmarket now. "So — are you as wiped as you look? Did you get any sleep on the plane?"

"A little."

"We could go by the yard first," she suggested.

"I haven't seen you in a week," he said. "Jay can wait."

She grinned. "Where is my head?"

"Really."

She wasn't convinced there'd be a whole lot of *that* happening right away. He did look worn out, like he hadn't slept since she'd left.

Rory had promised he'd look after Jay for the rest of today, so technically she was free until the morning, but that wouldn't keep her from checking on the horse later when she had the chance. Nate would understand she couldn't relinquish all sense of responsibility just because he'd arrived.

When they reached the flat, she showed him in and said, "There's not much to the place. It's not a four-star hotel in Dubai."

Nate gazed around, his weary eyes glazed over at this point. "Cosy."

That's exactly how Liv found it. It was enough. All she needed was a place to eat, read, and sleep.

He wandered through the living room with a glance to the kitchen on the left, the living area to the right, and easily found the bedroom. She followed as he dumped his bag next to the bed before wrapping his arms around her. He caught her lips, one hand cupping the back of her head while the other tugged her t-shirt free from her jeans, but the kiss was sweet rather than savage. Her hands pressed on his chest, their knees bumping as he reached the edge of the bed and crumpled into it, bringing her with him.

Nate groaned and buried his face in her neck. "I can't. I'm sorry. I'm exhausted."

He was asleep in seconds. As Liv watched him, she couldn't help thinking keeping him on Jay might be a mistake.

CHAPTER EIGHT

It didn't matter that the surroundings weren't familiar when Nate came to, because the wrap of Liv's arms around him was. He rolled to face her, and she kissed him.

"What time is it?" he asked, his throat feeling like he'd swallowed gravel.

"Six PM. Feeling better?"

He nodded, admitting, "I haven't been sleeping so great."

"Has it really been that bad?" she asked.

He didn't want to burden her with everything stuck in his head, knowing it was important to her to stay focused on Jay's race. It could wait till after. "I don't know why. All good now."

Pulling her closer, he hoped she didn't figure out that wasn't exactly true. For now, this was what mattered; that regardless of what was going on around them, they were fine.

Last summer he hadn't felt his past haunting him the same way it had other years. There'd been too much to look forward to, between the anticipation of taking Feste and Chique to Saratoga and his relationship with Liv finally seeming on a true course. It had all gone south, though, piling fresh tragedy on old scars.

Liv had her own feelings about Saratoga to deal with, some of which he'd borne witness too, but he couldn't help thinking she'd overcome her past with no help from him. The Liv in his arms was worlds away from the one he'd found, drunk and dishevelled in the house she'd stayed in near the New York track after her riding career had taken a nosedive. What was that, four years ago? It seemed like a different dimension now.

"Let's go see Jay," she said, springing off the bed.

He pushed himself up more slowly and decided he didn't care what they did as long as they were together. Once his head cleared, he'd be better. It had been amazing to get some decent sleep. Hopefully, by morning he'd feel almost normal.

When they reached the yard at the racing stable, he immediately recognized Jay's head poking out of the box Liv headed toward. Nate grinned at the glint in the big chestnut's eyes, the lift of his generous forelock exposing the star normally hidden beneath it. Large nostrils fluttered with the low rumble of a greeting. Nate followed Liv into the stall.

"He looks incredible," he said, running a hand down Jay's smooth neck, over the clear-cut definition of muscles layered over his shoulder.

Nate hadn't expected to notice so much of a difference in the big horse's fitness. He hoped he was up to the job tomorrow, that his jet lag and the stress he was feeling didn't make him an unworthy partner.

Liv remained silent at Jay's head as Nate's hands continued to travel over the chestnut's broad back, the only sound that of the horse's lips flapping against her palm. Now he felt it, the excitement finally finding him. All that power wrapped by a hide that was sleek without tension — and Nate would be part of it tomorrow.

The appearance of a human face at the door interrupted his immersion. Liv glanced over her shoulder.

"Hey, Rory," she said, her tone casual, not the first time the greeting had passed her lips. "Nate, meet Rory."

Nate sized the guy up quickly. Rory was a little taller than he was, but wiry. Maybe a couple of years younger. His quick grin and curly dark hair probably entranced a lot of girls. Nate went with professional, smiling as he stretched his arm out to shake the head lad's hand over the half door. "Nice to meet you."

His formality lasted about five seconds before Rory herded them off to the pub like it was the only logical thing to do now that Nate was here, which he supposed was true. He couldn't blame Liv for caving to Rory's relentlessness. The guy's charisma made him hard to turn down.

The pub could have been anywhere. Nate settled on a bench next to Liv. Neither she nor Rory was trying to make him feel out of place, but he could see she'd assimilated when he wouldn't be here long enough to do that, and part of him just wanted to go home and get things back to normal.

But wait, Miller, remember why you're here. It's not to make friends, or to see the sights. It's to ride at Ascot, and how many Woodbine jocks get the chance to do that?

Rory wasn't hard to like. Nate had figured that would be the case, because Liv didn't warm to many people and had been relatively kind in her comments about him. It wasn't long before the head lad's charm started to affect Nate, too. Rory insisted on buying a round to start things off, and while he respected Liv when she waved off his offer, he wasn't having any of it from Nate.

And Rory made sure everyone in the place was aware they had visitors from Canada.

Nate knew he was in trouble then. The head lad and other

locals considered it their duty to show him the bounds of their hospitality. How had Liv kept this guy at bay all week? If Nate didn't watch it, he'd end up both literally and figuratively under the table.

He leaned into Liv. "I'm counting on you to lay down the law so I don't end up soused here. *Boss,*" he added dryly. "Because you were wrong about him. He isn't harmless at all. I was right to be worried. Just not about you."

She grinned. "I'll do my best. Though, Rory thinks I should ride the horse. This could be his master plan."

Nate figured that might not be the worst idea, all things considered, but he kept that thought to himself.

Liv ordered a salad when it should have been him eating light. Though really, with the weights over here, he didn't have to worry. She talked him into fish and chips and promised to help him with it. Nate was beginning to think he might actually go into that race tomorrow reasonably well-fed and rested.

"Has she been earning her keep?" he asked, savouring both the food and the alcohol so he wasn't served more of either. There was already another pint lined up for him, courtesy of some well-meaning regular.

"She's done brilliantly," Rory said. "I tried to buy her lunch to thank her, but she wasn't having it."

No one could say Liv was leading this guy on. She'd told Nate they'd come here on the condition she pay, and she'd ended up with the chance to live out one of her horse girl dreams. Which, in Liv's case, was not to hook up with a handsome Scot (*sorry about your luck, buddy*) but to ride a hurdler.

"Maybe I was saving it for tonight so you'd have to pay double," Liv responded, helping herself to Nate's chips.

Before they knew it, Rory was checking the time, to Nate's relief. He wasn't sure how much longer he'd be able to nurse his beer.

"You have to go back to the barn?" he asked.

"The yard, you mean?" Rory quipped. "A barn is for cattle."

"Sorry about the language barrier," Nate quipped. "No wonder you all want to come to North America. You're at the barn — sorry, *yard* — all the time."

"So you'll give me a job then?" Rory grinned, but there was a hint of seriousness in his eyes. "I'll come and help you revolutionize North American racing."

So that was it. The guy was buttering Liv up for a ticket to Canada.

"Your boss won't welcome us back if we steal his help," Nate said.

"We could do an exchange," Liv suggested. "I'll stay here, and Rory can go back in my place."

Jokes on both of us, buddy, if you really are hoping to start something up with her. Nate glanced at Liv. "You wonder why I didn't sleep as soon as you left."

"Relax, Miller." She wrapped an arm around his neck and kissed him.

Once Liv had asked three times if Rory was sure he didn't mind doing Jay's last feed and water off of the day — something that probably killed her to accept — they returned to the flat.

"How many times do they go back after training in the morning?" Nate asked.

"Three."

"Wow. That would never fly in North America, would it?" Grooms went back mid-afternoon to feed and normally they took turns so it wasn't every day — and a trainer typically hired someone to water off in the evening.

"It would not," Liv agreed.

He'd had just enough food and alcohol that all he wanted to do was sleep again, and fought to stay awake as Liv got ready.

It was as if she was taking her time. Maybe because she didn't want to keep him up, but just as likely because her nerves were setting in.

Tomorrow, it was here. Race day at Ascot. He'd bet she'd be the one having trouble sleeping tonight.

CHAPTER NINE

Liv stretched the girth to meet the billet strap, the tremor in her arms from nerves, not lack of strength. She clung to the familiar ritual, focusing on the moment. *Deep breath. Do this, finish your part. Then toss the baton to Nate and let Jay carry them the rest of the way.*

Muscle memory took over as she finished saddling, something she'd done enough times now she didn't need to remove her hat, though her whole outfit had been carefully selected — with Faye's help, of course — to be practical and appropriate for the venue.

This is Ascot.

She shivered as it pushed into her thoughts. It made Canada's most prestigious race, the Queen's Plate, look like child's play. This was what it was all about. Not the Kentucky Derby. Not the Breeders' Cup. Not the Dubai World Cup. This was where those Arabian stallions had first been bred to English mares, creating the ideal combination of speed and stamina. Liv knew that history as well as, if not better than, the story of human civilization she'd learned in school.

She tried to push the wonder of it all back as she joined the Triple Stripe contingent in the parade ring, her smile quick and nervous, transferring the familiarity from task to people. When she'd met up with her parents to see Roger Cloutier and his wife, Hélène, were with them, she'd choked up. That Roger and Hélène would arrange their travel plans to be here helped ground her. Her parents, the Cloutiers — all of them were here to witness the stable's first runner at this famous racecourse, outfitted as they would have been for the Plate — the men in their top hats and tails, women in tailored suits and conservative millinery. It made her forget, almost, the cold reality in the background of what the future might hold for Jay.

Nate put his hands on her shoulders as if to help keep her feet connected to the grass beneath her flat shoes. Not a bad idea, because she felt like she was hovering.

"Are you okay?" he asked.

"As long as you are. That's all that matters."

Yesterday, she'd worried Rory was right, that she should have used one of the local riders for this race. That she'd have to make a last-minute change if Nate was in no condition to pilot Jay on a strange and demanding course where he couldn't afford to be less than fully alert. He'd bounced back though, and now she was sure it was the right decision — both keeping him on Jay and not telling him about the terms of the syndication. She'd carry that weight herself.

She gripped her elbows so he wouldn't be tempted to grab her hand, needing to maintain some scrap of decorum. "Do you think I'd be this bad if I were riding?"

He laughed. "No. Sorry about that."

"Sure you are."

The grin he flashed was full of confidence that wiped away any of her remaining doubt, and she half expected him to break into some song or another. What would it be, today?

"You look great, by the way," he said. "Do you think Em is kicking herself for not coming?"

Liv missed Emilie's nervous energy, which somehow always diffused her own. It still surprised her that her sister hadn't changed her mind and been on the flight with their parents — this was a 'move heaven and earth' kind of trip, after all.

Jay looked brilliant, the made-to-order sunshine reflecting off his honed muscles, his sleek copper coat highlighted with gold. They'd had enough time to talk about race strategy that there was really nothing more to say until she threw Nate up onto Jay's back.

"*Bonne chance.* Safe trip."

And then they were gone, swallowed up by the throng.

Nate wasn't really sure how things worked here; whether it was actually Rory's job to lead Jay up or if he'd just stepped in because it was *This Race* and Rory felt an allegiance to Liv. Nate didn't really care, or was maybe even glad to have a familiar face to take the edge off nerves he'd never admit to having.

"You going to be all right out there?" Rory quipped, glancing over his shoulder.

"If you mean, can I control the horse without a pony, yeah. But I could get lost. Are there road signs?"

Rory laughed, but Nate wasn't sure he'd been joking. They didn't use lead ponies over here to escort racehorses to the starting gate, and at home with a horse like Jay, Nate didn't need one. All tracks in North America had the same basic oval configuration. Ascot was shaped more like a gigantic triangle.

Jay hadn't been here before either, but the big chestnut was his usual collected self without the benefit of studying racing forms and videos, so Nate owed it to him to match that confidence. He found his way back to embracing the thrill of being here on a horse that could win this race.

The warmup blended their muscles together and melded their minds, so that by the time the small field loaded into the starting gate, their backs to the buzzing crowd, they could have been running on the moon for all Nate cared. The sight between the points of Jay's ears was as welcoming as the locals at the pub last night, though the faces to his left and right were those of strangers, their accents foreign to him. The grandstand was a vibrant, breathing thing, droning with brown noise. One beat, two, and the gates burst open with a scattering of colour — the Triple Stripe red, white and blue alongside more famed silks of cobalt, and green, white and pink.

Nate took a hold and Jay settled at the back of the small field, the others within range as they galloped downhill to the first turn to where the course levelled off — Swinley Bottom it was called, four furlongs into the mile and a half race. Places here had such storybook names, that one sounding straight out of *The Hobbit*. It was the lowest point of the undulating terrain, right-handed when they raced strictly left-handed at home. The first quarter mile seemed to pass in the blink of an eye, and Nate chased Jay after they rounded the bend, beginning a steady uphill. They needed the momentum to maintain their position.

The incline set Jay back on his haunches, his front end lifting, reaching, pulling him forward, making him feel invincible. He had all the room in the world, the four rumps between him and the horse on the lead packed in a tight cluster. Nate envisioned swooping around them when the time came to fly. Eight lengths separated them from the frontrunner, easy striking distance for a horse with Jay's turn of foot.

Climbing to the last turn, they charged toward the wall of noise coming from the screaming crowd. Nate pulled Jay from the rail, asking for the next gear, tucked low over the big horse's back. Jay's response was explosive, but these horses weren't coming back to him like they did at home.

In the fury of the final drive, straightness seemed like a suggestion. A bay horse swerved under the flailing whip of his jockey, right into Jay's path, forcing Nate to check hard, change course. It felt like the bodies around them had multiplied. They were all over the place. Catching sight of room on the rail, Nate ducked Jay toward it before the hole closed up. And it would have, because as soon as Jay scooted up the fence, his neighbour was squeezing him against it. All four horses behind the leader converged, advancing like a crashing wave of surf. Nate's urging was economical compared to the pumping and rocking of his rivals, and he funnelled all his energy forward, pressing toward the finish post, willing Jay's nose in front.

He didn't stop riding until they were well past it, didn't look around to see if the other jockeys' faces gave him any clue who had won, because Nate had absolutely no idea.

Liv dashed from her seat, trusting her parents and the Cloutiers to find their own way with only a twinge of conscience. Pushing through the press of the crowd, she hoped she was going in the right direction, her chest feeling like a rock was wedged against it. She didn't know if Jay's effort, however tremendous, had been enough. At Woodbine she could usually predict how a photo finish would turn out, but the sightlines here were too unfamiliar.

Come on Jay, it had to be you.

Someone grabbed her arm, and she yanked it away before

seeing Rory, a broad smile dominating his face. His expression revived her hope. Did he know?

"Come," he said. "Your horse can run a bit."

She wished Jay had run just a bit more, making the result obvious.

"Did he win?" she asked, hoping she didn't sound desperate. Rory didn't know how much was riding on the answer to her question, so she attempted a smile.

The way he reset his lips dissolved her spirits again. "Maybe we'll know by the time we get to the winner's enclosure."

Liv was admittedly glad for his company as they wove their way to where the horses would be unsaddled. Between Nate's face and his slight shrug as he and Jay approached, Liv figured he didn't know how this would play out either.

Keeping an ear tuned for the announcement and both eyes on her horse, she scanned Jay for any signs of distress — surprised and grateful he was allowed a drink, and Nate was permitted to remove the tack even though the result wasn't yet official. Score another point for the way things were done here. Jay's nostrils flared and his sides heaved, but none of it was beyond what she expected from a horse who had just run a mile and a half on an uphill course, finishing strong.

Nate disappeared to weigh in, and while Liv was happy Jay was being cared for, the difference in routine gave her a bad feeling about the result. Before Nate returned, they'd determined the winner, and it wasn't Jay.

Third.

It wasn't as if Nate could fault Jay's performance, except he'd really thought they could win that race; that Jay was better than those horses. *A nose.* Not even, really. He'd seen the photo. It was more like a hair, but that wasn't an official margin of victory. Such a letdown, to come all this way and get beaten by someone just plain luckier.

Tonight he wished they were out with Rory, because he could have used the endless pints the locals had been willing to pour down his throat last night. But with Liv's parents and the Cloutiers here, there was no way to say no to dinner, so Nate sat through the endless words of consolation. No one blamed him, but he still felt it was somehow his fault. He'd rather be mocked by Rory and the others in the pub than listen to this polite disappointment.

Liv's relative silence wasn't unusual, especially given Jay's placing. It had to be hard for her too, after a week of buildup. She clearly loved it here, and a win would have filled out the experience perfectly. But knowing her, she was already on to what was next for Jay because there was no point dwelling on the defeat. Today wasn't a failure, there was nothing to fix.

It wasn't until they were back at the flat that Nate had the chance to wrap his arms around her the way he wanted — no win meant no joyous embrace immediately after the race. Even if they weren't brooding about it, it was all right to sit with the anticlimax for a moment, wasn't it? He felt her release a sigh before pulling away; there was still a limit to what she would accept. She wasn't big on commiseration. You win some, you lose some.

"How late does the pub stay open here, d'you think?" he asked, grinning, but her face remained stoic. "You okay?"

She glanced at him, arms crossing, hands clutching her elbows. "The syndicate manager from Triumph Stud spoke with my father last week. He strongly implied Jay should go to an American to train up to Breeders' Cup."

Nate gaped before finding his voice, not sure what bothered him more — that development or the fact she hadn't told him about it as soon as she knew. "Seriously?"

Liv shrugged. "I thought if he won today, they'd lose some ammunition. But they're not going to care that he was only beaten an inch. The chart says he finished third. I know they weren't pleased about me bringing him here in the first place. In their minds it was probably foolish, and they'll use Jay losing to prove their point: I'm not experienced enough to manage a horse of this calibre."

"Why didn't you tell me?" They'd talked on the phone every day, and had plenty of face-to-face time since Nate had joined her. She couldn't have found a moment to share this with him?

She ducked his eyes, a glimpse of the old Liv; the one who had always kept so much to herself. "What good would it have done? You didn't need that in your head out there."

"That's not the point. We're supposed to talk about stuff."

Her gaze levelled on him. "This was business. Don't take it personally."

"I thought we were in this business together."

"I'm standing by my decision, Miller. I felt bad not telling you, that has to be enough. Your safety wasn't in jeopardy, but it could have been if you'd known what might be at stake. That kind of pressure could have affected the way you rode, made you reckless, and I wasn't taking that chance."

He couldn't completely argue with that, as much as he wanted to. "I rode the horse. Blame it on me. You've done it before." He cracked a smile.

She gave him a small shove, and almost smiled too before her lips fell again. "What good would that do? They'd just question my judgement all the more because I kept you on when I should have secured a top rider from over here. There were only five other horses in the race. How hard could that have been?"

"Maybe you should have," he said, his irritation returning. He was trying to be rational about this, but the words stung.

"No. You deserved to ride him. How fair would it have been to take you off?"

"Don't worry about doing what's fair on my account. I'd rather think you had me ride him because you believed I was competent."

"You are. But those hardboots in Kentucky won't see it that way." She rounded the couch and collapsed into it. "This is the problem with me being a trainer. The whole conflict of interest argument isn't going to go away. And how can I help making decisions based on how I think they'll affect you?"

He slid his eyes to the kitchen, wondering if there was beer in that fridge. Unlikely. Liv didn't drink it, and he doubted she'd have thought to stock some for him. Instead of checking, he sat with her. Because she was right, this wasn't going to go away, so running from it wouldn't help anything.

"I'm sorry," he said.

"You put together a campaign for a horse and everything goes right... until it doesn't." She shrugged, rolling her head toward him. "I'm not going to dwell on this. No looking back, right? It sucks to put this much work into him only to have someone else get the credit. Because he's going to win the Classic." She said it with admirable conviction. "But I'm not the first person this has happened to. Welcome to the big time, right?"

"Yeah. But I'm still sorry," he said.

She let him put his arms around her, curling into him, and he exhaled.

"Maybe my father can convince them to send him to Don," she said. Her father sometimes had a horse or two with Don Philips at Belmont in New York, and Jay had spent the winter before last in his barn. "At least then he'd be with someone who already knows him. But see, that's me just being sentimental, isn't it? It's not as if ending up with one of the big names in the US would be a terrible thing for a horse like Jay. He's so easy. I'm not vain enough to think he's done as well as he has because of me." She sighed. "We've had a good year. Next year, after Jay retires, we might not be so lucky. That syndicate money will go a long way. He'll run in my father's colours in the Classic. That's the only thing I want to be sure of."

Nate wanted to fight for her, fight for Jay to stay. But Liv was right. There wasn't any point.

CHAPTER TEN

The rain fell. Not enough to keep the horses from training, or even, really, to wear a jacket, but it was enough to dampen a mood that was already flat. Liv's head was upside-down from jet lag, though it wasn't as if she could mope at home and dwell on the less-than-ideal way the trip had turned out, waiting to find out whether Jay would be taken away.

It didn't really change much. Losing Jay was not a get out of jail free card that freed her to go back to riding races. The horses in Ontario still needed a trainer. And if Liv looked back on the last eight months, it hadn't felt like jail. Even if she removed Jay from the equation, she'd won the Oaks with Reba, just missed winning the Queen's Plate again, and was pleased with Trop's turnaround. She was handling it, this training horses thing, even if a bunch of men in Kentucky didn't have faith in her ability. They didn't matter outside the bubble around Jay, only her father did.

Woodbine's main track oval, which had always been second only to Belmont Park in her mind for expansiveness, seemed claustrophobic and so very even after the gallops in Newmarket. Trop galloped more strongly than Liv would have allowed before the trip, stretching over the surface at a clip just shy of what would get him caught by the clockers. Trop didn't seem to mind. When she returned to the barn, she rode him into his stall so Jo didn't have to catch him outside in the drizzle.

Jo glanced up before Liv dismounted, catching Liv's eyes with a wry smile — no doubt seeing more flare to the gelding's nostrils than was normal after a routine mile and a half. "How'd he go?"

Liv kicked her feet from the irons and hopped off, landing lightly in the straw. "He feels good," she said, running up the irons, unbuckling the girth, and dragging the saddle off. "We need to talk about where we're going to run him next." She gave Jo the courtesy of discussing such things, welcoming the assistant's input. Maybe it was an unconscious hope that Jo would step up and run the show after all.

If she intended to make the changes that bounced around her head after Newmarket, though, as Rory had pointed out, she could only do so as the head trainer. Nate was on board, and Liv would always value his perspective, but as much as part of her still wanted to shrink away from her responsibilities, she was the one who called the shots. On most things anyway. Because her father, who was still bankrolling the entire operation, had the final word.

She needed to figure out a way to take what she'd learned overseas and make it part of the routine here. They'd come up short with Jay at Ascot, but the trip to England had been positive in many ways. While Liv couldn't replicate that way of doing things, it didn't mean she couldn't incorporate a thing or two.

"We'll talk at the end of the morning, okay?" Liv said as she pulled the bridle over Trop's ears, Jo nodding and slipping on the halter. "When Nate gets back."

Nate had galloped Cam as usual, his first mount of the morning before he left to work horses for other trainers. He'd set out before her and been gone before she came back with Trop. At least today was a dark day, no racing this afternoon, so they could sleep when they went home if they wanted to.

She took the tack to her next horse, a bay waiting tied to the wall. A clean saddle cloth and girth cover were draped over the rubber stall guard. Sue wasn't nearby, so Liv ducked under the guard and began getting the horse ready.

The text from her father came mid-morning.

It was short, but Liv knew what it meant, and wasn't sure she liked it. He was going to be in town for a couple of days for work. *Lunch Friday?*

Friday. Well, at least she had Jay for a few more days.

What a year it had been. What a horse. A horse others had decided was too good for her.

Needless to say, they hadn't taken a couple of extra days to sightsee in London before returning to Canada. The reception they'd received at Woodbine wasn't bad — it was sympathetic, really — but it would have been a hell of a lot better had they won. *Duh.* Nate had left to a chorus of good lucks, and returned to an endless stream of condolences, to which he responded, "Can you believe it?" Because he still couldn't.

Maybe if he'd known the course better, he would have broken sharper, moved sooner, pushed Jay in that split-second he'd held back, beaten those horses in the last jump. Made it that barest of millimetres in front. He was going to second-guess his actions forever.

"You taking that horse to the Classic?"

He heard that question more than once. The first few times

it took a second before he remembered, the brain fog of jet lag blanking the truth from his mind. The real answer was, he didn't know, so all he could do was give a rote response.

"We'll see how he comes out of the race."

Not that it was his decision to make, but everyone assumed he was in the know about all things Triple Stripe. And usually he was. Or so he thought.

The Breeders' Cup Classic at Del Mar Racetrack was where Jay had to go if he wanted to have any hope of being named Horse of the Year, so unless something happened between now and the first weekend in November, Jay would run there, with or without them. The Dubai World Cup, while huge, wasn't enough to take the North American title in a year when a three-year-old had collected two jewels of the American Triple Crown. That colt, Chaotic Good, would surely show up in the Classic, and he was who Jay needed to beat to be Horse of the Year.

And what did the title give him? Bragging rights, essentially. Stallion appeal.

Jo and Liv were already holed up in the office at the end of the morning, looking as if they were waiting for him.

"Does she know?" Nate asked, eyeing Liv, seated behind Roger's desk — because it still felt like Roger's desk even though Rog had been away since the previous November.

Liv merely nodded in answer.

"So let's say, for the sake of argument, they don't take him away. What are you going to do with him?" Jo asked.

Liv fingered the top of a pile of condition books. "I guess we've got a couple of choices," she said. She glanced at Nate. "We stay here and run in the Woodbine Mile, and pay to enter the Classic. It makes no sense to fly him to California for the Pacific Classic at Del Mar to try to earn a free berth there when that's where Chaotic Good is headed. If we're going to face him, I'd rather wait till it's all on the line, even if it might be nice to have raced over the track." She took a breath before adding, "An alternative is Saratoga. The Jockey Club Gold Cup Stakes. It's also a 'win and you're in' race for the Classic."

Now she held Nate's eyes. *Saratoga.*

Just the name made a fist tighten around his heart. It squeezed, other fingers pressing on his windpipe, making his breath come short before he forced himself to suck in air through his nose, inhaling deep before letting it escape through his lips. It wasn't as if they could avoid the place forever.

To think once — days before it all changed — he'd compared it to Disneyland, quipping, *did anyone ever want to leave?* Now the thought of going back set his nerve endings on alert, and speaking its name leached colour from Liv's face.

"You're the boss," he said. "I'll go where you want me to go."

There was gratitude in her grey eyes, a sad little curve of a smile on her lips at the memory of what they had lost there; what had almost taken them out.

"I'm going to think on that a couple of days, to be sure I make the decision for the right reasons. And maybe by then, it won't matter anyway." She shuffled the plain booklets and pressed one open in front of her. "Now, moving on... I don't think there's any point running either Can't Catch Me or Reba in the Breeders' Stakes. It's not right for either of them at the moment."

Jo, leaning back in the old loveseat, arms crossed, nodded in agreement.

"We could still be the spoiler, though," Nate said.

Liv's head tilted slightly. "What are you thinking?"

"Trop. I think he's ready to play with the big kids."

Liv frowned. "He's only won one race. There's a nice spot

for Ontario-sired non-winners of one other than in the next book."

Sure, that was the usual progression — a race for horses whose only triumphs had come in maiden or claiming races — but Trop's impressive success first time out had convinced Nate the gelding was better than that.

"Trop's above average," he said. "Capable of skipping a grade."

"Why is it wrong to want to build his confidence? He's not been an easy horse."

"He broke his maiden like a pro. Do I need to make you watch the replay of that maiden race to remind you how easy it was for him?"

"I don't want to be around when you two have kids," Jo grumbled, and ducked the glare they both gave her.

Not going to have to worry about that, Jo. He turned his frustration back to Liv. "I thought you were past playing it safe." *You took a horse to Dubai. We just got back from Ascot.*

"I don't need to look like I'm running horses over their heads right now, Miller."

So, that's what this was. She was worried. About what, exactly? Looking like she didn't know what she was doing? "You have to let go of that. Jay wasn't over his head in that race." But Nate wondered maybe if he himself had been. *Follow your own advice and let it go.* "Don't project your own self-doubt on your horses."

Liv's eyes narrowed on him, and he expected a sharp comeback. Then her gaze dropped to the desk a beat before she turned to Jo. "Care to weigh in?"

Jo hesitated. If she didn't want to be the tie-breaker, Nate could make a guess on her opinion from her expression. "He's training great right now. You said it yourself."

"So you agree with Nate?" There was a carefully contained bite behind Liv's words.

Jo raised her hands, palms out. "Don't put me in the middle of your domestic dispute."

"It's not —" Nate and Liv spoke over each other. He smirked, and she scowled.

Liv tossed the condition book she'd tucked into a tight roll onto the small stack on the desk, and they all stared at it as it unfurled, the edges remaining curled.

She sighed. "Let's work him and Cam on the turf. If I'm happy with how Trop goes, I'll consider nominating him."

"And Cam?" Jo asked.

"Maybe he'll like the turf too," Liv said. "He's bred for it. But — I don't know. I'd really like to see him win a race this year. It might be best to just run him in an allowance and try to break his second-itis."

She looked pointedly at Nate as if she was daring him to challenge her on that, too.

While part of him wanted to prove Cam could beat Big Sensation — he was tired of getting out-nosed by that horse and was sure their colt had it in him — Liv's idea was a sounder one.

They ran over plans for the other horses, and Nate felt himself fading now that he was sitting still. Jo stood just in time to keep him from nodding off.

"Ready to go?" he asked Liv.

Liv turned to Jo. "Anything else you need me to do?"

The assistant trainer shook her head. "Go have a nap. Try and negate the effects of your jet lag."

Liv came around the desk, holding the Porsche's keys with a twisted smile. "I think I'd better drive."

She seemed to have no trouble making that decision.

CHAPTER ELEVEN

As soon as they shed their jackets and shoes in the foyer at the house, Holly the Labrador was there, her body swaying with the swing of her thick black tail. She gave each of them a chance to greet her before trotting in front of Liv to the kitchen.

"I'm having that nap, as suggested," Nate said. "You coming?"

"Probably. I'll be up in a minute. I just want to say hi to Em." Liv hesitated. "It's supposed to stop raining in a couple of hours. We'll go see the foals and yearlings then?"

"Sure. I'll set an alarm."

The black Lab led the way to her person, Emilie parked in the breakfast nook with her laptop. Em's eyes shot from the screen when she noticed Liv, and she hopped to her feet.

"Hey! Welcome home!"

Liv squeezed back when her sister embraced her. "Thanks, Em. It's good to be home." *Mostly*.

"I want to hear everything. Was it totally amazing?"

"It was, until the last bit," Liv answered dryly. She refrained from teasing Emilie about not going and didn't mention the situation with Jay. When she had something concrete, she'd share it with her sister.

"I need to talk to you," Emilie said, settling back behind her laptop once she was satisfied with Liv's rundown of the trip. "I have the best idea."

Liv grinned, her mood shifting. Emilie was always coming up with ideas, usually for potential fundraisers for the local retired racehorse charity. The horse show Liv had taken part in before she'd left for England, as a "celebrity entrant," had been only one of many such schemes. She didn't really think she was much of a celebrity, but it had been fun to have an excuse to hop on a horse preparing for his next career and dip her toe into a part of the horse world she'd been dedicated to before racing.

"What is it this time?" she asked, grabbing a water bottle from the fridge and sliding onto the bench opposite Emilie.

"A clinic. For new and prospective off-track Thoroughbred owners. Something to help people learn what's involved in transitioning a horse from track life to riding horse life. We'd have it after show season and before racing ends — you know, when we face that last-minute onslaught of horses needing homes. "

"Once again, that is brilliant, Emilie."

Emilie waved a hand and rolled her eyes in an *of course it is* gesture. "Maybe a seminar is a better way of thinking of it. We could have demonstrations, show them what the horses do and don't know, have presentations from different industry people like a vet and blacksmith, and so on. Cater lunch and snacks, maybe a few select vendors, door prizes. Kind of like music night at the café, except with horses."

"And you want to have it here," Liv said.

"Yes. And I want you to be a presenter."

Liv frowned. "I'm sorry?"

"You'd be perfect. You used to ride show horses, and you were a jockey, and now you're a trainer. You're ideal."

"Em —"

"I'll have to run it past the board," Emilie continued, ignoring Liv's objection. "But I can't see them having a problem with it."

Especially if Emilie did all the legwork, like she always did. Though, Emilie never seemed to mind.

"I'm not a public speaker." A horse show was one thing, but the thought of standing up in front of a group gave Liv flashbacks to obligatory presentations in university. Just the memory bumped her pulse.

"You'll do fine. I have faith in you. Please?" Emilie pressed her hands together, eyes imploring.

Liv sighed. "All right. Keep me posted." She slipped back out of the seat, standing. "I should probably try to get a bit of sleep."

She left the kitchen, but wasn't sure she would manage that. What made Emilie think she was a teacher? Oh well. It probably wouldn't be the last time her sister dragged her into something out of her comfort zone. It certainly wasn't the first. If she could take a horse to Dubai and Ascot, surely she should be able to speak coherently to a group. Her brain started running through what she'd say.

Nate hadn't waited for her to fall asleep, already passed out on their bed. He was likely still operating at a deficit. Liv didn't feel tired enough; positive if she tried to join him, her mind would decide it was the perfect time to obsess over everything — Jay, and now Emilie's request. Something that would relax her was needed. Something active. Pool or treadmill? Deciding on the latter, she changed into shorts and headed to the basement.

The exercise room had been part of the renovation

completed after her parents moved back to Montreal. When their family had all lived here together, Liv and Emilie had originally occupied rooms on the second level, but now Emilie had an apartment on the main floor. The basement was a nod to Nate — the home gym, a music room, and an updated TV room. Nate hadn't insisted on any of it, but Liv had left him and Emilie to work out the details.

Now that the gym was there, Liv loved it. She'd always been content to run outside or do laps in the long, narrow pool in the backyard — more than exercise, it was a tool to keep her head calm and organized — but the treadmill had worked its way into her regime. Sometimes it was good to put earbuds in, blast the right music, and zone out, thinking of nothing but her stride and breathing. Running around the farm or on the roads, she always felt she needed to be aware of her surroundings, listening, for safety. On the treadmill, she could block it all out, not worry about cars or a horse who might need attention. Plus, there were no bugs.

She was coming out of the shower when Nate stirred. He didn't look as if he'd moved from where he'd landed, so he probably didn't know she hadn't crashed next to him, unless the bathrobe and towel on her head gave her away.

He reached for his phone to check the time, muttering, "Five minutes," like he regretted waking before the alarm. He pushed himself up and ran a hand over his eyes before focusing on her. "Did you — go for a run?"

Liv shrugged, not sure how he'd figured it out until she remembered she'd left her damp clothes draped over a chair. "Treadmill."

Nate shook his head. "Well, that makes total sense."

She grinned, scooping up the shorts and t-shirt that had given her away, and turned toward the walk-in closet. "The rain's stopped. Get dressed so we can go see the babies, okay?"

Liv waited as Nate squeezed through the fence boards to visit with Chique: their first stop. She had the sense he still felt a little lost without his original claim to fame in training. He visited Chique daily, without fail, unless he was away. That was kind of the problem with racehorses who were worthy of contributing to the gene pool. They transitioned to this life, instead of a more active one. If Chique had been a gelding, Liv had no doubt Nate would have been hopping on for a hack around the farm just about every day. Chique had his heart as much as Claire had hers. She couldn't wait for this foal, partly because it would ground Nate again. Right now he seemed so... unsettled... and it worried her. He'd told her about his concern for his parents, but she wasn't sure that was enough to explain the underlying disquiet she'd picked up on.

After Chique, the yearlings were next. And while Fleur didn't join the mob of fillies at the gate, her ears pricked at their approach, a little less aloof than she'd always been. Maybe the attention her minor wound had brought her had stirred something in the filly. Kerrie had assured them the filly's scrape was healing nicely, the early precaution of a dressing to keep it covered no longer necessary.

Liv didn't want to feel the conflict flooding her as she studied the Sotisse yearling from a distance, but she couldn't help thinking Fleur was a casualty of living in the shadow of her older siblings — Chique's success, Feste's loss — leaving her surrounded with a certain apathy. While on the one hand it might be good not to have an agenda for the filly, the truth of it was, it was self-protective. If Liv didn't have expectations, she couldn't be disappointed. Or worse, gutted like she'd been with Feste.

"I think we should start them ourselves this year," Nate said as he played with one of the group vying for his attention. With Fleur, it was the other way around — he would have to vie for hers.

He ignored Fleur, like the two of them were secret friends no one else could know about, though the dark filly's expression gave away her curiosity. If anyone could win over a reticent soul, it was Nate. Liv had seen it before, been the beneficiary of his patience and intuition.

"Your turn for the Sotisse?" she asked.

He'd started Chique, she'd started Feste. It had been circumstance, not intent, that things had gone that way, so there was no assumption they should alternate. But if Liv were being honest, it fed her apparent avoidance of dealing directly with the broodmare's third foal.

"If you want," Nate said, eyeing her. Liv felt called out, but he didn't push. "And if she'll have me."

Liv laughed.

"You think I'm kidding," he said.

She didn't, though. She laughed because of the truth in it. "I think we should ask Marie to come from the track to help, and Jillian here on the farm. Jillian's been helping Em with the layups and project horses and seems keen. Time to pass on the old ways."

Maybe Emilie wasn't as far off the mark on her request for Liv to present at the clinic as Liv had initially thought, though Nate was definitely a better teacher than she was. He had more tolerance for humans — but Marie and Jillian were both easy to work with, eager to learn. A group of strangers worried her more. She thought of Geai, missing the old farm manager — her mentor — every day. He'd been truly one of the last of a different generation. They owed it to him to share the knowledge he'd so selflessly given them.

"Spend five minutes online and you'll hear someone saying

horsemen are a dying breed," she said. "Maybe we can do a little something to delay extinction."

"Except they're women." Nate's grin became wry.

"Because that's the future, Miller." She elbowed him, then began walking again, anticipating their next destination, because among the new crop was Léa, the foal who stirred her hope more than any of the others. The one she thought could help her past Feste's memory the best.

Logic told her Fleur, not Léa, should have facilitated that, and a twinge of guilt jabbed at her, that she didn't feel this free affection for Sotisse's yearling. It wasn't Fleur's fault she made Liv think so violently of Feste. *You need to get over it.* Nate was making a point of conquering his same feelings, and she had to do the same. She'd just agreed to his suggestion they start the babies, right? They'd deal with the inevitable grief that came along with that together.

She wasn't sure she was ready to go to Saratoga, the scene of so much sadness a year ago, but if the decision remained hers to make and it seemed the right thing to do for Jay, she would face those ghosts head on. She'd done it before, though this spectre overshadowed the first one. Losing the mount on Claire because she couldn't hold her riding career together seemed trivial compared to the death of Feste.

The flashy foal and her equally decorated mother chased away the filaments of sorrow, drawing Liv as if there were an affinity between them — electrons to her atom, or the other way around. When both raised their heads, their movements in perfect sync, Liv wished she had Emilie's fancy camera. They were a perfect picture, set in a landscape of vibrant green pasture, white fences, and blue sky.

Claire and Léa strolled over like the queen and princess they were, Claire's long, black tail swishing lazily at flies while Léa's shorter one worked double-time even though her dam's swept over her, too. The other inhabitants of the field cleared the way, keeping their distance as mother and daughter came to the fence to meet their loyal subjects.

Liv entered the paddock and encircled Claire's neck with her arms, inhaling her perfect scent. Léa nibbled at the edge of her t-shirt until Liv finally turned to the youngster.

"You grew in my absence," she said, her smile as automatic as the warmth spreading through her. "It's almost weaning time, you know. Overdue, really."

She could feel Nate's eyes on her, a spectator of the interaction. In this moment she set aside her usual fears, the endless list of things that could go wrong and keep them from getting the filly to the races. Léa would be her do-over, the one who benefited from all she'd learned between Claire and now. The emotions that surged in her felt childlike. She wanted it to be a year from now, when she'd be a month away from getting on Léa for the first time. There would be no discussion on that. She would start Léa. Liv couldn't wait.

Claire and Léa watched their departure as Liv and Nate slipped away, on to their next stop. The path through the woods was slick from the rain, drops that clung to the leaves falling as they brushed branches aside. She'd have to ask Kerrie to get someone to cut them back, because they'd use it for the yearlings once they were ready to go on walkabouts around the farm. Emilie and Jillian hacked through here with the older horses, but it wasn't ideal to be ducking out of the way of low-hanging limbs on yearlings only starting to learn to balance with a rider on their backs.

They walked past Kerrie's cottage, but the manager wasn't there, likely still puttering in one barn or another while the crew finished up the day's tasks. The stallions were already in their stalls, Just Lucky's rumble demanding they greet him first. Liv could no more deny Lucky than she could Chique, a reminder that most of his offspring were gregarious, like their sire. What was it that made Fleur so different? Liv expected Lucky's foals to be outgoing by nature, making Fleur a genetic puzzle she couldn't figure out.

Nate watched while she ducked in with the small, dark bay horse. Liv didn't let Lucky nuzzle because he'd get carried away, leaving her with bruises from his quick teeth. It still stirred an ache in her that Geai hadn't lived to see Lucky's success at stud.

Next door, Starway nosed the hay under his feed tub and lipped up the alfalfa leaves that had fallen free, indifferent to their arrival. Nate bypassed him, moving on to Jay. Liv joined him in the chestnut horse's stall. Jay got peppermints.

Jay had come straight here from the airport. Stay or leave, it would be the last break he got, possibly until his retirement. Liv was going to have to train him if the decision about the syndication wasn't coming until Friday, but he could stay on the farm for that. Maybe Emilie would like to get on him. For old times' sake.

She'd told Nate about the text from her father on the drive home, so there was nothing more to say on the subject. All they could do was wait in a state of limbo for the verdict; no amount of wishing it was sooner would help. Maybe she should better appreciate the time she still had with Jay instead of steeling herself for the worst outcome, but this was the best she could do.

Nate broke the silence. "Still planning to send Claire to this guy next year?"

"Definitely. And if Trop keeps improving, his dam too."

"Too bad he can't stay here."

It was, but Lexington was the centre of the Thoroughbred breeding universe — at least on this side of the pond — and Jay had proven himself worthy of a place there. She could feel sorry for herself for a heartbeat, but that was it. Whether he left next week or stayed until the end of his career, he'd be gone once the season was over, putting them back to square one with their small racing string. She'd face the next group of untried prospects, wondering if any of them could ever fill the big horse's shoes. The racetrack circle of life; a wheel that kept turning until you jumped off, and she wasn't ready for that.

Sure, they had a few older horses. Reba was consistent, Cam had talent, and Trop was showing promise, but they might wait a long time before getting another horse like Just Jay. As excited as she was about Léa and Chique's unborn foal, neither came with a guarantee of success.

"I need to go to Calgary for a few days."

Nate's statement jarred her out of her head, tension racing up her spine. "Is everything okay?"

"No one's dying to my knowledge, but everything isn't okay."

It seemed unimaginable that Nate's parents were having trouble, but what did she know? She hadn't seen them since last Christmas and she'd expected the holiday to be hard for the Miller family, the first one since the death of Nate's older brother and his wife. Liv hadn't forgotten how difficult the first Christmas without Geai had been — how she'd spent it alone, except for a brief appearance at Roger and Hélène's, and regretted it. Her own experience had made agreeing to go to Calgary last winter automatic.

"Do you want me to come?" she asked.

The flicker of his eyes made her wonder if he was remembering the first time she'd asked that — when he'd just received the news of the car crash that had killed his brother and sister-in-law, who was also Nate's ex-girlfriend. That marriage was the thing that had driven Nate away. It even surprised Liv that she hadn't hesitated to offer, even though nothing had been certain about their relationship at the time.

Nate shook his head, his gratitude less obvious than it had been that day, but apparent just the same. "You being there would just give my mother an excuse to avoid talking to me. I never realized how good she is at steering conversation away from herself. When you're young, it's all about you, right? When you're going through shit, you never consider your parents might be going through shit too."

It was true. She'd been no better, and even now, it wasn't the kind of conversation Liv could imagine having with her parents if she or Emilie suspected something was wrong. Nate had a more open relationship with his mother, if not his father, but he was a whole lot braver than she was. Add it to the list of things she still needed to work on.

"I guess all of us are selfish as kids." She couldn't think of what else to say.

"A reminder it's smart not to have them," he said, eyeing her. "It seems like signing up for a bunch of heartache."

His comment caught her off guard. It sounded like a challenge, when she'd been completely upfront with him about not wanting children. Was he testing the waters? *Don't, Miller,* she almost snapped. It was bad enough that people assumed — you get married, then you have kids, right? But Liv checked herself. *You're reading more into this than you should.*

"Not so different from horses," she quipped, unsure if it was a happier topic at the moment, between Jay's syndication and the looming anniversary of Feste's death.

CHAPTER TWELVE

Turf training was always late, so it was the end of the morning when Michel legged Nate up onto Can't Catch Me, Liv already aboard Trop. An idea had formed in his head: the Canadian Derby at Century Mile, just outside of Edmonton, Alberta. It might be a good spot for Cam, and it would give Nate a reason to be in his home province so he didn't make his parents suspicious with a random visit.

Maybe this morning Cam would dislike the green stuff enough that running on dirt would make him happy — or he might like it so much Liv would change her mind about skipping the Breeders' Stakes and Nate's idea would be squashed before he even shared it with her.

Either way, he still had to go to Calgary. Everyone here could live without him for a few days while he determined the state of his parents' marriage. Tim would never confront them, so it was up to him. Nate could imagine their mother scoffing at his concern. *Everything's fine. Don't worry about us.* Then the next thing they'd hear would be the "D" word.

Cam was possibly more aggravating since the Prince of

Wales, like he was ticked off he'd lost the race. *Your own fault, buddy. If you'd just run in a straight line, you'd do us both a favour.* Nate wished they had a big, tough gelding to work the colt with. Someone who wouldn't take his shit, who'd teach him a lesson or two. Too bad Paz wasn't a little younger. Nate wouldn't want to ask the old pony horse to take that kind of abuse.

"How old is Paz now?" he asked into the walk-out silence that had fallen between him and Liv.

"Paz? I don't know. I've lost track. Twelve? Thirteen?"

So, not that old, really. It just seemed that way around a bunch of much younger Thoroughbreds. Paz had still been a racehorse when Nate had first met him, though he'd been retired shortly after. Not before he ran off with Nate the first day Nate had been on Woodbine's main oval. A few days later the gelding won by twenty lengths in what ended up being his last start.

They galloped once around the track before entering the turf course, the warmup taking some of the edge off his unruly mount. Even though Trop didn't antagonize Cam anymore — before Trop had been gelded, there was no way they would have trained these two together — Nate still kept the big bay colt a few paths wide of his company.

The grass was springy beneath them, the lush course wide and inviting. Cam seemed to have one eye on Trop and one on the lawn before him. They let the three-year-olds roll, accumulating speed until they were breezing, manes flicking along their pulsing necks.

Nate fought to keep Cam from dropping closer to Trop. To an observer, it would look like he was lugging in, when in reality, he was eyeballing his workmate like he might reach over with his teeth and take a chunk out of him. *Wouldn't put it past you.* Nate glanced at Liv, noting the smile on her lips, her eyes hidden behind goggles, ponytail trailing down her back. He'd bet she was back on the downs in Newmarket — far, far away from this smoggy spot next to the Toronto airport.

The turn was long, gradual; a steady declining slope until they swept into the homestretch. Cam's nose tipped toward the big, white tent on the other side of the outer rail, drifting slightly, and Nate straightened him and chased him back up alongside Trop. In the final eighth, Liv unleashed Trop, letting him run on. Only then did Nate let Cam drop closer, testing to see if his colt would focus on keeping pace instead of playing games.

But Cam tried to do the same thing he had in the Prince of Wales — leaning on his workmate like he still thought he was a yearling colt intimidating his pasture buddy. *You're gonna have to beat him without taking him out, dude. If you don't stop that, you'll be the next one having a date with the vet to lose some special parts of your anatomy.*

Trop, all business, appeared well within himself as he flashed under the wire a neck up.

Nate could have pushed Cam more than he had, but the horse had just run last week. They were going to hear flak about this as it was, like they were being too hard on him. Other Breeders' Stakes hopefuls who'd run in the Prince of Wales might gallop over the course, especially if they'd never competed on the grass, but breezing? Probably not. But it wasn't as if Cam hadn't come out of the Prince of Wales with energy left over. If he'd kept his mind on running instead of being stupid, he probably would have won the race, and he'd be having a nice gallop on this course like his foes instead of being out-worked by his stablemate.

Of course, if Cam came out here just for a gallop, he'd probably run off.

Liv looked pleased when they turned in, kind of like a girl

who'd just beaten a boy in a spontaneous match race on their ponies. Hadn't every kid who rode horses done that? Probably not Liv, come to think of it. Her early days on horseback sounded more like military school.

"I've got a really stupid question," he said as they passed through the gap to the main track.

"What's that?"

"Why the hell have we never put blinkers on this horse?" It felt like Amateur Day, the way he wanted to smack himself between the eyes with the heel of his hand. Except, of course, with Cam, both hands needed to stay on the lines at all times.

Liv's laugh came easily. "Good question. You've just always accepted he was a total jerk, maybe. Why take away your fun?"

"Because he's not winning races. And it's not really fun." Chique's quirks had always seemed to amuse him. Cam's made him question his vocation.

Liv grinned. "Blinkers on it is, then."

"Trop looked great," he said. "He deserves to be the Triple Crown spoiler."

"Sounds like you've got an agenda there."

"Maybe because someone spoiled it for me," he admitted as they reached the tunnel to the backstretch. Chique had missed successfully completing the series by the slimmest of margins, thanks to playing her own games. Okay, so maybe that day her quirkiness hadn't been so amusing. "So — seeing as Cam isn't running in the Breeders' Stakes, what do you think about taking him out west for the Canadian Derby?"

"Never thought of that."

"Of course you didn't, Easterner," he said with a droll twist of his lips. Naturally, it was on his radar. It was hosted in his home province. How often did people at Woodbine look west instead of south to the US for opportunities? Though to be fair, the Canadian Derby was the only race out there worth worrying about. “I was thinking I could talk to Al,” he continued, mentioning the trainer who had given him his start out there. “And have that visit with my parents.” Two birds, one stone. Mask his intentions with a business trip. Stealth attack.

Liv caught his eye. “Confront them, you mean.”

“Potato, Potah-to.” He shrugged, returning his gaze to the dusty screenings on the horse path between Cam’s ears. “If that’s a wash, at least the trip wouldn’t be a complete waste of time.”

She snorted. “We’re talking about Cam here.”

“True.”

“What’s the date?”

“End of August. I have to look up exactly when.” He exhaled. “I don’t know if I can do anything about them, but I at least want to pre-empt any big surprises. And I guess it’s feeling like it’s time I went back to where it all started.” Even if the timing wasn’t great — it was right around the anniversary of his frantic departure.

“Figure it out and let me know,” Liv said.

Jo and Michel waited for them on the apron in front of the barn with two men, both of them familiar. Nate hadn’t noticed Claude Lachance and Roger Cloutier on the rail, but if they were here now, he was sure they’d arrived in time to see the horses work.

He and Liv exchanged a glance. Was Roger’s presence just a friendly visit, a meetup of friends? Or was he going to be at this lunch, and why? Nate couldn’t help thinking it was connected. If the syndicate didn’t want Liv training Jay because they didn’t trust her way of doing things, maybe Claude had negotiated a compromise. Roger resuming his position as Triple Stripe’s trainer would be a best-case scenario, at least. Liv would be free to go back to race riding. It was what she wanted, wasn’t it?

They dismounted and removed the tack, Marie and the hotwalker, Marc, stepping in to hold the horses for their baths. Nate shook hands with both men once his were free.

"I'm sorry you can't join us," Claude said.

"Me too. Good to see you, though." He touched Liv's elbow and kissed her quickly. "See you after the races."

He'd have to wait until then for the news.

The Woodbine Club was as good a place as any for lunch. There was nothing suspicious about it; owner and trainer, father and daughter sharing a meal in the grandstand's fourth-floor members-only restaurant. Even the presence of Triple Stripe's former trainer, Roger Cloutier, wasn't likely to arouse more than passing interest, but Liv had to make a conscious effort to act normally; to keep her eyes from darting around the dining room, reminding herself to take actual bites of her choices from the buffet instead of abstractedly pushing food around her plate.

On a Friday afternoon it wasn't particularly busy, but Liv didn't want this news getting out any sooner than it had to. It was better that the world learn of her predicament through a formal announcement rather than gossip. She was sure Nate had come to the same conclusion she had when she'd seen Roger. It was the perfect solution to keep the syndicate manager happy. Bring back Roger to train Just Jay. Respected. Experienced. *Male.*

When she'd learned from her father's text she'd have to wait until today for the verdict, Liv had assumed he had a reason for wanting to do this in person. It had to be because of Roger. Claude had indulged his daughter's gallivanting back and forth over the ocean, but it was time to reel her in.

Look on the bright side. She could go back to riding, conscience clear. It was just ironic it came when Liv had begun to truly accept training was her place. She reached for her water, wishing it were something stronger.

Her father set down his cutlery, brushing his lips with the serviette he lifted from his lap. "The deal is off."

Liv straightened, pushing her back to the chair, and couldn't speak, almost asking him to repeat it.

Claude continued. "Jay's loss in the King George is no indication you're incapable of training this horse. The Dubai World Cup proves that. It doesn't matter to me if anyone thinks I decided to leave the horse with you because you're my daughter. I believe a good number of people would side with me." He glanced at Roger, who was nodding. "This is our first Breeders' Cup horse. I think it's only right that you continue to train him. And apart from everything, I believe you're the best one for the job."

Finally, Liv found her voice, quiet but steady. "That means a lot. Thank you." She turned to Roger. "Though it should be you training the first of our horses to run in a Breeders' Cup race."

Roger shook his head. "You've earned the right to be there as much as Jay has. It's your training that got him there, not mine."

She controlled a smile. "Lucy the butter tart lady could train this horse, you know that."

"Stop selling yourself short." It was a reprimand. "Are we back to this? You still want to ride instead of train?"

"I'll always want to ride, Rog," she admitted.

"You're more than a jockey, Liv. You were always meant to be more. We thought it would be as a vet." Roger glanced at her father. "But it's not a secret to anyone, including you, that you were meant to end up running this place."

She just hadn't expected it to be this permanent, this soon.

"You've surrounded yourself with good people," Roger continued. "We need fresh blood in this business. People like you and Nate who are bold enough to do things differently. To be the change this industry needs to survive."

Liv dropped her eyes to her plate before forcing them back up. "That sounds like a huge burden to take on. How am I supposed to do that?"

"You're doing it already," her father said.

"I've only just scratched the surface."

"So you see? You have more to accomplish," Roger said. "You are capable of great things. As you said, you've only just scratched the surface. Don't keep looking for a way out."

She pressed her lips into a tight line, then laughed softly. She didn't say it to Roger, but it hit her that his words were exactly what Geai would have said. Had said, even, when her debate was about remaining in vet school.

Liv turned to her father. "So I have free rein? Because I have ideas."

Claude smiled. "Do these ideas cost money?"

"They do, though I haven't investigated just how much. And it won't be immediate. We'll win the Classic to fund it." She grinned, a deviation from her practiced business front.

"Science is your strength. It's an advantage you have over others." There was a note of pride in Claude's voice. "Give it to the end of next season. We'll assess at that point and see if it's working."

"But what now, for Jay?" Liv asked.

"There are other interested parties. It might not mean as much money, but it would be more in line with what I believe is best for the horse," Claude answered.

The small talk came after. A year ago, Liv never would have imagined she'd be sitting across from Roger Cloutier listening to stories from the travels he and his wife, Hélène, had made this summer. She never would have predicted she'd now have his job, or that her parents would have returned to Montreal.

Liv asked about her mother and family in Quebec. The only time she'd been back was for her grandfather's funeral last fall. She thought of Nate and his plans to visit his parents, but she wasn't ready to entertain the thought of anything with her estranged extended family — and wasn't convinced she ever needed to. It wasn't like Nate and his mom and dad. She'd never been close to any of them. Unless you counted her grandfather, and that hadn't been the good kind of close.

Liv had never been one to show much emotion to her father, and vice versa — it's just how they'd always been because of the damage *his* father had done — but much had changed since that man's death. So when they parted, Liv hugged Claude, hoping he would stop overcompensating for the past. She'd proven she could handle adversity, hadn't she? And she believed him, that this was a business decision. Mostly. Because she'd recognized sentiment creeping into his choices before — though to her, it wasn't a sign of weakness, it was a good thing.

After her father and Roger left, she stayed around to watch the races, remaining mostly in the outside seats, keeping to herself. Nate was her ride home. Liv wasn't avoiding him, exactly; she just didn't want to distract him, because he'd be trying to figure out by her expression how things had gone over lunch. It would be better to wait until the drive home to fill him in, though she supposed a smile and a thumbs up would put his mind at rest. She sat in their empty box, thinking about it all.

She'd never much questioned the North American way of training racehorses, always just gone along with it. Never challenged it. Made fun of Nate when he'd suggested an unconventional approach to dealing with Claire, when Claire had developed a respiratory issue as a three-year-old — but Liv had respected him too, for thinking outside of the box and speaking up at a time when she hadn't been very receptive. Since then, she'd begun to admire the few who took a different approach to conditioning.

Why couldn't she be one of them? Was it just a matter of confidence? Because now that she was back on Canadian soil, she wanted to change everything.

When have you ever cared what anyone else thinks? How many times had she heard that? From Nate, mostly. She was the girl who'd dropped out of vet school with just a year to go, abandoning the promise of the surgical internship that awaited her, post-graduation An internship many of her classmates would have killed for.

So it wasn't that she wasn't brave. You had to be to ride racehorses for a living. But she didn't like to stand out. Didn't like to attract attention. When she was on a horse, it didn't matter. But on the ground? Different story.

That's why taking over the job of training for her father hadn't been something she wanted. They'd always had a small but successful string under Roger's care. When he'd stepped aside, he'd left big shoes to fill. With Chique, it hadn't been the same. One horse. With Nate. The filly had been their little project. Training the entire barn was a much bigger responsibility.

Liv had done it, though. For nine months, so far. The person who had taken Jay to Dubai and Ascot was not afraid of what other people thought.

So what bothered her about the idea of doing things differently? That she might discover that what she thought was a better way, wasn't? She'd look like a fool.

But her biggest fear was more than that, one she wasn't sure she could live with. What if Geai was wrong, and these North American Thoroughbreds *needed* to be babied? That they *were* bred with an expiry date, not to last beyond a handful of starts?

What if she tried it, and one of them broke?

She knew she couldn't have prevented Feste's death. He could have died the way he had without ever training a day of his life. But how many horses would be able to stand up to a more demanding exercise regime?

Once the races were over, Liv waited for Nate outside the jock's room, pacing on the concrete floor. The riders coming out acknowledged her, some friendly, others polite. They'd been colleagues, once. Not even a year ago.

Finally Nate appeared, his gaze sweeping before landing on her, questioning. She stopped her pacing and tried to keep her face neutral until he was in front of her.

"Let's do it," she said, eyes steady on his.

Nate's narrowed. "What?"

"Saratoga. With Jay."

"He's staying?"

She nodded. "He's staying."

Nate grabbed her, spinning her around with a whoop before stopping for a kiss. He pulled back with the grin she hadn't seen enough of recently. "We're taking back the Spa."

CHAPTER THIRTEEN

Big Sensation was the overwhelming favourite to become the next Canadian Triple Crown winner, more so even than Chique had been when the title had been hers to claim two years ago. Trop wasn't a longshot, at least. When reporters had questioned Liv about Can't Catch Me's absence today, she'd given one of a million lines trainers kept tucked away. *We worked him on the turf and he didn't really take to it.* His performance breezing on the grass with Trop had been public, so anyone paying attention might have deduced that for themselves. Her colleagues were probably speculating he was injured. When the nominations for the Canadian Derby came out later this week, the news he was headed to Alberta would break without her needing to utter a word.

She loved Trop. And now that it was happening, she loved Trop in here — even if she hadn't been sold on the idea at first. Following with her binoculars as the outrider led the way, the horses and their pony escorts jogged up along the turf course to the gate positioned in front of the grandstand, heads held high. It wasn't a Plate Day-sized crowd, but there was still a buzz.

Not the mob that would bury Belmont Park with an American Triple Crown on the line, and not even the numbers this track would have seen twenty years ago, but a bigger-than-average group for a Sunday in August.

Trop was one of the first to load, his position number three. Liv could see his face, his tiny ears pointed forward with Nate quiet on his back, while the gate crew slotted the rest of the field into their stalls, one after another. She poised on the edge of her seat, jealous of the fans crammed at the rail, which was really the best place to watch a race on the E.P. Taylor turf course because the action was right there.

"And they're off!" The cheer that rose from the grandstand nearly swallowed the announcer's call.

Trop looked just like his sire and Chique as he leapt cat-like to grab the lead, the field trailing him into the clubhouse turn in a vibrant sea of colourful silks. Ears still forward as he zipped along, he rated, letting Nate control his speed. So far, the race felt exactly like Chique's effort two years ago. Would Nate have done anything differently if he had another chance at the Crown with Chique? But only Liv would think that at this moment. Nate was on Trop today. *Leave the past in the past. There's no changing it.*

The gelding skipped easily over the springy turf as he traveled along the backstretch, and Liv glanced at the fractions. Nate had slowed the pace, but Big Sensation was tucked just off the rail behind him, in striking distance as they rolled down the sloped, gradual turn before swinging into the homestretch. A lot could change in that long straight to the finish.

The field was so far away, even with binoculars Liv had difficulty differentiating the competition, but the race call helped clear the picture. Big Sensation's rider pulled him from his neat pocket and began the chase.

Nate wasn't moving on Trop, but the gelding quickened,

giving Big Sensation something to run at, the two of them separating themselves from the pack. With a quarter of a mile to go, Big Sensation inched to Trop's flank — then Nate asked. Liv jumped to her feet, eyepieces pressed to her face, only remembering Emilie and Tim were next to her when they followed suit and started rooting Trop home. He was holding the favourite off, his forelegs firing out, lengthening his stride with Nate flush to his withers. The black and white eighth pole flashed past, and Big Sensation crept up to Trop's shoulder.

"Come on Trop!"

Emilie's scream rang in Liv's ear as she muttered the same words, adding, *Come on, Nate.*

Nate cocked his stick and threw in some extra left-handed encouragement, Trop digging in, holding his rival off as they blurred past the aqua and white sixteenth pole. Both horses were flat out, driving to the wire. Liv lowered the binoculars, not needing them anymore, riding every stride with Nate and the gelding. Trop wasn't letting Big Sensation past. He had this. Nate pushed him through the finish, then tucked his whip away, Trop galloping out like he'd be happy to go around again.

Emilie squealed, bouncing and throwing her arms around Liv before squeezing out of the way to allow Tim to give her a more reserved embrace.

"Picture time!" she said, nudging Liv forward and grabbing Tim's arm.

On the trackside apron, Big Sensation's trainer shook Liv's hand, and she gave him an apologetic smile. She couldn't help it. She'd felt that disappointment, being denied a Triple Crown. Now they'd all press reset and try again next season. Except at the moment, Triple Stripe didn't have a standout two-year-old who made her think *Queen's Plate.*

Before Trop even returned from the test barn and was cooled out, grazing on the lawn, the mini celebration began. The liquid in their cups wasn't the champagne they would have been drinking two years ago if Chique had won the Triple Crown, but they toasted the victory with an assortment of beer and cider and coolers. Emilie had purchased a few food trays from the grocery store, and Liv selected an assortment of fruit and veggies and cheese, famished. She could never eat properly before a race.

Roger Cloutier had always been their unofficial bartender at these stake parties, but Michel assumed the role in Roger's absence. Michel was tougher — rationing the crew and scaring off moochers, popping a whip against his jeans as he stood next to the tub full of ice water and cans. While it wasn't like they couldn't afford to be generous, Liv appreciated his taking control so they didn't have to deal with any overindulgence.

"I have to admit, I still can't get over Michel being so responsible," she said to Nate.

"He's kinda scary," Nate said, nursing his beer like he didn't expect he'd be allowed another. "Mean Dad."

Liv couldn't help laughing. "Speaking of, have you talked to your parents? Not that I'm suggesting either of them are mean."

A smirk passed over Nate's lips. "Yeah. You know how it is. Mom's excited. Dad's probably trying to come up with things that will keep him from being around."

"I think that's why I like your father. I understand such avoidance of social responsibility."

He snorted. "If his personality inadvertently prepared me for you, I should be grateful, I suppose. Though I'm not sure it's working out for him anymore, so I'm hoping you're not really the same."

Nate's strained relationship with his father had come a long way in the last year, but he apparently wasn't ready to let go of all his resentment. Her own experience with Reid Miller had been nothing but pleasant, but she wasn't about to judge. The dynamics were different. She had only to think of her mother, though much of the tension between them had eased.

"Will your parents come to Cam's race?" she asked.

"I think that remains to be seen. Please refer to my comment about my dad." Nate grinned. "Not that my mom will be able to watch me ride, but she'll probably come just because I'm in the province."

Liv's own mother had admitted she'd never watched Liv in a race. If she had a child of her own, would it be different? Pity the poor kid whose parents were both jockeys. But she would never wish herself as a mother on anyone. Not having kids was an easy decision because as much as she realized she had grown and changed, that the past was the past, it was still part of who she was, and wasn't.

Could you think of the present, for once? Sometimes she felt as if her brain volleyed from past to future without appreciating the now.

"I'm not sure how to take this," she said, her gaze drifting over their happy crew and the little racehorse who had stepped up big-time to win today. "Things going well."

"I know what you mean," Nate said.

Liv glanced at him, but he was watching Trop now, looking distracted. She'd expected his usual stream of reassurance. Like his words the day he'd proposed, and she'd accepted. *We've put ourselves through such hell, maybe the rest of our lives will be easy*. Because this year was what easy looked like, wasn't it?

Liv drove home, like she always did when they ran a horse. It was like she needed it to restore the balance between them, because her control-freak self would forever struggle with being left on the ground while he rode. Nate was happy enough to be in the passenger seat, if that's what it took.

"We won't make a production of it. Just ship him, give him a gallop over the track, run him, and come home."

She was talking about Saratoga, now that arrangements had been made for Cam's visit out west for the Canadian Derby. Her tone was full of conflicted energy, hands gripping the wheel, eyes locked on the road.

"Micro-dose?" Nate quipped.

Last year, the plan had been to spend the entire meet at the historic track with Feste and Chique. Instead, they'd been back in Ontario in less than a week. Three of them, anyway.

"We can handle that much, right?" Her jaw was set in something resembling grim determination. "I told you after the spill at Santa Anita you had to stay for the rest of the winter, because if you left, your reputation would be shot. If I refuse to go back to Saratoga because of what happened there last summer, I'm a hypocrite."

After the accident in California, Nate had wanted more than anything to go back to Florida with her. The pre-dawn scene on the beach, waves of the Pacific crashing in the background — it was burned in his memory, a defining moment in their history. *If you ever want to ride on this side of the border again, you need to show everyone that spill yesterday didn't rattle you — even though it did.* Her bluntness had convinced him, and she'd left him at the airport with a kiss and direct orders, like she was sending him back into battle. She had been, in a way. Saratoga was their next fight.

But Saratoga would be harder. At Santa Anita, it wasn't their horse who had died on the track. It wasn't Nate who had passed away later in hospital. Saratoga had come much too close to being all of that. But there would always be risk —

physical, emotional — and if they wanted to stay in this game, they couldn't let it back them off.

"So how's the new deal for Jay coming?" he asked, wanting to nudge the conversation in a different direction.

"They'll sign it after Saratoga, I guess to work out the final amount. Either way, it's less money than the one with Triumph, so I'm not sure we can afford to keep a controlling interest." She pressed her lips together. "I hate that this is about money."

It was the price of Jay's success, but not a terrible fate by any means. He'd work five months of the year breeding mares, then live the high life in the Kentucky bluegrass the rest of the time. If he didn't make it in Lexington after having everything go his way, they'd bring him home, and stand him in Ontario. And if he had no better luck here? Well, Emilie had already established the big chestnut could have a future as a show horse — unless not having that controlling interest got in the way.

"So what happens if Jay doesn't win at Saratoga?" he asked.

The Jockey Club Gold Cup Stakes was another "Win And You're In" race for the Breeders' Cup Classic, so victory there gave him an automatic expenses-paid entry.

"As long as he comes out of it healthy and sound and the Classic is still the goal, it means we fork out a big, fat entry fee."

Which would look like peanuts if Just Jay captured the winner's share of the Classic's six million dollar purse.

CHAPTER FOURTEEN

The burnt orange tips of Just Jay's ears framed the view: a cooling breeze rippling through a viridian sea of alfalfa, fluffy clouds drifting across the deep cobalt sky. The August sun scorched Liv's shoulders, her t-shirt dampening under the closeness of her safety vest.

What am I doing?

Sitting on one of the top-rated racehorses *in the world*, about to gallop him in a hayfield. Was she insane?

"You're not sure about this, are you?" Emilie asked from where she sat on Curtis, who'd been officially known as Excursion when he was at the track. Now he was Emilie's eventer, the first horse she'd taken as her own, thanks to Tim. Tim had approached Liv on the sly about buying the horse for Emilie, convinced Em needed to keep Curtis instead of selling him, as had been Emilie's intent. The gelding was supposed to be her project horse. Because it was for her sister, Liv had given Tim a considerable deal. It was the grand gesture of all grand gestures for a horse girl, and had melted even Liv's cautious heart. Tim acquired Curtis for the princely sum of one Canadian dollar.

Both her sister and the gelding were loving this new direction, and seeing Emilie and Tim together was admittedly satisfying. It would make things convenient for the holidays as well, the two sisters ending up with brothers. Practical things like that made Liv happy, too.

Except that happiness was fragile. Nate had left for Calgary today. If his parents split, everything would get a whole lot messier.

"I'm not," Liv admitted, her mind returning to Emilie and what brought them to the hayfield. There wasn't much she could do about what might be happening with Nate's mom and dad, except give him whatever support he needed. "But we'll be sensible. And he's been out here before."

Before he won the Dubai World Cup. Before he ran at Ascot. Liv had to wonder what the insurance company would say about this. Her heart had almost stopped at the quote that had come back when they'd upped his coverage after that first trip overseas. Like Nate had said at the time, a chunk of the money Jay had earned in the big race in Dubai had gone to pay the premium.

"He's just come back from galloping on the downs in Newmarket, Liv. He'll be fine. He can handle it. He won't break."

"He'd better not." They hadn't signed the deal with the new syndicate yet. After Saratoga, they'd said, bringing the pressure Liv had felt before the race in England right back. If their trip to the Spa wasn't successful, what then? She just wanted Jay's future secured — as much as it could be in this business.

"Come on," Emilie prodded. "Let's go."

Liv nodded, crossing her lines and directing Jay to the right. The two horses transitioned from walk to trot. She gave with her hands, Jay dropping his head, his mouth soft on the bit as she stood in the irons.

She focused on the steadiness of her horse's gait as he jogged. This wasn't the carefully maintained main track at Woodbine. Even the Newmarket gallops received care. Here, the path was worn from Emilie and Curtis's conditioning days, but there were hazards. Rocks and stones. Unevenness. Inconsistency. But it was supposed to be good to train horses over different surfaces. There was science behind that, wasn't there? She'd heard tales from one of the old-timers in the area, of the days when the roads around here hadn't been paved.

We used to breeze horses on Dufferin Street.

Any time the usual argument jumped up — *horses were tougher then* — Geai's voice snapped right back, insisting it was softer training, not breeding, that had created today's Thoroughbred. Add in the darker side: excessive drug use. When racing became about ROI, shortcuts were taken on the way to getting a horse to the races as soon as possible.

Her father had given her permission to test Geai's theory. Did she have to do it with the nicest horse they had, though?

We're just jogging, Liv reminded herself. Soon Jay would return to Woodbine, to a surface with a cushion. To his carefully curated life, preserving his health and soundness until he retired to a fancy stud farm in Kentucky. Her priority needed to be getting him there in one piece.

Then she forgot about all of it, because this was wonderful. Fresh air, blue sky, the green trees rushing past on the perimeter feeding oxygen to the atmosphere. The vapour trails left by airplanes were far away instead of immediately overhead like at Woodbine, where jets took off and landed at the nearby International airport, the cloying odour of their fumes tainting every breath. She let Jay pop into an easy canter up the gradual incline, revelling in the power beneath her.

The horses' ears flipped forward, heads rising, catching the figure standing in the field before their riders did.

"Tim," Emilie called to Liv, grinning. "I begged him to come out and take pictures."

Both Jay and Curtis were sane, heads dropping back into their work, though not without the swivel of an ear here and there. Emilie sang out, "You're the best!" as they galloped past, Tim following them with the telephoto lens, the upward curve of his lips visible behind it.

What would it cost to put in an all-weather gallop on the farm? They would need something proper to train any faster than this casual exercise. The farm's training track was suitable for breezing, but an uphill stretch would be a brilliant addition. She'd investigate. It was one of those things on her mind when she'd told her father Jay would probably need to win the Classic to pay for it.

When they'd finished the circuit, ending on an active jog before easing into a walk, Jay's nostrils fluttered as he released a breath, ears flopping with each nod of his head. His neck was warm beneath her touch as she ran her hand below the line of his mane, but the soft wind had removed any traces of sweat. She was aware of Tim still taking photos as they strolled out of the field. Emilie would have some incredible shots for the farm's Instagram account.

"I'm not taking any yearlings to Florida this year," Liv said, glancing at her sister. "That will let Jillian continue with them. You'll help?"

Emilie nodded. "Should we hire someone new? If Jillian's going to be doing more riding, we really need someone else mucking stalls."

"I'll talk to Kerrie."

Kicking her feet out of the irons on the walk back, Liv let the steady pulse of Jay's head lull her. She could feel good about this horse contributing to the gene pool. Well put together. Sound. Sensible.

Emilie let Liv have the wash stall first, and she scrubbed bubbles into Jay's burnished coat, watching it darken to liver, then rinsed them away until the water ran clear. He shook like a dog, scattering droplets all over her, and she laughed before scraping him off and drying his face and legs with a towel.

Outside she let him graze, the breeze quickly drying his coat to its usual tint. Emilie joined her, the two of them co-existing in companionable silence. The horses provided a soothing soundtrack, tearing at the blades.

Leaving Emilie doting over Curtis like a kid with her first horse — which he was — Liv returned Jay to the stallion barn, wishing she'd taken a moment to trade her galloping boots for running shoes, because it was a long walk and her feet were sore by the time she turned him loose in his paddock. Jay rolled immediately inside the gate, raising a cloud of dust and grunting happily. So much for being clean. He shook and wandered a few feet before beginning to nibble the grass.

Sore feet aside, the long stroll was relaxing after a ride, and Liv was reluctant to see it end as she left Jay behind and started back to the house. She considered tugging her boots off and walking on the berm, then decided what the hell, doing just that, stockinged feet picking carefully through the parts where she had to pass over gravel.

Nate would still be in the air, but by the time she had a shower he'd be close to landing. As she went through their room to the ensuite, the piano seemed lonely without him, too.

The cool water washed the sweat and grime from her skin, her mind running over the next few days. She'd leave for Calgary after morning training the day after tomorrow. Emilie would gallop Jay while she was gone, and when they returned after Cam's adventure to the west, it would be time to ship Jay into Woodbine to prepare him for Saratoga.

The New York track brought a rollercoaster of memories. First year: good. She'd had her all-important fifth winner as a jockey and placed in her first stakes race on Claire, and Geai had been there to witness it — thanks to Nate. Second year: bad. She and Claire had both been struggling, and Liv, for one, had not handled it. At all. Third year: good. She and Claire had redeemed themselves with a convincing win. Fourth year — last year: devastation.

If the pattern continued, this should be a good year. Was that superstition or statistics?

Superstition. She'd done statistics courses. There was still a fifty-fifty shot of getting heads or tails when you flipped the coin.

She'd just wrapped herself in a robe, her hair gathered under a towel on top of her head, when her phone rang. Nate, preventing her from tumbling further into that spiral. Sometimes he had the best timing.

"Hey," she said, smiling. "How was the flight?"

"Fine. I'm on my way to pick up the rental. How's your day going?"

"I galloped Jay in a hayfield. Am I crazy?"

He chuckled. "Just maybe don't go letting that out until that deal is signed. Or better yet, until he's retired."

"There might be photos."

"Emilie?"

"She had Tim come out, yeah. Should I confiscate the memory card?"

"Hopefully he took some cleverly lit artsy shots where no one will be able to tell. Make sure those are the ones Em shares."

"I think we should start to train more off the farm."

There was a pause, like he'd stopped, and she pictured him standing in the middle of the Calgary airport, phone pressed to his ear. "That's what I was saying after Dubai, wasn't it? Not in so many words, but — yeah. What is all this stupid money for if we can't do things the way we want? It's not like anyone can stop us."

"For now, we can only do so much. Because what it doesn't buy us is another farm where we can grow more hay if we sacrifice a hay field for a gallop."

"But we don't need the entire field. So we start off with something wide enough to take two abreast. That should be enough at the beginning. The biggest challenge is going to be time. And help."

"Jo can handle things at the track. She's used to it by now." Liv grinned. "I can go in once a week or something." She was running with it now, entertaining the idea of an alternate regimen, even though implementing it was a ways down the road.

"So where does that leave me?"

Liv thought she recognized a taint of worry behind his comment. "You might still have to be the track guy. We'll still have to ship in for official works."

"You know this will make people suspicious, right?"

Of course it would. She raised a distrustful eyebrow at the outfits that trained on the farm, shipping in only to breeze and run. The big ones that seemed to have horses everywhere. She'd heard the gossip about what it let them do away from the scrutiny of the track.

"Let them be suspicious," she said. She'd have to, if she did this, trust in the knowledge that she wasn't doing anything nefarious. "So, do you have a plan for this weekend?"

"I'll go to see Cam and check in with Al now," he answered. "I told my mom I'd be there for dinner. I don't want to get into anything tonight. I'll just try to get a read on things, I guess."

"You're a good son."

"Am I? I don't know. Maybe I should just leave them be. Let the chips fall where they may. I'm not sure they'll appreciate me butting my nose in. Does anyone?"

"True."

"Sorry, I've gotta go. Talk to you tomorrow? Love you."

It still did something to her when he said it. The utter panic of the first time he'd strung the less-casual three words together had been replaced by a calmer certainty that demanded a response.

"Love you too, Miller. Good luck."

CHAPTER FIFTEEN

THE DRIVE to Al Wilson's farm was still so familiar Nate could have done it with his eyes closed, though the Nissan Rogue they'd given him at the airport was nicer than his old Mustang had ever been, while he'd been driving it. This would be a good car for Liv, he decided. She was overdue a new vehicle. An SUV like this would be handy — for the dog they didn't have yet.

It was the fourth time he'd been back to Calgary since his grand departure six years ago, and it still wasn't easy. This city would never be what it had been for him when he'd been twenty-one and thought he had life all figured out. Now that he was closing in on thirty — far too rapidly — it was as if the older he got, the less he understood.

The timing of the trip didn't help. The end of August was exactly when he'd left — right after his brother had married his ex. He'd bolted immediately after the reception for a wedding he never should have attended. But that memory had shifted into something different, because how could he hold on to the pain and anger of it now that they were gone? Their anniversary would be a tough reminder for his mother. He'd put money on her going completely overboard for his birthday just to balance out her sadness. Even though he'd be gone by the actual day, she wouldn't let him leave without something.

She'd offered to pick him up at the airport, but he needed the car. He'd had to fly, of course; there wasn't enough room in his schedule to retrace that two-thousand-mile-plus road trip, but one day it would be a cool thing to do. *Like when, Miller?* When he retired, maybe. Retired from what? Once he was done riding, whenever that ended up being, there would always be some way to stay connected to racing, especially with the farm.

Al was looking out for him. Nate pulled up in front of the cedar-sided bungalow and the trainer appeared on the wraparound porch, hiking down the steps to greet him with a hearty hug.

"Nice to see you again, kid," Al said, stepping back with his hands still resting on Nate's shoulders.

Nate wondered if he was thinking *I used to know you when...*

When you were down and out and had given up. One step away from living on the street. Well... that might be an exaggeration.

Al dropped his arms, gesturing to the side. "Let's go see that horse of yours, because I know that's the real reason you're here."

Nate followed the trainer to the nearest barn. It was an enclosed shedrow-style stable — a back-to-back block of stalls surrounded by an aisle wide enough to jog horses when the weather was bad, or to leg up horses coming off an injury. The animals they passed didn't pay them much attention before the big bay's familiar head jabbed over his webbing.

"There's my favourite asshole," Nate muttered. "Looks like he traveled well."

"He's a good-looking horse, eh? I like him a lot," Al said.

"Play your cards right, maybe we'll leave him here."

"Trying to get rid of him, are you?"

"He's a pain in the ass. He needs to win a race." That might help make him more appealing as a stallion prospect out here. Cam's pedigree was nothing to sneeze at. "If he doesn't, maybe we can throw a western saddle on him and see how he likes cows. Or teach him how to pull a chuckwagon."

"Doesn't sound like you like him that much."

"I'm not sure that I do." Nate grinned. Deep down, he had a warped affection for Cam. "I'll like him a lot better if he makes this trip worthwhile."

He ducked into the stall and took hold of Cam's halter, directing the colt to the wall tie and snapping it to the side halter ring. No peppermints for Cam. Nate had learned that early. Cam didn't discriminate well between small candies and fingers. Or arms, for that matter.

Nate ran his hand down each leg and felt the colt's feet — not that Al wouldn't have done exactly the same thing after receiving the horse into his care. He made sure he brought the colt with him to the door before turning him loose and slipping out so he didn't get nailed in the back.

"You want to come in for a beer?" Al asked.

Nate shook his head. "Told my mother I'd be home for supper."

"Just like old times," Al said, his lips spreading into a smile. He glanced at his watch. "You've got time."

"Just one, then."

There'd been lots of beer, even before he was of age. Horsemen like Al didn't care about legal stuff like that, so turning eighteen had meant little to Nate besides being old enough to vote. He'd consumed a significant amount of alcohol those months he'd lived at this place.

The ranch house hadn't changed at all, everything just as it had been the first day he'd been here. Fifteen years ago. It didn't seem possible. Area rugs were scattered over hardwood distressed by time and use instead of in a factory. It was messy without being dirty, bright despite the rich wood that made up the walls. A couple of original paintings — western scenes — and some framed and laminated posters from the Stampede. Only the flatscreen television was new, bigger than the one Nate remembered. This home was straight out of an episode of *Heartland*.

Al wanted to hear all about Dubai and Ascot, which was fine with Nate. Being here was enough to deal with, without regurgitating the past. He asked how Al's horses were doing, how Al's father was. Safe catchup stuff.

"I'll see you in the morning," he said before he climbed into the rental. *Just like old times.* Back and forth between here and the city — sometimes twice a day, before and after school — before he'd withdrawn from university and his dad kicked him out. At least he'd saved money on gas once he'd lived here.

He drove back toward Calgary, leaving the foothills and thoughts of Can't Catch Me behind and shifting ahead to his mother. It was too early for his father to be home, so he'd have some time with her alone. He'd let her dominate with her own queries, like she always did, and wait for tomorrow to bully his way in with some of his own.

The house looked small and was as much stuck in time as Al's place. A modest garden decorated the front, mostly shrubs and perennials, and the lawn looked freshly cut. He grabbed his bag from the back seat, throwing the strap over his shoulder, and tapped lightly on the side door — the same old screen one that had always been there — before letting himself into the booming chorus of two Golden Retrievers. They rushed down the short set of stairs, crowding the landing as they swarmed him; zero parts guard dog, one hundred percent welcoming committee. Nate laughed as he leaned down to greet them.

"Go on, get out of the way," he scolded lightly. "Let me in, will you?"

Connie Miller waited at the top of the steps, and he pushed his way past the dogs, though the two of them threatened to trip him as they bounded up with him. He let his bag slide to the floor, which forced at least one dog into the kitchen to the right, and enveloped his mother in a hug.

"So good to see you," she murmured into his shoulder, and when he released her, her eyes were shiny as she looked him over. She would try to feed him in four, three, two... "How was the flight? Are you hungry?"

He smiled. "I can wait for supper."

"Tea, then?"

"That would be nice." He should have brought some butter tarts. Would they have allowed those in a carry-on bag? The filling might be considered a security risk. Hazardous things, butter tarts.

"You went to see the horse first?" she asked as she boiled water in what looked to be the exact same kettle she'd had before, pulling out an actual china teapot he knew she'd inherited from her grandmother. She didn't pull out the matching cups and saucers, though. He wasn't that special.

He nodded, leaning against the fridge with his fingers tucked into his pockets as he watched her. "He's good. Maybe the flight will have unsettled him enough to make him easier to deal with."

His mother pressed her lips together, not looking at him.

She didn't like it when he said things that reminded her that his job was a little dangerous. Fair enough. His brother had died in a car on the highway though, so what could she say? And he'd tried to go to school. Have a normal life. Would have, if Cindy had said yes. When she'd turned him down it had wrecked him, but now, if she'd still been here, still been alive, he'd have had to thank her. *You were right. This is better.* Not easy, but better.

"When is Liv coming?"

"She'll fly out the day of the race and stay overnight. You'll come to the race, right?" *Both of you?*

"We'll come," his mother replied.

She'd said *we*. That was a good sign.

After bringing the teapot to the kitchen table, she returned to the counter and handed him a plate of cookies. He set it next to the pot, but couldn't help it — he reached for one. He might have to sleep in Al's tack room again the night before the race just to be sure he made weight.

"What are you really doing here? You've never brought a horse here to race before. Is everything okay? With Tim being there? With you and Liv?"

Oh, the irony. She'd always seen right through him, but her vision was a little blurred this time. "Everything's fine. I've never seen Tim happier. I almost don't recognize him. And I can honestly say everything's great with us."

"That's so good to hear. I can't wait for the opportunity to get to know Emilie better. I think if Tim hadn't finally made things right with her, I would've had to drag him back there by the ear myself."

It hadn't exactly been as simple as only Tim figuring things out — Emilie had needed to work through a thing or two, as well. "Even though it meant him taking a trade to Toronto?"

"Isn't that the most romantic thing? If that's not a grand gesture, I don't know what is."

Nate grinned. "You and Emilie are going to get along just fine."

"I know that already." Her smile was contented as she grasped the teapot's handle to pour.

Connie got along with everyone. Except maybe his father. That's probably why his dad kept the Golden Retrievers. Nate thanked her as she pushed the cup toward him, resolving not to have another cookie. Then he went through the same routine he had with Al, getting all the updates.

"You'll probably want a shower, and maybe a nap before dinner, hmm?" she asked once they'd finished their tea. Connie looked from the remaining cookie to Nate as if she was about to try to convince him to eat it before reconsidering and taking the plate and her empty cup to the sink.

Nate followed, setting his on the counter next to it. "I think so, yeah," he said. "I'm just going to sleep downstairs. Is that okay?"

"Of course. We'll eat about six."

He kissed her on the cheek before scooping up his bag and retreating to the basement. The memories down here were uncomfortable because they made him think of Cindy — the beginning, middle, and end of their relationship. He thought about calling Liv again before his shower, but decided instead just to text her. He needed to deal with this on his own.

Nate didn't sleep, though, because he wasn't sure he could. Damn, he hoped this wasn't becoming a thing. Instead, he found an old guitar, tuned it, and played that until he heard the door, the excited dogs. His father was home. Nate waited until he heard footsteps going down the hall and jogged up the steps, hoping his mother hadn't set the table yet. He wanted to be doing something when he saw his father.

It wasn't so bad. His dad gave him a gruff hug, but that was as much as Nate would ever expect. They were more or less back to where they'd been before Nate had become the family's great disappointment, dropping out of school to gallop racehorses full time because a girl had broken his heart.

But dinner was awkward. His mother chatted to him while his father silently ate. Was it always like this? Did they even eat together when no one else was around?

"I have the twins Sunday afternoon," his mother said. "I bring them home with me after church to give Julie and Kevin a break. You'll still be here, I hope? What time is your flight?"

"Not till two-thirty, so yeah, that's good," Nate said. His father showed interest for the first time, watching him. "Liv will be gone, though."

"That's too bad," his mom said.

Liv wouldn't think so. The kids would probably give her an anxiety attack.

"Which day would be better to have cake, then?" Connie asked. "Because we'll celebrate your birthday, seeing as you're here so close to it."

See? There it was. "Sunday, I think. The kids will like that." And Nate didn't need to be eating cake the night before a race. Liv would be disappointed she missed out on that, though.

Connie cleared the table, giving him a stern look when he half-rose to help. "I'll take care of this."

Nate knew what she was doing. She was making her escape. In that glance he saw something else. After a quick swipe with a dishcloth over yellow Formica countertops that almost matched the harvest yellow walls, she left them. Alone. Was this more, or less awkward?

It wouldn't be so easy to confront his father as it would be his mother. They'd had two serious conversations since he'd moved to Ontario — one after Phil and Cindy's funeral, the other last August when Nate had come out here after his accident, his life once again a mess. Both those times, the talk had been about him. *His* life. *Selfish, selfish, selfish.*

So for now, they talked about work. Nate could understand his father's job better than his father would ever understand what he did. All Reid Miller would grudgingly admit was that Nate was good at it — the Eclipse Award that still, surprisingly, occupied a place of distinction in the living room, proof.

"Can I take you out for breakfast Sunday?" Nate asked. It was hard to shift their stilted conversation in that direction, make it sound like a casual thing that fathers and sons should do. Apparently some had relationships like that — just no one he knew.

"Your mother is probably hoping you'll go to church with her."

She would be, and Nate felt bad about that, but this was more important. He wondered when Reid had stopped going with her. "She'll understand."

Reid's gaze appraised. "I play golf on Sunday morning. You could come along and we could eat after that."

Nate gulped back the mouthful of water he'd just taken, in danger of choking on it. Golf? Him? He recovered, saying as if he hadn't nearly laughed out loud at the suggestion, "Sounds like fun. Count me in." He glanced at the time. "I'd better get to bed. Early morning."

"Good night," his father said simply.

He was tired, but not ready to climb into bed just yet, so he flipped on the TV and swiped open his phone. Screen time, times two; probably not the best idea given his recent sleep problems.

Emilie had posted on the Triple Stripe Instagram account. *Oops*. But the photos of Jay and Curtis galloping around the hayfield were amazing. *PC📷 @tim_miller Cross-training with the Big Horse with @liv_lachance #bighorse #triplestripebred #canadianbred 🇨🇦 #horseracing.*

He checked Liv's account afterward, finding more discreet images: an ears pic from the tack and a grazing shot of the big chestnut outside the training barn. Next weekend they'd be in Saratoga, worlds away from down home here in Alberta. Maybe it would seem easy after this.

CHAPTER SIXTEEN

Tacking up in the dimly lit stall took him right back, the saddle the same one he'd used every day when he'd worked for Al, though the stirrup leathers looked new, and the billet straps had been replaced. Al took care of his equipment. He'd always been a safety-first kind of guy.

Nate had spent his darkest days here, the tack room he'd slept in for almost eight months in this very barn. Even if he gave Triple Stripe the credit for his success as a rider, it was Al who had saved him. Al, and these Alberta-bred horses.

He could do it now — return to ride races and not worry he'd be hit so hard by what had driven him away. Last year's events changed that. Changed him. Brought the important things to the surface. His exodus had spread the fracture line in their family that Phil's betrayal had incited, but Nate had to give his brother and Cindy the credit for being the ones to try to put a screw in the break so it could begin to mend. They'd had to ambush him. Seeing them had been hard, but he was so glad they'd made the effort, as difficult as it had been to have the past he'd so neatly smoothed over dredged up. The accident that had killed them both so soon after had been a tough thing to swallow.

That's why he was here. If his parents' marriage was in trouble, he wasn't going to wait until their family cracked further to... what? Did he think he could prevent it, if that's what was happening?

Al came out to the track with him, riding the pony Nate had learned to gallop on when he was fourteen. The old retired racehorse had to be in his twenties now, but he looked great. Will's grandfather and Al's dad were friends, so Nate had the elder Mr. Callaghan to thank for making the connection. Probably tired of Nate clambering up onto his old draft horses and begging to race his cow ponies — though he accepted the free help come hay time willingly enough.

"I don't know what you're talking about," Al said, one hand loosely holding the pony's reins, the other resting on his thigh. "Your horse isn't any trouble at all."

Cam was, remarkably, on his best behaviour as they meandered to Al's modest half-mile track, like the mountains rising in the distance had him transfixed. Nate couldn't blame the colt. They'd forever do something to him, too. They would always be a part of him, their majesty resonating with his soul, a reminder of something greater than himself. He'd taken Liv up there last spring after the funeral, but he wanted to convince her to go on a ski trip in Banff sometime. Seeing as he had yet to talk her into taking any kind of holiday at all, he didn't like his chances.

Nate couldn't recall his parents ever taking a vacation.

"He must like it here," he said. "I think he wants to stay."

Al laughed and parked the pony just inside the gap once they were on the track. Nate sent Cam to the left, jogging, and the big colt settled like he was channelling Jay.

Nate had been around this small track more times that he

could count. Liv would like Al; he was all about jogging horses three miles in the early days of their training. Six circuits of the little oval. It drove a lot of exercise riders crazy, but Nate had learned to just put himself in a zone. Sometimes there was singing. He jogged once around with Cam before lining him up next to Al and the pony.

"Did you give him something?" Nate asked wryly.

"He looks happy," Al said.

Nate shrugged and set off to gallop, and Cam was just as agreeable for the three laps he made at the faster gait. Whatever the reason for the big colt's positive attitude, he'd take it.

Al asked him if he wanted to get on a couple of other horses, and of course Nate obliged. It was easy being here, easier than what would follow, and the regular help didn't mind one bit when he said he'd clean the tack. Contentment settled over him. This was the version of simpler times he'd been missing lately.

Before leaving, he checked in with Liv, mostly to finalize details for tomorrow while he had Al there, then he headed back into Calgary in time for lunch with his mother.

"Al said he's happy to drive you and Dad up to Edmonton tomorrow," he told her as he helped bring the food — too much of it — to the table. "I've got to leave early and pick Liv up at the airport."

"That's very kind of him," she said. "I'll check with your father once he's home."

Oooh, communication. At least they still talked to each other sometimes.

His mother joined him at the table, said grace, then, releasing his hand, gestured to the salad she'd prepared, smiling. Nate filled his plate with greens and added a chunk of cold salmon, then resisted her attempts to get him to eat more.

"You can feed me Sunday, okay?" After Saturday's Canadian Derby, he wouldn't ride again until Wednesday night.

"All right," she conceded. "What kind of cake would you like?"

He grinned. "Surprise me."

It would have been easy to forget what had inspired this trip, to let go of the questions he'd brought with him and just enjoy this time together, but he needed to get to it. He couldn't put it off any longer; it was time to dive in.

"I'm not just here for the race, Mom," he said, pinning her with his eyes. "I'm here to check up on you."

His mother laughed. "Me? Why ever would you think you needed to do that? I'm fine."

"Tim says he's worried. About you and Dad."

That beat of silence before she scoffed at him was a dead giveaway. "Everything's fine with your father and me. Tim worries too much."

"Liar," he said, and wanted to laugh when she stared at him, horrified. Didn't she know he knew her as well as she knew him? "Just because I'm not around anymore doesn't mean I can't see through your bullshit."

She gaped at him. "Nathan Miller! How dare you speak to your mother like that?"

"Oh, don't give me that."

"I'm sorry to disappoint you, if you're here thinking there's something to fix. I hope your horse wins, coming all this way."

That didn't sound defensive at all. "Tim wouldn't just say he was worried unless you'd given him reason to be."

She avoided his eyes, reaching distractedly for her water glass, but she didn't bring it to her lips. Her gaze remained on her plate, and she sighed. "It's been hard. Losing Phil — and Cindy — was hard."

She'd been so adamant at first there was nothing wrong,

Nate had almost been convinced, wanting to think Tim was way off base with his concern after all; that this was a fishing expedition in an unstocked pond. But there it was. An admission.

He hadn't been around to feel it. Their deaths had affected him, of course they had. He'd come home to comfort his parents, to sing at the funeral, failing to make sense of something that made no sense at all. But then he'd gone back to his new life in Toronto, where he'd been without them for five years anyway. He'd had no contact — until the day Phil and Cindy had shown up at the farm in Ontario, when the two of them had reached out. If he'd known that was the last time he'd ever see them, he'd have played things differently.

How could he judge, if this was his parents' reaction? Feste's death had nearly been the end of him and Liv. Losing a human child — two, really, because his mother had loved Cindy as much as her three boys — had to be unfathomable. Your kids weren't supposed to predecease you. It wouldn't be fair of him to go on about those three months last summer, but it's the closest thing he had to compare it to. *The two of us are like this massive black hole right now,* he'd told Faye, of all people, trying to explain why things were so wrong with Liv as he lay in a hospital bed wondering if he'd walk again. *It's just way too much grief in one place.*

If that's what his mom and dad were dealing with, how could he not understand?

"I get that," he said finally. "But you'll work through it. Get past it. Right?"

"I don't know, Nate," she said.

"You sound like you're not even trying."

She shot him a look so hard he almost ducked. Yeah, that was out of line. But if she said "people change," he was going to have to walk out.

What could he do? Their shared commitment to Chique was what had made the difference for him and Liv, but he didn't know what would hold his parents together now.

"I'm sorry," he said, because it was all he had.

"For what?"

"For last year. After the funeral, I just tucked it all away neatly and left as if nothing had happened."

"I'm sure you did no such thing. You called. You checked in. Then you had much larger things to deal with. That horrible accident."

"Don't make excuses for me. When I came back in August, too. It was all about me. I should have considered how rough it was for you."

He'd returned for his own self-absorbed self. Sat at this very table and not seen any of it as he wallowed in his own mire. Then Christmas. The holidays were always like some kind of performance. Peace on earth, good will toward all. Everyone set aside grievances — or pretended they did — and looked for the hope of the season. His mother, especially. His father just played along. Maybe he'd been playing along for a lot longer than Nate could know.

"None of this is your fault, Nate. I don't know what's going to happen, but it will never be about you."

The slap in the face was he'd done it again — tried to make it all about him. "All right," he said quietly. "I'll shut up now. Just don't shut us out, okay? Me and Tim. Can I ask that much?"

He wasn't sure what that meant, but she nodded.

So that was it? Thirty-five years. How? He'd always thought they just worked. They were the ultimate grumpy versus sunshine, the foundation on which he'd been built. But everything he'd thought he believed about his parents — about marriage, about family — suddenly felt upside down.

His mother rose, and he jumped to help clear the table; it was ingrained in him, but this time it was as if he needed to follow her around or else everything he'd known might disappear. Next time he came, this house and all the memories it held could be gone.

Swiping his phone from where he'd left it on the counter, he opened the music app and flipped through his playlists. He had one for her, something he'd listened to when he missed her most and it wasn't the right time to call. When he hit play and the first notes rose from the inadequate speaker, his mother turned from the dish towel she'd just hung on the stove, a smile coming to her lips. He held out his hand.

Most middle-grade boys thought dancing was silly. Each year the class moaned when it was time for the unit in gym class where they were forced to learn how to waltz and square dance. *Swing your partner!* They'd try to launch each other across the gym floor as if acting stupid covered up the embarrassment. What did dancing have to do with sports?

The other kids didn't have a mother who used to do professional ballroom.

He'd gone along with her teaching him because it made her so happy. She'd cajoled him until he agreed because his father wouldn't dance with her. Really, Nate didn't mind. Seeing her happy made him happy, and it had impressed the girls at school dances that he could do more than shuffle his feet on the gym floor.

So now, they danced in the kitchen like they had countless times before and she didn't correct him when he held her tighter than he should have.

CHAPTER SEVENTEEN

Nate didn't offer, and Liv didn't ask how things were going with his parents. There wasn't really time to get into it on the short drive from the Edmonton airport to Century Mile, so discussion centred around the business at hand: Cam and the race ahead. The rest would wait until after; or maybe Nate wouldn't want to talk about it until they were home. He was preoccupied, though. That much she could tell, so she suspected the news wasn't positive.

Once they reached the track, he went to the jock's room and she went to find Cam. The newness of Century Mile was a stark contrast to the likes of Ascot, and even to the revamped Woodbine. The stable area felt temporary, as if they didn't expect racing here to last. A casino carried the place.

Al's foreman, Stubbs, had traveled with the colt. Liv wondered how he'd gotten that nickname but didn't ask. The track was full of them and sometimes it was best not to know. He wasn't short or tall, and he had all his digits, so it wasn't that. Maybe he liked early equestrian art.

Stubbs held the shank and updated her while she checked

Cam, running her eyes across the colt's body and her hands over his legs. Cam had traveled well and settled in fine. She told Stubbs she'd stay with the horse until she had to go to the grandstand to meet Al, and Nate's parents. They were both coming, at least. Stubbs nodded and scooted away, and Liv left the colt to relax, parking herself on the tack box to the right of his stall. She slouched against the wall, her silk tank top and dress pants probably branding her as a Woodbine trainer, and scanned the evening's card of entries on her phone.

This was worlds away from the most exotic place they'd run a horse this year, but it might be the most significant. It was Nate's homecoming in a sense. He had a busy night, the local trainers jumping on the opportunity to put a top Woodbine rider on their horses. It undoubtedly ticked off the local riders, though. He hadn't mentioned it, but she wondered if that contributed to his low-grade brooding. He knew what it was like to be on the other side from times when big-name American jockeys came to Woodbine for an important race and picked up mounts on the undercard, displacing the regulars. Now Nate was the interloper.

Her phone pinged with a text from Al — he'd arrived, with the Millers. They arranged where to meet, and when Stubbs returned, she peeked in at Cam one more time to make sure he was still all right. He dozed, one hind leg cocked, looking right at home.

Connie Miller greeted her with open arms, and even Reid gave her an awkward hug. Al settled for a warm handshake and they exchanged words about the horse after she was done thanking him for all his help.

"This is a good crowd for Century Mile," Al said, showing the way to the restaurant. "Our boy's a draw."

There was a note of pride in Al's voice. Nate, the home-grown talent who'd left and made good. Connie beamed. Hopefully Cam wouldn't let them all down.

Connie looped her arm through Liv's as they walked. "I still can't believe you're here with a horse," she gushed.

"It was Nate's idea," Liv responded, glancing from Connie to Reid, looking for clues.

Maybe she shouldn't do that. Raw reactions to Nate's visit were probably complex. They were both likely setting emotions aside, trying to enjoy this. Their successful son, riding in the province of his birth for the first time. It was meaningful. It just might have been easier to digest if that had been the only reason he was here; if it hadn't been all twisted up with the troubled marriage of his still-grieving parents.

Their seats gave a view of the racing oval, a big sky above the barren infield that looked strange after Woodbine's lush landscaping. Nate announced his presence by winning with his first mount. Liv didn't notice if Connie watched. She wanted to assure Connie he'd be fine, but knew better than to make such assertions.

Liv excused herself when it was time to get Cam ready, turning down Al's offer to go in her place. Maybe staying with her in-laws was the right thing to do, but this was still who she was. The horse came first. Connie promised they understood.

Cam was easy to get ready. She didn't really need to be there. All she did was supervise as Stubbs knocked the dust off him, wet his mane, picked his feet and the shavings from his tail before the bridle went on. It was warm enough, Liv hosed the big colt with cool water before sending Stubbs on his way, then fished the blinkers and foam girth channel from the tack trunk and hopped in Nate's rental. She beat Stubbs and Cam to the paddock.

Nate greeted Stubbs like they were old buddies, and who knew, maybe they were. He waved to his parents standing on the other side of the rail with Al — they'd declined Liv's invite to come inside. Then his expression reverted to seriousness. Call it his game face, but Liv thought it was more than that.

Once saddled, the colt strutted around the parade ring. Cam was on the muscle, decked out in the navy blinker hood, but he didn't look as if he was on the verge of his usual shenanigans. He was easily the best-looking horse in the field, unruffled and ready, and the crowd made him the favourite.

"Maybe he's afraid we're going to leave him here, so he's decided to be on his best behaviour," Nate said dryly. "Al likes him. A lot. I told him if he plays his cards right..."

His usual grin was almost there. She'd press him later about how it all felt — coming home. Big fish, little pond. Knowing Nate, he wasn't all that comfortable with it.

With the riders up call, the hum surrounding them rose. Liv passed along her usual *bonne chance, safe trip* as she legged Nate up, Cam bouncing, feeling the building energy.

This was when she was used to shutting out all distractions, wanting to rush to their vantage point to get binoculars on her charge as soon as possible to assess every step, every muscle twitch. Al would get it — or maybe he was one of those laid back trainers who, with years of experience under his belt, took all this in stride.

"This way," Al said, ushering them forward when she joined them.

Liv smiled in gratitude. There would be plenty of time to chat after the race, maybe even a celebration to be had.

The horses were on the track when they arrived at the seats, Liv immediately finding the red, white, and navy Triple Stripe silks at the end of the line of horses and ponies jogging up to the front of the grandstand. Nate seemed more at ease now, his back straight but his features relaxed as he chatted with the pony rider. Liv had left it up to him to decide if he'd warm up Cam on his own or stay with his escort, and wasn't surprised when he went solo. Cam carried him swiftly to the backstretch before turning, meeting up with the others behind the gate. He was the last one in.

The doors crashed open and the crowd roared.

Right off, a horse veered sharply, slamming into his neighbour, and on the edges of her vision Liv saw Connie cover her eyes. The drama was far from the Triple Stripe pair, for once. Nate kept cool, holding Cam back as the commotion sorted itself out. By the time they raced into the clubhouse turn, two runners had separated themselves from the pack, setting a zippy pace that would suit Cam perfectly. He trailed nonchalantly several lengths behind, looking like Just Jay, the way he rated so kindly. Clearly the blinkers were doing something. They hadn't sharpened him, which happened with some horses, but they seemed to help him keep his head. *Why, again, did we not think to try them before this?*

If the other jockeys were expecting Cam to be on the front end, like he'd been in the Prince of Wales, they were probably wondering what was up. His position didn't change until midway down the backstretch when he started passing the horses, Nate choosing — wisely, Liv thought — to keep him to the outside when there was room on the rail. Not that Cam wasn't brave enough to go up the inside;, it was just that he'd yet to prove himself trustworthy of such a trip. There'd been enough mayhem in this race without Cam showing what he was capable of in that department.

The cautious choices saved him again when another horse swept in abruptly, knocking his rival into the rail hard enough to unseat his rider. She noticed Nate glance over — that could have been him if they'd gone inside — then he sent Cam on.

It wasn't a flashy ride, but she'd take workmanlike over brilliant any day, especially with this horse. When Cam kept his head in the game, no one here was going to beat him, and he was demonstrating that. Nate gave him a couple of cracks with the whip — left-handed, keeping his attention — and Cam steadily wore down the still-battling leaders, driving past far enough in the middle of the track they probably didn't have time to react with an extra effort by the time they realized he was there.

Connie's fingers closed around Liv's elbow, her fears apparently gone as she bounced up and down on the balls of her feet like a teenager, reminding Liv of Emilie. Liv grinned, glancing sideways at her. Connie's other hand was a fist, pressed to her mouth. Okay, maybe not all gone. Bounding past the wire, Cam careened around the turn, galloping out as if he was just starting to roll. Nate didn't even bother to try to pull him up, allowing the colt's momentum to diminish naturally somewhere around the far turn.

"New track record," Al said, slapping Reid on the back before reaching for Liv's hand. "He made it look easy."

Nate's father looked bemused, as if he wasn't sure exactly how he should feel.

Liv nodded, controlling the wry tilt of her lips. "I didn't know that colt had easy in him."

There was a proper grin on Nate's face when Stubbs led Cam into the winner's circle.

"It was a little wild out there," he said. "Weird it wasn't us."

Liv gently helped arrange her in-laws for the photographer. It was fun to feel the excitement of people who'd never been in a win picture. With Reid next to Stubbs, Connie clinging to Liv, leery of Cam's power as adrenaline still pumped through his exposed veins, the photographer captured a few shots. Cam even had the decency to stand still.

Nate hopped off, Connie and Reid retreating as Liv stepped forward. He kissed her before peeling the tack off and weighing in. Then he hugged his mother, who looked both joyful and relieved he was alive. He only hesitated slightly before embracing his father when his mom finally released him.

They all went back to the barn. Nate joined them after he'd changed, Cam his last mount of the day. Cam wasn't the kind of horse you got up close and personal with, and Connie had already shown she wasn't comfortable around him. So, while Liv gave them the usual safety instructions — stay on the inside of the shedrow, close to the wall — Connie and Reid huddled inside the stall as they watched the big colt once he returned from the test barn. When he was ready to go in, Liv steered them well clear.

"Stubbs will do him up," Al said.

"Looks like they've bonded," Nate quipped, and Stubbs threw him a crooked smile as he began gathering the bandages. The nice stake bonus the foreman would get from Nate made Cam especially easy to like right now.

"You must be tired," Connie said, resting a hand on Liv's arm.

"Those two hours do catch up with you when you've been up early," Liv agreed. She was running on Toronto time.

She was relieved they all agreed it was best to return to Calgary instead of going somewhere for dinner. Al offered to supervise getting Cam to his farm and this time Liv accepted his help, thanking him. She tried to stay awake for the three-hour drive back to the Miller's house, but it wasn't long before the soft back-and-forth conversation between Nate and his mom faded away. She woke when the car stopped moving. It was after one AM, which her body told her was three.

"I'm sorry," she whispered, but Connie hushed her and ordered them all to bed.

"I'm awake now," she said when she climbed under the covers.

"But what time's your flight?" Nate asked.

"Right," she said, sitting up and reaching for her phone to set her alarm. "Are you sure you still want to drive me to the airport?"

"I have to be up early anyway," he said. "You'll love this. I'm going golfing with my dad."

Liv snorted. "You? Golf?" Nate was the guy who scoffed at the jockeys and agents who played.

"I know, right? Don't let me make a habit of it, okay?"

"You'd never hear the end of it, trust me. I will require photos, however."

"Huh," he said. "Selfies with my dad? Not sure that will happen."

CHAPTER EIGHTEEN

The last place Nate thought he'd be this weekend was a golf course, yet here he was. With his dad, no less. Quality father-son time, right? Such a thing had never existed between him and Reid Miller. Except for the handful of times Reid had helped after Nate bought his old Mustang, it had been hockey or nothing.

Can't Catch Me was on his way back to Toronto, as was Liv. Nate had seen them both off at the airport in the wee hours this morning. Part of him liked the idea of Cam staying, but Al's interest in the colt might have saved the big bay's reproductive organs. Something to keep in mind when it came time for Cam to retire. There was an incentive program for Alberta-breds, and some decent stallions ended up here. Unless the Canadian Derby became the turning point of the colt's career and, like Jay, he was destined for bigger things.

Nate had to keep himself from swinging the golf club around like a baton. Probably poor etiquette. If he concentrated, he was sure he'd be good at this. He could shoot a puck; how hard could hitting a golf ball be? And he wasn't going to lie to himself. It was important to him to be exactly that — to catch on like he was a natural. To get one of those looks of approval from his father. The thing he'd told himself he didn't care about, but did — and hadn't quite managed last night after winning that race, despite being considered one of the best jockeys in the country. Back here, in his hometown, it felt as if he still had to prove himself.

"Too bad Liv had to go back so early," Reid said as they strode to their starting point.

What was it called? The first hole? Were they teeing off? Something like that. It would look bad if he googled it. He should have spent some time watching the pros on TV, except he found golf so boring.

Reid continued, "Your mother would have liked to have spent more time with her."

"Liv's still learning to, you know, relax." She could have stayed later — as early as she'd left, she still wouldn't be back in Toronto in time for morning training — but she'd insisted she didn't want to interfere with whatever he was hoping to accomplish with this visit.

"Ah, because you've mastered it?"

Nate caught the glint of humour in Reid's eyes. "Hey, I'm here, right? Playing golf." He'd never live it down if he took up the pastime. Or was it a sport? He had trouble thinking of it that way.

His father smirked. "Playing might be a stretch."

"How's it working for you?" Because one thing was for sure, Reid Miller had a solid work ethic, which was a nice way of saying he immersed himself in his job. "Preparing for retirement? Do you think you could do this all the time?"

There was something in the way Reid paused that seemed off. Finally his father said, "What else would I do?"

"Dunno. Go on a cruise with your wife?"

"Could you picture me on a cruise?"

"Maybe not." Nate couldn't picture himself on one either. "Fishing?"

"Could you picture your mother fishing?"

That was a no, too. Was that the problem? That now that their kids were grown up, they had nothing to share? How had they ended up together in the first place? He and Liv would always have the horses to bind them, so if outside of work they had other interests, that wasn't a bad thing. But his mom and dad — they didn't work together, or play together.

"Didn't think so," Reid said, tossing a ball with one hand. "Are you ready?"

"Sure." *Let's do this. Let me show you how quick I catch on.*

It didn't exactly work out that way. For an hour and a half, Nate tried. With anyone else, he would have made a joke of it. Maybe he and Tim would have to take golf up, learn together so they could better bond with their father. A lot of pro hockey players golfed in the off-season, right? At least his father didn't make fun of him.

"Time for brunch?" Reid asked.

Nate nodded, relieved to be done with this golfing fiasco, reminding himself to leave room for the cake his mother would push when they returned.

It surprised him when his father stopped to introduce him to the people they encountered. *This is my son. He came to ride in the Canadian Derby. Won it, too.* The praise took the edge off the chip Nate had balanced on his shoulder on the golf course and helped start brunch off on the right foot. But Nate wasn't done with his line of questioning, which would probably put an end to it. Except his father nailed him with a look as soon as they sat down.

"What is this, exactly?"

Nate didn't think he'd ever heard his father sound defensive, but Reid's tone was exactly that. He hadn't really fooled either of his parents with this visit, had he?

Nate took a deep breath. "Do you remember, after Cin and Phil's funeral, we took that walk? You told me Liv kicking my ass on the track would keep me humble." She'd just decided to go back to race riding, a year after the injury on Claire that had seen her put that career on the shelf, and for the first time they'd be competing head to head on the track.

"Now that she's a trainer, I guess you're missing that."

Nate ignored the dig. "I asked you who did that for you. You said it was me." He threw his arms open. "Here I am. Mom's already admitted things aren't good with you two. Let's hear your side. Do you just not like each other's company anymore? Did you ever?"

His father set down his knife and fork, placing a hand on either side of his plate and Nate thought for a second he was going to leave.

"You remember the story of how we met?"

Nate shook his head. It embarrassed him he didn't, not exactly. Another reminder he'd been a selfish kid only caring about his own stuff. And how many boys really cared about their parents' romance? Maybe he didn't want to hear this, because maybe it wasn't a romance at all.

"We worked at the same camp when we were teenagers. She was a counsellor, I was on maintenance. It won't surprise you that everyone liked her, and the guys were all after her. She was cute and smart. Great with the kids. Led chapel services singing with her guitar. A girl that couldn't help but catch your eye."

It was easy to picture Connie in that setting. How many times as a teenager had Nate accompanied her on piano at church or even just in their living room while she sang?

"We barely exchanged two words all summer. I was a lot

like Tim. Way too shy to even think of talking to her. No matter. She insisted she had a guy, so nobody got anywhere with her." Reid reached for his water, took a sip. "Next time I saw her was at a dance competition. My sister was in it, so I got dragged along. Seeing Connie there made me glad I'd gone after all, but I guessed her dance partner was the guy she'd talked about at camp. The two of them were incredible together. Made me jealous, to be honest."

Nate almost interrupted. *So what's the deal with that? Would it kill you to dance with her?* Instead, he let his father continue.

"But again, it didn't matter. Never even talked to her that night. I was pretty busy anyway. Finishing school, working a part-time job, playing hockey and expecting to get drafted. Which I was, the next summer."

"Wait —" Nate cut in. "Why the —," he stopped himself before continuing, though his dad wouldn't care as much as his mother if he swore. "Did you never tell us that?"

"Wouldn't have been fair, really, would it? Would have made it more obvious that the reason I put so much pressure on you and Tim was because I was trying to live out my dream through the two of you."

"What happened?"

"I got hurt. My knee, just like Tim, only it was worse, and my surgeon wasn't as good. It finished me."

How had all of that never come out?

"Anyway. My parents couldn't afford to help me with school, so I went full time at the plant. Learned a job from the inside out. Worked my way up. I ran into your mother again at the wedding of a couple we both knew from the camp. Found out from our mutual friends she was single. Was confident enough by then to ask her out. Got married a couple of years later. Had three great kids. We were good at that. Balanced each other out. She got to be the sweet one, because she is sweet. I got to be the hardass. It worked. All three of you boys turned out all right. None of you ended up in prison or strung out on drugs," Reid said with a hint of a wry smile.

"Not yet, anyway," Nate responded, aware he'd mirrored the expression. He hadn't heard his father string so many words together. Ever. Even Tim and Liv seemed chatty next to this man.

"I made a lot of mistakes. You succeeded, despite my failure."

"What makes you think you were a failure? If you hadn't been such a hardass and had actually supported my decisions back then instead, I never would have left." He'd let those thoughts drift through his mind, time and again. *What if Cindy had said yes?* What would his life look like today? She'd be alive, at least.

"It was hard on your mother when you left. I won't say you were always her favourite, because it's not like that, but you were always closest to her. Because of me, you stayed away. Then Phil and Cindy... that feels like my fault too. Because they went to see you."

Nate was tempted to fight his father for the blame, but that wouldn't help anything. "You're being a lot harder on yourself than you should be," he said instead. "And now Tim's moved, too."

"I'm happy for Tim," Reid said. "Even if he's not playing for the Flames." That hint of humour again. Tim had started out playing for the Calgary team. "I appreciate you care enough to come, but I'm not sure anyone can change the facts. No one ever tells you that sometimes once the nest is empty, you're not sure it's somewhere you should be anymore."

There had to be something Nate could do to make it better. Maybe they just needed a reset. He could send them on a trip.

Buy them a house in the country, if the old nest held the wrong memories. But money — the money he had, which he'd never grown up with so didn't know how to handle — would not fix this. Why was he having so much trouble admitting there was nothing he could do?

"They're pushing me to retire."

Nate's jaw went slack, and he could only stare at his father for a moment before he found words. "What are you talking about? That's insane. The plant would fall apart without you."

"They can get a younger guy to do the job and pay him a lot less. That's just how things are now."

In the end, was everything about money? He wasn't close to his dad like he was with his mom, but he'd figured out enough — that Reid Miller's world had always been his job and his family and golf wasn't going to make up for both those things evaporating.

"I haven't told your mother," Reid said quietly.

Nate was sure, despite everything else, his mother would be sympathetic if his dad would just open up. But that would be a big jump for Reid Miller. He'd never been one to talk about feelings, and would struggle to accept her help to navigate this next chapter. Just when he needed it most.

"How long have you known?" Nate asked.

"They've been hinting about it for months. Recently it's become a lot more than that."

Nate kept himself from screaming, *you need to get over yourself and just tell her. There's nothing you can't fix here.* But maybe it was all too much, that after years of ticking along with work and kids, not having either anymore meant losing the only thing that had held them together.

"That sucks, I'm sorry." It seemed the only thing he could say to either parent.

His mother's car was in the driveway when they returned.

No announcement was necessary when they pushed through the side door, immediately met by a tornado of three-year-olds and Golden Retrievers. Nate stood by, petting the dogs as his father somehow scooped up both of the twins, one in each arm.

It slammed him in the chest, seeing his niece and nephew. It was just the second time. They'd been subdued those brief moments he'd met them after the funeral; wide-eyed as they clung to Cindy's sister Julie. They wouldn't remember him, and in time they'd forget their parents. Was it better not to know what you lost? There was just no way to work that through to a satisfactory conclusion.

In the year that had passed, the resemblance to Phil and Cindy was more pronounced, driving the emotions deeper. These two perfect beings were his blood. He wished he lived closer so he could help. Help his mother, help Julie, and help these children understand who their parents had been.

It came back yet again. How things would have been if Cindy had said yes to him instead of his brother; imagining himself having completed the kinesiology degree he'd started. Maybe he would've been a trainer for the hockey team his father had hoped he'd play for. Consolation prize for the career he was supposed to want. *Settling, settling, settling.*

But he might have had *this,* and he hated the contrary voice in his head that tried to tell him he'd made a mistake. Because with Liv, he never would.

If Reid had ever been as relaxed as a father as he was with his grandkids, Nate didn't remember it. He entertained the kids in the living room while Connie was busy in the kitchen, and soon Nate found himself dragged into the shenanigans. Reid told the kids he was a jockey, and before long they'd warmed up to him enough to play horsie, fighting over whose turn it was to ride their uncle.

"Who wants cake?"

Tanner did a flying dismount with Skye hard on his heels at the sound of their grandma's voice. Nate rolled onto his back to stretch it out and breathed for a moment before he followed them to the kitchen. Not because of the physical strain. It was the inner turbulence he needed to reorder.

The twins were helping her push candles through dark chocolate icing, and he was glad they couldn't count high enough to know there weren't enough. Twenty-nine. He shook his head.

"Come sit down, Nate," his mother said.

He did as he was told and watched as she lit the haphazard arrangement of candles before leading the chorus of "Happy Birthday" and setting the cake before him.

"Make a wish!" the kids insisted.

That was easy.

Then he blew out the candles and looked around at the faces, struck by how happy they were, and let himself believe this is how it could be again. That his parents would rediscover each other, that these kids would grow up whole, and that he'd be truly satisfied with his own future, instead of always wondering what he'd lost.

CHAPTER NINETEEN

THE AIR outside the terminal was dank and heavy with the smell of exhaust fumes. After midnight, the airport wasn't busy so it was easy to pick out the familiar car swooping into the curb in front of him. Nate reached for the handle, pulling the passenger door open and throwing his bag behind the seat.

"Thanks for picking me up," he said, snapping on the seatbelt.

Tim shrugged. "Made sense. I'm the one technically on vacation right now."

"Any excuse to drive the Porsche, right?" Nate had needed to talk Liv out of coming. One of them had to be rested in the morning which, for them, came in four hours.

Tim just grinned as he shifted into gear and eased the car forward. After spending most of the day with their dad, Nate was struck by both the similarities and differences between his father and younger brother.

He was tired but not sleepy, so it seemed as good a time as any to update Tim. "You weren't wrong."

Tim's eyes flitted from the road. "That's too bad."

"It is."

"How dire is it?"

Nate sighed. Five hours on a plane had eroded the image he'd clung to when he'd left: Connie and Reid as grandparents enjoying the next generation — together. "They're still living in the same house, so that's something. But neither of them gave me promises they were going to work through it, so I guess we need to be prepared."

"I suppose it's better to know than to wonder."

"Yeah." It still didn't feel great. "Hey. Why don't you and Emilie come to Saratoga?" The idea popped into Nate's head now that he was back on Toronto time and had to focus on what was on the horizon.

Tim cocked an eyebrow. "That's this coming weekend?"

Nate nodded. His trip west had kept him from thinking about it, but now it loomed. "You know Em's never been?"

"That's a huge omission, I guess, is it?"

"Major." Nate grinned.

"I can't see her saying no. She's still going on about missing Ascot. Can youi figure out the track stuff?"

"Cam will be on the farm and we'll have Jay, so I think they'll manage. It's just a short trip for us this time. Saratoga's only six hours away. We'll drive there Friday and come back Sunday."

"That's crazy."

"That's life. Hang around here, you'll get used to it."

"You let me know if they can do without her at the track. If that works, I'll see if she can rearrange her schedule at the clinic."

"I'll talk to Jo and Liv in the morning." Nate didn't expect either of them would have a problem with his plan. "It'll be fun."

"It'd be more fun if we had more time, wouldn't it?"

Right now, the quick turnaround felt perfect. Microdosing, as Liv had said, with the added benefit of Tim and Emilie to dilute the associations of last summer. "It's Saratoga. You make the best of what you get."

He was trying to go into this with a positive approach. *Remember your first time there, Miller?* It was everything a visit to Saratoga was supposed to be. A road trip with Geai, a fun day at the races, New York pizza from the grandstand concession. The weather forecast for this weekend looked great — steamy but blue skies. Bright, instead of the rain clouds that had opened up last year like they'd been scripted for a tragic movie. That first mini-break was proof Saratoga could be good. Saratoga could be fun. And they were due.

Only good things.

Liv stirred when he climbed into bed, even though he'd tried to be quiet. "So?"

It was too late to answer that fully. "It's good to be back." And it was, because having reality here, under his fingertips as he wrapped himself around her, put this — the two of them — back into perspective. "What's up for tomorrow?"

"Tim helped Emilie take Jay to Woodbine this afternoon. He'll breeze. You can sleep in. I can get on him."

"Nah. I'll come. All I'd do here is think too much." Horses helped disrupt the complicated thoughts clogging his brain.

She was already falling asleep again. He was hopeful he'd follow suit, his body and mind stuck somewhere between two worlds.

Nate said he was fine, despite four hours of sleep, but the good thing about Jay was you didn't have to be totally awake to breeze him. Liv went out with them on Paz. At least he didn't have to get on Cam this morning. It was the three-year-old's turn for a mini-vacation on the farm, so he was Kerrie's problem.

"Probably as close as I'll get to a vacation myself until the end of the season," Nate quipped when they'd agreed after the trip out west that the aggravating colt was due a holiday.

Liv was sure the visit with his parents was on his mind, but it wasn't distracting him. He'd achieved what he'd set out to accomplish, gotten the story firsthand. Even if he didn't like it.

And now they had Saratoga to look forward to. *Ha.*

The thing was, she found she *was* looking forward to it — at least partly. The part that had been in awe of the place on her first trip to the famous racetrack, because it had been memorable in a good way. She'd finally ditched her five-pound bug and just missed winning her first stake race on Claire, with both Geai and Nate in attendance. Nate hadn't had any idea how huge a gesture that had been, how much it had meant to her. Maybe his motivation for making the trip had been selfish. She knew now he'd been running from bad memories — everything he'd left behind in Calgary. He'd needed a distraction, but in the process he'd done something massive for her. To this day it stood out in her mind how wonderful it had been. If she'd been a normal girl, that would have been it. She'd have been head over heels. She wasn't though, so it had taken her considerably longer to get there. Thank heaven for Nate's legendary patience.

Jay didn't need to be broken off; Liv just backed up with him and let Nate get the big horse to the pole on his own, watching them drop to the rail from behind as she cantered Paz to the five-eighths marker. All horses should be this easy to train. But where was the fun in that? That's what Nate would say. She hoped he still felt that way when it was Chique's baby he was dealing with.

"What are you thinking about?" Nate asked when he pulled up beside her, facing the infield, Jay's nostrils blowing lightly after his effort. "That's an almost wicked smile."

"Not wicked. Amused, maybe."

"So?"

"Your monster baby."

"Ah." He laughed. "Counting the days, are you? What brought that on?"

"The comparison. Between this one, and what that one will be. Are you ready?" *For Chique's baby? For Saratoga?*

He grinned. "Can't wait."

CHAPTER TWENTY

Emilie looked as if she needed to pinch herself, an expression of wonder on her face each time she dropped her camera from her steady gathering of shots. Liv remembered feeling that way — in awe of finally being here. The emotions tied up in this place weren't so simple for her anymore.

Saratoga appeared the same. The trees were still plentiful and lush on the backstretch; the quality of horses still top tier. But the past had shifted the perception, the track's reputation as "the graveyard of champions" for its history of beaten favourites a literal graveyard for her. It was hard not to think that Bad Things Happened here. They weren't supposed to admit that it affected them, that the grief lingered like toxins collected in adipose tissue — but how could they not?

If any horse could turn things around, it was Just Jay. *Today was the day.*

Don Phillips' crew was much the same as it had been previous years, headed by his assistant, Jeanne Dufour. Their plans had been too last-minute for them to stay at the house Jeanne rented each season like they had last year. It was already fully occupied, so they'd snagged a hotel room in town — to the tune of a lot of money — and had been lucky to get it. Saratoga Springs was overrun on the final weekend of the always popular meet.

"Jay's gotta win so we can pay for it," Nate quipped.

"If you'd given me more of a heads up, I could have found you something," Jeanne said. "Though I figured the way you two have been traipsing around this year, sleeping on an air mattress in the living room would have been beneath you."

"I'd sleep on a cot in the stall next to Jay if that were a possibility," Nate said. "Which it might have come to, if there *was* an empty stall."

"Sure you would," Liv said, but agreed it wouldn't have been the worst option. Forget the cot, the way these stalls were bedded with straw, thick and banked up the sides, it probably would have been more comfortable than the bed they'd slept in at the hotel last night.

"Hey," he said. "It's only been six years since I was living in a tack room. I don't intend to forget it."

He kept saying things like that, reminding her he wasn't comfortable in his new skin, someone who didn't have to worry about existing one degree away from living on the street. Liv didn't really think it would have ever come to that for Nate because as long as he could ride, he'd have work — though being here was a stark reminder how quickly that ability could be taken away. If he hadn't been able to come back from that injury last year, she'd have helped him any way she could if he'd let her. Which might have been the sticking point, the way things had been between them then.

That was probably how so many previously successful people around the track ended up living in obscurity, dying in poverty. Once someone had been on top of the game, it could be hard to ask for, and accept, help. She wasn't allowed to judge. Asking for help wasn't her strongpoint, either.

There was only one way to deal with the barrage of feelings. "Got something for me to get on, Jeanne?"

Jeanne nodded, and called down the shed, "Mo! Put the tack on your gelding. Liv can gallop him with Jay. He almost ready, Michel?"

Michel had joined them this time. He hadn't been able to make it to Dubai or England, so at least he got to visit one elite racing destination on Just Jay's grand tour, this pursuit of Horse of the Year. With Emilie also deserting the Woodbine crew, they'd be short-staffed, but Jo and Liv had agreed some of the other horses could have a couple of days off to make things easier. All Michel had to deal with was the ire of Sue, who hadn't appreciated it when Michel promised to bring home t-shirts for her and baby Leo.

"You want to get on the pony, Emilie?" Jeanne asked.

"I would *love* to get on the pony," Emilie said. "A day on the back of the pony at Saratoga is better than —" She waved her hands around, then frowned. "That sounded better in my head."

Liv laughed and tugged her helmet on. She'd been surprised that Emilie and Tim had decided to come along. It'd been Nate's idea. A good one, because having them here, experiencing this place for the first time, helped distract Liv from her own perception.

"Can I walk him out to the track?" Michel asked, looking from Jeanne to Liv as he stopped Jay, Nate stepping forward to run his hands over the tack.

Jeanne shrugged. "Sure. We've got everything under control here."

"You're covered, Miller," Liv said. "Groom's walking you out and you have the pony."

"Can't be too careful with the Big Horse." He grinned, ducking around from Jay's off side to gather the lines and cock his leg for Michel to toss him up. "It means I can nap. Wake me up at the gap, Mike."

Tim followed them, now in charge of Emilie's camera, pointing the lens from the surrounding scenes and back to the three of them riding out. There were always photographers around the Saratoga backstretch, from professionals to amateurs. Jeanne had even pointed out a group of equine artists she'd befriended who came every year for a few days. Liv would have to ask if Jeanne had their website info or social media accounts, to both see what shots they captured and check out their work.

"If you'd let me put you on a horse, this could be you," Emilie said when Tim fell into step next to her, the camera cradled against his chest.

"I'm good down here, thanks."

Nate began singing Meat Loaf's "I'd Do Anything For Love," with a strong emphasis on, "but I won't do that," making Emilie snort.

Liv smiled and thought it again: it was a good thing, having them here. Emilie steered the pony to the right as they went through the gap and found a spot on the outer rail while Liv and Nate backed up to the wire.

"Let him run off with you a bit down the lane," she said as they paused, the two horses standing pointed toward the infield.

Nate gave her a sly look and a nod, but didn't say anything. A move like that the morning of the race would attract attention, but Roger and Claude had agreed science was her strength, and she was using it.

As she let Nate go on ahead with Jay so her mount wouldn't be drawn into Jay's energy — she was only galloping this one — Liv wished Jeanne had given her something less tractable. It would've kept her mind better occupied as they went around, so she didn't keep thinking, *this track, that spot right there,* almost expecting to see a wreath of flowers to mark where Feste had gone down.

The gelding she rode was happy to travel at a workmanlike pace, and she resisted the temptation to close her eyes as they passed the dreaded landmark, but there was no way she wouldn't feel it, even if she didn't see it. Jay's short blow out let Nate fly past it, but Liv wondered if he was experiencing the same battle in his head.

It was a relief to reach the backstretch, easing the gelding and pulling up where Emilie waited. Jay danced off the track with Michel at his head, a light in the big chestnut's eyes — a spark ignited that would erupt into flames this afternoon.

"I hope you know what you're doing," Jeanne muttered as Liv pulled the tack off the gelding. Because on the backstretch, even if you didn't see, you heard.

"I won the Dubai World Cup, didn't I?" she answered, sounding more like Nate than herself. It made her smile.

The morning wasn't the rush of constant action it was for them at Woodbine. They were tourists on this backstretch, visitors to Jeanne's show. Cameo appearances in a month-long production, brought in for the finale. It left them with time to kill between now and when they'd need to prepare for the race.

"Can we go to Mrs. London's?" Emilie looked apologetically at Nate. "Sorry, Nate. We'll get you something to have later."

The wait would feel longer to him, sequestered in the jock's room. He'd have his own psychological war to wage in there, though the post-race carnage hadn't involved that space for him. He'd been unconscious after the spill. By the time Liv had seen him in hospital, he'd only known his own status. She'd had to break the news to him about Feste, and that under her tortured guidance, Chique hadn't been able to win the race that had come after — one Liv was sure the filly would have captured had Nate been on her.

"Come on." Emilie grabbed her shoulders and directed her toward the car, like she recognized Liv needed to be rescued from her thoughts. "I need pastry."

A proper lunch would have been too much, but the lure of the French bakery trumped the queasiness in Liv's stomach. Something about the steamed milk in a cappuccino always settled her nerves.

The downtown café was jam-packed, much smaller than Faye's place at home. They stood in line, and Liv laughed as Emilie and Tim gawked at the filled display case.

"We have to take something back for Faye and Will," Liv said.

"She's so mad that I'm here," Emilie said. "You help me pick, but I'll buy. It's the least I can do."

"One of these times we'll get her here." Someday, when she could manage to be away without the responsibility of a horse. Liv was jealous of that small group of artists and their annual Saratoga escape.

The pastry was as delectable as always. She couldn't remember coming to the bakery last year, though she must have. All she could recall was the bad, none of the good.

Liv glanced at her sister and Tim. "Thanks for coming, you two. It breaks up the clouds a bit."

"You know I bring sunshine everywhere I go," Emilie said, and Tim grinned.

When they returned to the track, they watched races until it was time to go to the barn and prepare Jay. Liv left Emilie and Tim at the seats, and even though her presence wasn't really required at the barn — between Michel and Jeanne there wasn't anything for Liv to do — she couldn't stay away. When it was time to go over, she walked with Michel.

That day had been grey and drizzly; today was sunny and clear. That day had started with hope and excitement; this one hummed with cautious optimism. The Labour Day weekend crowd had a different feel from the one gathered that afternoon last summer. It had been early in the meet, attendance nowhere near the peak it would see as the days wore on. Spectators stood layers-deep at the rail of the pretty walking ring, the statue of Sea Hero presiding over the routine. Dashes of colour from the red and white umbrellas and awnings blurred into the background when the horses and jockeys arrived.

Hadn't it been Labour Day weekend when Nate started working on the farm? Liv remembered sitting by the pool with Faye, being teased about the good-looking New Guy, dismissing her best friend's taunts. If Liv had been typical, she might have gone along with the plan Faye suggested. *A late-summer fling is exactly what you need.* Instead, she and Nate had simmered and sputtered.

Now, there was this.

This horse, Jay, capable of setting their world straight.

This race, somehow bigger than Dubai. Bigger than Ascot.

It was for Feste, and for Chique. It was for them. For all of them.

Nate joined her, Emilie and Tim disappearing from her consciousness so that it was just the two of them and the big red horse circling around them.

They'd stood like this at racetracks across the world. She'd watched him ride numerous times since that moment last summer, before he and Feste went down. For the first time, the fear she'd always been able to keep submerged threatened to break loose. She wanted to toss decorum out the window, throw her arms around him, hold him tight, in case this was when he didn't return.

"I don't care if you win, Miller. Just come back safe. Both of you."

There was no fear in his eyes, though.

Do you ever get tired of being so reassuring?

"We will," he said, a promise he had no business making. "But we're here to win this."

It was a relief to be on Jay, away from Liv, when the rest of the time he could never be close enough. Right now he needed distance because his life literally depended on it. When he'd been in front of her, eye to eye — standing where they'd been with Feste just over a year ago — he hadn't been able to block the anxiety that simmered below her surface. As much as she tried to keep it there, it threatened to infiltrate the thin wall of confidence he'd set in place. It was like someone had lifted the edge of a scab, exposing raw flesh that had yet to heal into merely a scar. He had no room for fear.

The warmup centred him; it became just him and Jay, his focus only on their partnership. A quarter of a mile from the wire, the starting gate waited. They would pass over the spot where Feste had gone down twice, but on Jay it would be meaningless — a flash, a tick on the clock as it recorded fractions.

Saratoga would not defeat them today. All doubts needed to screw off. Nate pulled down his goggles as the starter's assistant led them into position. As soon as the rear doors closed behind them, Nate shut out all uncertainty along with the chatter around him and the buzz from the grandstand. Even harrow lines converged in the distance on the track before them, an invitation to claim their ticket to the Breeders' Cup.

He remained just aware enough of the activity around him to be ready for the break once the final horse was loaded, grabbing a chunk of Jay's thick red mane, feeling the big horse's weight shift with his own. Then with the deafening clang of the bell, the front doors slammed open, Jay dropping before those powerful hindquarters thrust them free.

The whoosh in Nate's ears muffled the cries of the riders around him as the speed horses flew to the front, leaving Jay and Nate in their own bubble, content to fall behind the fray. The harrow lines marred, dirt pelting his face, and he settled his horse to the inside, falling even further back where the sting of the kickback was less harsh, saving ground, conserving the chestnut's energy for the stretch run. Charging into the clubhouse turn, the leaders disappeared around the bend first, Jay happy to trail, his hooves reaching, digging, pushing off as they clung tight to the rail.

The furlongs flew by on the backstretch. Jay relaxed, taking Nate along for the ride. It was almost peaceful, the announcer's voice and hum of the crowd distant so that the pervading sound was the hypnotic thrum of horses' hooves and Jay's rhythmic breaths. It wasn't until they rounded the turn for home that the wall of noise hit him, the roar of the fans a growing din as the real running began. He pulled Jay off the rail and let him roll.

The horse to his inside staggered and Nate's heart lurched, but Jay powered on with enough heart for both of them. There was nothing but open stretch from here to the wire and he picked up his hands, threw them at Jay's ears, asked the big horse to fly. And Jay flew, an explosion of muscle accelerating past his rivals — taking all the pain and heartbreak this place had burdened his people with and shoving it far behind. The wire was a blur as they swept under it; the others forgotten in the wake of Jay's might.

Nate let the big horse gallop out all the way into the backstretch before pulling him up, turning Jay to stand, facing the grandstand. He released a long breath, Jay's ribs rising and falling underneath him, their hearts beating together, fast and strong. *Safe.*

When his feet hit the ground in the winner's circle after the photo was taken, Liv launched herself at him, and as he caught her, it felt as if they'd won something much bigger than a race.

CHAPTER TWENTY-ONE

As Liv sat at the desk in the office at the track, it finally felt a little more like hers and a little less like Roger's. She studied the walls of win photos, surrounded by victories — something that wasn't easy to get her head around. Some of the old pictures, accumulated when Roger was Triple Stripe's trainer, would forever stay, the big composite of Just Lucky's Canadian Triple Crown dominating — but it wasn't about the photos and the wins they represented. It was about the team working with her, and finally starting to believe in herself.

It would take time to process the emotions woven into Jay's triumph at Saratoga. Being back at Woodbine was like a sigh, a modicum of normalcy in a year that had been anything but ordinary. She wouldn't complain about any of it, but needed to remain grounded when the surface beneath her feet kept shifting.

Everything was an awful lot like it had been a year ago when Chique had retired. They'd made their decision. The syndication agreement was signed. Jay was going after the American Horse of the Year title, the coveted Eclipse award, instead of the Canadian version. He would have been a shoo-in for that just by running twice more at Woodbine, but the US title would hinge entirely on his performance in the Breeders' Cup Classic. No playing for small potatoes. Jay was officially a commodity. She hated it.

The big chestnut was on the farm again, the next two months a countdown to the most important race of his career. Hers and Nate's too. Trop was slated for a start in the Woodbine Mile — *is that enough of a show of confidence for you, Miller?* The gelding would be a longshot, but if he could pull off an upset against the big turf milers that would come to Canada to play, he'd have his own ticket to the Breeders' Cup. He'd be cutting back a full half mile from the distance of his last win, but Liv had faith he had enough speed to be a contender. Chique had won the Mile two years in a row, with similar breeding behind her.

Cam, Liv didn't know about. It would be good to get him another easy win, preferably not two thousand miles away. She needed to know if the Canadian Derby triumph had been a fluke. Either way, he was back to his daily head-butting sessions with Nate. It gave Nate something legitimate to complain about. That made her smile until she thought of his parents. He wasn't saying anything about that. Either there was nothing new to report, or he was keeping it to himself.

She circled a couple of potential starts for Cam on the stakes schedule. There was a race for Reba the same day as the Mile, but it would be a big move up for the filly; she could wait instead until the following weekend for a softer spot. Then there were the other horses. And they were starting the yearlings this week...

When the door creaked open, she expected to see Nate or Jo, but it was Michel. He looked strangely sheepish as he stepped through, letting it click shut softly behind him.

"Can I talk to you a minute?" he asked.

"Sure," she said. They'd known each other so long, it seemed strange to have him approach her as the boss, but this had to be work-related. "Want to sit?"

He nodded and eased onto the battered love seat, sinking into cushions that had long ago lost their structure. She should probably replace it, but somehow it seemed as much a part of this place as the photos on the walls.

"I — ah," he began, clasping and unclasping his hands between his knees. "Sue and I have been talking."

Just spit it out. This tentative behaviour from the guy who usually bordered on arrogant set her on edge.

"We're not going south this winter."

Liv frowned before catching herself. Michel had been traveling to Florida from the beginning with Roger. He couldn't not go. But she had to find words of understanding. Things were different now.

"Okay," she said, forcing herself to sit up straighter, lacing her voice with sympathy instead of disappointment. "I guess it would be hard, with Leo and all, now."

He glanced at her with a smirk that made her think it was always hard. She had to give him credit, though. She'd never heard him seriously complain. He'd levelled up. He and Sue were looking to buy a house. All of it so adult for a guy who she sometimes still thought of as an annoying brother figure. *When did we grow up?* Her married. Michel with a kid.

"You'll come to the Breeders' Cup though, I hope?" she said.

"If Jay's going, I'm going."

"Good." She smiled with a twinge of sadness. "It's going to be weird without you two at Payson."

"I don't know what I'm going to do with myself. I'll probably drive Sue nuts and get myself kicked out, so you might hear from me." He grinned, looking more like the brash young man who'd come to Ontario from Quebec around the same time as Liv's family.

"Well, if you decide you need to work, we can probably use the help on the farm," she offered. Many racetrackers who stayed home over the winter could collect unemployment insurance, but that probably wouldn't cut it with a baby around.

"That might be a good idea." His lips twisted. "Keep me out of trouble."

"You're both coming back in the spring though, right?" She couldn't entirely keep the plea from her voice.

"Of course. The farm might do for the winter, but I'd rather be here."

She needed to talk to Kerrie soon; make sure they had something to offer him on the farm before he started looking around. An experienced groom like Michel could work anywhere he wanted. She couldn't risk him finding a job elsewhere that might become permanent.

"Thanks for giving me lots of warning," she said.

He rose, rubbing his palms on the front of his jeans. "Yeah, well, thanks for understanding."

Like she had a choice.

Liv watched him leave. His sometimes abrasive personality aside, Michel had always been loyal to Triple Stripe, but now and then, she wondered why he stayed with them. Most guys with his experience would be itching to have their own horses. He was capable of passing his trainer's test, but had never asked to take it. As much as she wanted to keep him around, she and Jo would both give him the support he needed to get his assistant's license. She could understand him staying right now, with a horse like Jay making him lucrative stake bonuses, but what happened next year? Cam was all right, but he wasn't in the same category. She didn't picture Michel as someone who would only ever be satisfied rubbing horses. All the more reason to figure out a place that presented a more attractive future for him.

Liv pushed herself up from the desk, leaning out the screen door when she reached it, hoping to find Jo nearby. She was in luck. The assistant trainer was ducking out of the first stall.

"Jo? Let me know when you've got a minute?"

Jo nodded, grabbing some brushes. "I'll just finish up here."

The spot on the loveseat was probably still warm when Jo settled into it, wiping the halter she'd pulled from her charge.

"Has Michel said anything to you?" Liv asked.

Jo paused as she rubbed the halter's brass nameplate with the edge of her t-shirt. "No — what's up?"

"He just told me he and Sue aren't going south this year."

The assistant was silent a beat before answering, her expression sober. "So, we need to find two grooms. I'll keep my ears open. Ask around. There're always people looking to go south for the winter. Or we could wait till we're down there and pick up a couple."

"I'd feel better if we had things set sooner rather than later. And I'm not sure how that would work anyway. Are we allowed to hire American help? My dad would definitely not approve of doing anything under the table."

"I'll ask Elliot. Maybe he knows."

"You still keep in touch?" Liv hoped she didn't sound suspicious. She'd never known Jo to have a relationship of any sort, and definitely not a fling, so when the assistant had hooked up with the trainer who'd shared their barn at Payson Park last winter, Liv had been worried they might lose Jo to the American. Thank goodness it had ended when they'd left Florida. Or at least Liv thought it had.

Jo shrugged, but Liv caught the hint of a smile. "A bit. It's not as if I see him though."

Maybe they'd pick up where they'd left off this winter. *None of my business.* But it dredged up her worry. It felt as if her entire crew, the team she relied on, was in jeopardy of disintegrating.

The door creaked, sending both their heads toward it. Nate. He stopped just inside, looking from one face to the other.

"What's wrong? Did someone die?" There was no humour in his voice.

"No," Liv said quickly, then told him. In comparison, it didn't sound so bad.

"Shit." He said. "Oh well. I can rub a couple, you can rub a couple... we'll get it done."

This is why Liv loved this man. Because he would do exactly that, if required.

"We'll find people," Jo assured them. "At least he gave us a heads up."

"And he said he'd help at the farm," Liv said.

"It's just one big old personnel shuffle." Nate shrugged.

Jo rose, carrying the halter and sponge. "We'll get it sorted out. I'm going to feed lunch."

Nate stepped out of her way, then dropped onto the side of the couch, opposite where Jo and Michel had sat, his arm draped over the edge. "Guess it's not really a surprise."

"No," Liv agreed. "Still sucks, though."

"You remind Marie we're starting the yearlings today?"

"Yes." She glanced at the time. "We should get going."

Liv straightened the pile of booklets and swiped her phone from the desk, sending Kerrie a text asking her to bring in the yearlings, mentioning she wanted to chat about help. With Michel's announcement, she had to rethink everything.

CHAPTER TWENTY-TWO

The back of a yearling felt like home to Nate, even if Fleur wasn't exactly making him feel welcome. Sure, she'd stood as he'd draped his body over her like a sack of potatoes and hadn't batted an eye when Liv lifted him right up so he had a leg on each side. The filly went along with it when Liv led them around the stall, but Fleur wasn't having any part of his plan when Liv exited the box and he asked the filly to turn with him up top. She locked her legs, and he decided not to push her. Maybe she'd be happier outside.

The day the babies graduated to the sand ring was his favourite step. It required his entire focus, letting him shut everything out — including the audience that inevitably collected at the rail. Geai had always banished the farm help, but Kerrie didn't, and Nate didn't care. It wasn't as if he was going to give them a show. They'd leave disappointed. This year Liv had Jillian and Marie watching because she wanted them to learn, making this a demonstration of sorts. It was her job to give the commentary. He just rode.

Cash was the obvious choice for demo horse because the colt was a quick study, reminding Nate so much of his full brother, Just Jay, both physically and mentally. He picked up on Nate's open rein and bodyweight cues, displaying a wobbly change of direction through the middle of the ring, and growing in confidence as he trotted along the rail. Nothing else existed in Nate's head as he gave the colt his first lesson under saddle. It was a version of himself he recognized, when some days it still caught him off guard if someone commented on things like Jay's win at Saratoga, and heading to the Breeders' Cup. Like, who was *that* guy?

He kept the session short — it didn't take long for the babies to tire. Nate halted the colt in the centre of the ring and scrubbed Cash's neck lavishly before hopping off, Liv meeting him and snapping the shank to the halter Cash wore under the bridle. She handed the lead to him and they started walking toward the barn, Jillian opening the gate, then falling in step with Marie.

"That was boring," Jillian complained.

"It's supposed to be," Nate said. "You'll be plenty happy when it's your turn."

"When does that happen?" Marie asked.

"Liv and I will get them going this year," Nate said as he pulled the tack off in the stall. "They'll all still be green enough by the time you get on them, you'll get a sense of what to do without getting stuck."

"Getting stuck?" Jillian asked.

He laughed. "Yeah. The thing with babies is you have to have more gas than they do. Pro tip: if you're not already working out on the side, it wouldn't be a bad idea to start."

Jillian's eyebrows arched. "You want me to go to the gym? I ride every day plus work here from seven till four. Isn't that enough?"

"Sorry," Nate said, his grin completely unapologetic. "Trust me, it's so much easier when you cross-train."

Maybe he should let them try to replicate what he'd done, just to expose how unfit they really were. He knew he made it look easy, and that wasn't vanity talking.

By the time they were ready for the last two fillies, the whole farm staff, including Kerrie, had gathered to watch. Nate hoped they were learning something, because it hadn't been a very exciting performance.

"You want to do Fleur?" he asked, glancing at Liv.

She caught his eye before hers shifted to the ground. "That's okay. You go ahead."

He'd thought she might be ready, that the untroubled trip to Saratoga might have softened Feste's memory enough that she'd open up to the filly, but he had to let her do it on her own time. She'd worked through a lot in the last year. Faced the abuse in her distant past that she'd never realized had shaped her. Dealing with it was huge. It had allowed the two of them to move forward, something that would've been impossible otherwise, so he'd keep cutting her slack.

And it wasn't as if he wasn't still dealing with his own shit. That was why he was glad he was doing this, when most jocks of his calibre wouldn't be caught dead breaking babies. Remembering where he came from was the key to balancing his sometimes heady success.

Marie and Jillian had helped with the first few days of groundwork, and tacked up the next set. Fleur certainly didn't care that Nate wasn't the one doing it. Daisy, the filly Liv opted for, was a sweet thing, and when Marie unsnapped the lead rope after walking them around the sand ring, Liv bumped the filly with her heels, lines drooping, and Daisy popped forward into a trot. Liv's voice rang with praise. Fleur was content to supervise her underling's jaunt around the perimeter. Nate let her stand for a minute before gathering the lines.

"All right, Jillian. Walk her on," he said, ready to join in on the fun.

He waited until Liv went by on their outside – having a lead for motivation wouldn't hurt – and nodded at Jillian to turn Fleur loose, giving the filly a burst of encouragement. Fleur kept ambling like a lesson pony who'd had one too many kids on her back.

"Are you serious?" he muttered. He couldn't remember the last time *that* had happened.

Liv circled around alongside them, letting Daisy deflate to a walk. "What happened, Miller? Forget to put gas in her before we started?"

"Is that what you mean by getting stuck?" Jillian called from where she'd retreated to the other side of the fence. "Did you miss too many days of going to the gym or something?"

Nate smirked at her, then looked at Liv. "Pony me."

She shook her head. "Daisy doesn't want to be that close. Fleur isn't exactly friendly."

"Maybe you're going to *have* to ride her," he said. "You two might be kindred spirits."

"I can't believe you just said that," Liv said, feigning mortification, then added, "Horses always like me better, though. People, not so much."

"What did you do, Nate? Insult her?"

Great. Emilie had joined the peanut gallery. This probably wasn't the show any of them were hoping for. It was a non-event. He steered Fleur to the centre of the ring. It seemed to be her happy place. The filly's weight shifted as she rested one hind leg, tail swishing with a snap.

"Do me a favour, Em?" Nate asked, feet dangling free of the stirrups at Fleur's side.

"Maybe."

Nate rolled his eyes. "Grab me the driving lines? And some gloves."

Liv steered Daisy back to the rail to finish the other filly's session and was off and leading Daisy out before Emilie returned. Nate hopped off as Emilie went to Fleur's head and stroked the filly's face, rubbing the star in the middle of her forehead while he figure-eighted the reins and tucked them under the cantle. After he accepted the long driving lines, Emilie pulled her fancy riding gloves from the back pocket of her breeches and waved them at him. They were a little tight. If she got mad at him for stretching them out, he'd buy her a new pair.

Fleur didn't care when he draped the off-side driving line over her rump, but when he let it slide down to where her buttocks tied into her Achilles, she tucked her tail and scooted in a circle around Emilie, firing out with one hind leg.

"Turn her loose, Em," Nate said, and Emilie scooted away as he snagged Fleur in a circle around him. The filly crow-hopped a few steps before jogging, and Nate slowly let her out. With a huff she settled, ears turned back at the pressure hugging her quarters. He was going to have to ride — or long-line — this out.

Finally, the filly lapsed into a walk. Nate moved behind her for a couple of steps, then circled her the other way before driving her around the ring, changing direction across the diagonal. Easing her to a halt in the middle, he blew out a long breath, and Fleur echoed him.

"C'mere."

Liv seemed to know Nate meant her. She ducked through the fence boards and held Fleur's head while he organized the lines. He handed her the left one, and wrapped up the other, leaving her standing with the filly while he handed the line to Emilie. Liv's eyes didn't leave him as he walked back to her.

"I need you to get on her," he said, and as she met his eyes, he thought she was going to refuse. But she nodded.

Liv sprang lightly from his leg up and adjusted the irons a hole before knotting the reins. She rested her hands on the pommel. "What now, Boss?"

He gave her a crooked grin. "Just sit there to start."

Nate was worried that without the second line around Fleur's butt they'd be back to square one, but when he backed away a couple of steps and flicked the end of the rope, Fleur stepped forward.

They walked and trotted both ways, then Nate set them free. Liv's face was all soft focus as she jogged Fleur around. She was a nicer rider than him. A little lighter, too. He didn't think it was either of those things. Nate didn't know what the actual difference was, but it seemed like Fleur had made her choice.

"She's yours now," he said after Liv dismounted. And though he couldn't read Liv's expression, she didn't disagree.

CHAPTER TWENTY-THREE

"Do you remember that colt you started the first year you were here, Nate? He was kind of feral."

Emilie's comment knocked Liv out of her head as she walked toward the barn next to Nate — followed by the entourage that had gathered to watch the yearlings. She was still trying to pin down her feelings after the session with Fleur. Every few strides Fleur snorted as if she was releasing something, and Liv noticed her own neck and shoulders were more relaxed, like maybe she'd let go of something, too.

"Arthur?" Nate said, a smile coming to his face. "He wasn't that bad. Just a little worried about life."

"He was one of Dean's," Liv recalled. "The owner tried to call him 'Miller Time' but of course the Jockey Club rejected it."

Nate laughed. "I never heard that."

"Aw," Jillian said. "Why'd they reject it?"

Emilie explained. "Against the rules. Commercial slogans aren't allowed. They called him Make A Dent instead. I helped find him a home when he was done racing. He's turning into a pretty decent hunter."

They'd had seven yearlings to start that fall, and Liv liked that she knew where all of them were. Claire and Just Gemma were broodmares. Excursion was Emilie's eventer, Curtis. Sans Défaut was a sport horse stallion. One of Dean's was a track pony, and the other was still racing, and still trained by Dean.

Kerrie helped put the exhausted yearlings back into their pastures. Liv had shared Michel's news with her, but they hadn't really talked about the current staff situation. This time of year they managed with fewer people because most of the horses lived outside, but as that changed and the yearlings' training progressed, riding would occupy more of Jillian's time. There would be a gap to fill between then and when Michel finished at Woodbine in November.

"Are you coming to Florida with us this year, Marie?" After Michel's news, Liv wasn't taking anything for granted.

"Yes! For sure. Will I be doing the same thing?" Officially, Marie was their swing groom. She filled in on Sue and Michel's days off, the rest of the time helping gallop and walk.

"Yes, mostly. Probably," Liv hedged. "Michel and Sue aren't coming, so we'll have to figure a few things out."

"What?" Emilie exclaimed. Liv hadn't told her sister.

"Can I come?" Jillian interjected.

Liv's eyebrow quirked. "You want to?" She exchanged a quick glance with Kerrie. That would help with one problem but create another.

"Yes! Can I gallop?"

"We need to replace two grooms, so that's the job. But we might be able to fit in some riding, at least once Nate and I are down."

"You would abandon me?" Emilie said to Jillian, her tone all mock hurt. "I thought you didn't want to gallop."

"Not at the track where all the crazies are. But a training centre? In Florida? That's not the same thing."

Jillian was right. The atmosphere at Payson Park, where they took the Triple Stripe horses, was almost as nice as being on the farm. Plus, in the middle of January, it was — usually — a lot warmer.

"Michel said he'd come help here," Liv mentioned.

"You'd better tell Sue we'll need her too," Emilie said. "But we need riders. I can't do it all myself. I have a job, remember?"

Emilie worked full time as a physiotherapist in town; retraining the retired racehorses was her hobby. Her schedule was too packed to ride the yearlings and racehorses who would winter on the farm.

A thought came to Liv's mind. "Michel rides."

Emilie gaped. "Seriously? I've never seen him on a horse."

"He got too big to gallop at the track, but he'd be fine on the older horses. And he's decent enough to not ruin a riding horse."

Emilie grinned. "Like me! That's exactly what Jodi told me after my first lesson."

Jillian laughed. "Gotta love a coach who doesn't mince words."

"Did you all remember your bathing suits?" Nate interrupted.

"Yes!" Jillian's voice led the chorus from the farm staff. "Pool party!"

Nate's idea — the good ones were usually his. He'd suggested the get-together with both the farm and track crews, seeing as, thanks to Michel's news, there would now be overlap. Normally, the two worlds rarely intercepted.

Michel and Sue were the first to arrive at the house, carrying bags of chips and other snacks. Liv had a flashback to an impromptu gathering at her condo in Florida when Chique had been a yearling. After setting up the shedrow on the first day, Nate had proffered a less-welcome invitation to their crew. He and Liv hadn't exactly been on civilized speaking terms that November, four years ago, Chique the fragile filament that had connected them.

"Come in," Liv said, ushering them into the front foyer.

Sue collapsed on the floor, making a fuss over Holly. "I miss having a dog so much. Maybe when Leo's older we'll get one. We have two cats, for now. Michel tried to make me leave them with my mom when we first moved in together but I told him the cats and I were a package deal, so..."

Emilie laughed. "He chose wisely."

"They're not so bad," Michel conceded.

"Why do guys not like cats?" Sue said. "It's like they think it's not manly."

"Will does," Nate quipped. "I think the cat he babysits might be the true love of his life. Don't tell Faye I said that."

"Where's the hot tub?" Michel quipped, steering them away from a conversation that had become just a bit strange as he wandered to the sliding doors that opened to their back patio.

"No hot tub," Liv said.

"C'mon, Mike, you don't think Liv actually relaxes, do you? It's sixty lengths in that pool, or nothing." Nate gave her one of his smartass grins.

He wasn't wrong, so she just shrugged.

"Can Sue and I stay here while you guys are in Florida?" Michel continued, his head tipping up toward the cathedral ceilings. "I think we need to work that into the farm deal."

The thing was, Liv wouldn't care if they did. Emilie had her own apartment and even when they came home, this place was so big there would be room — though the idea of sleeping in the same house as a baby set her on edge.

Potluck instead of ordering in or getting a caterer had been Kerrie's suggestion. It made it easy — all Liv had to do was grab some things for dessert from Faye at the café while Nate picked up drinks. They had enough people that there was no shortage of food.

Once everyone arrived, introductions were made, drinks served, and plates filled. A couple of the farm staff had brought their boyfriends, but women still outnumbered men. Nate took pity on Michel and drifted over to him, and Liv found herself with Jo and Kerrie. Part of the inspiration for this get-together was planning for winter, so she didn't feel bad about bringing it up.

"Sue and Michel will make your life easy," Liv said, nursing a glass of wine. She didn't want to gallop horses tomorrow with a headache.

"I'm pretty excited to have them on board," Kerrie admitted. "Everyone we have is great, but knowing those two can handle anything is a huge bonus. I won't feel bad in the least going to visit my parents out west for Christmas."

"So you're from Calgary, too?" Jo asked.

Kerrie shook her head. "Originally from Northern Ontario. My parents moved to Alberta a few years ago, and when my daughter decided she wanted to go to Olds College, I took a job nearby and we moved in with them. She graduated in the spring, so I felt I was free to take this position."

"Is it wrong to say you don't look old enough to have a daughter who's finished college?" Jo asked.

Kerrie didn't seem offended. "I had her young."

Emilie had taken care of hiring Kerrie as manager, but there were questions you weren't allowed to ask in interviews, and Liv both hadn't been around much of the year and was still disinclined to make personal inquiries about the farm manager's past. She'd heard all about Kerrie's hockey career and Liv had collected some of the other details here and there, like Kerrie having family in Alberta but growing up in Ontario. The fact she had a daughter was news.

"What did your daughter study?" Liv asked.

Kerrie laughed. "A bit of everything, but always with animals. She has an Animal Health Technology diploma, a Farrier Science certificate, and she did the groom course."

"She doesn't want a job, does she?" Jo said dryly.

"She's been working at the track out there all summer," Kerrie said. "But they're done for the season soon. She will need something."

"Would she be interested in grooming for us this winter in Florida? If that's okay with you, of course," Liv added. To think she and Nate had been out west just a few weeks ago. They might have crossed paths without even knowing it.

"She's twenty, so I can't tell her what she can and can't do," Kerrie said with a combination of humour and regret. "I'll talk to her. If she's going to work in this industry, it would be good to know she was with a solid outfit like this. Where would she live?"

"I was going to suggest Jillian could stay with me," Jo said. "There's room for another. When the rent is split three ways, it's pretty affordable, plus they get an allowance to help pay for it."

"It sounds too good to be true," Kerrie said.

"I think this calls for more wine," Jo proclaimed, looking at her own nearly empty glass. "It would be a weight off my mind to have a full crew arranged for the winter."

"I'll grab a bottle," Kerrie offered.

Liv watched her go to the kitchen, then turned to Jo. "You'd be okay as den mother to a couple of twenty-somethings?"

"I would do a lot for reliable help," Jo said, then added with a wry smile. "If they misbehave, I'll dump them on you and Nate."

Kerrie returned with the bottle and topped their glasses up. "I may need to drink more of this if she says yes. I'm sure she'll be thrilled, but I might not sleep at night."

Liv took another careful sip of wine. Jo wasn't a mother, and neither was she. Liv wouldn't pretend to know what it would feel like. She still identified better with the daughter being both scared and excited to strike out on her own — new adventures, chasing a dream.

"Cheers," Jo said, holding out her glass.

"It sounds like a wonderful opportunity for her," Kerrie said. "If she doesn't want the job would it be wrong to take it myself?"

Kerrie was joking, but the thought of losing their farm manager when they'd finally found someone who fit so well made Liv twitch. The years between Geai's death and when Kerrie had started had been frustrating.

As happy as Liv was to have the staffing situation a little closer to set, it was a relief once everyone was gone. Emilie helped clean up, then disappeared. Liv slipped out to the patio, peeled off her t-shirt and shorts to reveal the bathing suit beneath, and dove into the pool. Water was second only to riding as a way to rebalance.

Her face submerged as she pulled herself along with steady strokes, she heard a muffled splash, so it wasn't a surprise when Nate met her partway after she'd turned. She stopped, treading water. He was grinning. He knew what was happening, and she could have been irritated he'd interrupted her — or ignored him and swum past — but she was trying to get better about sharing even the uneasy parts of herself with him.

"They're a great bunch, but humans are still exhausting," she said, adjusting the kick of her legs that kept her afloat as he snaked his arms around her. When he kissed her, all she wanted to do was stay right here forever. But they climbed out of the water and Nate handed her a towel.

Liv wrapped it around her shoulders. "Kerrie said her daughter might be interested in going to Florida this winter. She graduated from Olds and is working at the track out there."

"I didn't even know she had a daughter," Nate said as he dried off. "Find out who she works for. I'll ask Al if he knows anything."

"I trust Kerrie," Liv said.

"We don't really know that much about her."

"She's been here seven months and she's been outstanding."

"And how long was Austin here before he revealed he was actually a jerk?" Nate's eyebrow quirked.

Just the name raised Liv's hackles. Austin had seemed all right when he'd started as their manager. He wasn't Geai, but no one was. Liv had just begun to believe the guy might work out when he'd made a pass at Emilie then quit — right before Christmas, when Nate and Liv were in Florida and had no way of knowing Emilie hadn't had the situation as much under control as she'd claimed.

"I think Kerrie's proven she's far superior to Austin," she said.

"That doesn't mean her kid is perfect. You need a character reference who isn't her mother." His tone was insistent.

"I really don't think that's necessary."

"When did you become so trusting?"

Wait, now he was criticizing her for being less wary?

"If we'd done a better job of vetting Austin, we would have saved ourselves a lot of grief," Nate said. "The things I've heard about him since he bailed on us... it was all there, if only we'd asked around."

Liv could barely remember hiring the guy. They'd been so desperate for a manager, and last year had just been so… extra… it was true she hadn't done much investigation.

She scowled and blew out a breath. "Fine. I'll leave it with you."

CHAPTER TWENTY-FOUR

"Where'd you get a horse like this?" Nate stood, arms crossed, sizing up Wayward Sun, fresh off the van from Illinois. He looked as if he ate smaller Thoroughbreds — like Trop — for breakfast. "This horse wasn't with you in Florida last winter. I would have remembered this horse."

Elliot, the trainer they'd shared a barn with last winter at Payson — and Jo's winter fling — returned a broad smile. "Scaring you, is he?"

Wayward Sun filled up the front of the stall as he gazed into the distance, ignoring his haynet. *Maybe. A little.* Both the horse and his past performance were impressive, and he'd be the one to beat in the Woodbine Mile.

"We have home team advantage," Nate said, just because he had to say something.

"Which one is yours?"

None of them, he almost responded, but he knew what Elliot meant, leading him down to Trop — who would look like a midget next to Wayward Son. He silently dared the Chicago trainer to say something derogatory about their little dark bay gelding.

But Elliot said, "I watched his last race. He was strong in there. He probably won't mind shortening up with that pedigree. He's got some speed, huh?"

If Elliot was playing nice, Nate had to, too. So much for the fun of a little rivalry. "He does. I think he'll do all right in there."

"Hey, Elliot." Jo strolled down the aisle, fingers jammed in her pockets, her shoulders slightly rounded. The corners of her lips tipped up into a coy grin. This woman did not resemble their assistant trainer.

Uh-huh.

Nate made a show of looking at the time on his phone as Elliot crushed her in a hug. "I've got to get going," he mumbled. Jo was flushed when Elliot released her.

"I was hoping you guys would let me take you to dinner," Elliot said. "You and Liv and Jo. After the races, I guess?"

Nate glanced at Jo, thinking, *You sure?* But he supposed they had all afternoon to... catch up. Because if he was reading it right, that's what they'd be doing. "I'll run it past Liv. I'm in if she is. Catch you later." But he guessed — and hoped Liv would nix the invitation.

He slipped into the office on his way out. He wasn't in a hurry — he'd only wanted to get away from Jo and Elliot — so he dropped on the end of the couch. "Nice looking horse, eh?"

Liv looked up from the desk, pen poised over the training record. "He is. Elliot's had a good year with him."

"He wants to take us to dinner tonight."

Liv frowned. "Tomorrow would be better. I don't really want to be out late tonight."

"Makes sense. And if we beat him?"

"I'd be more than happy to pick up that tab."

Trop was on his toes, Liv following his orbit in the walking ring. Had it been only a year ago she'd been here with Chique, watching the small, dark filly circle under Woodbine's willows? She missed the feisty freak show and wondered if Chique's foal would inherit those traits that had made her so special. The larger-than-life personality, quirks and all, that had been so challenging, and often frustrating — but made every victory especially satisfying.

Nate nudged her, and she swung her gaze from the gelding to catch his eye.

"Where were you?" he asked.

She smiled. "Thinking of the last horse we ran in this race, when I should focus on this one."

"So you're saying I shouldn't join in on the nostalgia?"

"Maybe not right now. There'll be plenty of time for that on foal watch."

He held a hand out palm-up and used the other to count off fingers. "October, November, December, January... only four months."

"So close, and yet so far away." She grinned.

There wasn't much to say about this race, because nothing had really changed since the overnight had come out with the entries. Elliot's horse was the favourite, and the five-year-old looked the part. There was a lot at stake. The winner's share of a million dollar purse, a free pass to the Breeders' Cup Mile — and dinner at the restaurant of the loser's choice.

The paddock judge called for riders up and Sue cut Trop closer to them. Liv legged Nate up and sent them off with her usual words. Luck and safety. It's what this game came down to, wasn't it?

Emilie and Tim stayed close behind her as she made the

trek from paddock to seats. Dean waited in the box with Faye and Will. Liv was sure the biggest reason they'd accepted her invitation was the opportunity to meet Elliot. She'd given him a stall in her barn, so it seemed ridiculous not to ask him to join them in the box. He could have watched from upstairs, but this was a much better vantage point.

She wouldn't apologize for leaving Emilie to introduce him, only vaguely aware he trailed when she planted herself next to Faye. No one here would be insulted that she ignored them, her binoculars already focused on the horses coming onto the track.

It was more than a little remarkable Trop merited consideration in this spot and she still couldn't believe she'd decided to give him a shot here. The gelding had been a puzzle. Like many of Just Lucky's offspring, he'd inherited his sire's personality — they were feel-good horses, but sensitive. When he'd still been a colt, Trop had been a thick-skulled, hormone-driven pain in the ass. Thankfully diminishing those hormones had done the trick. He was a different animal. He had a brain. It was a miracle. Okay, not really. A blessing, then. His performance in the Breeders' Stakes suggested he was going to be a racehorse after all, but this was a bigger step up in class than the one he'd made from maiden win to Triple Crown race.

Somehow he looked diminutive alongside these foreign invaders, when she hadn't felt that way with Chique — even though Chique was physically smaller than the gelding. Wayward Sun, galloping next to his pony escort, looked every bit the part of a highly touted favourite.

Nate took Trop off on his own, giving the Triple Stripe entrant a sharp warmup on par with the European imports. Liv felt one of those pangs she sometimes still got as she watched him, wishing she was the one on Trop's back. She galloped him in the mornings; she breezed him — but it was Nate, far on the backstretch, turning the gelding to face the grandstand, reaching up to stroke Trop's neck. She kept her binoculars on them as they jogged a loopy figure-eight, waiting for the rest of the field to catch up, before an outrider led them through the gap to the turf course where the gate stood.

At least Trop didn't have Chique's penchant for holdups at the start. He had a long wait, the first to go in. Liv tried not to grumble when Elliot's horse balked, dragging out the process. Of course he'd be the problem of the group. It took one assistant starter at his head and two with locked arms around his quarters to funnel Wayward Sun in. She held her breath, unable to see what the delay was, imagining Wayward Sun causing problems again. Liv bit her lower lip, not daring to look away — then finally the starter set them free, eight horses bursting out onto the turf.

Trop shot to the front and was three lengths up by the time Nate reeled him in, the field settling into position behind him. Liv felt a drip of sweat trickle down the channel of her spine. In restricted company, Trop might pull off gate to wire, but the same strategy would be a lot tougher in here. He added another length as they rolled along the easy downhill slope of the massive E.P. Taylor course, its generous turn not demanding a display of his handiness, and Liv found her thoughts leaping ahead. If Trop could steal a win here, get himself in that Breeders' Cup Mile on an inner course in California, he'd love the tight turns and hard going.

Even with her binoculars, the horses were merely dark specks with flags of colour on their backs as they entered the long stretch. Trop led the way with the Triple Stripe red, white and blue, but Liv spotted the green helmet atop Wayward Sun, splitting horses to begin his pursuit. Nate remained still as Elliot's horse whittled away at Trop's lead inside the quarter pole, and she wished he would start asking Trop, make

Wayward Sun work harder to catch him. *Go already, Miller. Go!*

At the eighth pole, Wayward Sun was at Trop's rump, inching up to Nate's boot, and now Nate was riding. Liv sprang to her feet, dropping the binoculars from her eyes and screaming so hard her throat ached.

"Come on, Miller! Come on, Trop!"

Nate drove, Trop's ears laced to his head, but Wayward Sun still gained, shrinking Trop's advantage — a neck, a head. Trop battled hard as his rival stared him down — matching strides, matching intensity. With a thrust of his neck, Wayward Sun shoved his nose in front, but the smaller gelding pushed right back, drawing even once more. The wire loomed, and the duel carried them right through it.

It came down to the bob of a head — and it looked heartbreakingly as if the match would go to their guest. Liv crumpled into her seat, the hum around her turning into a steady buzz in her ears. She felt a hand on her shoulder from behind.

"Wow Liv, your horse ran huge."

She glanced over her shoulder at Elliot. "Thanks. So did yours, damn it," she croaked, her voice gone, the upward curve of her lips resigned. "We'd better get down there."

By the time they reached the apron, the order of finish lit up the tote board, the result announced an agonizing moment later. Liv closed her eyes and shook her head before plastering on a smile and spinning to face Elliot. He accepted her handshake.

"Congratulations!" she said. "Looks like dinner's on you. I'll pick somewhere extra-nice."

After the horses were cooled out and tucked in for the night, they met at the restaurant.

"Will you take him to Del Mar anyway?" Elliot asked.

Liv shook her head. "I'm not going all that way for a race I don't think we can win."

The Chicago trainer eyed her. "So you think you can beat Chaotic Good in the Classic with Just Jay?"

"Absolutely."

She'd show the syndicate manager from Triumph Stud what a mistake they'd made.

CHAPTER TWENTY-FIVE

Nate turned off the television after replaying Chaotic Good's Pacific Classic victory. He didn't know how many times he'd watched it in the last month, sizing up Jay's most significant challenge for the Breeders' Cup Classic. The west coast-based colt had won with conviction, his time two-fifths of a second faster than Jay's in the Jockey Club Gold Cup, on the same track over which the championship would be decided — Del Mar. His rider, Huey Harrison, was last year's top apprentice and the hottest jock in North America right now. That's all Nate knew about him. All he needed to know. It wouldn't matter on the first Saturday in November who the guy was. Nate couldn't wait. Three years into his riding career, and he had a mount in the Classic with a legitimate chance to win.

He climbed the basement stairs, heading outside. Knowing he had it easier than Liv these days, he left her alone when they had free time, so he didn't know where she was. He spent most of his time riding other people's horses and it gave him a diversion. She was all Triple Stripe, all the time, with the Classic looming on the horizon like a towering monolith. It was the ultimate achievement in this game, and in a small stable like theirs, opportunities to take a shot were rare. He was giving her space to get her head around that.

Chique picked her head up when she saw him, stopping mid-chew. Nate ducked through the fence boards and ambled over, smiling as her molars resumed their grinding. She waited for him, like he was her humble servant. Which he was. He knew his place. Chique bumped him with her nose and he presented a peppermint. *Just call me Pez, dispenser of candies.*

Two years in a row, Chique had earned one of those free spots in the Breeders' Cup by winning the Woodbine Mile. The first time, he'd thought they might go because it was held at Keeneland that year, but she'd sustained a minor injury in training. Last year, Liv had said no from the outset because it was at Santa Anita. Too far, too much to ask, but Nate was sure the real reason was much like what she'd said after Trop's race.

"I'm not going all that way for a race I don't think we can win."

Nate couldn't disagree, though a lot of owners would put up the money for the possibility just for the chance. It was horse racing, after all. Anything could happen. As much as his soft spot for Chique demanded he think she was capable of anything, though, she'd already given them enough by that point in her career. At least now, with Jay, they were finally going.

"Maybe we'll take your kid one day," he said, giving her another peppermint.

He still couldn't get used to Chique's new shape, even though she wasn't really that big yet. Glancing over his shoulder toward the gate, he saw the two rope shanks hanging from the top rail. Was that a stupid idea? Other than going for a hack last winter before she'd been bred, he'd resisted the temptation to hop on her since she'd retired, but why? It wouldn't do any harm. He wanted to be on her again, even if it was just to walk around.

"What do you think, Cheeky? It'd be fun, right?"

Her head rose a little higher, ears tipped, when he returned with a lead in each hand. After snapping one to either side, he crossed the ends over her withers and vaulted up. Chique swung her head around toward his leg. She had enough fat on her it was comfortable, and even sitting here relaxed him, but when he picked up the makeshift reins, she stepped forward and her rolling walk felt like home.

Claire, her companion again now that Léa was weaned, seemed only to roll one of her wall eyes before continuing to graze — always the sensible one. The third mare, Stella, fell into step behind Chique like they were playing follow the leader.

Nate let Chique wander, like his mind. There was no destination, no intent other than coexisting. The paddock she shared with her companions was about five acres, so it wasn't as if they'd go far, but putzing around on her back let him forget who he was for a while. It brought to mind his first days on the back of a horse, though that reminded him of Calgary, which made him think of his parents.

When his parents had needed him, he hadn't been there. And Chique sure didn't need him interrupting her evening, but he was grateful she humoured him, because he needed her.

He nudged her into a jog, and after only a couple of trot strides she broke into a canter. Stella's hooves thudded on the ground behind them, and a glance over his shoulder gave him a glimpse of Claire, jogging. Not joining them, but monitoring what was happening like a disapproving school marm. Then Stella pinned her ears and flattened, pulling up alongside Chique, and Nate felt Chique's back come up underneath him

— and not in that good way he'd heard Emilie going on about after a dressage lesson.

He sat back, trying to keep Chique's head up when she dropped her nose and crow-hopped. The second buck had him worried. The third was pretty damn athletic for a broodmare, her spine twisting, heels in the air, and he was airborne.

Somehow he landed on his feet, but Chique and Stella were off, bucking and farting like a couple of weanlings. He fell in a heap, laughing. Claire raced past him to join the romp, shedding her sense of responsibility.

So much for your Black Stallion on the beach moment, Miller.

He climbed to his feet and Chique let him approach — once she'd decided the game was over — and he unsnapped the leads from her halter. He could say what he wanted about her quirkiness, but she'd stopped as soon as she'd been rid of him, the ropes dangling harmlessly. The old turnout halter she wore was so cracked around the hardware it would have broken if she'd stepped on one of them, so it wasn't a safety hazard.

"Have you completely lost your mind?"

Oops. He should have known his little adventure would not go unnoticed. Wherever she'd been, Liv appeared now, glaring at him from the other side of the fence.

"She's fine," he said, a little sheepishly, embarrassed that he'd come off.

"I can see that. It's not really her I'm worried about, believe it or not. All I need is for you to break your skull. If you're going to do stupid things, could you at least put on a helmet?"

"I landed on my feet. Did you see that part? Maybe get a video?"

"Will you leave those poor mares alone and get out of there?"

He gave Chique his last peppermint and vacated the paddock before Stella and Claire swarmed him.

"What were you thinking anyway?" Liv asked, hands on hips.

He had to keep himself from grinning. It had been a while since he'd pissed her off — she was always hot when she was pissed off — but he restrained himself. There was probably a better time.

"I miss her. I miss our adventures."

"Could you save any ideas you have for further adventures until after the Classic?" She dropped her hands to her sides and ducked through the hedge that lined the fence, emerging at the circular drive in front of the house. Nate followed as she asked, "Are you hungry?"

"What are you suggesting? Or have you taken up cooking to distract yourself?"

She scowled at him. "I thought you might have ideas."

He quirked an eyebrow, but left it alone. "How did you see what happened anyway?"

"I noticed they were running. I came to check it out. In case there was a predator." Finally, she grinned. "And so there was."

Her humour put him back at ease. "I'll throw some food together."

If Liv was already this tense, the next month would be hell. He hadn't seen her this bad since — well, Chique's final race, probably. Or what they'd thought was her final race, until the racing secretary had written a special one to drag her out of retirement so she'd be eligible to be voted Canada's Horse of the Year. It was a shame Jay couldn't have two more starts so that he'd be the champ in his home country when he was hands down the best Canadian-bred in training this year. He needed three races on home soil, but he only had two.

Nate left Liv in the living room with a book after they ate

and went upstairs to call his mom. He was due his weekly check-in. She answered after only a couple of rings, and he imagined her getting dinner ready — checking something in the oven, pulling dishes from the cupboards, cutlery from the drawer.

"Hey, Mom."

"Nate. How are you?" She was trying to sound casual, but her cheeriness seemed forced.

He'd play along a bit, to keep her happy. "Okay. Things are a little tense right now, I guess, but it's nothing to worry about."

"Are you sure?"

"Yes, I'm sure." He sat on the bed, propped against the headboard with his knees up. "I was thinking about Christmas this year. I haven't talked to Liv yet, but what about coming this way this time?"

Her hesitation made his mouth go dry.

"What's up?" he asked. "You promised you wouldn't shut us out." Though he knew Tim didn't invite the same directness. His brother waited for updates that came filtered through Nate, as if that degree of separation made them easier to swallow.

His mother's sigh was audible. "We've decided to just —" She paused, her words uncharacteristically stilted. "Try a trial separation. So I'm not sure what will happen at Christmas this year."

He wanted to protest; he wanted to hang up and call his father because he'd bet Reid hadn't told his mom about the retirement thing.

Don't overreact. Don't overreact.

Nate closed his eyes, forced himself to take measured breaths. Still, he couldn't keep the bite out of his voice. "We'll talk about it again after the Breeders' Cup, maybe."

By then his parents would have had a month to realize splitting up was a mistake, and his and Liv's lives would be something close to normal again. Everyone's heads would be clearer.

"Everything will work out as it should," Connie assured him.

He had to believe she was right — but couldn't help thinking what *should* happen was that they'd stay together.

For now, he'd focus on the Classic. He didn't want this next month to rush past. He wanted to experience all the hype and fever leading up to the event at Del Mar. Most importantly, he wanted Jay to win, to be Horse of the Year. But he'd be lying if he didn't admit part of him craved the calm that would come after, regardless of the result.

With the Classic on the horizon, Liv wanted more than anything to keep Just Jay on the farm indefinitely, to shield him from the growing buzz. Who was she kidding? She wanted to shield herself. But there would be no staying in the shadows leading up to the big race. The best she could hope for was being prepared for what was to come. At least Woodbine wasn't a hot spot. There were more live Breeders' Cup horses at Belmont and Keeneland and Del Mar. Up here, sometimes she could even pretend her horse wasn't one of them — but they'd be in the thick of it soon enough.

The past month had been an experiment of sorts, though she still thought her first Breeders' Cup horse probably wasn't the best choice as her initial subject. She'd galloped Jay three times a week on the farm's training track, and the days in between they'd gone to the hayfield, negotiating the hilly, imperfect perimeter. Some afternoons were hot, which would better acclimate him to San Diego temperatures than the cooler mornings in Toronto as autumn descended. He needed to breeze at Woodbine, though, and once he was in there he'd stay until his flight west.

Nate galloped him the first morning he was back at the track — before dawn, taking Jay to the field by himself. She didn't know what to say to Nate after hearing the news about his parents, and was angry at herself for wishing Connie had kept it from him until after the Breeders', but they were adults. They had to take this stuff in stride. Life happened, but it couldn't get in the way.

She kept her eyes open for his return, sending Nicole and Marie out on the first set without her. Jay appeared like a mirage in the mist, colours muted by the sky's low ceiling, and she wasn't positive it was them until Jay's aluminum-shod hooves rang on the asphalt apron in front of the barn.

"You should run him," Nate said as he dismounted, releasing the girth as Liv unbuckled the throat latch on the bridle and unsnapped the martingale. "You should have nominated him for the Durham Cup, but you could still find him an allowance."

"What?" She waited next to Jay's head as Nate came around to slide off the bridle.

"Run him. A race would do him more good than a work. He can handle it."

Nate walked away as she buckled the halter and wound on the shank, not giving her a chance to figure out a response. She heard him call, "See you at the end of the morning," after he dumped the tack in front of one of Michel's stalls and left the barn.

She passed Jay to the hotwalker and put Nate's words out of her mind because she had enough other stuff to fill it right now. Her first horse of the morning waited for her.

When she returned from the main track with Trop, Liv noticed two strangers standing in front of the office. It made her uneasy. Sue waited in front of the barn with Trop's halter, the hotwalker with her.

Liv glanced at the shedrow before dismounting. "Who's Jo talking to?"

"Not sure," Sue answered, passing the shank to the hotwalker once the halter was on.

After setting the tack in front of her next horse, Liv walked down toward the office where Jo stood with a woman holding a notebook, and a man — Liv now noticed — who had a camera. Media. How did they know? Already?

There are few secrets on the backstretch. She might have said that herself.

Jo waited while the reporter introduced herself and the photographer to Liv, then she backed away with an apologetic slant to her lips. Liv didn't try to remember either name. Social media would probably tell her soon enough.

"Can I help you?" she asked, making no attempt to sound friendly.

"Can you confirm Just Jay shipped in last night?"

There was no point denying it. She nodded.

"What are your plans for him leading up to the Classic?"

"It's the middle of training and I have horses to get on, so I'll have to ask you to leave." She wished she had her whip to help usher them out of the barn. This was just the reminder she needed to set up additional security for Jay. When did training horses become this complicated?

She knew she couldn't duck the reporters forever and would have to come up with something to say so she was ready the next time. Have a set of pat answers.

"Media were here this morning. Someone was clocking you and Jay in the field. Can you believe that?" she told Nate when he showed up at the end of the morning.

"And so it begins," he said, parked in the same spot on the

old loveseat as she updated records. "Did you think about what I said?"

She would have loved to tell the reporter Jay would run again before the Classic. That would shake everyone out there up. It would show them that a real horse could handle it. Because she believed Jay could — but she had to stick to her plan.

"I don't need you second-guessing me, Miller. I got him to the Dubai World Cup without a race after the Pegasus. That was the same timeframe as this."

"Yeah," he said, pushing himself up from the loveseat. "You've got this." But it wasn't said in encouragement. "Can I have the keys? I'll wait in the car."

Liv grabbed the fob from the drawer and tossed it to him, then watched as he disappeared though the door. She sank her head into her hands. What had she said? Why was he so touchy? It had to be his parents. She tidied the desk hastily and dashed after him.

He was behind the wheel of the Porsche, the music playing. She ducked into the passenger seat and just listened, searching for a sense of his mood. Nate's song choices were always intentional.

I am still running...

But the song came around to something less troubled. Something about building a home, "the only place I ever will belong." She had a sense it was bigger than just her.

"Sorry," he said. "Sometimes it seems like things never change."

"You're not, though. Running." She kept her gaze on him, but his eyes stayed on his phone, scrolling too quickly to really be seeing anything. "Seems to me you're facing everything head on. And I'm sorry I'm letting myself get caught up in my Breeders' Cup panic already."

His laugh was quiet, more a lift of his shoulders and a slight snort. It said, "Is that a surprise?" though he didn't speak.

"I listened to a video on Instagram this week," she started. "Some woman talking about her relationship, and how it's unreasonable to give a hundred percent all the time. So you agree that between the two of you, you make up that hundred. Some days you're the sixty, some days you're the eighty."

He looked at her sideways. "What do you think we are right now?"

"You tell me what you've got, so I know I have to make up the rest."

"Good to know where to go for marriage counselling," he said, finally meeting her eyes with a wry grin.

"Probably cheaper than my therapist." She straightened and snapped in the seat belt. "Let's get out of here."

CHAPTER TWENTY-SIX

It wasn't so bad that their first Breeders' Cup wasn't closer to home like Keeneland, or somewhere familiar like Santa Anita, or epic like Churchill Downs. Because this was Del Mar, famous and historic in its own right, a beautiful storied locale next to the Pacific Ocean.

It was hard to put words to the emotions of being here. Calling it another box on the bucket list didn't seem enough. It was two wishes rolled into one. Her list needed a better name. Destination List. Dream List. *I Can't Believe I'm Actually Here* List.

The media in Toronto had become progressively worse, but it was nothing compared to how cloying they were here. Liv would never get used to it, and still wasn't very good at handling the attention. All she could do was try to be honest but not effusive. Jay had breezed at Woodbine so they wouldn't be expecting another move before the race, and anyone could see how tremendous her horse looked. An entourage followed her out to the track every morning, and there was no shortage of photographers. She liked that part — looking through the endless gorgeous pictures of her Big Horse on social media when she was alone again, after her morning responsibilities were complete.

It would all be over soon. Just a few more days, then she could retreat to her relative anonymity. There would be some aftermath if Jay won, but that part would be worth it.

Jay was stabled with Wayward Sun and Elliot, so she had an ally in this unfamiliar place. Nate would join them Friday, catching a plane after the races at Woodbine. Michel was so happy to be here with the horse, he was almost like a stranger — not nearly as snarky as he was at home. He deserved this break from that life, working hard six days a week and helping raise a baby. Liv shuddered, and tried not to make derogatory comments about that part of his life in their downtime, which, with only one horse to care for between both of them, was frequent.

There had to be something wrong with her. She was the person who anxiously waved people off if they asked her to hold their squirmy, tiny humans, and the baby smell others cooed over made her stomach churn. It was more than not knowing what to do. It was not knowing what to say. How to act. How to be appropriate. So she avoided speaking her mind around Michel. *This must be nice for you, having a reprieve from all that. And what were you thinking? Really?*

She was a horrible, horrible person. But here she was with a horse to run in the Breeders' Cup Classic. You didn't have to have a good soul to be here. Right now she was surrounded by trainers who were evidence of that.

The ocean drew her at the end of each day. Del Mar was a stone's throw from the beach so it seemed wrong not to catch the sunset. Solitude wasn't common for her anymore, but it was never far away, and nothing she feared. There was even something delicious about feeling Nate's absence, looking forward to seeing him, sharing another incredible experience with him. It was too bad post time for Saturday's Classic was late enough they'd miss the chance to catch the beauty of the descending, fiery orb after the race.

Nate's flight got in late, long after the sun had disappeared below the horizon line where the expanse of sky met the vastness of the Pacific. She'd lost track of the airport visits this year. He greeted her quickly at the curb and they climbed into the rental, sweeping away from the terminal.

"So how are you?" he asked before she had the chance to question him about his day.

Liv realized she'd tightened her grip on the wheel, and loosened it, one finger at a time. "You know. Fine, as long as I don't think about it too much. But I mean, really. Dubai. Ascot. Del Mar for Breeders' Cup." She shrugged, feigning nonchalance. "Just another horse race, right?"

He grinned. "Right."

"It's been okay. Of course the media part is..." She lifted a hand from the wheel briefly, then replaced it, as if that explained. Nate would get it, because he got her. She snagged his eyes. "We're here. We did it. Got a horse here. Together."

"The best part is yet to come." He held onto her gaze until she had to return it to the road.

"Do you mind if we go check on him?"

"Of course not."

The barn was quiet, the nearby highway like white noise in the background. She imagined she could hear the crashing ocean just beyond in the darkness. Low nickers greeted them when they walked down to Jay's stall, Liv nodding at the security guard. Jay dozed quietly, but at the sound of their voices he turned, shuffling in the straw. Nate slipped in behind her, peppermints at the ready.

"Hey, Big Horse," he murmured.

The minty scent wafted to Liv's nostrils moments after Jay crunched the sugary disc. He pressed his muzzle to her next as if suggesting a candy was the cost of admission, the price of disrupting his nap. She searched her pockets and didn't let him down.

"Do you think if I end up training for twenty or fifty years, I won't feel as if I have to come the night before a race like this to check my horse?" She glanced at Nate.

"You? Nope. Never."

"Guess we should let him have his peace. Get some sleep ourselves."

"Let's go to the beach first," he suggested. "Grab something to eat, maybe. Sit for a bit."

She was reminded of the last time they'd been in California; the two of them on a stretch of sand further north, predawn instead of night. A visit, after she'd encouraged him to ride here that winter — to put his career before them — thinking it was the right thing to do when she had to admit she'd been pushing him away. It had taken near-disaster last year to let her see the two of them the way he did. Like this. Together, side by side, ready to tackle everything before them.

"They used to take horses to the beach here," she said, as if he didn't know. "How fun would that be?"

She wasn't surprised when he started singing, "Where The Surf Meets The Turf."

"I really need to add riding a racehorse on the beach to my list," she mused.

"You're not going to eat that, are you?" he asked.

She looked down at the pita in its waxed paper wrap that had seemed like a good idea when she'd ordered it. "Apparently I can't eat anything right now. Nerves, I guess."

He slipped a hand to her neck, pulling her to him. His kiss was a lot of things, but tense was not one of them. He didn't seem to be affected by anxiety like she was. Probably because he got to be on the horse, in more control of the outcome, not stuck in the grandstand wishing they could trade places.

"Let's go back to the hotel."

She nodded, and he climbed to his feet, offering her a hand.

The next morning, she sent Nate and Jay out to the track as early as possible with the same instructions she'd given at Saratoga.

No one had to ask her how fast her horse went, because the clocker caught his time.

If Jay won, she'd be a genius. If he lost, she'd be a fool.

Either way, in twelve hours, everyone would know.

CHAPTER TWENTY-SEVEN

Huey Harrison, Chaotic Good's regular rider, looked like his name. He was a caricature, with red hair and freckles and a round face that was begging to be punched. What was he, eighteen? He reminded Nate of the kid who had played Alec in *The Black Stallion* movie, except he actually had red hair like the book Alec, when the child actor had not.

"Hey old man."

Nate looked around, from Ricky Acosta, who was at least five years older than Nate was, to Wes Holden, still riding at the top of his game in his early fifties. Nate wanted to be *that* twenty years from now. But was the kid talking to him?

"I just saw your horse on TV, back at the barn, *eh?*" Yep. That voice was coming from Huey. "He's having a nap. You got time to have a nap before the Classic, *eh?*"

"You watch too many YouTube videos of Bob and Doug McKenzie there, kid?" Not that Nate never said "eh," but Americans rarely used it right when they tried to make fun, so the joke lost its effect. It was good to know Jay was relaxed, though. Nate had missed that pre-race clip.

Huey looked confused. "Bob and Doug who?"

Guess not.

"Maybe if you'd been older and more experienced, you wouldn't have lost the Preakness and you'd be sitting on a Triple Crown winner this afternoon." It wasn't the best comeback, but Nate didn't really want to play.

"Maybe if you'd taken a nap before that race at Ascot you'd have had the energy to win it."

Wes Holden, whom Nate had ridden with the winter he'd spent at Santa Anita, put an arm around his shoulders. "You walked right into that. *Eh?*"

Nate shook his head and could only laugh. *Truth.* The kid would have to do better than that to rile him today. He'd learned from experience — and threats from Liv — to stay out of these things, so all it did was feed his determination to win. A couple of old guys, him and Jay. They just had to beat Chaotic Good and the kid. Nothing else was acceptable.

He had a long wait in front of him and envied the guys who had more than one mount. For a while he watched the TV to see if they showed any more clips of Jay or Liv. Elliot's horse won the Mile, looking even stronger than he had at Woodbine. Just as well Trop had stayed home.

If only he had a guitar, he could keep busy with that. Instead, Nate played countless games of ping-pong, taking on all challengers, when normally he didn't have time for that in the room at Woodbine. If he'd sat down, he might have found himself having that nap Harrison suggested. He wasn't used to this much down time. As post time drew closer, he put in earbuds and cranked some music, walling himself off from everything.

Then finally, finally, he was getting ready: putting on Triple Stripe's red, white and blue silks, weighing out, and joining Liv in the paddock. Maybe he was biased, but Jay was the best-looking horse there. The sheen of his chestnut coat was dazzling, the low rays of the early evening sun catching the checkerboard quarter marker pattern Michel had brushed along the top of his hindquarters. The big horse walked with what Nate could only describe as authority.

After shaking Claude Lachance's hand, kissing Liv's mother, Ann, on the cheek, and hugging Emilie, Nate joined Liv. On the odds board, Jay and Chaotic Good swapped the position of favourite back and forth like one of the table tennis rallies he'd had in the jock's room.

"No song?" Liv asked. It was a brave attempt to ignore her nerves — Nate could see she was practically vibrating.

It only took a second for the last tune he'd played to rise again in his mind, and he sang, *"This is how legends are made..."*

Liv seemed satisfied.

"How much you got?" he asked.

It was a beat before she seemed to understand what he meant. She held up her hand, making an "O." "Completely tapped out."

"That's all right. Jay and I have the hundred."

It could have been any track, anywhere. It didn't matter. It was a mile and a quarter of sandy loam and it was Nate and Jay's job to cover it faster than the competition.

Who was he kidding? It was Del Mar. It was the Breeders' Cup Classic.

He was glad he'd taken Jay around the oval this morning; it had been worth the snarky comments afterward. *You think that horse is Secretariat, blowing him out like that?* No, Nate would never compare Jay to that horse, even though they were both big and red. Jay was good. The best of his generation, maybe. But he wasn't *that.* Besides, Nate was pretty sure Secretariat had never breezed a quarter the morning of a race, and no one did stuff like that these days. For someone who could be so careful, Liv had been bold, bold, bold with Just Jay.

He shut out the chatter around him once they were in the gate, their position in the middle of it ideal. The horse beside them was anxious, flipping his head, the starter's assistant perched on the partition cursing and the jock looking ready to climb onto the frame of the metal barrier. Jay stood square, merely flicking his ears at the disturbance. Nate was aware of the others in his peripheral vision, being slotted into stalls, the energy building, fuelled by the buzz of the crowd. The slam of the final set of doors closing came, Jay on his toes, ready to pounce... then the doors crashed open.

Jay's power catapulted him out and Nate capitalized on his horse's eagerness, vying for the best place in the fray. As Count Kazoo and Fundamental rushed past to battle for the lead, he settled Jay in their wake. Glancing around, he didn't see Harrison and Chaotic Good. No matter, it just meant they were behind Jay, and could stay there. Nate liked where he was, a couple of lanes out from the rail, where no one could trap him. Jay was on top of the program, staying closer to the pace than he had in the past.

On the first turn he let Jay drift in, tucked mid-pack but still off the rail. Nate resisted the temptation to look behind, locate Harrison. *Put the kid out of your head, and worry about what's in front of you:* another three-quarters of a mile of running. Nate was sure he'd have to contend with Huey soon enough.

The kid showed up, floating Chaotic Good up the rail on the backstretch. Nate dropped Jay closer so that the co-favourites galloped along like they were on a friendly country hack, but if Harrison was expecting Nate to be a polite Canadian when he needed room, the kid was dreaming. There was a wall of three horses in front and a fleet of them tight behind, and Nate had every intention of keeping Chaotic Good boxed in.

Entering the stretch, the leaders continued head in head until one broke free, going for it — leaving the slower two an impenetrable barricade in front of Harrison's horse. Nate didn't chase the frontrunner, not yet, trusting Jay's explosive kick. The flight directly in front of them slowed with fatigue but he wanted to keep Harrison flat-footed a while longer — until it was time to set Jay loose down the lane. They needed that head start. He eased Jay out just enough to have a clear path, but Chaotic Good had nowhere to go.

Apparently, Huey Harrison didn't see things that way, because the move he made, looping his left arm out as he pulled on the right line, slammed him into Jay with enough force to knock the big chestnut sideways. The sliver of room created still wasn't enough, and Jay was game to fight this fight, but *shit,* there would be carnage, so Nate gave the kid enough space to keep them both from dying, and the race to the wire was on.

Fundamental was still on top, and Chaotic Good had exploded, getting the jump on Jay. Nate yelled in Jay's ear, lighting a fire under the big horse because the advantage he'd tried to preserve was gone. Jay drove, regaining the ground he'd lost. Nate let him fall in again, becoming a three-horse blanket with his two foes in the charge to the wire. It was so tight Harrison had no room to use his stick, but Nate put his own away. Not to make it a fair fight, but because now it was up to his hands — and Jay's heart.

Liv was deaf from the cacophony around her, and dumb from her own raw screeching for Jay and Nate as they stormed down the stretch. She was numb all over as the three horses swept past the wire, only then breaking apart as they galloped out around the turn. Emilie's nails dug into her arm, making her jump, and forced her to shift her focus.

"Come on!" Emilie said. "We have to get down there!"

So. Many. People. Liv didn't think they were ever going to make it trackside. Emilie bowled through the crowd like an icebreaker, clasping Liv's hand so they didn't become separated, tugging her along when she hesitated to stretch up as she tried to keep her eyes on her horse. Snatches of speculation reached her, predicting the victor, fists clutching mutuel tickets with rewards that relied on the result.

Michel beat them to the track, rushing up to Jay, snapping on his shank. The valet released the overgirth so Nate could remove it; let Jay breathe more easily while they waited. Chaotic Good's rider brushed past Liv with a scowl. He didn't make eye contact, but Liv glared in his direction anyway. Nate's discretion could have cost them the win, but it had probably saved that kid's life.

She reached Jay, stroking his neck when she wanted to hug both of them. Nate shrugged with one shoulder like he had after the King George at Ascot, not offering a gut response. Did it matter, really, with that performance? Jay had defeated Chaotic Good, his competition for Horse of the Year. If Fundamental had won, they couldn't possibly give him the title on that score alone — could they?

"They're taking forever," Emilie muttered after several minutes had passed, stealing glances at the numbers on the big screen in the infield. Then her mouth fell open, a wall of sound descending from the grandstand as fans erupted. Liv spun to see the board for herself.

It took a moment to compute. Her heart, which had been pounding so wildly as she screamed Jay home, seemed to stop.

The photo finish sign was gone, official payouts flashing up, and Just Jay's number was on top.

Liv's legs almost gave out. Because though she'd predicted it, believing it would happen, she'd never truly imagined the moment coming to pass.

Nate's arms shot in the air, the overt display one she'd never seen from him, even after winning the Plate. Recovering, Liv had to keep herself from dragging him out of the saddle when he dropped a hand to grab hers, and she braced her free palm against Jay to support herself as she stood on her toes to reach his lips.

"Here you go, boss," Michel said, holding out the shank.

She shook her head. "No way, Michel. You deserve this."

They gathered in the winner's circle, Jay adorned in the traditional Breeders' Cup purple and gold blanket of flowers for the photo, their group small compared to others on a day like today. Then came the trophy presentation, while Michel led Jay to the test barn. When the microphone was pushed into her face, Liv stepped aside. It was her father's horse — his vision responsible for their success.

But Claude Lachance deferred. "We would not be here without the hard work and determination of my daughter and her husband. Their teamwork made all of this possible." Her father's gaze, his warm smile, turned to Liv and Nate.

Nate's hand curled around hers, out of sight of the persistent camera. A prompt. There was no avoiding it, she realized. She swallowed back the anxiety that threatened, and found her inspiration.

"Just over a year ago, this horse was standing in a paddock on the farm. We thought he was done. My sister Emilie threw the tack on him one day and started hacking him around, thinking she'd turn him into an event horse if we didn't have any interest in him as a stallion. He looked so good, Nate said we should give him another shot. And here we are. I'm grateful for the crew back at Woodbine and wish they could all be here for this. To his groom, Michel Larouche, who's looked after him since he was a yearling. And to my father, for having the faith to let me train his horses and do things how I wanted. Jay is evidence that a horse doesn't have to be finished at three or four. That medication isn't necessary. And that we don't have to buy into thinking today's Thoroughbred is too fragile to last. When you take the time to do things right and listen to the horse, this is what can happen."

Nate nudged her, reaching for the mic, edging it away like he thought it might explode. "He's an incredible horse," he said, his tone a combination of wonder and modesty. "We're very grateful to be a part of all of this."

Then he pushed the mic back and tugged Liv away, staring at her like she'd said something wrong.

What? Liv asked with her eyes.

"Later," he rumbled in her ear.

Of course, Claude insisted on taking everyone out for dinner. This was a landmark victory for the farm, after all. A celebration was mandatory, even when Nate was sure this win would take days to sink in.

No one else seemed uncomfortable, or else they were faking it well, but Liv's soliloquy had siphoned off some of his joy. Was he really the only one who thought those words were going to come back to bite them?

The hotel room was mercifully quiet after the constant noise of the restaurant, but it didn't translate as peace. Nate tried to talk himself into keeping his mouth shut. *Leave it, Miller. Leave it for another time.* Maybe it wouldn't be as bad as he thought.

But his phone was lighting up, and it wasn't all congratulatory texts. He should have shut it off as soon as he'd got back to the jock's room, to spare himself the early reaction to Liv's declaration.

"That was some speech, honey," he said, tossing his jacket on the bed. "Way to shake them up. You went from hiding from the media to standing in front of a TV camera that was blasting a signal probably to Mars, on the biggest day in racing, telling everyone they're doing it wrong." The words spilled out.

Liv wheeled, the ice of her irises grey instead of blue. He'd seen her bristling as soon as he dropped "honey" in there, like his unconscious wanted to antagonize her. It worked.

"Maybe they need to be told."

"Ever heard the expression, 'pride comes before a fall?'" he drawled.

"It's not pride, it's truth."

"Maybe, but a little diplomacy goes a long way. You basically called out the entire industry."

"I thought you'd be on my side. We're supposed to be in this together."

That hit him with a bolt of guilt, but it wasn't that simple. "We are. I am on your side, it's just —"

"How am I hurting anyone?" she challenged, giving him a palms-up flip of her hands before crossing her arms.

"That's just it. I still have to ride for those trainers. I don't have the luxury of operating in the Triple Stripe bubble. So I guess the answer to that is you're hurting me." And he hadn't really realized that was what had come to the surface until it seeped up. Maybe he really was blowing this out of proportion.

"So this is about you," she snapped.

"You don't understand. If they think I'm too good for them, my business is going to end up in the toilet pretty fast."

"You say that like I'd let you end up on the street or something."

"I need my career, Liv." Because he wasn't so different from his father, was he? "I can't just let you take care of me. If the shoe were on the other foot, you wouldn't want to rely on me for support. So don't expect me to be happy with it."

There, finally. Something had made its way through to her, the tight line between her brows easing, her hands leaving the tuck of her defensive stance to grip her elbows instead.

"You know what I hate?" she said. "I hate that you're right. That I should've just kept my mouth shut about that stuff. That I should just quietly do my own thing and let them all think I'm just like everyone else."

And that was what she'd always done, wasn't it? Liv wasn't one to attract attention to herself. She didn't seek the spotlight. Jay had forced her into it, and she'd — inadvertently — added opera glasses to herself by speaking out tonight. He should be applauding her bravery, not lambasting her, but for some reason, he couldn't bring himself to apologize.

"In a week, everyone's going to forget what I said," she muttered. "They're not going to change. All they'll do is laugh at me and keep doing what they do. This is why no one should let me talk into a microphone."

Nate was inclined to agree at the moment, but he wasn't so sure this would be easily forgotten. *Everything lives forever on the internet.*

"Here they come." Liv wrapped the chain around the noseband of Jay's halter and handed the shank to Nate. "I think it's best if you do this."

"Is it, though? It could be your chance to redeem yourself." He grinned.

"To backtrack, you mean?" Her anger threatened to resurface. "I may not have chosen the most diplomatic way to say what I said, but none of it was a lie. I'll never be voted Ms. Congeniality. That's why I have you." She might have kissed him if she wasn't still mad at him. "Plus, they always love it when they get shots of the jock with his Big Horse. They could sell posters of the two of you. Have signings."

"Do I get a cut?" he quipped. "Can we license our images? Monetize this shit?"

"We're not that far from LA. Maybe you can find yourself a different kind of agent before we go." She put her hands on his back and pushed him forward. "Go be my frontman."

Facing reporters was bad enough at the best of times, but after last night's diatribe the prospect would be that much worse. Could she hide here in the stall? Nate glanced over his shoulder as he led Jay out. She'd just hang here for a minute, admire the movie star good looks of her Classic winner and his partner.

"Where's the trainer?"

Had she really thought she was off the hook? Liv sighed, and emerged from the darkness of the stall, summoning the closest thing she could find to a friendly but unapologetic smile, and left the security of the barn.

"Nate's my official spokesperson," she quipped. "As of yesterday."

That got a laugh.

Nate leaned back, whispering in her ear. "See? You're not a total lost cause."

"I think you're wrong about that, but whatever."

She stayed just behind him, thinking Nate and Jay were the most photogenic pair in horse racing, but of course a pack of sportswriters wouldn't let her remain in the background. She missed Chique. Chique would have spun her hind end into the pack and scattered them all. Jay was far too well-behaved.

Nate became the mediator: filtering questions, deflecting the ones with potential to get her in trouble. It was a temporary measure, but he managed to keep the focus on Jay's accomplishment.

"Will he be retired?"

Liv stepped forward. "He's going to Willowmark Stud from here. If he comes out of this okay, we'll talk about the possibility of the Pegasus in January. He'd come to Payson Park in Florida with us to train, then that would be his last start."

It was a script any of them could have written; a common path to add one last million-dollar race to the tally. For Liv, though, it meant she could hang onto her Big Horse just a little longer.

CHAPTER TWENTY-EIGHT

THE CLOCKS always went back an hour on Breeders' Cup weekend for Daylight Savings Time. It hadn't affected them in California — they went with the daylight, not the clock. Monday morning at Woodbine, though, it was obvious. From training horses before dawn under the lights on the main track, to the bi-annual moaning from employees about why the legislation was still in place. At least they gained an hour of sleep in the fall, but it felt like going from autumn to winter overnight, plunged into the darkness of the impending change of seasons.

Michel and Sue had the day off, so they were short-staffed. Liv and Nate stopped at Triple Shot for coffees and pastries on the way in, both a mini-celebration for the weekend's success and a way to ease the damper of the time change. They walked what horses they could, but with a race this coming Saturday, Cam had to train. So, Liv got on Trop, who she was considering giving one more start in Ontario before he went south with the rest of the string.

They backed up together in silence, jogging to the front of the grandstand and turning in at the wire to face the infield —

like they had hundreds, or maybe thousands, of times — then she let Nate go on ahead of her, setting Trop off briskly in his wake. She could see Cam looking around as he galloped, like he expected zombies to leap out from the shadows on either side of the rail. Some days, he was like a bigger, more powerful version of Chique. Nate had to let him go fast enough to keep him occupied, or he'd find dangerous ways to amuse himself.

Liv didn't know what to do with the big colt. With Michel not going south, if she and Nate stayed in Ontario until after Christmas, Jo would have to take care of him, which would not go over well. And who the hell was going to gallop him down there? They couldn't just turn Cam out at Payson until Nate arrived, or the colt would be a nightmare to start back up. It would involve a healthy dose of tranquilizer to make him safe.

Don't let anyone hear you say that, after that monologue at the Classic. She wasn't against drugs; sometimes their use was warranted. The issue wasn't as black and white as people on the outside wanted to think. It was the stuff that pushed the envelope with ethics and regulations that she wanted no part of. Her goal was just to prove a horse could be trained without that, but it felt like a losing battle; not because it couldn't be done, but because who besides her really cared?

Nate didn't wait for her when he'd finished galloping Cam, which told her all she needed to know about the colt's state of mind this morning. She saw Cam duck off the track as she pulled Trop up, Nate too preoccupied with handling the tough colt to acknowledge her. The stream of dialogue he released as Cam threw his head back and tried to gallop down to the tunnel was not friendly. She shouldn't laugh — if Cam dropped him, not only would it hurt, it would cause mayhem for the surrounding horses. But it was such a normal thing for this horse, and Nate had survived it hundreds of times before; she had faith he'd live through this one to fight a hundred more.

Her return to the barn was more leisurely, and by the time she got there, Nate was leading Cam out front to the rolling pit. She stopped herself from saying what she wanted: *are you sure about that, Miller?* Trop, at least, was showing a level of maturity she was grateful for, because the sight of a rolling horse and Cam's subsequent trademark display of athleticism — standing on his hind legs with his forelegs striking the air — would set a more fractious horse off.

"Good boy," she said, scratching his withers as she let the gelding stand to observe. "How so very grown-up you are, mister." Cam, on the other hand, had a ways to go.

Nate stayed long enough to cool out Cam — it was too cold for baths. Liv wondered if he'd get the pushback he was expecting when he went to breeze horses in other barns. No one had done more than congratulate them on the walk to and from the track, but people would say things to Nate they wouldn't say to her. She nearly always heard things secondhand. Or read them online. She hadn't been able to keep herself from looking, even though Nate had warned her not to.

"Has anyone said anything to you?" Liv joined Jo in the tack room once Nate was gone.

Jo raised her eyebrows briefly before reaching into the box of pastries. "You're worrying about it far too much. Who listens to the presentations anyway? I was too excited after watching the race to really even pay attention to what you were saying."

But she'd obviously heard, or replayed it.

"Haters gonna hate, Liv. Thanks for the pastry. I've got horses to do up." Jo raised the croissant in her hand in salute as she left.

And with Sue and Michel off, Liv had her share of work too, so she carried on with the morning routine.

Nate didn't share anything about his morning on the drive

home, and Liv kept herself from asking. When they got to the house, he opted for a nap — but her? That wasn't happening.

For once she didn't feel like going for a run or a swim. Ontario in November was cold after California and the morning at the track had left her tired and chilled. Holly's tail thumped against the wall of her plastic crate near the kitchen when Liv opened the fridge for some water. So maybe a walk. Her life hadn't settled down enough this year to think about her and Nate finally getting a dog of their own, but now that the Breeders' Cup was behind them, it could be the right time. For the moment, she'd borrow Holly.

She snapped a leash on the Lab and headed for the training barn. Emilie squealed a greeting to her dog, and Liv let go of the lead, letting Holly rush up. Curtis, standing in the crossties, didn't care about the canine intruder. Liv went to the horse, not surprised her sister didn't acknowledge her until she'd lavished attention on her dog.

"Get Jay settled in his once and future digs?" Emilie asked when she finished fussing over the dog, Holly snuffling around in search of grains somehow missed in the clean-swept aisle.

It had been hard to leave Jay at the stud farm in Lexington, to not be the one assessing how the horse was doing in the days after the biggest race of his life, no matter how incredible Willowmark was. The cost, again, for having a horse who was too good to keep to herself.

"We did. Poor guy, living in luxury."

"Do you know what the plan is yet?"

"We agreed to give it a few days. They'll make sure he came out of the race okay, and we'll go from there."

"Kind of sucks, doesn't it?" Emilie said with a sympathetic frown as she checked her girth.

"Yes, it does," Liv admitted. "It should be me seeing how he comes out of that race. At least, if there's a chance he'll run again. But I guess that's how it is now. Hopefully we'll get him back for one more start, then look forward to his babies."

"You have to be just a little bit excited about the thought of the foal Claire's going to have by him."

"I don't know how I could possibly love anything more than I love Léa, but yeah, I am." She reached for the bridle hanging near a stall and handed it to Emilie. "I wanted to talk to you about something else, Em. I don't think it's such a good idea for me to do the clinic anymore."

"What?" Emilie stopped short of accepting the bridle. "You can't back out now! You don't get to tell me you can't do it after that speech at the Classic."

"That's exactly why I can't do it," Liv groaned.

"Liv, you were a rock star! The whole thing has gone viral, haven't you seen?"

"Unfortunately."

"You haven't seen the right stuff then. It's all over the equestrian groups. They love you. We'll get so many people wanting to come just to hear you talk, we'll have to add a second session."

"Em —"

"Liv! This is it, all right? You've opened up the can of worms. You need to own it."

Liv snorted. "Just what I've always wanted. A can of worms."

"Please, please, please say yes. You can't just hide. It just makes it look as if you think you did something wrong when you didn't. And at this thing, you'll have a friendly audience. These aren't racetrackers, but they're people who might want to get into racing."

Liv sighed. Emilie was giving her the response she'd expected from Nate. At least her sister was in her court, so she had to trust Em was right. "Okay. But you'd better double-check with the New Chapter board."

"How could they have a problem with it?"

"Do you forget that board is made up of key people in the industry? Most of them likely didn't appreciate what I said any more than the rest of them."

"But that's so backward! It will look bad for them if they don't agree. Their whole mandate revolves around helping horses."

Liv leaned against a stall door. "Politics, Em."

Emilie hadn't made a move to put the bridle on Curtis yet. "Why don't you get on a horse? You seem a little lost."

Was she? How could someone in her position be lost? But what better way to find herself if that was true than on the back of a horse?

Liv pushed herself from the wall. "Who should I get?"

Emilie thought for a moment. "That little bay filly. Her name's Mabel."

"You have an extra pair of boots around?" Liv knew she had a spare helmet here.

"I have my galloping boots in the car, and my chaps are in the tack room."

Mabel was a sweet thing, one of those fillies Liv wasn't surprised had shown no interest in racing. It was always tempting to believe she might find that will to run in another trainer's reject, because everyone was convinced they could do better than the other guy. Emilie had turned Reba around when, a year ago, the filly looked to be a hopeless case. Reba had been more the exception than the rule, though.

Liv treated Mabel much like she would a yearling, even though the filly knew more than the babies. A fresh off the track Thoroughbred's muscles weren't accustomed to this kind of work — Mabel was used to going around a mile oval, not this comparatively small indoor ring. There was a big difference between galloping fitness and flatwork fitness.

The filly was happy to jog along the outside on a loose rein and Liv gave her a couple of circuits before she shortened up and circled, working on reshaping those muscles — first one direction, then the other. It got Liv's mind off everything for a while until she and Emilie were cooling their mounts out.

"I think you should do that for the clinic," Emilie suggested. "Or seminar. Whatever we're calling it."

"Do what?" Liv absently flipped the stray piece of mane that had flopped to the left side of Mabel's neck.

"Hop on something straight off the track so they can see a first ride."

"You can do that, Em."

"But I'm not a celebrity." Emilie grinned. "Maybe we could livestream, too. That would open it up to even more people. What do you think?"

Liv rolled her eyes, bringing Mabel to a halt in the middle of the arena and hopping off.

Emilie followed suit. They put the horses away, and Liv stashed her borrowed gear back where it had come from. "Do you want me to take Holly to the house?" she asked when Emilie released the dog from her bed in the tack room.

"Could you? Thanks for giving her some time."

"She was good while we were riding. Why don't you bring her more often?"

"She's a distraction." Emilie's grin was sheepish. "I'd be stopping between horses to play with her and I'd run out of time." Emilie operated on a tight schedule.

Liv let the Lab off lead for the walk. She stopped to say hi to Claire and Chique, both of them, and their third wheel, Stella, coming over. Looking back, Claire and Chique had been the beginning of this journey, though Liv hadn't been aware of it. She'd endured strange looks and wisecracks while logging twice the usual mileage every day when she'd interval trained Claire, and Chique had raced without medication.

Both mares carried the next generation of racehorses. The attendees of the upcoming clinic – most of whom would likely be young women – might represent a new generation of humans, ready to make a difference. Hadn't she told Nate young women were the future of this sport? She'd just never imagined herself as any kind of leader.

CHAPTER TWENTY-NINE

BACK IN THE Woodbine jock's room, Nate's Breeders' Cup win made him a hero for about five minutes before the playing field levelled and he was back to being one of them. That's what he loved about this job. You could be a star for a heartbeat, riding the wave of a big win, but if you didn't remember tomorrow you might be a nobody again, either someone would remind you, or something would come along to knock you down. All he had to do was look around him, see the older guys battling weight and scrabbling for mounts to realize that could be him one day. That smartass Huey Harrison at Del Mar aside, Nate was just hitting his prime. He was nowhere near done. But another ten, fifteen years of this was the best he could probably hope for.

He was in a three-way race for the Woodbine riding title with Cory MacDonald and Jiro Watanabe — a title he'd lost last year, thanks to a delayed return from the winter in California, then that fateful trip to Saratoga. The spill had knocked him out of the standings because he'd been off for over two months, leaving him with no hope of making up the lost ground. When he'd started back riding, none of it had mattered. He was lucky to be back at all. Now, the two younger riders were giving him a run for his money, and some days he cared more about winning the title than others.

The first Wednesday night after the time change, when the temperature just might reach freezing before the last race, it didn't seem that important.

With five mounts tonight, three of them looked like good bets to win. Maybe he'd lost out on a couple of rides because of Liv's comments after the Classic, but it might work in his favour: cut out some of the less desirable barns. Did he really want to be riding for trainers who felt threatened by what she'd said? Liv was probably right. It would all blow over with no significant damage.

The overnight entries for Saturday were out, and Nate scanned the printout, stopping on the Autumn Stakes. Can't Catch Me, post position five. Two imports from New York among the starters. Nate was curious as much as anything how Cam would do facing older horses and open company for the first time. The three-year-old colt wasn't the poster child for anything outside the box, like Jay. If he won, there would be no speeches. Liv might just suggest Cam was finally putting things together, and Nate would quip he was happy the horse hadn't hurt him yet. The reporters here were almost friends, not the vultures that covered the big American races.

Once Cam's race was done, what was left? Maybe one more start for Trop, but Liv had mentioned possibly waiting till Florida so he could run on the turf, because grass racing was done for the season at Woodbine.

Florida sounded good right about now.

"That was some speech, Miller. What a load of bullshit."

Nate turned, cranking an eyebrow up. Chris Hill,

yammering about something. Nate folded the overnight and reached for his silks for the first race, ignoring the other rider.

"Come on." Hill wasn't shutting up. "That horse has been at the farm as much as at the track this year. And Liv was almost a vet. Oh, but it's all about how she's a better trainer than anyone else. I bet there's stuff in that horse's system no one's ever heard of. She worked for Doc Baines back in the day. He's always ahead of the curve. I bet she learned lots from him."

Nate clenched his hands into fists. Forced himself to release them. *Big breath in — let it out.* He tucked the silks into his breeches.

"I bet you're in on it," Hill goaded. "Those big warmups away from the pony. You're probably doing something the outriders miss."

What? This guy really needed to shut up. Nate played with the goggles on his helmet, then pushed it onto his head. *Ignore him.*

"You had a horse drop dead at Saratoga last year, didn't you? One of those *unexplained* things. Yeah, right."

It took him three strides to get to Hill. Nate didn't say a word, he just returned Hill's sneer with a patient smile. Then he dropped the guy so fast Hill didn't know what hit him. He shook out his fist, knuckles stinging — but seeing the guy's nose bleeding all over the floor made the discomfort worth it. That punch was the first thing that had really taken some of the pain out of Feste's death.

Liv ran through the darkness, the cool air invigorating, though it was nearly ten minutes before her muscles warmed. She needed this, to destress after sitting with pen and paper, trying to tame her thoughts into coherent paragraphs for the upcoming retired racehorse presentation.

Her words had to be informative without being preachy — and she needed to be ready for the tough questions, like why do they need to use drugs? And why do horses break down?

Somehow she had to come up with diplomatic answers. She'd put her foot down on Emilie's livestream idea, though that wouldn't stop anyone from videoing. No matter how careful she was, if anyone wanted to make her look bad, all it would take was some clever splicing. Everyone had a phone these days, and banning them at the event wasn't an option. It would only feed suspicion.

Surprisingly, she'd gained some online allies since the Classic. Private messages of support showed up in her inbox and she'd received friend requests — which she carefully vetted before accepting. There was a small but growing community of like-minded people out there. Sometimes the social media was bad, but sometimes it was good.

That afternoon she'd met Ryn, Kerrie's daughter. The twenty-year-old had her mother's smattering of freckles and tall, athletic build, her hair strawberry-blonde. Nate's inquiries uncovered nothing unusual — all he'd learned was that Ryn was green but reliable. No red flags. Liv and Kerrie agreed Ryn would help at the farm until the racehorses went south. Now that the yearlings had completed their initial sixty days of training, Jillian would switch to the track, learning the ropes from the staff in there. If either Jillian or Ryn didn't work out or changed her mind, Liv decided she'd just send fewer horses to Florida this year. She didn't have the bandwidth to worry about anything more.

Back at the house she climbed into the shower, the hot water chasing away the chill spreading through her. It felt indulgent to pull on flannel pyjamas afterward, knowing Nate was at Woodbine to ride tonight. Night racing should be outlawed; it was that miserable this time of year.

She watched the first few races, happy to see him bring home a couple of favourites, then drew a blanket around her shoulders, curling up in a chair in the main bedroom with her book. Within a few minutes the post-run calm had her head nodding, the book tumbling to her lap. She gave in, closing her eyes.

The sound of Nate returning woke her, though he wasn't noisy. She stirred and yawned, stretching.

He chuckled softly. "You were ten feet from the bed. Too far?"

"I didn't intend to fall asleep." She gave him a sheepish smile. "How was your night?"

He blew out a slow breath and sat on the edge of the bed, facing her but not meeting her eyes. "Won a couple, but had some unnecessary drama."

She sat up straighter, suddenly awake as her mind jumped to what that could mean. He looked okay, but hiding injury was part of the job description. "Are you all right?"

"I'm fine," he said, glancing at her. "Chris Hill's face is not."

She frowned, staring. "You didn't."

"He started running his mouth, saying it was a load of crap that our horses are clean. That you were practically a vet and Jay spent more time on the farm than off so who knew what was going on away from the track."

"That was reason enough to punch him?" None of it was unexpected. Someone had just finally voiced it.

"He thinks I must be doing something. During the warmups. Like, how? I've got a syringe tucked up my sleeve? I don't know."

"Still not a good enough reason, Miller!"

"He brought up Feste." Nate's voice was flat.

Now he met her eyes, and Liv had to look away. Yeah. Of course there would be those who suspected Feste's heart failure had been because of some nefarious drug. How many times had she thought the same thing in sudden deaths? It had to be suspicious, didn't it? Until it had happened to her.

"He said you worked for Parker Baines. Is that true?"

Dr. Parker Baines. Just the man's name made Liv's skin crawl.

"It's not how it sounds," she said. "I used to help our vet, remember? When I was still in school. Baines was a newish associate in the same clinic. He'd already made a name for himself as, you know, one of *those* vets. I went around with him a few times when Jake wasn't there. I learned a lot. A lot of stuff I didn't want to know." She pulled her knees tight to her chest, arms wrapped around them. "I was so naïve."

He walked past her, dragging his sweater over his head on his way to the closet. She followed him with her eyes.

"Hey. It's not as if I think you're giving horses stuff on the sly that I don't know about," he said over his shoulder. "I knew you used to help Jake. It just makes me so mad to have anyone question your integrity."

"It's probably not new. And you predicted there'd be push-back because of what I said at Del Mar." She sighed, unfolding her legs as he returned to the bed once he'd changed, sitting again on top of the covers. "So do you get suspended for that stupidity, or just a fine?"

"I don't know. Guess we'll see." He rubbed his knuckles absently.

Liv hoped they hurt, but not enough to keep him from galloping Cam into Saturday's race. If the stewards set him down before that, Nate could appeal the suspension, but she doubted they'd let him off. So much for his riding title; they might as well go to Florida with the horses.

"I'm sorry," he said.

She tilted her head, watching him. "For what?"

"For after the Classic. I am on your side. We are in this together."

"I think defending my honour by punching a guy out proves that. And while I appreciate the sentiment, you don't have to do that. Like, please, don't."

"Come to bed," he said.

As if that would make everything better.

CHAPTER THIRTY

CAM WAS STRONGER THAN EVER.

You will not run off with me the day before the race. This wasn't Jay. There had been no sneaky instructions when they'd backed up under the lights in the predawn darkness with Liv on the stable pony. Cam didn't need any sharpening. Nate was almost wishing Liv had stayed with him instead of telling him she'd wait at the gap. She had more faith in his strength than he did.

Then — he felt it right away, something subtle on the left side, front end. When Cam swapped leads sooner than usual as they rounded the turn into the backstretch, it was even more obvious. But that didn't mean Cam wanted to pull up when Nate asked him. The colt fought, because *hello,* he was still as hard-headed as ever. Each stride they battled, and all Nate could think was that whatever was bothering the colt, it was getting worse with every step.

The pressure of a horse coming up the inside only made Cam more determined, but then Nate realized it was Liv on Paz. She swooped in, the old gelding's ears pinned to his head, a curl to his lip. Liv snatched the left line, rocking her bodyweight back, and Nate relaxed.

"What's wrong?" she said as she eased them to the outside rail, concern dominating her features. Both horses fell into a jog, Paz giving a hearty snort, all proud of himself after his rescue mission. Liv turned them both to face the infield.

"Thanks," Nate said first. He would have got the colt pulled up, but her quick action might've saved Cam further injury. "Left fore."

She nodded like he was confirming what she already knew and walked them off the gap.

The vet and his assistant were packing up the x-ray equipment when Nate made it back to the barn at the end of the morning. He greeted them as he passed them on the shed and continued to Cam's stall where Michel was putting on the colt's bandages, Liv watching.

"What did Jake say?" Nate asked.

"Radiographs didn't show anything. We're going to send him to the clinic for a nuclear scan." Her phone rang, and she fished it out of her pocket. "Hey. That soon? Okay. I'll figure it out." She disconnected. "They'll take him today, if we can get him there. They're not that busy this time of year."

"I saw Dean's rig," Nate said. "Maybe you can catch him before he goes home."

Liv pulled out her phone again. That would freak Dean out. Liv was one of those people who only called her friends in emergencies.

After assuring Dean it was nothing serious, she turned to Michel. "He'll be here in half an hour."

"I've got to go. Keep me posted," Nate said, satisfied he knew as much as there was to know for now. He had an afternoon of racing ahead.

Dean didn't comment as Michel walked Cam up the ramp of Northwest's four-horse gooseneck trailer. It wasn't until they were on their way out of the East Gate that he asked, "What did he do?"

"Not sure. Nate pulled him up on the turn when he was galloping. Nothing showing up on the x-rays but he's off. Guess I'm scratching out of the Autumn Stakes."

"Are you planning to run anyone else before the meet ends?" Dean asked.

"I think that might be us done for the year." She was leaning hard toward saving Trop for turf racing at Gulfstream. "Though with Sue and Michel not going south with us, I might have to keep everyone here a bit longer. My help situation isn't the most solid right now. I should have tried to steal one of your grooms for the winter." She grinned at him.

"You stay away from them. I don't need them getting a taste of what life could be like."

Liv laughed, because it was true. She was so used to spending four months in Florida now, it would be hard to endure an entire Canadian winter. Leave in November, come back in April. That was the way to do it.

They left Cam at the nearby clinic. He'd be there for three days — one to receive the isotope, another for the scan that would show them any areas with significant uptake, indicating injury, then the third to allow the radioactivity to drop to levels safe enough for his release.

"Do you want a ride home?" Dean asked when they climbed back into the cab of his black Chevy truck.

"That would be great, thank you."

She did not feel like spending the afternoon over at the races waiting for Nate, wondering what people were saying behind her back. But — *you don't care. You've never fit in anyway. It should surprise no one that you're different. You've always been different.* Opening her mouth about it was new, though. But Emilie was right. She needed to own it. Make it her strength, instead of her weakness.

She didn't have to worry about Dean, at least. Because, of course, the topic came up on the forty-minute drive back to the farm.

"I'm jealous, actually," he admitted. "You have the option to do what you want and you're doing it. Having a public stable can be such a soul-suck sometimes. Each time I have to sell a piece of one of our homebreds to stay afloat, it's like selling part of my heart."

"We need to find you some new owners," Liv said, probably not for the first time. "Good owners."

He chuckled. "You just let me know where you find them, okay? Owners like your dad? I think you know your father's a unicorn."

She laughed. "I've never thought of him that way, but it's true. Should I get Emilie to design a t-shirt for him? A Christmas present." She tried to picture her father's face as he opened such a gift from the daughter who had always been just as reserved as he was. "I like it."

He's a unicorn and I'm a princess.

The thought knocked her back. It would forever be how the backstretch viewed her. Riding had been her attempt to escape that label, but it had followed her, all the way to New York City where she'd thought she could be free of it. Geai had predicted it: *that's what you're going to get. They'll say the only reason you have the mount on Claire is because your father owns her.* And sure enough, it had taken all of five minutes in the Belmont Park jock's room for Ricky Acosta — jockey idol, teen crush —

to slap the title on her like a sticker to her forehead: *this ain't high school, princess.*

Nothing was really different now, and it wouldn't change. But without her father, she never would've had the chance to ride a horse like Claire. To train a horse like Chique. To travel the world with a horse like Jay. She knew she was only as good as the opportunities presented to her, and she was beyond grateful for them. It was time to accept what she was and run with it.

She had the report for Cam by the time Nate got home after the races the next day. "It's an avulsion fracture."

"Ouch," Nate said. "Isn't that where a ligament gets pulled off a bone?"

Liv nodded. "That solves one problem anyway. He'll be off for a couple of months, so I don't have to worry about them dealing with him in Florida. He'll come down after Christmas when we'll both be there." She sighed. "Is this where things go bad?"

"It's a blessing in disguise," Nate insisted. "Which will become my nightmare when I have to get on him again."

She chuckled, thinking again of the dose of tranq the colt would get when that time came. No amount of herbal calmer would make Cam safe after that kind of layoff. "I'm going to book the van tomorrow. The Woodbine horses will go in two weeks. And I confirmed it with Willowmark today: Jay's going to run in the Pegasus. They'll start galloping him again in Kentucky and send him to Payson once our horses are there."

Nate nodded. Liv understood his subdued reaction. It was just a deferment, but a good thing just the same. A reliable, if temporary, raft in a sea of uncertainty.

"What's the latest with your parents?" she asked. "Do you think they'll come for Christmas?" Inviting them was the right thing to do, but the thought gave her an adrenaline spike. How would she manage that? There was no way she could put together a Christmas dinner that could come any way close to Connie's.

"Nothing's changed. My mother's being very noncommittal, so maybe she's hoping they'll figure it out and both come."

"If everything goes smoothly in Florida and we don't need to go rescue Jo once the Woodbine meet is over, what about staying here until Christmas? Take the truck and trailer down then, with Cam."

"Like a staycation?" He quirked an eyebrow.

"Yeah."

Nate gave her a crooked grin. "Sounds like progress."

CHAPTER THIRTY-ONE

Payson Park was like an old friend, the open shedrow barns and sandy paths a welcome sight. Elliot's familiar beastly Magnum was parked on his side of the barn, horses' heads poking out over webbings. In comparison, the Triple Stripe side looked empty — left almost exactly the way they'd abandoned it last spring.

Liv pulled up onto the grass between barns and climbed out of the rental. All that had been available was a minivan, and she was sure it would take Elliot no time at all to rib her about that. She wasn't sure in what universe she'd ever need a Dodge Caravan. If she started training dogs instead of horses, maybe.

The heat smothered her as soon as she left the comfort of the vehicle's air conditioning and she escaped to the shade of the shedrow. It was still too hot in November in this part of Florida for her northern blood. She envied the bigger Canadian owners who had farms in Ocala where it would be marginally cooler, though with horses to run, she appreciated the convenience of being closer to Gulfstream Park.

"Hey," came Elliot's Chicago twang as he rounded the corner, the accent discordant to her ears after not hearing him for a while. "You made it. When do the others get here?" He crushed her in a bear hug before she could object. It was Elliot, what could she do? That's just how he was.

"The riders, Nicole and Marie, will be here late tonight. Jo and our two grooms should arrive in a couple of hours," Liv predicted, restoring equilibrium to her lungs when he released her. "Our hotwalker is taking his vacation time, so he'll start later."

"Jo told me you had two newbies to break in this winter." Elliot grinned, rubbing his hands together like he was prepared to torment them as part of the process. "I've got a new guy too. He's not new to horse racing, at least. Hey Stan?" Elliot called over his shoulder. "Come meet Liv."

The man who appeared around the corner from Elliot's side was rangy — taller than Elliot. Stan's sky-blue t-shirt, remarkably clean at the end of a morning's work, was tucked neatly into worn khakis cinched with a leather belt. His dark skin and tidy appearance contrasted with Elliot's paleness and resemblance to PigPen. The only time Liv had seen Elliot anything close to neat was in the suit he'd worn for Breeders' Cup. The rest of the time he looked more like the help than the trainer.

Liv offered her hand and traded close-lipped smiles with Stan, meeting his eyes — one introvert to another, she guessed.

She asked, "Where's the pig?" Last winter, Elliot had a pig as a companion for one of his horses, but he wasn't part of the welcoming committee.

"Got too big. A friend of mine gave him a home. We had to retire the horse."

Liv didn't know if he was serious about the horse, or if that was just his ever-present sense of humour.

"We power-washed the stalls for you a couple days ago," Elliot said as Stan retreated. "They should be dry and ready to bed."

"That's amazing." Jo was probably responsible for that. Liv walked to the first stall. The mats were even down. Laying mats was probably the most hateful of all the setup tasks, but as much as she wished they could leave them in place from year to year, someone would steal them if they did — and replacing rubber matting wasn't cheap. "You're both saints. Thank you."

Elliot gave her a toothy smile. "Don't be letting that get around. I have a reputation to maintain, you know."

Liv rolled her eyes, positive that he did.

"Speaking of reputations," he drawled. "Are you sure you're okay having me in the same barn? I don't think I can live up to your rigorous standards."

She should have known he'd have some crack about her post-Classic diatribe, though she was still surprised he hadn't commented on the minivan. Liv smirked and moved on. "Can I borrow your wheelbarrow?"

Filling the stalls with shavings from the transport trailer parked at the end of the barn was hot work, the dust settling on her sweaty arms and face. Liv thought of Nate stuck riding this afternoon in the Ontario cold and chose not to complain. He hadn't argued when she'd decided she should come down and help get things going; it made sense with their less-experienced crew. She didn't tell him she had an ulterior motive. Between the strain she'd felt after the Classic and the presentation she'd done for the off-track Thoroughbred seminar, this brief visit was a much-needed reboot.

The seminar had gone well, but she was relieved to have the talk behind her. It had caught her off guard, the number of questions she'd received about working at the track. That had led to discussing a potential partnership with a representative from Equine Guelph. The not-for-profit educational organization at the university ran an employee training program. Liv hadn't committed to anything. The idea pulled her in opposite directions. There was more of a shortage of experienced help than ever right now, and hadn't she and Nate talked about passing on their knowledge to the next generation? It was what had inspired having Marie and Jillian help with the yearlings, and why she'd taken a chance on Ryn, but that didn't mean she wanted to start a school. Except, if she was going to train more off the farm next season she'd need extra help, and it wasn't the worst idea to start with fresh blood and teach them right from the ground up.

Once the stalls were bedded, there wasn't anything left to do. Jo was bringing the hardware — snaps and eyehooks — another thing that would be stripped if they left it behind. The stall screens, wall plaques, water buckets, and feed tubs would come on the van with the horses tonight. Sneezing, Liv mopped the sweat dripping into her eyes with the edge of her t-shirt and stopped to take a drink. She probably looked like Elliot's bedraggled sidekick.

As if summoned, he walked down the shed with a beer. "Want one?"

Beer would be colder than the bathwater in her bottle, but, "No, thanks. Hey — I was just thinking. Could you keep an eye out for a decent used car down here? We'll be bringing the truck and trailer down after Christmas, but I think that's the only time we're going to be driving."

"What, no Porsche?"

"This time of year there's no guarantee it won't get caught in a snowstorm along the way, and I don't want to think about that." Never mind Nate was still driving it — in November, in Ontario. He needed to put it away for the winter.

Elliot laughed. "That would be bad. So, something like

what you've got here?" He nodded toward the van.

"Please, no," Liv begged. "Something less embarrassing."

"I'll see what I can do."

She was levelling the shed — with Elliot's tools again, because the Triple Stripe implements were also on the van with the horses — when Jo's car pulled up next to her rental, two more vehicles in tow. A weary driver stumbled from each one.

"What is *that?*" Jo said, after reaching her arms to the sky in a groaning stretch. Her hand shaded her sunglasses as she pointed at the gleaming white minivan.

Liv pushed back the damp strands of hair that had worked loose from her ponytail and wiped more sweat from her eyes. "That's the rental I'm stuck with."

"I can't picture you as a soccer mom, Liv."

"Thank goodness for that."

Jo joined her on the shed, looking down the freshly raked aisle. "What's left to do?"

"Nothing, really. You've all been driving anyway. It wouldn't be fair to put you to work. I'll finish this up, then how about we go to the beach? We'll have to pick up some food, though. I left the cook at home." She grinned, and Jo laughed.

Turned out the minivan served a purpose — it had plenty of room, so Jillian and Ryn climbed into the back seat while Jo rode shotgun. The two younger women found a second wind when they saw the ocean, running to its edge and wading in. Watching them made Liv feel old — or maybe the minivan had done it.

"The drive go okay? You seemed to make decent time," she asked Jo.

"No problems," Jo said. "Ryn and Jillian both seem like good kids."

"You still all right with playing den mother?"

Jo laughed. "Part of me says no, not really, but the rest of me knows I've already been doing this for a few years." She stared across the water, then glanced at Liv. "It's going to be an even stranger winter than last year, isn't it?"

It was, and not just because of the new human faces that would be around the barn; it was Liv's own involvement, always feeling as if she needed to be two places at once. Six years ago when she'd still been in vet school, being at this training centre with the bulk of the Triple Stripe horses in training was exactly what she'd wanted. Now, her heart was split between the farm and Payson Park. The arrival of Chique's first foal was something Liv didn't want to miss, but if Chique didn't cooperate, Liv would need to leave to be back in Florida at the end of January to saddle Jay in the last race of his career. And when did Chique ever cooperate?

Once they were all inside the condo, Liv took a moment to call Nate as the other women dove into the food. She updated him on everything so far, leaving out the part about the perfect sky, the warm sand, and the glorious ocean.

"So what's your plan from here?" he asked.

"We'll clip the horses tomorrow, then I thought I'd take a couple of days and work out a routine. I'm kind of making it up as I go along."

"And dragging Jo with you," Nate said, laughing.

"I'm counting on her to let me know if it's too much, but hopefully the plan will work."

"It's a good plan," he said.

"Do you really think so?"

"Yeah, I do."

Her idea was to try a partial version of the British model she'd witnessed during her stay in Newmarket — Marie and Jillian would each groom a couple and ride. Ryn would just groom, and Nicole would just gallop. Jo would do what Jo did

— take care of a couple of horses herself while overseeing the crew. Marc — currently the lone guy — would continue his role as hotwalker. Come spring back at Woodbine, they'd reorganize all over again. Liv was counting on Michel and Sue coming back to work at Woodbine, and Jillian and Ryn returning to the farm.

"It's nice to be here, even if it's just for a few days. But I wish you were here," she added, meaning it.

"When I suggested getting away, I did always picture us together." His wry tone came through clearly.

"I'm looking forward to having you here on this beach."

"You are, are you?"

Walked right into that one.

"I'll talk to you tomorrow. Stay out of trouble, Miller." He was laughing as she disconnected.

Jillian and Ryn brushed past her, running down to the ocean again. They were going to end up with sunburns on their first day. A couple of guys who looked to be the same age ambled up and Ryn didn't hesitate to chat with them.

"She's friendly, I know that so far." Jo joined Liv, closing the sliding door behind her.

Liv asked, "Is that going to be a problem?"

"What was it Kerrie said? She's twenty. Not much we can do about it but hope the answer is no."

"I'm only twenty-eight, Jo. Why does twenty seem so young?"

"Because it is," Jo said. "You've packed a few lifetimes into those eight years. Most of us do."

"It looks like summer camp over here," Elliot said with his usual smartass grin. "Who needs a leg up?"

Four horses stood tacked up and tied to the walls of their stalls. Jo handed Elliot a shank. "If you're volunteering to help, take that one a turn." She pointed at Trop.

"Yes, boss," he said.

Elliot towered over the small dark bay, and his strength practically placed Liv in the saddle, little effort required on her part.

"Thanks, Elliot," she said, knotting the lines and snugging up the girth before she adjusted her irons. "You can turn him loose."

She waited until the others were up, all four of them walking around the shed. "All right. Let's go."

It felt like leading a trail ride, Nicole bringing up the rear on Happy. Liv wanted to show Marie and Jillian the paths and trails around Payson, and warned them about the possibility of seeing wild boar in their travels. *Really? Yes, really.* When Marie had started working for them last winter, she'd had a cast on her arm so she hadn't been riding. Tomorrow, they'd go to the turf course. This winter Marie and Jillian would become very familiar with that course, because it was the best place to do the long, slow distance work Liv had planned.

"This *is* like summer camp," Jillian gushed. "Only better because we're getting paid."

Liv glanced back, one corner of her lips crimping as she caught Nicole's eye roll. No one had asked Nicole if she wanted to play camp counselor. The novelty would wear off for Jillian soon enough. It always did.

Yesterday, they'd clipped all the horses. Jillian had earned bonus points because she knew how. It was nice that Liv and Jo didn't have to do it all for a change. Nate always got out of it, though Liv would put money on him being capable. Apparently, there were still things she didn't know about Nate Miller.

After the tour, they filed onto the dirt lane by Payson's

office near the front of the property for the walk home. Liv pulled Trop to the side so they could walk four abreast.

"I want all of you to feel like you can speak up, okay? If the job's not working for you, say something to Jo or me." *But I really hope it works.* Both Marie and Jillian nodded.

Back at the barn, Elliot helped with baths. For possibly the first time, Liv was glad Jo was sleeping with him because his assistance came in handy right now. To be fair, last winter they'd helped him a lot. Marie had been working for him when she'd broken her arm, so they'd done some galloping for him, and Nate had even ridden some races for him.

The horses didn't need to be walked after their leisurely hack, so they hand-grazed on the lawn until their coats were dry. Every day wouldn't be this easy, Liv tried to warn them.

At the end of the morning, Liv caught up with Nicole as they cleaned tack, because she'd failed to predict there might be a hitch in her plan. She was used to everyone being content at work, more or less. "Are you okay with all of this?"

"It's going to take some getting used to. I've never had seniority around here. And I am not a supervisor. Or maybe I should say babysitter." There was no humour in either her voice or expression.

Liv felt queasy. If Nicole felt put out and quit, they'd really be screwed. She quickly said, "That should probably come with a raise." More money might help — for a little while anyway.

Nicole's eyebrows twitched, and she didn't exactly smile, but her expression was more amiable. At least as an exercise rider she'd always be the first one done every day, so she could escape.

"Plus, you get to gallop Jay," Liv added.

Nicole's face lit up. "When's he coming?"

"He's on his way." Apparently she should have mentioned that before the money.

"Ryn! Come finish doing up your horses!"

Jo's bellow made Liv glance out to the shed before putting the last of the saddles away. Ryn jogged across the grassy area between barns.

"What the hell was she doing over there?" Liv muttered.

"How much of a raise?" Nicole asked.

Liv sighed, slipping past her and pausing in the doorway of Trop's stall where Jo brushed the gelding. "I'll talk to her."

She'd been spoiled her first year in this job. Jo was easy to get along with; they worked well together. The rest of the crew knew their responsibilities, and any issues Liv had encountered had almost been like bickering with siblings: easily resolved. She hadn't needed to assert any authority. Now it was necessary. She couldn't leave it all up to Jo.

Jo had assigned Ryn two easy horses to start and everything was simple right now — no standing or training bandages. It didn't take Ryn long to finish up her charges once she finally settled down to do them up. Liv sucked in a breath and approached her when Ryn started cleaning her halters.

"I wanted to let you know the same thing I told the others when we were riding," Liv began. "This winter's different for all of us. It's a work in progress, so speak up if you have a problem with anything, okay? Talk to me or Jo."

Ryn nodded like the others had.

Liv continued. "From our side, there's only one other thing we expect, other than taking care of the horses properly, and that's that you stick around until your work's done. You should be finished by noon every day, and Jo's got it set up that you only have to come back to feed every third day." Did Ryn have any idea how cushy a job this was for the track? "When you're done, you're free to do what you want. So save the socializing for then, all right?"

Ryn ducked her steady gaze, but nodded again.

"And if you decide it's not for you, that's okay," Liv said. "Just please give us some warning. Don't leave us high and dry."

"I'd never do that," Ryn insisted, finally meeting Liv's eyes.

"You'd be surprised how common it is." Their former manager, Austin, came to Liv's mind.

Liv resisted bringing Kerrie into it, even though she felt she had a responsibility to both keep an eye on the manager's kid, and report back. *I don't want to have to tell your mother about this* was not a phrase she wanted to use. Sure, she'd given Ryn a chance because of Kerrie, but she felt she owed it to the kid to treat her like an adult. *She's not even old enough to drink in this state.* Hiring Ryn felt like one of her less brilliant decisions, the more she thought about it.

Jo dragged Liv over to Elliot's side when everyone else was gone. All that was left to do was to wait for Jay to arrive.

"Sit," Jo insisted, nudging an overturned bucket in her direction. As Liv obeyed, Jo ducked into Elliot's tack room and came out with a cold can. She handed it to Liv.

"I can't drink that," Liv protested, though the perspiring aluminum was gloriously cool in her hands. "I have to drive to the airport."

Jo disappeared again, returning with a plastic cup. "Half, then. I'll drink the other half."

Liv acquiesced — sort of. A third, not a half. She handed the can back to Jo. The beer was bitter, but she had to admit it was refreshing. "Is this going to be a disaster? I feel bad about leaving you."

"Don't worry about it. Think of the next while as your vacation, and when you come back, you get to take over while I have mine. Maybe if we're lucky, by then all the kinks will be smoothed out."

"I hope you're right," Liv said.

CHAPTER THIRTY-TWO

Like every other time he'd stayed right until the end of the season — four years now, when these cold, dark mornings made it feel like forty — the backstretch started to empty out the nearer they got to closing day. November saw a gradual winding down as the best horses from the bigger outfits headed to warmer destinations, leaving mostly cheap horses to populate lonely shedrows. The track surface had the potential to be problematic. Everyone watched the weather with the dedication of a meteorologist, wondering if it would affect the races.

The Triple Stripe barn was stripped down and barren. Michel and Sue helped Nate drag mats into storage where they could be locked away, safe from scavengers. They dutifully unscrewed any eyehooks that remained. Nate took a hard rake to the shedrow one last time.

"I don't know why you're bothering," Michel said, tying off the last bag of garbage. "It's just going to be dug up by the cats using it as their litter box all winter."

Sue came out of the tack room with a box of dry food for said cats and filled up a couple of dishes. She'd joined the league of backstretch workers who looked out for the feral population. At the sound of the kibble hitting the metal dishes, a few of the residents appeared, one of the bolder ones weaving through her legs.

"Sue would take them all home if she could," Michel said with a scowl, but Nate was pretty sure he detected a hint of affection in Michel's voice.

"You have the lock for this door, Mike?" Nate asked when he'd finished raking up. He'd just tuck the tools in the same space as the mats.

"Catch," Michel said, tossing it.

The grey day left the inside of the unlit stall dark, and Nate started when something moved in the corner. A rat or a possum, maybe?

"You'd better get out of there," he called to whatever it was.

A weak mewl answered him. *Shit.*

The cat was an adolescent with patches of gold and white on its otherwise black coat, and it didn't look one hundred percent healthy. It was hard to tell, but he thought it was favouring a leg, too.

"What are you doing in here?" he said gently. He peeked around the corner to the shedrow. "Hey, Sue?"

Michel followed her down, and they each peered into the corner.

"Should we catch him?" Nate asked. "I think he might be hurt or sick. And possibly stuck."

"Her," Sue corrected. "Calicos are always female."

"Huh," he said. "I did not know that."

"We can try," Sue said. "I've seen her around, and she's friendlier than a lot of them. Don't move."

Did that matter? The calico didn't seem to be going anywhere. Sue came back with a cardboard box and handed him a blanket.

"You want me to play cat wrangler?" He gave her a dubious look.

"You're a rider. You should have better dexterity than me, right?"

"But I also need my hands. Cat bites are bad, right?"

"You're wearing gloves. Also, that's what the blanket is for. If she is hurt, hopefully she won't be moving too fast."

"C'mon, Miller," Michel goaded. "You ride big tough race-horses and you're afraid of a kitten?"

"Fine. But you explain to my agent that I can't finish the season if I end up with an infection from a cat bite or scratch."

Michel only laughed. "You've got backup."

"You know how to do this, right?" Sue asked.

"Why do you think I should know that?"

"Just drop the blanket over her and snatch her up."

He gave Sue a look, then shrugged. *Here goes nothing.* Except maybe his face. He was satisfied his hands and arms were covered well enough. The blanket fell on the cat and he scooped her up, tucking her — squawking — into his chest. He could feel her little heart pounding. It melted his, just a bit.

"Sorry, little girl. We just want to get you fixed up." He looked at Sue again. "Now what?"

"We either put her in this box, or you hold her while we drive to the vet."

"I've got her now," he said. "Let's go. But where are we going? No backstretch vet is going to look at a cat."

That's where he was wrong. He'd underestimated the power of the backstretch feral cat network. It was like a secret underground he'd somehow never encountered. Possibly because he never gave the cats much thought. The only cat he knew was Will's very pampered, part-time feline friend.

The vet somehow examined the pint-sized terror before plunking her in a small plastic crate.

"Nothing feels broken. She's just dehydrated. Call when she's a few weeks older, then we'll get her spayed and you'll be good to go." She handed him feeding instructions and shooed him out the door before he had a chance to protest. It was as if she thought he was adopting the thing. That wasn't happening.

"Come on, Nate. You have that huge house almost all to yourself," Sue said.

"Not forever! And do you forget Emilie has a dog?"

"She has her own apartment too, doesn't she? I'll get you everything you need. There's a fund."

Of course there was. "Fine."

He set the crate on the floor in the front of the Porsche where it should be safe and headed back to the farm. At least the kitten was older — the vet had said she was about four months — so the feeding schedule wouldn't be too demanding. Where was he going to put her, though? He didn't want the thing keeping him up all night. Cats were nocturnal, weren't they?

Thank goodness Emilie was out when he got there, so Holly was in her kennel. It gave him a chance to settle the kitten, deciding on the bathroom on the second level because no one used it right now. Would the cat just know how to use a litter box? How long would it take for her to figure it out? They liked to be neat, right?

It's probably best we're not having kids if I can't even figure this out.

"Good to have you home," Nate said, opening the passenger door.

"Except for the weather, it's good to be home," Liv replied as she stashed her bag and slipped into the seat.

"What's the matter?" he asked as he climbed behind the wheel. "You're looking kind of on edge."

Liv released the death grip she had on her phone and stopped the fingers on her other hand from drumming on the door. "It was not the relaxing getaway I'd hoped for," she admitted. "My big idea might have been a big mistake. I knew it would be an adjustment with new people on board, but I'm worried that hiring Jillian and Ryn will backfire. They're both so... immature."

"Of course they are. Don't forget they're supposed to be immature at their age, just because you never were."

She slid him a withering look. "Nicole is less than impressed, and I feel terrible leaving Jo to manage everything. We'll be lucky if Jo and Nicole both don't quit."

"They won't quit. Jo's got Elliot close by, and you think Nicole's going to give up galloping Jay?"

"I guess."

"It's just growing pains," Nate said. "They'll sort it out."

"I hope so." She leaned back into the bucket seat, pressing into the headrest. "But what if it doesn't? I think Jillian will be okay once she settles into the routine, but what if Ryn can't cut it? I don't relish the idea of having to tell Kerrie I had to fire her daughter."

"Kerrie doesn't strike me as an overprotective parent."

But if she was, she'd be a momma bear.

"Give it time," he said. "If you have to go back down, you have to go back down."

"You seem pretty chill, Miller." She didn't want him to see the conflict roiling inside her. It was her job to be there, with the racehorses. But she'd told him she'd stay here till Christmas. This was for their relationship. She'd screwed her priorities up before, insisting career came first.

"Only because the end of the racing season is in sight." His lips twisted as he glanced at her.

"Isn't it time you thought about putting your baby here away for the winter?" She'd finally stopped twitching and ran her hand over the Porsche's dash.

"Past time," he admitted. "I've been in denial."

"What have you got on tomorrow?"

"The usual. A few workers. One for Dean."

"I'll come in with you. Maybe he'll give me something to do for a few hours, and I'll do one more sweep of our barn." She didn't intend to lounge around the house. It would do her no good to be idle right now.

"If this keeps up, maybe we'd better take your car," he said, peering out at the dark sky, the precipitation hitting the windshield as ice before slowly melting. He flicked the wipers to intermittent.

When they arrived at the house, she didn't object as he grabbed her bag and carried it for her. She could let him do these small things from time to time, and didn't even make a face anymore.

"I've got a surprise," he said, as they climbed upstairs. "Follow me."

He left her bag on the landing of the second level with a smile in response to her raised eyebrows.

"As long as it's a happy surprise."

"That could be a matter of opinion." Cracking open the bathroom door, he slipped his hand in to flip on the light over the mirror. "Close the door behind you."

She slid in after him and did as she was told. Her eyes went from the tiny crate and covered litter box, then back to his smile. "What's this?"

When he crouched down and peeked into the kennel,

something hissed and spat at him. He laughed, and Liv peered over his shoulder. *A kitten?*

"Aw, poor thing. She's terrified." Liv backed away, giving the cat its space. "Are you going to tell me what's going on here?"

"I found her yesterday, stuck in between the wall and a stack of mats in the stall we stored them in. How the hell she got there, I'll never know."

"It happens," Liv said wryly.

"Sue and Michel were with me, and Sue is part of the crazy cat lady network. So, long story short, the vet — you know Dr. Keith? She checked her over and said she's just dehydrated — and somehow I got roped into being the designated foster person."

"You'll never cease to amaze me. One day you're punching out a colleague, next you're rescuing a cat. There's just no end to the surprises with you, is there?" Liv laughed. "I see exactly how this is going to go."

"You think so, do you? You don't want a cat."

"It wouldn't be my cat."

"We're supposed to have a dog."

"We will, eventually. It'll happen when it's supposed to happen. In the meantime, what are you going to call her?"

He could have the cat, especially if it satisfied his hankering to be a parent — something he wasn't great at hiding.

CHAPTER THIRTY-THREE

Seeing Liv breezing an unfamiliar horse with a different trainer's saddle pad probably shouldn't have surprised Nate, but it gave him pause. It reminded him she'd never asked for this training gig she'd taken on, something she'd been silent about for a while now. Even though he wasn't responsible for the turn of events that had put her in the position she was in, he felt guilty that he got to ride but she didn't. She was a good trainer, but riding was her truest passion — something he'd felt the first time he'd watched her work a horse. She'd quit vet school to do it. That wasn't something someone did unless they were serious. He could give her all the jewelry, flowers, and fancy dinners another woman might adore, but figuring out a way to get her riding races again would be a thousand times more meaningful.

When he got off his last horse, there was a text from her telling him that she was — no shock — at Dean's barn. She'd been spending a lot of time there, and once that might have made him jealous, but she'd married him and not Dean Taylor, so he could let it go. He found her underneath a horse, picking out feet, putting on bandages. Breeders' Cup winning trainer, playing groom.

Dean walked up behind him. "I've got the best help."

"Yeah." Nate grinned. "Free help."

Liv stood after finishing the bandage she'd been working on. She reached down to pick up some brushes before snapping a rub rag from where it had draped over the stall guard. "At least I'm working."

"Who's riding my horse in the Valedictory?" Dean asked.

Both Liv and Nate looked at Dean. The horse in question was Ride The Wave. Liv had been up for The Wave's first win when Dean was already touting the colt as his Queen's Plate horse, but because, as the owner's daughter, she had to partner the Triple Stripe hopeful in the big race, Nate had acquired the mount — and won. After Nate's injury, Liv had taken the ride back and won the Breeders' Stakes while Nate watched — resentfully — from his apartment over the barn in King City. So, in a sense, Dean's question was a fair one, except...

Liv finished running the rub rag over the horse's coat and pulled off the halter. "I'm not licensed to do so, so I guess that would be Nate."

Nate's eyes flitted to her, but she avoided his gaze, ducking under the bar and pulling the stall screen shut. "Your horses are in Florida," he said. "I'm pretty sure you could dust off your tack. It's not as if they're going to refuse to re-issue your jock's license."

"And ride a mile and three-quarter race out of the blue? Like I'm fit enough to do that."

Like she wasn't.

"Why are you trying to give away mounts, Miller?" She pushed past him to scoop a sponge out of a bucket of water, grabbing a bar of glycerine soap from the rail.

He tilted his head, cracking a smile. "*Mi casa es su casa?*"

"Right," she said, the word long and drawn-out. "Not when it comes to rides."

Why not? She'd done the same for him a year ago, giving up mounts on horses she could have piloted — and won on — herself, just so he could get back into things after his injury. Okay, so one of those had been Cam, but before he'd broken his maiden, the colt hadn't known what this racing gig was all about and he'd been easier to deal with. Racing had made Cam a cocky monster.

"Can you just assure me it will be one of you?" Dean said, eyes darting between the two of them with a laugh in his voice.

"Sure," Nate said, glancing at Liv again. "Right?"

"I'm positive you have the number of Nate's agent, Dean," she said, refusing to meet his gaze.

"I might be busy that day," Nate said.

Liv quirked an eyebrow. "Closing day?"

"Yeah. Looking after my cat."

She laughed. "I'm going home now. Have fun at Will's."

Liv caught Faye at the mid-morning lull, when the café was quiet before the lunch crowd came through. Triple Shot only offered items that were quick grabs, not full meals, even though there was a sit-down area. As soon as Faye saw her, she smiled and started packing fresh grounds into the espresso filter. Liv grinned. *Yes, I will have a cappuccino, thanks.*

"Butter tart? Brownie? Muffin?" Faye asked.

Liv pressed her lips together and shook her head. "Just a cappuccino, thanks."

Faye eyed her with suspicion, like Liv had just refused

wine and was about to announce she was pregnant. She shuddered away the thought.

The high-pitched squeal of steaming milk delayed further conversation. Nate was headed downtown where he got together most weeks with Faye's boyfriend, Will, and some other guys to play music. They did it mostly for fun, though when Nate had been off with his injury last year, they'd had their first gig. Normally, Nate's life didn't allow for such diversions.

Faye set the ceramic cup on the counter. "Or should I have made it to go?"

"I've got time to sit if you do," Liv said.

"Tuesdays are usually slower, so I've got a few minutes. My life will get crazier as the holidays get closer. And you're going to abandon me soon. I have to take advantage, right?" Faye followed Liv and pulled out a chair at one of the small, round tables.

"It's not as if I'm much help." Liv grinned. She could be useful to Dean with the horses, but with her lack of culinary expertise, not so much for Faye. "We are planning to stick around till Christmas, though. We won't be going to Calgary this year. "

"Will told me Nate said there were problems there." Faye frowned in sympathy, then leaned back, crossing her arms. "So what's up with you?" No surprise she'd sensed Liv was agitated about something.

"Your brother and Nate seem to think I should ride Ride The Wave in the Valedictory. Ridiculous, right?"

"If you thought so, you'd have the butter tart. I mean, why not? It's a horse you know."

Why not? Because it would only be a one-off. What was the point? Nate should just go after his title and not think about her. It would only be a taunt for her, make accepting her reality harder. "I don't get why Dean suggested it. It's not as if I've been riding regularly. The Wave deserves someone who's sharp."

"So ride a few races before then. You know you'll have no trouble finding trainers to put you on horses. They love you."

Liv snorted. "They might have, before."

"Is that still a problem? It's been a few weeks."

"It might always be a problem."

"I think you'll find several trainers would be thrilled to have someone with your experience. You're just riding the horses, you're not training them. It's only an issue when you're telling them they're not doing their job right... right?" Faye paused for effect, one eyebrow raised. "This would be their chance to turn the tables and tell you that *you're* not doing your job right."

Faye's wry smile made Liv smirk because even Nate chided her about that. Trainers were always complaining about riders messing up. "Maybe. The truth is, I can't commit to riding anything right now. Just because my horses aren't here doesn't mean I'm not still responsible for them. I feel as if I need to be ready to drop everything and head south at a moment's notice."

Faye rose, returning to the counter and display case. "I think you need the butter tart." She came back with a tart on a plate. "What's going on?"

Liv brought Faye up to speed about her concerns with the help at Payson. "I should be there, not here. But I'm trying to put this relationship first, like you always said I should." She didn't want Nate to see how conflicted she was. He'd seemed so happy she'd agreed to stay in Ontario until after Christmas. "But it's my job to be there. Jay's retiring in two months. I should be there for him. But how do I do that and be here for Nate too?"

"Is he giving you a hard time?"

"No." He hadn't even said *I told you so* when she'd

mentioned the troubles with Ryn. "But that could be just because he didn't want me to give him a hard time about his cat."

Faye nearly sputtered the mouthful of water she'd just taken. "A cat? Nate?"

"He rescued a feral kitten from the track. I'm putting money on that cat becoming a foster failure. I'm sure he'll tell Will all about it. They're probably bonding over cat talk while we speak."

"So, if you have to go back to Florida, no problem. He's got a cat now. He'll be fine." The bell on the door chimed as a customer came in. Faye leapt up. "Kerrie! What can I get for you?"

Liv straightened. She hadn't seen Kerrie since she'd come home — all she'd done was send a text to mention she was going into Woodbine this morning. How much should she say if Kerrie asked how things were going so far with Ryn?

Kerrie came over as Faye ground fresh beans. Liv smiled and gestured toward the extra chair.

"Ryn says she's loving it so far," Kerrie said as Faye brought over her cup, then disappeared into the kitchen. "She enjoyed being on the farm here, but what she's doing now is her dream job. Is she handling it okay?"

Dream job. I'll be an ogre if I take that away from the kid. "It's a bit of a learning curve for her I think," Liv said cautiously. "She'll learn a lot from Jo if she's serious about it, though. It's a more relaxed environment than at the track here, so that will help."

"Should I be worried about her? Do you want me to talk to her?"

Liv forced her eyes to stay on Kerrie's and mimicked what Nate had said. "It's just growing pains with the new crew. We'll give it time." Then she had an idea. "Why don't you go down for a week before Christmas? We'll be at the farm. You could stay at the condo. It's beachfront. That will let you have a break before foaling season, spend some time with Ryn and see for yourself how she's doing. The only condition is... you have to come back."

CHAPTER THIRTY-FOUR

NATE PILOTED Ride The Wave in the Valedictory — the cat didn't require his services. Liv watched from the grandstand with Faye and Dean, and only felt a twinge of jealousy. Or so she told herself.

She and Nate flew to Florida for a few days after the racing season was over. Liv needed eyes on Jay, not just a video — live or otherwise — of him training; and it gave Nate, who knew how the big horse felt at his best, the chance to gallop him and provide his own assessment. The staff was getting along, and Jo was satisfied with Ryn and Jillian. Kerrie came down, and Liv and Nate went back to the snow. Then after Christmas was taken care of, they returned south for the rest of the winter, sort of — bringing along Cam, ready to resume training, and the cat — dubbed Goldi, for Goldikova, a famous race mare.

Big sigh. Everything had not blown up.

It surprised Liv how busy they'd ended up being at home leading up to the holiday. She'd insisted Faye let her help at the café when Nate's mom had announced she and his father would come, because Liv desperately needed Faye's help to pull off Christmas dinner. Connie had come for a week, which was lovely once Liv got over feeling the pressure of entertaining Nate's very domestic mother — something that hadn't taken long because Connie had jumped in to help Faye too. Reid stayed only a few days. Nothing seemed resolved there, but that was only part of a very upside-down Christmas celebration. Everyone seemed to enjoy it anyway.

It was a relief to be back in familiar territory. She had space to focus on Jay, leaving the care of the incubating mares in the capable hands of Kerrie. Liv let her mind fall back into the routine of honing their Big Horse for his final start. She would take a break from worrying about Chique and Claire's approaching foaling dates, for a week or two.

The Payson crew chattered about their own holiday celebrations. Marie and Jillian had prepared a big meal at Jo's and invited Elliot and Stan. Ryn went to visit her grandparents for Christmas with Kerrie. Now Jo was on vacation, and Nicole had taken a few days away. All the horses but Jay and Cam were getting the week off.

For New Year's Eve, Nate bought a bottle of champagne and poured as they sat on the beach, the sun setting behind them, the same place they'd been exactly twelve months ago. They'd agreed to wait until this night to celebrate all the things. What a year it had been, so full and so good.

"Here's to making it to New Year's Eve without Cam killing me," he began.

Liv laughed. It wasn't funny, but it was.

"And here's to another good New Year's Eve, and to forgetting the bad ones of the past." Nate still didn't hold out his glass. "And, of course, here's to your birthday." He leaned in and kissed her.

It was the perfect amount of fanfare for her to mark the

occasion. She hated a fuss. The start of the last year of her twenties. It seemed impossible.

"And here's to us, one year in."

At last he proffered his glass, and she clinked. Their actual anniversary was before Christmas, but there had been too much going on at home to do a proper job. Other than to acknowledge the date, it had been more practical to hold off until now.

"First anniversary is paper, right?" he said.

Liv took a sip, the dry bubbles popping at the back of her throat. "You're asking the wrong person, Miller."

"Right. Forgot. Guess you're going to have to trust me on that, then." He handed her a manila envelope.

Her eyes slanted in his direction before she accepted it, and he offered to hold her glass.

It was indeed paper. Thick, like currency; pinkish-brown with blue embellishment, *The Jockey Club* in old-fashioned script across the top, details filled in with black type. A second certificate was stapled to it from the Canadian Thoroughbred Horse Society, then two smaller slips. One the Breeders' Cup nomination, the other a Lasix slip, medication the horse identified here had only run on once, Liv knew — in her second race. The steady beat of her heart ticked a little faster, her lips slightly parted as she studied each familiar element, unable to utter a word.

Paper. *Papers*. Registration papers. *Certificate of foal registration. This is to certify that the dark bay or brown filly named Chiquenaude ...*

Liv flipped it over to the list of Chique's wins written over the sepia-toned monochrome of the old painting of Lexington.

Unfolded it to expose the transfer of ownership. Her name, and Nate's. Her father's signature.

"You bought me a horse." Her lips lifted into a smile of

wonder. And in less than a month, that one horse would become two.

"Can't have my brother outdoing me on grand gestures, can I?"

"That was a little different." She didn't think her father had sold this mare for a dollar. Claude Lachance was only sentimental to a degree. "How?"

"Your dad gave me a break. Not like you gave Tim, but we made it work."

She might hear what kind of deal they'd made, in time, but it would ruin it to ask right now.

"I know it really says I bought us a horse," he said. "But that foal's gonna have to run in your name, so you'd better design some silks."

"I can't believe you did this."

"It's about time, don't you think? Time we had something that's ours. You know, besides a cat."

"I don't know what to say. Except, it's perfect. Thank you." Then she pushed him down to the sand, and hoped her kiss expressed what her voice couldn't.

"Is this when you have me on the beach?" Nate's mouth twisted against hers.

"Is that even legal?" Liv arched away, eyebrows raised.

"One of these days, you'll actually let me take you away to another, more exotic beach."

"We have a beach right here. A perfectly fine beach." She climbed to her feet, pulling him up. "And we have a perfectly fine condo on our perfectly fine beach."

New Year's Day, they turned everything out. Even Jay got the day off. Stalls were mucked and bedded, water buckets filled, then Liv sent Ryn and Marie home. She and Nate would hang around and bring the horses in after a few hours. Elliot served Mimosas and snacks.

Liv sat down and mapped out the next month, working backwards. The Pegasus World Cup, Jay's last race. The Eclipse Awards, where Horse of the Year would be announced. The dates of each of Jay's works. Chique's due date. Claire's due date.

The last two were just numbers, roughly eleven months from their breeding dates, because mares rarely adhered to exact timelines. All that mattered to Liv was that at this stage in each pregnancy, both foals were viable. They'd made it that far. It would be best if they waited at least a couple more weeks to show up, though. Whether she and Nate would actually be there when they foaled was uncertain.

Like a lot of things were uncertain, as they faced a new year.

CHAPTER THIRTY-FIVE

The Pegasus was less than a week away, but Liv didn't feel the same pressure she had for Jay's other races. He wasn't campaigning for Horse of the Year anymore — this would just be a nice feather in his already plumed cap. He'd had his last breeze, and he was ready.

The tension she felt was from the way her heart was torn, once again, between Jay and Chique. She needed to be there on race day. She had to put the tack on Jay for this final bow. It was looking as if they would miss welcoming Chique's foal into the world. Chique was at that stage where she could hold off for a month, or drop her foal in two days. As of Sunday afternoon, the mare had yet to give a clear signal that said *come home, now*. There was absolutely nothing Liv could do to change that.

Nate was sulking because he felt it, too. "We really should have planned for this. I mean, did she need to foal in January? We should have bred for an April baby."

Liv's laugh caught in her throat. "I'm not going to get into the why of it because I'm sure you already know, but it's kind of late for that. Go walk your cat."

Goldi had transitioned to indoor life — at the farm in Ontario, cats were easy prey for coyotes — so Nate had gotten the calico accustomed to a harness and took her exploring with that. He joked he was going to start jogging with her. At least Liv hoped he was joking.

She'd just jumped off her last horse Monday morning when her phone rang — with Kerrie's tone. She juggled the tack in her arms, trying to grab it from her back pocket, when she felt Nate snatch it from behind and answer it.

"If you're coming, you'd better get on a plane." Kerrie's voice rose from the speaker.

Liv draped the tack over the rail and spun toward Nicole. "You'll get on Jay again while we're gone?"

"For sure. But I am not getting on Cam. Just so we're clear."

"We'll just turn him out if we have to," Jo said. "With drugs. Lots of drugs."

"C'mon, Nicole, you could gallop him with lots of drugs, right?" Nate quipped.

Nicole's gaze narrowed. "No. I could not. I would not."

"Can we not go on about drugs, please?" Liv begged. "All I need is for someone to overhear and think I'm actually running a horse on something." The flack had died out, but she was glad for the peace, *thank you*.

"Someone has to take care of Goldi," Nate said.

"I will," Marie volunteered.

Nate tossed her his keys. "Stay at the condo."

"You'll need help," Jillian said.

"Oh, yes," Ryn agreed. "Mine too."

"I won't," Marie snapped, and both Jillian and Ryn stepped back.

Liv almost laughed. Someone needed some alone time, apparently.

"I'll referee," Jo said. "Go. You have to be back for the Eclipse Awards on Thursday night, right?"

Do we, though? Liv had avoided thinking about the ceremony. Jay being named Horse of the Year was one thing; showing up to accept the bronze statue in front of other professionals who might still harbour disgruntled feelings about her Breeders' Cup comments was something else.

"My parents are going to be there, so if we aren't, we aren't. We'll be back Saturday, for sure." Her father would make the acceptance speech. Even if she made it back, she was keeping her mouth shut.

Nate found a flight as Liv drove, the Mazda Elliot had found them flying down the Florida Turnpike.

"Careful now," Nate cautioned. "I'm all for getting there fast, you know that, but I got a ticket on this highway once."

"When?"

He ducked her gaze. "Not important."

"Come on, Miller."

"Three years ago? After leaving your place, on my way to picking up Faye at the airport."

Of course Liv remembered that day. That conversation. The denial. She eased the press of her foot on the gas. "That was a strange day." Another reminder of how far they'd come.

Making the flight Nate booked depended on the drive taking exactly the time Google Maps predicted it would. Liv checked her speed again, because a ticket would definitely cause a delay. She dictated texts to Nate to pass on things she'd forgotten to tell Jo in the rush, and he sent Emilie their arrival time to see if she could pick them up in Toronto.

Was this the craziest thing they'd done? Probably not. It

could be a colossal waste. They could get all the way back there and find the new foal already on the ground. Or they could wait as long as they dared, and have to leave before it happened. That was the fun thing about Chique. About horses. They didn't come with guarantees.

CHAPTER THIRTY-SIX

"Here we are, legging up two-year-olds in January again, just like old times." Nate jogged Cash next to Liv on Fleur, fingers frozen on the lines. Even before they'd gone numb, he could barely feel the rubber grips against his palms because of the heavy gloves he wore. "Except you talk to me now."

"You're exaggerating," Liv said.

"Barely."

Yesterday, when they'd gotten off the plane from Fort Lauderdale, it had been minus thirty-one degrees with the wind chill and the horses were all in, their body heat needed to keep the water pipes from freezing. Today, it was a balmy minus fifteen. The arena was more tolerable — at least, if you were a fuzzy horse. When you were a human who'd been somewhere forty degrees warmer less than twenty-four hours ago, it was harder to take. But there was no sense grumbling and stating the obvious: *we could be in Florida right now. We don't have to be here.* Because they *did* have to be here.

Chique looked like a tiny black bear, though she was losing her thick winter coat like mares often did as they got closer to foaling. And she looked ready to pop. Like she might actually cooperate and release this baby to the world in the ideal window allotted for their stay. Chique had, all her life, reminded Nate that horses couldn't really read, and even if they could, she wasn't about to do anything the way "they" said she should. But maybe this one time she'd play nice.

He'd had a chat with her when they'd reached the farm, because of course they'd come straight to see her before settling themselves at the house. What was the point in getting settled at all, if the mare was as close to delivering as Kerrie had said?

Tonight would be good, Cheeky. Or tomorrow at the latest. Then we can have a day with you and the kid before we have to go back for Jay.

Last night sleep had come in snatches, though Kerrie was doing the night watch. Nate was too wound up. He couldn't wait to see this foal.

If Chique went over, would he actually stay — let someone else ride Jay in the Pegasus?

Anyone could ride Jay. Nate had always said that. He wasn't a necessary part of the equation any more than Liv's presence was required to saddle him. Her name would still be on the program, though. Her name on the past performance chart, even if it was Jo putting on the tack on race day. Nate would be the one leaving people wondering, in the future when they studied the big horse's racing record, why, after being the only one ever to ride Just Jay, he'd disappeared.

Injury? Suspension? Family emergency?

Nope. Chique was family, but foaling wasn't an emergency. At least, he hoped this one wouldn't be. Even if it was, Kerrie was here. Vets were on call. Dean was down the road. Any issues would be addressed efficiently.

But what if... things went really wrong? If the unthinkable happened and they lost her, and he wasn't here to say goodbye?

"Nothing's going to go wrong, though," he'd told her. "Your cheeky little bitch self is going to sail through this, and soon we'll be complaining about you and your cheeky little monster of a foal."

Chique's birth, six years ago, *had* been an emergency. And he wasn't kidding — Liv did barely speak to him back then. When she'd come to his apartment to ask for his help, she hadn't known how much of an emergency it would be.

"Do you remember that winter?" he asked as they slowed to a walk.

"I do." Liv shuddered. "I think that was the first time I heard the words 'polar vortex.' Of course Chique would be born in a polar vortex! We might have missed a naming opportunity there."

"You were so cute, coming knocking on my door," he teased. "'I'm sorry to bother you, but...' like you didn't really want help but knew it was the Right Thing To Do."

"I did not say that," she insisted.

"Close enough. Was that your phone?" He'd left his in the tack room to spare the battery from the cold, but Liv had tucked hers in one layer of clothing or another. She didn't allow herself to be without it when the horses she trained were in another country.

She brought Fleur to a halt, and it took her two tries to zip her jacket down far enough to reach in for the device, but she fumbled it, watching it tumble to the arena dirt.

"Stupid fingers," she mumbled as the phone stopped ringing.

"Liv! Nate!" Emilie's voice came from the barn. "Door!" She leaned in, waving her phone. "It's Kerrie. Chique's starting!"

Nate flew off Cash as if Emilie were a riding instructor

asking for an emergency dismount. "Come on, Cash! Hup hup!" But the yearling didn't break from a walk.

"Just put them in their stalls, pull the tack off and get going," Emilie said. "I'll take care of the rest."

Nate felt guilty unceremoniously dumping the tack outside the stall. He didn't wait for Liv, but she was right behind him. They sprinted to Chique's barn, the cold air biting their faces and scorching their throats, slowing only to slip through the door.

Inside, it was quiet, Kerrie standing silently outside the stall. She smiled at them as they snuck up next to her, but Chique, steam rising off her round body, could not care less about their presence.

An ear twitch. Weight shifting from one hind to the other. Head swinging, glancing back. *Something feels weird.* A turn around the stall — a pause. Another turn, then the magic bubble appeared: a beautiful, safe, pearly white.

"She's not wasting any time," Liv said quietly, the calm one this time.

Nate had to keep himself from rushing into the stall, piercing the membrane, reaching in to make sure the next step was okay, but he waited — and it wasn't long before the pressure of the fluid inside the amnion took care of that, releasing in a gush over Chique's hocks.

Liv glanced at him. "I know you want to. I'll hold her."

He shed his jacket and reached for the examination sleeve. Slid it on and followed Liv into the stall. His arm didn't have to reach far under the neatly wrapped tail to find what he was looking for. One foot, two, and a few inches behind, the little nose. He nodded, and they stepped out, standing by in the doorway, Chique already dropping her nose to the straw, dragging it over the long, golden stalks.

She crouched, sprang up again, walked some more. Stood a

moment and tossed her head sideways towards her hind end as another tremor ran through her, the foal's legs jutting out six inches now.

"Don't make us catch him, Chique," Liv muttered.

Again, Chique circled, then in one decisive move, dropped, flopped, and began to push.

"I knew you were smart," Nate said as he slipped back in. Liv stayed by the door.

After all the waiting, it was over in minutes. And there he was — because yes, it was a colt — forelegs sprawled in front of him, his tiny ribcage heaving, dark and wet and wondering what had just happened to eject him from his warm, safe haven into this cold, bright world. His little face had a spiky star and a snip that covered part of one nostril, and one of his hind feet was white just over the ankle. The colt released a throaty nicker and Chique, still resting on her side, rumbled back.

"Relax, mare," Nate said. "Welcome to the family, Junior." He grabbed the towel Liv had draped over his shoulder and swiped the nostrils clear.

"You're not going to call him that, are you?" Liv said.

"No. He is Kraken," Nate declared as he rubbed the towel over the colt's head and body.

"Of course." Liv's laugh was echoed by Kerrie.

Chique righted herself and lurched to her feet, spinning toward her baby, the umbilical cord snapping. *So much for relaxing*. She pressed her nose to the colt's, his unsteady head bobbing, and Nate thought it was the most perfect thing in the world.

"Boys are dumb," Liv said.

"Hey," Nate protested.

"Seriously. Fillies always get it faster." Chique squealed as the colt worked his mouth against her barrel then wandered right on by. "I'm sorry, momma. You'll feel better once he's nursed."

The colt had figured out his legs within an hour, but an hour after that, Kraken was still staggering around, looking clueless. Liv told Kerrie to go get some sleep, that she and Nate could handle it from here, but it didn't matter what they did. Liv had held Chique with her quarters in the corner while Nate directed. He'd squirted milk at the colt. He'd tickled the colt's butt. They'd switched places. And Chique was being so good. The mare tried to help, even lifting her hind leg out of the way and butting Kraken's fuzzy rump with her muzzle.

"I'm not waiting any longer," Liv finally said. "Let's milk her and try him with a bottle. Pray he takes to that, because what comes next isn't fun."

Chique was not impressed with the contraption Liv pressed to her udder, a hand-held pump. Nate latched onto the mare's upper lip to convince her to cooperate. The thick, yellowy colostrum gushed into the bottle, and when she was satisfied with the amount, Liv released the suction. She found the nipple and attached it, using gloves to keep everything as sterile as possible. Though, the way the colt had toured the stall for the last hour, checking out the walls and his mother's coat, the extra precaution seemed pointless.

But he couldn't figure out the bottle, either.

"I'm calling Chad," she said, punching the vet's name in her contacts before she was even out of the stall, walking close to the doors where the reception was better. Kerrie had confirmed he was on call. She thought it was going to voicemail when Chad finally answered.

"I'm at an emergency, but it's just around the corner from you. You can come and get my naso-gastric tube." He broke off, and she heard voices on the other end. "Pam says she'll run it over to you."

"I am not tubing a foal, Chad." *This foal.* She could probably still do an adult, but not this tiny, fragile thing. "You won't be that long. I'll wait."

"You could try something else," he said.

"What? I've tried everything, and he won't suck."

"The Madigan squeeze."

"He's not really behaving like a dummy foal though, other than not being able to figure out how to nurse."

"What have you got to lose?"

"You're right. I'll keep you posted." She disconnected and even before she turned to Nate, Nate was off.

Liv didn't know where he found it, but Nate returned with a length of soft rope — and Kerrie.

"Thought I'd better come," the manager said. "In case you need another set of hands."

"Sorry," Liv said. "I tried to let you get some sleep."

"It's foaling season," Kerrie said dryly.

While she'd waited, Liv had refreshed her memory about the details of the procedure. She'd never used it before, but it wasn't complicated. Definitely easier than getting a tube from nostril to stomach in order to deliver a foal's first meal.

Nate held the colt while she looped the rope. Then she applied the backward pressure, not entirely believing it would help, Nate easing the foal to the ground. Chique hovered with a wrinkle of worry over her eyes. Kerrie held her and started timing with her phone.

Then Kraken lay on his side, still.

"That's a little freaky," Nate said.

Liv pressed her lips together, eyebrows fused. "Pray it works."

The twenty minutes they waited was how long it usually

took a mare to foal. It seemed like forever when it was happening, but performing the squeeze seemed longer still. Liv studied the newborn laid flat in the straw. He was dry now, so the sprinkling of white hairs around his eyes was visible. It was no surprise the colt would be grey. His sire, Megalodon, was grey.

At last Kerrie said, "Time." Nate remained with a hand resting on the colt's head and neck as Liv unlooped the rope. Even before they'd backed out of the way, Kraken was sitting up and scrambling to his feet.

He shook his head, spoked his spindly legs through the straw to his mother's flank — and thrust his head under it, poking at her udder. Before long, Liv heard the unmistakable sound of the colt latching on and suckling.

"That's amazing," she breathed. *Note to self: start adding rope to all foaling kits.* "I'd better call Chad." When Chad picked up, she said, "You're a genius. Thanks."

He chuckled. "You always thought you were the smarter one in vet school."

"Well, you're top of the class today. Worked a charm. Makes total sense, now that I've calmed down enough to think about it. Chique shot that baby out like a cannonball, and he's small. It fits the theory perfectly."

The one that suggested that in the uterus, neurosteroid hormones were at play that kept the foal calm, and the act of being born shut them off as long as there was enough pressure on the foal's ribcage as it passed through the birth canal. Kraken had come too fast to turn all of his off, leaving him with a mild case of neonatal maladjustment syndrome.

If only she'd put the pieces together sooner, she wouldn't be worried that the colt hadn't received enough of Chique's vital colostrum to get the antibodies he needed. But they'd have to wait to test for that. Liv looked at the time. They'd check it first thing tomorrow morning.

"You got him?"

Nate nodded, Kraken finally quieting in his hold. He could feel Chique's breath on his neck. She didn't like this one bit, the way he pinned her baby against the wall, the stubby tail cranked up, his arm wrapped around the narrow little chest. Liv was wedged against him. She didn't stroke the colt because that would just make him worse.

"Okay." Liv's nod was a quick jerk.

Nate tensed, watching her prepare to jab the tiny needle into the foal's jugular to get the blood sample needed to check the colt's antibodies, wondering how she could be accurate with that fuzz-covered little neck. The colt squirmed, squealing like a piglet. He was a strong little sea monster.

"Hold him, Miller."

He didn't bother to respond, because it wasn't as if they could swap places for this.

Nate didn't see it coming, the foal's head flipping back, blackening his vision for a second. He gritted his teeth, sure he felt a warm sensation spreading down his face. But he had orders. He held on.

"Okay. Got it," she said.

He let the colt go and felt Liv's hand on his arm, dragging him clear of the tiny explosion, vaguely aware of legs flying too close to his ribs. Chique's worried murmurs as she fussed over her colt were drowned out by the ringing in his ears. Liv pushed something to his face and his fingers were sticky when he removed them to grab it.

"That's payback for knocking out Hill in the jock's room last fall."

His face was broken, and Liv was making jokes? *Thanks, sweetheart.* "I was defending your honour."

"Let me see it."

"No way. Last time you thought I might have broken something, you hurt me."

"That's because you wouldn't go to the hospital."

"We're done here, right? We can go." This was his nose they were talking about. That had only been his ankle.

"Consider this a pre-assessment."

"Did you become a plastic surgeon in your spare time? Some online thing? I didn't know that was possible."

"Just let me check it. It's going to hurt at the hospital, too."

"Yeah, but they have drugs."

"What happened here?" Kerrie. Her voice sounded close, and Nate saw her on the edge of his vision.

"Where were you?" he grumbled. "You could have held that little beast for his torture."

Liv snorted. "He's your little beast, remember, Miller? Besides, Kerrie will do her time with him."

"You might want to dig out your facemask," Nate muttered.

"I'll get you some ice," Kerrie offered.

"You keep ice here?" Liv said.

His nose was stinging now, the adrenaline wearing off. "How about ibuprofen? Got any of that?"

"Maybe not the best idea right now, when you've recently had a major nosebleed," Liv warned.

"Beer, then? Can you prescribe that, Doctor?"

"Only if you let me check it."

"Fine."

"Now stop being a baby and hold still." Her fingers were remarkably gentle as she palpated, starting between his eyes.

"I think it is broken, but not displaced. We'd better take you for x-rays. You could have a concussion, too. Any nausea?"

"Not so far."

Kerrie returned with an ice pack wrapped in a rub rag. "I'll look after things here. You go ahead."

"Can you do the IgG test for me?" Liv asked. "Or can you wait that long, Miller?"

"Just let me sit down."

It was cold — or was he shocky? The feed room was heated, and he eased into a chair while Liv dropped the colt's blood on the rapid test. Nate closed his eyes. No one had brought him a beer.

"Damn it," Liv swore quietly.

He cranked an eye open. "What?"

"It's low." She picked up her phone, pacing slowly as it rang. "Chad? Yeah, thanks. But his IgG is low. Do not suggest I do a plasma transfusion. When can you come?"

Nate heard her relay the information to Kerrie. "Unless you feel the need to supervise that?" Liv asked him.

"I think I can leave that to the professionals."

The emergency room wasn't busy, but they were still in no hurry to see him. It felt like a waste of time now, and he did feel like a baby for moaning so much. The x-rays, when they were finally taken, really just confirmed Liv's diagnosis. *Minor fracture, no displacement. Watch for signs of concussion.* The ache had spread to the back of his head and down his neck. It was Wednesday. He'd be fine to ride Jay on Saturday.

"I guess we'll make it for the Eclipse Awards after all," Liv said. "You and your pretty face."

"Great." It would be some lovely colours by then.

"It'll be fun," she said.

Nate stared at her. Liv never thought social events were fun, and had been dreading this one after her own self-inflicted drama at the Classic. "I don't even know you anymore."

"It's right to celebrate," she said resolutely. "Jay, and our new foal. Though at the moment, it just looks as if you bought us a few big vet bills."

CHAPTER THIRTY-SEVEN

NATE WAS self-conscious about the nose. When Faye had seen it, she'd offered to show him how to cover it up with makeup, but he hadn't taken her up on it.

"Go for the rugged look, then," she'd said, throwing her hands in the air in one of those *I am so glad you are not my problem anymore* gestures. "Maybe if you've got a bit of scruff, it'll distract everyone from the bruising."

Liv knew one thing: she was not going to the Eclipse Awards without him. His marred face did not get him out of it. It might even make an evening that was already promising to be awkward a little more interesting.

The tux almost made her forget her escort looked as if he'd been in another jock's room brawl and this time the other guy had come out on top — except her face hurt just looking at his, with its bruising under the eyes and a knot on the bridge of the nose. Nate insisted it didn't feel so bad, just a mild headache lingered. The plus was he wasn't drinking, so he could drive, though she'd be counting on him to make sure she didn't have too much herself. That's all she needed — to get up on that stage drunk because she'd consumed too much alcohol in an attempt to settle her nerves.

"I think it's that dress that's going to distract everyone."

The way he breathed it in her ear as they walked into the crowded room, wrapping an arm around her waist to pull her close, made her wonder what would happen if the award went unclaimed.

It should be her father accepting that heavy bronze, but a snowstorm that had delayed their own flight out of Toronto had nailed Montreal. Airplanes were grounded. Her parents still expected to make it for Saturday's race.

Their table, with just the two of them, made it even more obvious they were outsiders. They didn't belong. And Liv was fine with that because she didn't want to belong here. She wanted to go back to her farm this spring, bring along the young horses in her control-freak way, and vacillate between training there and running at Woodbine. But she would accept the recognition for Jay, because he did belong in this echelon.

As much as she'd insisted they needed to be here, she was tired and just wanted tonight over with. A day of travel, with the delayed departure, made everything a rush. Flying into Fort Lauderdale, checking on Jay who'd arrived at Gulfstream so he could gallop over the track the day before the Pegasus. Checking into the hotel to dress for the evening, then actually getting here in time. All of it left her longing for their quiet condo on the beach, or even the snow-covered farm back home. At least the event was in Florida instead of California this year.

"What the hell happened to you?"

Liv and Nate both glanced up, and it wasn't until Liv saw Elliot's familiar face that his voice had context. She'd completely forgotten he'd be here for Wayward Sun, who was up for top turf male. And that, of course, he'd bring Jo.

"You need to have her back by midnight," Liv quipped as

she was crushed in one of Elliot's hugs when she rose. He was more gentle with Nate.

"There must be a good story behind that," Jo said. They had their own seats with Wayward Sun's owners, but pulled out chairs to sit for a while.

A wave of gratitude washed over Liv as she let Nate recount the story. The presence of friends was all the sweeter because it had slipped her mind they'd come, and the table seemed empty again when they returned to their own.

Liv had considered asking Nate to accept tonight's awards — he had experience, after all, with his top apprentice trophy from three years ago to show for it — but she needed to do it, to stand up in front of these people and not say something ridiculous. Once more, the words ran through her head: *I might never have a horse like this again.* This would be her fifteen minutes, and she wanted to leave these people, peers who were strangers, with a more rational memory than her last time in the spotlight. Even if she'd meant what she'd said.

The presentations leading up to Horse of the Year seemed to go on forever, a repeated cycle of the listing of nominees with video of their performances, the announcement of the winner, the sometimes polite applause or sometimes cheers, before the acceptance speeches. She was so focused on Horse of the Year it caught her off guard when the title for older dirt male came up. Seeing the stretch runs of Jay's three big wins as the finalists were listed never got old. She'd watch that clip on a loop if she could.

Thank goodness the room was dark as the presenter spoke, pulling out the envelope, speaking Just Jay's name into the microphone. Nate kicked her under the table and grinned at her, knocking her nerves aside. She could hear Jo's whoop over the clapping. He sprang up and reached for her hand, lifting her from her chair and directing her to the stage, reminding her. *I need you, Miller, to keep me from running out the door.* Still.

He squeezed her hand when they reached the podium, then nudged her to accept the trophy — and took it from her, stepping aside, standing in shadow. *No, stay close, beside me,* her eyes pleaded, but he mouthed, *I'm right here.*

What did she do next? No one else had seemed to need cues, but she'd insisted her father email her what he'd intended to say for Horse of the Year. Had he set her up, so she'd have to say something original after all? She smoothed the creased hard copy of his message against the podium. She would read it now. Maybe she didn't need to say anything for Horse of the Year. Maybe *thank you* would be enough.

The words came quickly, her voice a strange quaver as she added a brief preface, glancing over top of the heads to the back of the room, avoiding eyes. "It may seem hard to believe here in Florida, but my father — who should be up here accepting this award as the owner — is not, thanks to a snowstorm in Montreal that grounded his flight. So you're stuck with me." There was laughter. Was she funny?

This was not the Academy Awards. These weren't movie stars. They were all people just like her. People who loved their horses, even if they did things differently from her. They were just dressed up, some of them maybe as uncomfortable as she was. Instead of picturing them naked, she imagined them in jeans and sweaty t-shirts. Dusty boots, cracked sneakers. *Relax.*

Blinking, she dropped her eyes to the podium, reciting from the page. Thanking the team, the family that had made this past year possible; thanking the voters for recognizing this horse. Thanking the horse, for taking them places.

Though it would have been shocking if Jay's name hadn't been called for Horse of the Year, her heart still pummeled her chest as the finalists were announced with brief introductions, because they'd all won their divisional awards. Then the focus was on the National Thoroughbred Racing Association president, standing on the stage. He said his own preliminary words of thanks before getting right to it.

"Canadian-bred. Canadian owned, trained and ridden. Oh, Canada."

She'd have thought it sappy if it hadn't made her feel more than a little proud, the prick of tears threatening her eyes as she and Nate approached the stage again.

Did she dare ad lib? She did not need to get herself into trouble again. No, she could do this.

"I'm going to repeat a lot of what I said earlier, but I have to thank my father for entrusting me with this horse." *When others didn't want to.* Liv inhaled, determined to do this out of her head, a more controlled version of what she'd said after the Classic. In future, she'd let her actions speak instead of words. "My assistant Jo St-Laurent." Elliot's whistle pierced the otherwise silent room and made her laugh, gave her a chance to breathe. Jo would only be mad at her if she made her assistant stand up. "Jay's groom, Michel Larouche. My sister Emilie for dragging Jay out of a paddock when we thought he might be retired. And this guy, here, for riding him in every race and just about every morning. And for helping keep me sane. It's not an easy job. And thank you again, for this."

No amount of money could have convinced her to stay for the after party. Once she'd satisfied the reporters and joined up with Elliot and Jo briefly, Liv and Nate got out of there as quickly as they could without seeming entirely ungrateful.

It was another hotel room, but still quiet. She kicked off her shoes and couldn't wait to get out of this dress. Nate would help with that, she had no doubt. He was already sweeping her hair to the side, his hands kneading the tight muscles of her neck, slowly easing the tension away, though he couldn't possibly rid her of all of it.

Two more days. Just two more days. She'd miss Jay, but she was ready to go back to being a nobody.

CHAPTER THIRTY-EIGHT

JAY BOUNDED down Gulfstream's homestretch, ears pricked forward, his gallop feeding Nate's joy. Liv was ready for this to be behind them, but Nate was relishing every last moment of the big horse's career. Tomorrow, the looming grandstand would be alive, tens of thousands here to see the brilliant chestnut tear up the dirt one more time. Jay was going to give them what they came to see.

Liv met them at the gap for the walk back to the barn — on foot. Jay didn't need a pony, so Paz had stayed at Payson — Gulfstream wasn't his favourite place. Some other pony rider would have the thrill of escorting the Horse of the Year in his final bow.

"He feels incredible." Better than ever. It really was a shame this was his last start.

"He looks pretty perfect," Liv agreed.

"The Payson crew obviously don't need us." He grinned. For all Liv's fears at the start of the winter, the team had meshed. "We could've just flown in for the race and left them to the day-to-day stuff. They did a great job."

Liv laughed. "So we can hang out in the arctic tundra and you can wrestle with baby monsters?"

"I was more thinking so we could go lie on that exotic beach." He wasn't giving up on the idea.

And Liv still wasn't giving in. "Sure, Miller. That sounds like us."

"We should, though."

"Should what?"

"Go somewhere for a couple of days. Before we go back to Woodbine. Don't you ever just want to go somewhere you know no one can find you?"

She glanced up, and for once, her face wasn't saying no. "Let's get this horse retired and get life back to normal first, okay?"

"Fair enough." The door wasn't shut. He'd let things calm down and try her again.

Liv grabbed Jay's halter when they reached the barn. Nate hopped off and stripped the tack, then held Jay for his bath. He took short video clips, like he was documenting the final vignettes of the big chestnut's career. He couldn't prolong it, but maybe once it was over, he could relive it just a little.

"Let me get my boots off, and I'll walk him," he said.

"You don't have to do that," Liv insisted. "I'm fine."

"I want to do it," he said.

"Then what am I going to do?"

"Go grab yourself breakfast, because I know you're not going to leave him after I go."

Nate was away to the jock's room with a couple of horses to ride this afternoon. A little tune-up before tomorrow's race to remind his body what its job was. Getting on layups in an indoor arena wasn't the same as race riding —he'd been off since the second week of December.

Liv planted herself on the footlocker outside Jay's stall and read. She wanted to just hang out with the horse, and it gave the security guard a longer break. It still felt weird to have the hired man lurking around, but they needed eyes on this horse twenty-four seven, and cameras were fallible. When he returned, she'd go over and watch a few races, then come back at feed time.

She should have felt nervous, the pressure of preparing for this finale, but the tension was all but gone. This was Jay's swan song. If he didn't win, it didn't really matter. There were no more accolades to be awarded. The Pegasus World Cup was just one last chance for the racing public to see their Horse of the Year before he began his career at stud. His fans would be sad, like Liv was sad, but there was already chatter about how much they were looking forward to seeing his offspring come along. *Me too.* Once Claire foaled — she still held out, back on the farm in Ontario — she would be one of the accomplished mares in Just Jay's impressive first book.

What a ride he'd taken them on. It was the end, and the beginning.

Emilie was doing her job, sending regular photo updates on Chique's foal. The ring of light hairs was becoming more distinct around the colt's eyes. It seemed hard to believe that Triple Stripe had never had a grey, but Kraken was the first. It felt as if that should mean something. They'd have to wait and see exactly what.

The way Claire was going, they might get to see her foal after all. Either way, Liv hoped it was soon. She wanted to send Claire and Chique and their babies on a van to Kentucky together. This year, her choice for Chique was one hundred percent sensible: Jay's sire, Extra Terra. When she couldn't breed Chique to Jay himself because they were too closely related, it was an excellent compromise.

The bruising under both eyes no longer matched the colours of the silks Nate wore in Gulfstream's walking ring. He endured the expected wisecracks and refrained from the typical response — *you should see the other guy* — because the other guy had been a day-old Thoroughbred colt. Embarrassing.

He and Kraken were off to a stellar start. Maybe he'd regret calling the colt that, but despite the foal's size being quite the opposite of the mythological beast, it seemed to suit his personality. At least he didn't have teeth yet. By the time Nate saw Kraken again, the colt would have incisors, increasing his ability to inflict damage. *Remember how much you were looking forward to this baby, Miller.*

Jay circled with Jo, defined muscles sliding freely under the rich orange of his coat, turnout in the Florida sun at Payson leaving it a lighter hue than usual. Tomorrow, regardless of today's result, he'd be on his way to Kentucky. Two and a half years, with many stops and starts, it seemed like the big chestnut was just now hitting his prime. But money talked, and sometimes you had to listen. At least he was six. Chaotic Good was two years younger and he was on his way to Lexington tomorrow, too — retired shortly after a stellar three-year-old season, like so many good colts these days.

Chaotic Good was Jay's main rival in today's Pegasus, back for a rematch, but nothing hinged on this meeting. Horse of the Year had been decided. If he beat Jay this afternoon, he couldn't take the top honour away from their Big Horse. But he wouldn't beat Jay. The way Jay felt right now, nothing could touch him.

Liv had warned her parents about his face at least, so Nate didn't have to explain, only accept their condolences. After gasping, Anne Lachance fell into mother mode, which was sweet, though it was nothing like his own mom's reaction would have been. He'd show Connie pictures later, after the black and yellow had faded.

The crowd was a steady hum around them, layers deep. Nate ignored it, ready to be on the horse, on the track, where he and Jay would create their own cooling breeze away from the cloying, still air of the paddock.

"Riders up!"

Liv repeated her ritual phrase — *bonne chance, safe trip* — and legged him up. Then Jo led them to the unnecessary pony and sent them off with more luck to take along.

One more post parade to introduce a horse who no longer needed introduction. One last pipe-opening warmup. One last approach to the metal barrier.

When Nate pulled his goggles down, they rested right on the broken spot, but he brushed aside the discomfort, the padded doors snapping into place behind them. He locked onto the harrow lines of the track through the burnt-orange tips of those perfectly pricked ears, blocking out the buzzing crowd, the cries up and down the line of riders and the starter's barked instructions as the field lined up.

When the gates crashed open, Jay launched, in stride with the wave of bodies on either side. The speed went. Jay settled. Nate eased him to the rail to save ground. Chaotic Good was mid-pack behind an honest pace; in Nate's sights. On the backstretch, room opened up in front of him, and he let Jay travel up the rail. The big horse was running easy, like he'd go all day. He felt so good. It put a song in Nate's head. He had a peaceful, easy feeling.

I'm going to miss this.

Everything went their way. They continued slipping up the rail, and turning for home, the path was clear. Nate couldn't remember having this much horse under him. They must've been feeding Jay Wheaties or something while he and Liv had been gone. Either that or he had amnesia and just didn't remember right.

Time to roll, Big Horse.

Jay surged to the lead mid-stretch. Nate saw Chaotic Good to his right, firing on the outside. Huey Harrison dropped him in tight to Jay. The kid was riding like a maniac, arms flailing. All that flapping might have backed off a more timid horse, but not Jay. He'd had enough, and so had Nate.

He picked the big horse up, chirped as he threw the lines, and set Jay free. Jay responded enthusiastically, leaving his rivals, and his magnificent career, in the dust.

CHAPTER THIRTY-NINE

THIS WAS LIFE, back to normal. Time to focus on the other horses, the next races. Trop running in a turf stake in a few weeks. Reba beginning her four-year-old campaign in an allowance. And there was no better way for Nate to land himself in the middle of reality than getting on Cam.

The incredible ride with Jay had stretched to Monday, when they'd flown to Lexington because Willowmark Stud wanted the photo op for their new stallion. Social media would keep Jay in the public eye. Next they'd traveled back to Toronto, where Claire had politely waited for Liv to be there to foal, or so Nate liked to think. She produced a beautiful bay filly, smaller but just as flashy as Léa. Liv had yet to name her.

Kraken was becoming everything they'd thought he'd be — a cheeky, boy version of Chique. Nate had kept his distance this time. The bump on his nose still hurt.

Jo claimed Can't Catch Me had trained just fine in his absence. Promised Cam had gone to the track every day. And when Jillian legged him up on the big bay colt, Cam didn't go leaping down the shed.

"I told you they don't need us," Nate said as Cam walked — actually walked — past Liv on the way out of the barn.

Jillian had fallen in love with the horse — begged to groom him when they'd brought him down after Christmas. Liv and Jo agreed to give the relationship a shot, but that still left the question of who would gallop Cam while they were in Canada. Jillian had solved that problem, too, finding an exercise rider from one of the other Canadian outfits to do it. It sounded suspicious to Nate, because anyone who had galloped at Woodbine would know this horse. Maybe the guy liked Jillian and wanted to impress her.

Winter seemed to be the time for new relationships to bud with their help. Sue and Michel had gotten together after coming down early one year to set up the shed. Jo and Elliot were obviously back on for the winter. And Nate had overheard Marie and Ryn whispering about someone — it had sounded like Marie was teasing Ryn. Was Kerrie going to kill him if her daughter hooked up with someone they didn't know? He'd better ask Jo if she had any intel. It felt like they had a responsibility to look out for these younger women. Marie was so quiet. How would they even know if something was up?

Cam stood squarely at the end of his gallop when Nate turned him to face the training track's infield. The colt had never gone that nicely. Maybe Jo had given him tranq and not said anything. It could be she'd decided to be better safe than sorry while Nate was gone, or whoever had been getting on the colt had insisted on it.

"Hey, there's my buddy!"

Cam swung his head at the voice, and Nate followed the colt's gaze. An exercise rider eased his horse after a gallop and lined up next to Cam. Nate recognized the colours of the barn Jillian had said the guy who'd galloped Cam worked for — and tried to pull the man's name from his memory.

"Billy Rowe," he drawled when it came to him. "I hear you two got on famously when I was gone."

Billy was on the larger side: not overweight, but too big to be a jockey. Black chaps with a fringe covered his legs and he must've been wearing a muscle shirt under his black safety vest, because his cut arms were on full display, making it easy to understand why he'd been able to hold Cam. The ball of Billy's foot rested in irons that were halfway down his horse's barrel.

"He's awesome. We got along great, didn't we, buddy?" Billy's fingers dipped into the pocket of his jeans and he leaned over, holding out a peppermint which Cam swiftly lipped up.

Nate laughed. "Oh, I see."

"He's a good boy. Lots of fun."

Fun. Not the word Nate would use. Maybe he was getting old. He thought of Kraken and what was in store with that colt. If he was breaking noses at a day old, Nate shuddered to think how he'd be full grown.

"Well, thanks for helping with him. Sounds as if he likes you a lot better than he likes me."

"I think it's because I ride so long. Takes the anticipation away, you know? You jocks ride so short, they're always thinking they might get to do something when you're on them."

"Good point. I'll try that. Thanks."

"My pleasure. Let me know if you need me again. I'm happy to gallop him."

Happy to gallop Cam. Nate shook his head, following Billy and his mount out the gap — trying not to take it personally that perhaps Cam just disliked him as much as he disliked Cam.

Once they were back at the condo, it was time for the beach. It was glorious to stare out over the ocean with no plans to cross over it, or any travel plans at all until April when they'd head back to Canada. Nate supposed Liv might want to hop up to Lexington to visit Chique and Claire and their foals, both of whom would be there soon to be bred, staying until they were well in foal. Nate had a couple of months to not think what a terror Kraken would be by the time they got back to their farm in Ontario.

As far as he knew, things were status quo with his parents. They frustrated him. Shouldn't they have themselves sorted out by now? He wasn't ready to accept that they were done. He left Liv reading on the sand to go in and call his mother, because he was overdue. With all the back and forth and here and there, he'd only spoken to her once since Christmas.

Connie sounded out of breath when she answered the phone. "Oh, hi there, Nate. I might have to call you back. I was just headed out the door."

"Is everything all right?"

"Oh, well..."

Uh-oh. "What's up?"

"It's Julie. She's in hospital."

"What's going on?" Julie — Cindy's sister — and her husband were the guardians of the twins.

"Pre-eclampsia. I'm on my way to pick up the twins from the babysitter. Julie's not going to be able to look after them, so I'll have to bring them here."

"Uh — wow. I guess." Because who else was there? "I'm sure Dad will help. You'll call him, right?" That would give Reid something productive to do now that he'd finally resigned himself to retirement. Connie's pause worried him. "Mom?"

"He's away right now."

"He's *what?*"

"It's all right. Everything's all right. I told him to go."

"Tell him to come back!"

"I'm not doing that. I'll be fine."

"Are you kidding me right now? You can't do this alone. Do

I have to come there?" Why was this sounding like a role reversal? If his father was AWOL — or, he guessed, Reid had Connie's blessing, so Nate could hardly blame him — and Tim was in the middle of hockey season, that left only one other option. Nate had to go.

"Just stay where you are," she said. "You have a job."

"Well, you're in luck. This is the off-season for me. They don't need me as much as you might think."

"Nate, really, you don't have to."

The hell I don't. "You don't get to tell me what to do anymore." He glanced at the time, then put the phone back to his ear. "See you when I get there. I'll rent a car."

And before she could protest — or he snapped — he disconnected.

He closed his eyes and made himself take a couple of deep breaths, feeling the air-conditioned condo cooling his skin. Goldi hopped off the couch, meowing and butting his leg, and he scooped her up and held her at arms' length, growling. Then he tucked her neatly into his elbow, her purring helping calm him further as he stroked her head.

The patio door slipped open. "What's your problem?" Liv asked.

He walked over and sat on the couch, Goldi nestling on his lap. "My mother. My mother is my problem. She's lost it."

"That doesn't sound like your mother."

"That just shows how little you know her."

Liv laughed, settling beside him, and Nate filled her in on the conversation. "I'm really sorry, but I have to go out there again. If she won't call my dad, I will. But even if he comes back right away, it wouldn't hurt to have an extra set of hands until they get things organized."

"I get it. I'm not going to even pretend to offer to come along this time."

"Ha. There's a surprise." He grinned at her. "You'll be okay?"

"I'll miss you, but I'll survive. We know Billy gets along well with Cam now, so that's my biggest concern put to rest."

"If I'd known it was just me that Cam hated, I'd have told you to find someone else to gallop him ages ago. Maybe you should get Cory to ride him when he runs."

"We don't have to worry about that right now," Liv said, "but I'll talk to her in case I need her to breeze him."

"You can breeze him. Now that we know it's not him, it's me."

Liv snorted. "Let's not make assumptions. All we really know is that he likes Billy."

CHAPTER FORTY

Liv ran her hands down Cam's legs. Billy outweighed Nate by at least forty pounds, she'd wager, but the colt was holding up to the extra burden just fine. She thought maybe Nate was right. Cam liked Billy better, so the horse wasn't as hard on himself when he trained. It wasn't always about weight.

"He looks great, Jillian. You're doing a good job with him," she said as she ducked out of the stall, and the younger woman beamed, her arms filled with cottons and bandages, ready to do Cam up.

Liv watched for a moment as Jillian kneeled at the colt's front end and squirted liniment into one hand. Cam was like a big teddy bear with her. *Just goes to show, horses for courses, horses for people.* And if Cam was happy, everyone was happy.

She stopped outside Reba's stall next, where Ryn was in a similar pose at the filly's left foreleg. "Looking forward to Friday?"

Ryn grinned. "Can't wait!"

Reba was making her debut as a four-year-old — and Ryn was making her debut taking a horse to the paddock. Liv had overheard Jillian and Marie bickering over who would go with her to help, and Liv had yet to break it to them: it would be neither of them. Jo was going because she actually knew what to do. Reba was easy, but Liv wanted someone experienced showing Ryn the ropes her first time at Gulfstream.

She wondered if what Nate had said was right, that Ryn was seeing someone. Liv didn't know what the three girls did in their free time and didn't care as long as they all showed up for work. And they did, none of them ever looking as if they'd had a rough night before, so she had no reason to believe they were getting into any kind of trouble.

The tack they'd used throughout the morning was scattered, and Liv gathered it, lifting saddles and pads from the rail, bridles from nails on stall doors. Saddles and girths got a quick wipe before she put them away, then she started on the bridles and martingales, because Nicole was off today. The new way of doing things was working well. Who cared if it was different from other barns, as long as the horses and help were happy and the work got done?

When her phone rang, her first thought was Nate. She wondered what his mornings looked like now, wrangling human youngsters instead of horses, and didn't envy him one bit. She'd take piles of dirty tack, all these stalls, and even throw in sheath cleaning over what he'd tackled. He was so good. Her? Not so much. She'd be lying if she said it didn't worry her. What if this time with the twins made him decide that's what he wanted, when he knew he couldn't have it with her?

Glancing at the screen, her throat tightened. It wasn't Nate. She left the concrete-block walls of the barn for better reception out on the lawn.

"Hello?" She couldn't help sounding like a frightened child as she pressed a finger to her other ear to block everything out. Radios playing, cars driving past, grooms bantering.

"Olivia Lachance?"

She flinched as he mispronounced her last name, then sucked in a breath. *Sound professional, damn it.* "Yes?" What would they want with her?

He didn't offer any clues. All she could do was agree. Note the date and time, wishing she had a pen in her hand — except she wasn't likely to forget.

"Liv!"

She whirled her head toward the barn, disconnecting the call after a stuttered thank you when it wasn't something she was in any way grateful for. Jo leaned on the rail.

"What's the matter? Have you got sunstroke?" Jo quipped.

Liv returned to the shade of the shedrow, acutely aware of feeling vulnerable standing out there, exposed, when news traveled fast in this business.

"What's going on?" Jo asked, her tone shifting from joking to concern. "You've got no colour in your face."

When Liv forced herself to meet Jo's eyes, the assistant's brow was furrowed, and she looked as if she was expecting the worst.

This was not the worst. But it was... confusing.

"That was the stewards," she said, her voice sounding strange even to herself. "They want to see me."

She had nothing to worry about. It was probably some minor thing, not even a rule infraction. Because Liv always followed the rules. She'd never even been called to the principal's office in school. Never cheated on a test. Never had a parking ticket. But she knew her stomach wouldn't stop churning until she went to Gulfstream and stood before the officials to hear what they had to say.

Cam would seem like a vacation after this.

There was no way in hell his mom could have managed two almost-four-year-olds on her own. Nate didn't know how Cindy had done it — or Julie — both of them several years younger than Connie. Their husbands, working full time, would not have been much help, but at least the men would have been around some of the time.

Meanwhile, Reid was golfing in the Bahamas with his buddies in some attempt to adjust to retired life, when he could be here, if his stubborn wife would just ask for help. Two peas, those two. Nate had given his mom a few days to come to her senses, but she had not, so as soon as the kids were down for their naps, he was finding the number of the resort and tracking his father down.

His mother had scolded him when he'd shown up, then hugged him so fiercely he'd thought she might suffocate him. Coming had been the right thing to do, but it didn't let his father off the hook. Nate couldn't stay forever, even if the kids tugged pretty hard at his heartstrings, and he wished he lived closer so he could both help his mom and be a more consistent part of their lives.

It was weird Liv hadn't called yet. She'd promised to, right after she saw the stewards at Gulfstream. Of course she'd freaked out. Who could blame her? She'd never had to appear before them before. Unlike him. He'd made his share of appearances. For riding infractions — or, you know, punching Chris Hill out in the jock's room in November. They'd only fined him for that because it was his first time — but he'd had a few suspensions. Jockeys were either riding too hard, or not riding hard enough. Either could get you in trouble.

He'd assured Liv it was probably nothing, because what could it be? The officials would say their bit and she'd be annoyed they'd made her drive all the way to Fort Lauderdale.

Maybe she'd wait to call once she was back on the beach with the breeze blowing her hair and soothing her frazzled nerves. Because he wasn't there to help. He was here.

Connie laid down while the kids napped, and Nate found the travel information his dad had left for her stuck to the fridge. He decided to wait, not wanting to be on the phone when Liv contacted him. Reid would probably be out on the green — is that what they called it? Nate could corner him later.

He was getting worried, thinking he should call Liv, when his phone finally rang. Snatching it up, he tried to sound chipper. "Hey! How'd it go? Did you try to enter a horse without shoes? Or forget you'd wanted to ask them if you could run with kinesiology tape?" Because he was sure it was something obscure like that. But she didn't laugh, or even speak. "Liv?"

"Jay came back with a positive test."

His heart seemed to thump too slowly in his chest, each beat distinct. "What?"

"He tested positive for Clenbuterol."

Nate remembered how incredible Jay had felt galloping the day before the Pegasus. *Better than ever.* How easily he'd won the race. "But — that's impossible."

"Apparently not." She sounded defeated.

"It has to be a mistake. You're going to appeal it, right? They'll find out it was an error when they do the split test."

"It doesn't matter. They'll have a heyday online," she said. "And you know everyone at Gulfstream probably knew about it before I did."

"You seriously need to stay off the internet until this blows over." He could feel her dejection, and it worried him. Not much mattered more to Liv than her integrity. "Want me to check the cameras? I can probably find some time, after the kids are in bed."

"I will. Who would do that, though, Nate?"

He snorted. "In this crazy business? I'm sure there's no shortage of unstable people, pardon the pun. Your little speech at the Breeders' Cup wasn't that long ago. And we were gone, right? When we were home for Chique. Perfect opportunity for someone with a little hate-on to get to the horse."

The security guard who'd been hired to watch Jay when no one else was around wasn't a horse person. It probably wouldn't have been hard to fool the guy. Or he could have been the one to add the drug to the horse's feed. An easy way to make a little extra cash.

"I've always known I'm not the most likeable person in the universe, but I never would have thought anyone would want to sabotage me," she said. "Maybe it was just a mistake in the barn. We were away, like you said. Clenbuterol, though. Jo would have told me if anyone had needed it."

"It's too suspicious. You'd better talk to everyone, see if they remember anything. This is a wake-up call. We're probably a little too trusting." Nate's brain had no problem coming up with suspects. It might not have been about Liv at all — it might have been about the one point six million dollars that would be stripped from Jay's earnings.

He didn't know what he could say to her to make any of this better. "I'm sorry I'm not there. The timing of all this sucks. I'll get back as soon as I can." As soon as he hung up, he was finding his father, because it was absolutely clear now. This was Reid's place. Nate's was in Florida, next to Liv.

"Don't rush, Miller. I'll talk to Jo, and we'll figure out what needs to be done. And I'll be all right."

But he wasn't sure she would be. He needed to get there.

There was nothing to say. Nothing to fight. Even if it wasn't her doing, it was still her fault. She was responsible for the horses under her care. Period. It didn't matter if she hadn't broken the rules, administered the drug. It had happened on her watch. She had failed to protect her charge.

What would they do if Willowmark Stud didn't want Jay now? They'd been excited about him because they could boast he'd raced drug-free. Maybe the earlier interest would resurface. Triumph Stud had been perfectly willing to send Jay to a trainer who wasn't concerned with avoiding medications. A trainer who brushed off positives as part of the business and carried on.

At least her father believed her. After Nate, he'd been the first one she'd called. It was really all that mattered, because she didn't train for anyone else. She couldn't control how outsiders viewed her, and would have to learn to live with them thinking she wasn't who she claimed to be. The way she did things was a sure-fire way to arouse suspicion, and there was no way to avoid it. Stuff like this stuck like dried clay to a horse's legs. She'd forever be remembered as the trainer whose horse had been disqualified from the Pegasus World Cup for having a Class-B substance in his system.

She waited until she was alone, back at the condo, to review the video. It was a daunting task, but while it still didn't change her base stance on the issue — regardless of what she found, she was still to blame — it might give her peace of mind, or help her prevent it from happening again.

There were a few people she didn't automatically recognize. It certainly gave her some insight into the social lives of her young staff. Billy hanging around longer than necessary after galloping Cam to talk to Jillian, and some guy whose face she never quite saw clearly chatting up Ryn. The secret boyfriend. She smiled, watching Marie. Should she feel sad for the girl, because other than Elliot obviously teasing her, no potential suitors visited her? Hope one day someone would get through, like Nate had to her? Or should she applaud Marie for being happy exactly as she was?

Wait. There. A chunk of time with nothing, three days out from Jay's race. It hopped from around one PM, the shed neat and peaceful after Jo had finished setting afternoon feeds, to six PM, a similar stretch with only the odd pass by Jay's security guard until the nightwatchman appeared, unrolling the hose to water off, topping up hay where needed. He didn't go into any stalls, just paused in front of each one, making sure the inhabitant was happy. Conversed with the guard briefly before he left.

Clenbuterol came in more than one form, including a convenient syrup that could be administered orally. Jay had never turned up his nose at medication in his feed, those rare times he'd needed it. It would have been so easy to pour a dose into his afternoon meal. Nate had raved before the race about how incredible Jay felt. No wonder. Clenbuterol was a bronchodilator. It opened up the airways, made breathing easier. Long-term, it had anabolic properties. That's what had led to heightened control of the drug. Withdrawal time was fourteen days. At three days out, it would have been easily detected in a post-race sample.

She called Jo, who had been as shocked as she was. "Who fed on the Wednesday before Jay's race?"

There was silence as Jo considered. "Ryn. Her friend helped her. A girl named Melissa who works for the same barn as Billy. She's helped Ryn before. Is there something on the video?"

"There's nothing. As in, it hops from one until six. Like it randomly stopped working."

"Or someone unplugged it."

Liv still didn't want to believe any of it was intentional. "There's something else. Have you met this guy that's been hanging around Ryn? He shows up sometimes, but I never get a clear view of his face."

"Yeah, I have. I don't remember his name, if I've even heard it. She says they're just friends, but it seems pretty obvious he likes her. And as she's never chased him away, she probably likes him back."

"Thanks, Jo."

Liv watched more, fast-forwarding through nights and mornings, viewing feed time carefully. Recent footage, since Jay had left, the security guard's contract ending with the horse's departure. The feed time pairs rotated. Sometimes Billy helped Jillian, and Melissa helped Ryn, with this guy whose face she could never see watering off or carrying a muck bucket. But there were no more gaps in what the camera had captured. The mystery guy never went into a stall. Never touched a feed tub.

Reba was running on Friday. If someone had got to Jay, were they satisfied that his disqualification and Liv's suspension had tainted her reputation enough? Even though the fifteen-day suspension the stewards had handed her meant Friday Reba wouldn't run in Liv's name, the transition was recent enough the filly was running on her training. *We're probably a little too trusting,* Nate had said. Now, maybe she was paranoid, or maybe she was just making sure this time no one tampered with her horse.

She packed an overnight bag and her laptop. Cleaned Goldi's litter box and left the cat food and fresh water. Sent a text to Jo to let the assistant know what she was doing and headed to Payson Park. What did she have to lose? She wasn't going to be able to sleep anyway. Her integrity had taken a hit. How would she ever get it back?

CHAPTER FORTY-ONE

LIV WASN'T EVEN sure she was allowed to be here. Staying off the grounds at Gulfstream went without saying, but Payson Park was a private training centre. They recorded official works, but was a trainer under suspension in the State of Florida banned from setting foot? It didn't matter. Her horses mattered. What was the saying? It's easier to ask for forgiveness than permission.

And now my life has become a Dick Francis novel...

Liv locked the tack room door, flipped open her laptop and, using her phone as a hotspot, opened the site with the camera on Stella back home. There was something comforting about watching the mare. With Chique and Claire off to Kentucky to be bred, Stella had new companions, but she was the next one expected to foal. Kerrie's most recent message had said she didn't expect it to be tonight. The mare nibbled hay, then lifted her head, her ears swivelling forward like something had caught her attention.

Liv shifted to her phone to replay a video Emilie had posted on the Triple Stripe Insta account before the two mares had shipped to Lexington. Kraken barrelled around, bouncing off of his mom. Chique allowed him a couple of body checks before pinning her ears and diving her teeth into his shoulder. It looked worse than it probably was, but Kraken stopped, shook, pivoted, and tucked his nose under her flank to nurse. This was better than television.

Dragging herself away, she checked the cameras in this barn. It was why she was here, after all.

Nothing. All was quiet.

She read a book on her phone and glanced at the laptop periodically. Nate would be upset if he knew she was here. But like most nights, Jo was staying over with Elliot in his tack room, so it wasn't as if she were here alone. They were right next door.

Nate could be right. It was possible someone had been paid off to compromise the cameras for a few hours — long enough to put the drug in Jay's feed tub. The tubs hung exposed, once Jo set them at the end of the morning. Every barn did it, so it wasn't as if they were being negligent. The cameras were supposed to pick up on anything suspicious. But someone had definitely messed with the cameras.

She hated to think it was one of the crew. Someone who'd been compensated well enough to do such a thing by, say, someone in the Chaotic Good camp who wanted to see the Pegasus' big fat purse redistributed in their favour. She'd actually rather it was a disgruntled stranger who wanted to smear her name.

Her pulse tripped. There was someone on the shed.

Liv peered closer, then zoomed in, but the resolution wasn't that good. Then, a sound from next door, like someone was leaving one of the other tack rooms. On the left, so Stan, not Elliot. His tall frame appeared on the screen, the person on the shedrow spinning. When she turned the sound up, there was a hiss that kept her from hearing what was being said. He looked sort of familiar — because she was almost a hundred percent sure the person was male — but his hood still obscured his face.

Stan thrust an arm forward in a half-crouch, and she caught a glint of something in his hand that made her heart lurch. Liv rushed to the door, but made herself stop. *Slow down.* She needed to intervene — this was her problem, not Stan's, and it would not go well for him if he was caught with a knife.

Breathe. Think.

The two men were still facing off, the intruder's hands raised, his weight shifting as he glanced out from the barn like he was planning to run. Liv grabbed her phone and texted Elliot. She prayed he didn't have his silenced because she didn't want to pound on his door. Then she took another deep breath, pulled a sweatshirt over her t-shirt and slipped out, closing the door soundlessly behind her.

By the time she peered around the corner, Stan had the guy face-down, straddling him with arms pinned behind his back with one hand, and the glinting thing still in his other fist, pressed to the side of the man's neck.

"Hey, Stan."

Elliot's drawl made her jump, her hands instinctively covering her pounding heart like she thought she could keep it from flying out of her chest. She glanced behind her as he sauntered by like he was going to ask Stan what kind of pizza he wanted. Jo hovered, eyes wide.

"I think you've got him, Stan. Want to hand me that?"

Stan's shoulders slumped, and he sat up, still straddling the prone man. His expression was sheepish as he held out an aluminum sweat scraper.

Liv exhaled. Could he still get in trouble for that? She'd feel horrible.

Elliot flipped the scraper casually through the air. "Payson's security should be here soon."

Liv had to keep herself from charging over, pushing Stan aside so she could flip this intruder over and see who had it out for her enough to sabotage her horses, her reputation. Jo's hand rested on her arm as an extra reminder. *Wait for security. Don't risk this asshole getting away.*

The security guard was a burly man, lumbering into the barn. Liv doubted he could outrun the lanky guy still facedown in the dirt. She could, though. If it came to that.

Stan stepped back as the guard drew closer. She wanted to hug this tall, quiet man. He'd taken a big chance. The security guard hauled the stranger to his feet.

But it was no stranger. Liv gaped, recognition flooding through her, a cascade of fresh anger tumbling through her. "Austin? What the hell?"

Once upon a time — as in, just over a year ago — she'd entrusted this guy with managing the farm. He'd seemed all right. He wasn't Geai, but he lasted longer than the previous hire. Then he'd left Emilie high and dry right before Christmas because, for all any of them could figure out, Em had agreed to have dinner with him and the evening hadn't ended as he'd apparently planned. Nate had been ready to kill Austin then. Good thing he wasn't here right now.

Jo gripped her arms from behind, like she thought Liv might fly at the guy. "That's Austin? He's the one who's been hanging around Ryn."

Jo had never met him. Ryn, too, would have had no idea of Austin's history. Jillian knew him, though. But Austin's worst offence, in Jillian's eyes, was probably that he didn't like to hear the word "no." Even Liv wouldn't have thought he'd do something like he'd done.

"You people think you're all better than everyone else.

You're God's gift to horse racing. And your sister?" he spat, pausing. "Don't even get me started. I hope her boyfriend's good enough for her. Has she let him kiss her yet, or are they waiting for marriage?"

Liv couldn't even speak, but she had to. She needed him to say it, with all these people around to witness it. "So you thought you'd drug Just Jay? The Breeders' Cup Classic winner?"

"That's right. Because no one believes you're so squeaky anymore, do they? You'll never live that down. All high and mighty with your *Big Horse,* like Lasix is something evil, when all anyone else is trying to do is make a living."

Liv wanted to point out that all the horses in the Classic and the Pegasus weren't allowed to run on Lasix now anyway. Was she such a poor judge of character that this guy had fooled her? She'd thought he was brighter than this. Emilie would laugh, though. She had no trouble calling Austin an idiot.

The security guard had Austin's arm gripped with one of his big mutton fists. "I need to call the police. This is outside my authority."

"Wait," Liv said. "I don't want to make a big deal here."

"You don't want to make a big deal?" Jo snapped. "This guy just admitted to giving your best horse a Class B medication. He's trying to ruin your name, and has cost you a lot of money. He needs to never be able to do that again. To anyone."

"But the police are going to want to question everyone, aren't they?" Liv said, holding Jo's eyes. "Including Stan."

"Stan didn't do anything any of us wouldn't have done."

"Maybe true, but he's going to be treated a whole lot differently than you or I would be."

"He pulled a knife on me!" Austin inserted. "He's an ex-con!"

Elliot chuckled, raising the aluminum scraper. Austin

cowered and Liv fought the urge to kick him in the shins, then glanced at Elliot. If Stan had a record, that made things that much worse.

"It was a minor offence," Jo told her quietly. "But I'm sure you can imagine how that went for him."

Liv frowned.

"We've got his back, Liv," Jo assured her. "It's our word against Austin's here."

"The damn sweat scraper is bent," Elliot said, pointing it at Austin. "It's not cutting anything, especially not your jugular. You're just terrified because you were caught, and now you're making shit up in your head. You were never in any danger. Just be glad it wasn't me that caught you, because you'd be really messed up."

Exhaustion piled on Liv like an avalanche as they waited for the police. All she wanted was to go back to the condo, crawl into bed. Spend tomorrow on the beach. Which, of course, she could do, because catching Austin didn't remove her suspension. They were going to have to scratch Reba from Friday's race, because she wasn't taking the chance that he'd got to the filly. One positive on her record was enough.

Then what? The suspension was only for two weeks. It would be over before she knew it. She just hoped the rumour mill that had so efficiently spread the word about her misfortune worked the other way, too. Because while the suspension would end, the stigma would not.

CHAPTER FORTY-TWO

NATE FOUND her on the beach, staring out over the ocean. It reminded him of a day four years ago. Not this exact stretch of beach; a little south of here, in Hobe Sound. It'd been a fluke to come across her that afternoon. He'd been walking, and she was sitting there, in that exact pose, preoccupied, her book abandoned. That might even be the same bathing suit she'd been wearing, a white two-piece that showed off her tan... and fitness.

He wouldn't apologize for taking a moment, drinking in the scene. Comparing then to now. He'd thought twice that day about approaching her, but when she'd looked his way, gazing just as brazenly back at him behind her sunglasses, loose strands from her ponytail whipping around her face, he'd thought, *what the hell*. Fools rush in, Emilie had reminded him once. Em had warned him about Faye — but it had applied just as well to Liv, for different reasons. Had he listened? Nope.

Hey, it had all worked out, hadn't it?

Now, like then, Liv glanced over her shoulder. He'd probably made a noise rather than her having some sixth sense, as he might like to think. She smiled, unlike that day four years ago, and he eased himself to the sand with a lot more confidence than he had then.

He hadn't bothered to change since getting here from the airport, only removing his socks and shoes, leaving Goldi squawking at him as he slid the patio door closed. Curling his toes in the sand, he mimicked Liv's posture, wrapping his arms around his knees, gaze lost to the waves. When he looked at her, her lips curved in amusement, waiting, because he didn't kiss her.

"I was just thinking about that time, when Chique was two, and I ran into you on the beach right before we were due to go back to Ontario. Do you remember that?"

"I think I do," she said, her expression changing slightly to something more chagrined.

"When I first realized it was you, I almost kept walking. Then I thought, what have I got to lose, except my pride?" He grinned, sure he'd felt that way with her on more than one occasion. "Which, you ultimately flattened."

The corner of her lips fell ruefully. "Sorry about that."

"I should probably thank you. It lit a fire under me. When I got back to Woodbine, it gave me the drive I needed for a pretty brilliant start to my riding career."

"It was pretty brilliant," she agreed, her mouth finding an upward curve again.

"Hooking up with Faye shortly after, not so much."

Liv shrugged.

"Maybe if I'd just done what I wanted to that day, we could have avoided all that."

"And what was that, Miller?" she asked, her smile turning coy.

He leaned in, reaching a hand to her face, but stopped short of kissing her, meeting her eyes first. She glanced down, then tilted her head, closing the hint of distance remaining between them, the touch of her lips soft but still electric. He imagined how it would have been then: dangerous instead of familiar, a fragile uncertainty instead of the sureness of this thing now between them. Where would it have gone next?

Her exhale was a sigh when he drew back.

"Hey," he said.

"Hey back," she replied. "How'd you leave things in Calgary?"

"All right, actually. They're good at it. Dealing with children. Had lots of practice, I guess. Probably easier this time, seeing as it's only one boy. Girls are easier."

"Maybe at that age."

"I don't know." He laughed, then sobered. "I hope it's what brings them back together. Maybe it's a second chance to figure things out so that when it's just the two of them again, they'll be better prepared to make things work."

It had marvelled him, watching his parents fall into their roles so easily. Whatever it was, he'd take it. He didn't know what would happen — if this arrangement would be permanent for the twins. He doubted Julie would be in any shape to take them back for a long time.

"I'm sorry I left," he said. "I should have been here."

"You had to go. Your mom needed you."

"You needed me." And Liv didn't deny it. "I went there wanting to fix everything, but if they work it out, it'll be nothing to do with me. It made me realize all I can do is take care of this." He reached for her hand, then said, because something told him she needed to hear it, "I think somehow I always thought kids were the ultimate happiness, what rounded out a relationship; that people get married because they want that. But now, seeing my parents... I don't want to get to my fifties and find out I'm living with a stranger. I want this."

She glanced down before meeting his eyes. "Even if half of this is jaded and disillusioned right now?"

"Especially. What did we say on this beach? For richer or poorer, in the winner's circle and in suspensions?"

"I'd rather that not be plural."

"You throwing out mine?"

She laughed. "They never hit this hard."

It was true. "You didn't do anything wrong."

"I failed to protect a horse under my care. The best horse under my care."

"You're not the first."

"How many of those do you think are legitimate, and how many are just stories?" she asked. "Unintentional contamination. There's always a quick excuse. But there's not even a quick excuse for this. He walked right in and laced Jay's feed. That's all it took. Sweet-talked a kid so his presence wouldn't be suspect."

"Like I said, we're all a little too trusting."

"It's sad that's a bad thing." She released a long breath. "You called it. Pride comes before a fall. I thought I could be the change, but I'm not sure it's possible to change anything."

"We might not be able to change the world, but we can change the world for our horses."

"That's not terribly original, Miller, and it's kind of corny, but I like it." She smiled, then pulled him closer. "Let's do it."

"What?"

"The beach. That mythical one you talked about, where we can go and no one knows us. You book it. I'll go wherever you want."

"You sure?"

"I'm sure. I've got nowhere else to be."

It did seem mythical, with sand so white and water an incredible turquoise blue; postcard-perfect palm trees against a deep cobalt sky. Liv didn't ask how Nate had found this place — if it had come recommended or he'd just done a deep-dive internet search for secluded getaways — but it was incredible.

Part of her never wanted to leave; the other part knew she didn't really want to stay. It was nice to forget the drama they'd left behind. Being here didn't wipe her memory, but it renewed her courage, fortified her, and reminded her she had good people around her — starting with the one who had promised to stay beside her through it all.

From this very beach, she'd composed a statement to post on her Instagram account. An apology, basically, to Jay and the fans. She'd let them down. She promised to do better. For the horses. For the sport. Accompanying it with one of the photos she'd taken from Jay's back, she'd sent it out into the ether. Then she'd shut off her phone. If anyone needed to reach her, they could do so through the resort's office.

She couldn't control what people thought, and even if she could, what did it matter? The public was probably justified in coming down hard, because they didn't know her. Most of the time, she didn't know who to believe, either. No source was without bias — and it really wasn't black and white. It wasn't a matter of blaming the track surfaces, or the breeders, or the trainers, or the vets. They needed to consider all those things, and all she could do was maintain a more critical eye on her tiny section of the sport. Breed for soundness. Train for soundness. Feed for soundness.

Ryn had been upset when she'd learned about Austin and needed talking down. Liv believed her when she'd said she didn't know, and convinced Ryn she didn't have to quit and go back to Canada — all things Ryn had insisted she must do as penance. Ryn wasn't to blame.

As Jo had stated, their word against Austin's had kept Stan blameless, too. Liv didn't know what would happen to Austin. It wasn't over yet. She was happy to put it out of her mind and enjoy this alternate universe for a few days.

She wasn't sure Nate had stopped beating himself up for being away when it had all gone down. Sure, Liv wished he'd been here, but she didn't think he'd been wrong to leave. She'd had Jo and Elliot and Stan for backup, and it was only her reputation, not her life, that had been in any kind of danger. It wasn't Nate's job to protect either of those things.

Nate bumped her shoulder, bringing her back to the tropical island. They'd been promised sea turtles and colourful fish and coral reefs, and she couldn't wait to get in the water. Next to the back of a horse, it was where she felt most at home. The pool at the house in Ontario was going to pale in comparison.

"What do you think so far?" Nate asked, then grinned. "This is our honeymoon."

"Only a year —"

"And two months —"

"Late." Liv smiled back. "So far, so good. I might even manage to do it again sometime."

"You did it! A whole four days." Jo grinned, hugging Liv. "I'm so proud of you."

"You're funny." But Liv grinned. "I don't know how people do it for weeks."

Though they hadn't just lain on the beach. They'd snorkeled and windsurfed and explored — and explicitly avoided horses. And Liv agreed she'd more than survived. They'd had an amazing time, but Nate would leave it a while before attempting to suggest an encore.

He ushered them through the living room to the patio facing the ocean, and gave Elliot a beer and Jo a glass of wine. Nate handed Liv the same, then brought Goldi out on her leash and harness. She twirled around legs and he spent most of his time unwinding the leash. Finally, he gave up and returned her to the condo. Goldi stood at the door, squawking at them.

There was a brief lull in the conversation when he returned. Nate noticed Jo square her shoulders, holding her wine glass in one hand, the other tucked in the crook of her arm.

"We've got some news," she said.

"No!" It was out of Liv's mouth before Nate could intercept her. "Sorry," Liv muttered.

Elliot cracked up. Jo held out her left hand.

"It's beautiful, Jo. Congratulations," Nate said, pushing past Liv to give her a hug. He shook Elliot's hand and slapped him on the shoulder. "Glad to see you spent your Breeders' Cup winnings wisely."

"There's more news," Elliot said.

Oh, shit. If Jo says she's pregnant, Liv's gonna self-destruct. Nate could see the tension in her neck as she clenched her teeth, and her hands were in fists at her sides.

Elliot was beaming. "I'm moving my horses to Woodbine!"

Liv almost collapsed before throwing her arms around him. "Oh, thank goodness. But I'm keeping my assistant trainer. Find your own."

"Actually, I'm hoping Stan takes the job, if I can get his paperwork sorted out. He's sure qualified. All he needs is some confidence."

"That would be great," Liv said. "I like Stan. I hope it works out."

If Nate had known the announcement was coming, he would have bought champagne, but they toasted with their beer and wine instead. Elliot wasn't really a champagne kind of guy anyway, though he'd sure come through with the ring.

"Welcome to the family," Nate said, and glasses clinked with aluminum cans.

They ate dinner on the patio, softly lit with solar illumination and candles on the glass table. It wasn't St. Vincent, but the Florida weather was being kind this February, the temperature comfortable, even as the sunlight disappeared. The food was good, the company was pleasant, and the conversation was easy. When he'd first met Elliot, Nate never would have thought he'd fit in the way he had, let alone steal Jo's heart, but here they were.

Once they were gone, Liv helped him clean up, then collapsed on the couch. Goldi hopped up next to her. Nate hesitated to rearrange them but did, joining them so Liv's head rested in his lap and Goldi curled up on hers.

"So, Jo and Elliot," he said.

"If she'd told me she was quitting, I would have gone straight back to St. Vincent."

He laughed. "So, what's next?"

Her suspension was almost over. Only Trop had run in her absence. There was another race for Reba coming up.

"We could go visit Chique and Claire. And check in on the two-year-olds at home. Be back in time for Reba's race."

"Sounds like a plan. And the bigger picture?"

"Have Chique in foal to Extra Terra, Claire in foal to Just Jay, and both of them home again. Keep Kraken out of trouble. Take a serious stab at training the two-year-olds off the farm. See if any get to the races this year."

Her eyes were closed, and he thought she was falling asleep. Goldi was peaceful, still except for the gentle rise and fall of her breathing.

Liv opened her eyes, looking up into his. "And this fall, start Léa." She grinned.

He smiled back, then turned serious. "When you're ready to go back to riding, you know we'll make it work, right?"

"We need to find a trainer first. Unless you want to swap."

"How about Elliot?"

"I like Elliot, but no." She closed her eyes again. "It's not time yet. When we find the right person, it'll be time."

It felt like they were aligned again — complete. Their family might look a little different from others — the two of them, a calico cat, a quirky broodmare, and her cheeky colt. The dog would come. Maybe they'd choose it, maybe it would choose them.

With the horses, everything was changing, again. Jay and some of the older horses retiring, Reba and Cam now four-year-olds, no sophomore standout, but some exciting juveniles — and a fresh season of racing ahead.

They were ready for the next thing.

EPILOGUE

This landscape was glittering whites with pale gold accents, cool blue shadows and grey skeleton trees. Winter in Ontario wasn't ready to give up its hold, but change was in the air.

There was still frost in the ground, and a rogue snowstorm had dumped enough white stuff to cover the makeshift gallop in the hayfield, but the fresh smell of the air promised it was winter's last gasp. The worst was behind them and the dark, cold season was ending at last. It was easy to endure a freak storm when soon enough the trees would begin budding, daffodils pushing up through the soil, promising renewal. March was being March, but April was just around the corner.

The snow made for perfect footing. As soon as things thawed, they wouldn't be able to use the field until it dried out – which would be sometime in April if they were lucky, but more likely not until May.

This was real. The cold, the snow, the ice; the echo of words from her doubters and critics. But the snow and ice would melt, the sun would travel a higher arc through the sky, the days would get warmer. The keyboard warriors would lose steam, or — more likely — find new targets. The American Triple Crown was coming up. That was usually good for some drama.

The farm was as far from the spotlight as Liv could imagine; where all that really mattered in the moment was these young horses beneath them, standing side by side. No one to answer to but Fleur and Cash, her only goal to listen to them, tuning into the unspoken.

Liv glanced over. Nate had his eyes closed.

"Are you all right?" she asked.

"Just imagining I'm still lying on that beach instead of freezing my face in a frozen hayfield."

"Are you done now?"

Fleur, in that moment, reminded Liv of Claire more than her full sister, Chique. The dark bay filly was still but for the gentle rise and fall of her ribcage, waiting for Liv's direction. Cash was a chestnut mirror, the pair of youngsters as responsible as two nerdy students. Without a word, Nate tugged his goggles down over his eyes and steered Cash toward the incline, Fleur stepping up beside him.

Why was it sometimes a horse glommed onto a certain person? Liv had allowed herself that with Claire. She was expecting it with Léa. But Fleur she hadn't bargained on. Everything about Fleur was unexpected.

The filly floated as she jogged, as pretty as a hunter pony in a hack class. Liv rode shorter than she would have in a horse show, but the equitation was still there, hard-wired and honed, her posting economical. Considering Nate hadn't had a single lesson in his whole life, he looked damn fine on a horse, so she didn't know if the abuse she'd endured to reach such a level of precision had been worth it. But those scars had faded. In comparison, this winter's trials were nothing. The past would not hold her back.

They jogged once around before letting Fleur and Cash pop into an easy gallop. Nate started singing, "I would walk five hundred miles," and Liv laughed. Always a song.

She was counting the days until Chique and Claire returned from Kentucky. They'd traveled through on the way back from Florida to check on the two mares and their babies again, living their days in the bluegrass. Both were in foal, but they'd remain in Lexington until they reached the forty-five-day mark of their respective pregnancies. It was one of the checkpoints along the way; if a mare lost her pregnancy before that date, they normally came back in heat and could be bred again. After that point, it was less likely, and time to accept a breeding year had been lost. Breeding was a game of waiting, and wishing, and hoping.

They finished with a jog, then eased to a walk. Liv's phone rang, and she unzipped the pocket of her jacket and tugged it out, glancing at the screen, just in case it was something serious. Curiosity got the better of her, her eyebrows creeping up, and she answered it, noting Nate's worried expression. She couldn't blame him. She rarely answered the phone, though she couldn't get away with ignoring it as much these days as she used to. The tension in his face eased when she broke into a grin.

"Rory Anderson. How are things?"

"My things are good," came the voice on the other end of the line. "How are your things?"

She stifled a groan. She was out of practice talking to the cheeky Scot. "Fine, thanks. What can I do for you?"

"I was wondering if you might need an exercise rider. Stable hand. Dogsbody."

She laughed. "You might be in luck. We're restructuring."

She glanced at Nate, all traces of concern replaced now with a wry smile. "Give me a day or two?"

"Certainly. Thank you."

"Either way, I'm sure I can find someone deserving of your talents."

Rory chuckled. "I'd be most grateful."

When she hung up and tucked the phone away, Nate eyed her. "What are you thinking?"

"We do need more people."

"He'll need a place to live."

"I'm sure we can help him find something."

"The apartment's empty."

"True, but I'm not sure the farm girls are ready for the likes of Rory Anderson."

"You mean the other way around," Nate quipped. "I could give him some survival tips." Obviously he hadn't forgotten his early days, when he'd been the new guy, the object of their shameless attention.

They turned perpendicular to the path and stood again, facing across the snowy field. The wind that blew over it created small drifts in the expanse of white, but there was no doubt: spring was in the air.

"Warmed up now?" she asked him.

"Yeah. But I won't be for long if we don't head back to the barn soon."

Liv nodded, and they walked the two-year-olds to the gap in the fenceline. The path they took looped behind the broodmare barn, then past the large pastures where the yearlings lived: boys in one, girls in another. The colts charged up to the fence, bumping into each other as they walked along it before the body contact regressed into roughhousing. The fillies were more civilized. In their midst stood the striking dark bay, her crooked blaze bright against her mahogany coat.

Léa was still fuzzy in places, shiny in others where she'd begun to shed out. Her mane was too long and her tail still only reached her hocks. She was taller and rangier than her mother had been at the same age, that awkward stage between baby and adolescent. The proverbial diamond in the rough.

"This is it," Nate said.

"Hmm?" Liv pulled her eyes from the filly.

"Triple Stripe, the next generation?"

It felt like exactly that. A new era, full of promise and possibility. This was where she belonged, and she let herself believe that the best was yet to come.

THE END

THANK YOU!

For some reason, this book was a hard one to write. I had more than one serious battle with imposter syndrome along the way, and the real world of horse racing is dealing with a lot right now. As someone who grew up loving the sport, it's hard to watch what it's become.

I wanted to write something that was relevant. I did a lot of questioning. I don't have the answers. The bottom line is, it's not black and white, and this story is just a fictional "what if." I really admire the people who are trying to do things differently, despite what everyone else thinks.

A little background on the cover image — you might look at it and wonder why the horse is a bay, when the star of the book, Just Jay, is chestnut. I shot the reference photo for the painting at the paddock before the Queen's Plate one year. His name was "Took The Time," and while he didn't win, every time I remember him, I think of one of the problems with racing today. It takes a lot of time to do things "right," and not many people are willing to do that. A horse like Jay might have been passed over. I like to think that he became the champion he was because his people were willing to take the time.

But... the Good Things Come series is now at a crossroads. I could end it here. If you want to hear more about Liv and Nate and the horses, speak up! You can email me at linda@ lindashantz.com or leave a review. That one accomplishes two things — lets me know you want to read more, and lets other readers know about the series.

Either way, I still plan to publish Faye and Will's "happily ever after." It's called ***Shiny Little Things*** and takes place at Christmastime, the same year as ***Horse of the Year***. If you'd like to read the first chapter, you'll find it after the glossary.

Take care and, as always, thanks for reading.

Linda

PS - You can also join my Patreon to read as I write. While after ***Shiny Little Things*** I might take a break from publishing, I'll always be writing, and everything new will appear there first. Check it out with a seven-day trial to start. https://www.patreon.com/lindashantz/membership

If you'd like to stay up-to-date on all my writing news and can deal with me sharing pictures of my horses, sign up for my newsletter at www.lindashantz.com/writes

Curious about the music mentioned in the book and what I was listening to as I wrote Horse of the Year? Check out the playlist: https://spoti.fi/45u5okw

Scan the QR code for the **Horse of the Year** *playlist.*

GLOSSARY OF HORSE RACING AND OTHER TERMS

The world of horse racing has its own vocabulary, different from that of other parts of the equine world. Below are some of the more common terms used in this series, from my experience of thirty-five years. In most cases they are specific to North America, but may vary by region.

Exercise:

Back up - to warm up at a jog going the "wrong" way around the track (clockwise). Horse and rider must stay to the outside rail.

Blow out - a short work a few days before a race.

Break off - to start breezing or working, or for a pony to accompany a horse to the starting point (the pole).

Breeze - a timed speed workout at a true gallop where the horse runs without urging from the rider. Also used as a verb. Breezing is done close to the inner rail of the racetrack.

Gallop - daily conditioning; a gallop at the track is a three-beat gait which will vary in speed depending on the horse's training program, Galloping is done in the middle of the racetrack.

Hack - a leisurely walk.

Jog - trot, a two-beat gait, faster than a walk.

Leg up - to assist a rider to mount; also to bring a horse back into work after a layoff.

Rate - to control a horse's speed (to rate the pace).

Run - what racehorses do in a race. Harness horses race, Thoroughbreds run.

Tack the shed - to walk on the shedrow with a rider up. Can also be called "shedrowing" or "tack-walking." Often done when bringing a horse back into training or during poor weather.

Work - a timed speed workout; also used as a verb. Like breezing, working happens on the inside rail.

People around the track:

Bug (rider) - slang for an apprentice jockey. Apprentices receive lower weight assignments depending on their experience/races won, denoted by an asterisk in the program known as a "bug."

Exercise rider - person who rides the horse for daily exercise. They can either be on salary for a trainer, or freelance.

Gate crew/starter's assistants - people who load the horses into the starting gate and hold the horses until the race begins. They also help teach the horses how to be loaded. This is known as gate schooling and takes place at the end of morning training hours.

Groom - person who cares for the horse, including stall cleaning, grooming, putting on bandages and equipment, and taking them over for the races. Grooming is also known as "rubbing."

Hotwalker - person who walks the horse after training or a race, or on a day off from training. Other duties include holding horses for baths and cleaning up the barn area at the end of the morning.

Jockey - person who rides the horse in races and often for timed speed works in the morning. Commonly called a rider. Real racetrackers never use jockey as a verb or "jockeying" as a career.

Jockey's agent - person hired by jockey to connect with trainers in order to find a jockey horses to ride, both in the morning and afternoon.

Outriders - mounted racetrack officials who oversee proceedings from the time the horses leave the saddling area until the race goes off.

Pony person - mounted person who leads the horse onto the track, though the post parade and warmups, until it's time for the horse to be loaded in the starting gate.

Starter - official responsible for overseeing the horses as they are loaded, and determining when to open the gates.

Racing secretary - official responsible for putting together prospective races and deciding which races will be used.

Trainer - person responsible for overseeing the horse's training schedule, entering races, saddling on race days and making decisions based on all the above, including medications and other treatments. Trainers might be private (on salary for a single owner) or public (paid by a day rate per horse).

Assistant trainer - second in command to the trainer, able to step in to saddle the horse on race days if needed. Daily responsibilities will vary depending on the trainer.

Places around the track

Backstretch - racetrack's stable area; also the part of the racetrack on the far side of the track (parallel to but opposite of the "home stretch." Also called the "backside."

Clubhouse turn - first turn after the finish line.

Chute - extension of the homestretch or backstretch which allows a straight start for a race (instead of placing the gate on a turn).

Gap - literally, a gap in the rail that encloses the track which allows horses on ("on-gap") and off (off-gap).

Paddock - area to which horses are brought to be saddled (saddling enclosure) and where the jockeys mount (walking ring).

Shedrow, shed – At the racetrack, shedrow-style barn has a block of stalls back to back, with a covered (and usually enclosed outer walkway around the outside. The shedrow (often shortened to shed) is a section of a shedrow-style barn assigned to an individual trainer. It's common to refer to people or horses being "on the shed," which refers to the aisle/walkway.

Test barn – controlled area for selected horses to be cooled out under supervision after a race, after which samples will be taken for drug testing. Normally 2-3 horses are tested per race, including the winner.

Equipment

Blinkers - hood worn with plastic cups to limit a horse's vision and improve focus.

Irons - stirrup irons.

Brace bandage - support bandage sometimes used during training. These are a stretchy Ace-type bandage. At the track using boots is rare.

Knot - racing lines (reins) are long, so the rider will tie a knot in the end to shorten them for safety reasons.

Leathers - stirrup leathers.

Lines - racetrack term for reins. They're an inch thick, have rubber grips, and are much longer than riding horse reins.

Neck strap - a loop of leather for added safety - something to grab if a horse misbehaves or if the bridle breaks. During training it is part of the martingale (and so attached to the girth) but in a race it is unattached (and not all trainers equip their horses with them).

Polos - soft bandages used during training to protect a horse from superficial injuries. At the track using boots is rare.

Rundowns - bandages applied, normally to the hind lower limb, to protect the back of the fetlock from burning as a horse runs.

Shadow roll - a noseband covered in thick sheepskin (usually synthetic) used to limit a horse's vision and improve focus.

Shank - lead shank, aka lead line, typically made of leather. Chain shank - lead shank with a chain at one end. Paddock shank - lead shank with only a snap at one end.

Sheet - a lightweight blanket. A quarter-sheet is a light blanket (usually wool or artificial fleece) that covers the horse's hindquarters during training when the weather is colder.

Standing bandage - bandages applied after training either to assist in holding topical leg treatments in place or for protection. Most horses are also shipped in bandages. Consists of two parts - an inner "cotton" for padding, held in place by a flannel (non-stretchy) or nylon bandage. Some people call them "wraps."

Race types:

Allowance - a race for which the racing secretary has set out certain conditions, such as the weight the horses will carry depending on their age, sex, past performance.

Claiming race/claimer - a race in which each horse can be bought for a specific price (= tag). The higher the claiming price, the better the quality of horse.

Condition race - after a horse had "broken" its maiden (ie won its first race) they can be entered in a series of races with specific conditions, ie, non winners of a race other than maiden or claiming, non-winners of two races other than maiden or claiming, non-winners of three races. Completing each step is known as running a horse through its conditions. Once they've accomplished that, races become more competitive and harder to win.

Condition book - booklet published every two weeks which lists prospective races trainers can enter.

Conditions - the criteria of a race, including distance, type of track, weights to be carried, purse money, restrictions (ie place of birth, sex, age).

Graded stake - a selected group of stakes races given a rating (one, the highest, through three), depending on the prestige of said race. Called Group races outside of North America.

Maiden - a type of race in which horses who have never won a race run. A race can be "Maiden Allowance, Maiden Claiming or Maiden Special Weight" depending on how good the horse is expected to be. Also, a horse who has yet to win a race. A horse winning its first race is said to "break its maiden."

Stakes/stake race - race for which nomination and entry fees are paid (also known as "added-money" races for that reason). They generally attract a higher class of race.

Terms that didn't quite fit elsewhere:

Ankle - what racetrack people call the fetlock joint, the joint between the hoof and the "knee."

Century home - historical designation in Canada for a house that is, you guessed it, over a hundred years old.

Cross - to "take a cross" is to cross the lines (reins) over each other so the rider is holding both lines, making it easier to control the horse. Called a "bridge" outside of racing.

Doing up — daily ritual performed by the groom after training each day and after a race that involves hoof care, application of leg treatments (liniment, sweats, poultice), bandaging and grooming.

Form - a horse's past performance; also short for The Daily Racing Form, a newsprint publication with the past performances off all horse racing in an area on a particular day.

Knee - carpal joint, anatomically equivalent to the human wrist.

Lay up - a horse resting from the track or rehabilitating from a track injury.

Longe - British spelling more commonly written as "lunge" in North America. A training exercise in which the horse travels in a circle on the end of a twenty-foot line while the handler pivots in the centre.

Pony - racetrackers refer to anything that is not a racehorse as a pony, regardless of size. Track ponies help escort horses from the paddock to the starting gate and also help with morning training. Also called "pony horse," "stable pony."

Rub - to groom; to care for a racehorse.

School - to train.

Start - to introduce a young horse to saddle. Usually a sixty-day period where the horse will progress to learning how to gallop. Also known as "breaking" though it is normally a very slow, gentle process.

Tag - claiming price.

Toque - a knit hat humans wear, typically in winter.

Thoroughbred Life stages:

Sire - father; "by" the sire.

Dam - mother; "out of" the dam.

Foal - from newborn to weaning time (aka suckling).

Weanling - from weaning time (5-7 months old).

Yearling - in North America, from January 1 following the horse's birth until the next January 1, regardless of actual birthdate.

Filly - female from birth through age four.

Mare - female five years and up; when used for breeding becomes broodmare.

Colt - male from birth through age four or until castrated.

Horse - male five years and up unless castrated.

Stallion - male used for breeding.

Gelding - castrated male of any age.

This list is in no way complete. If I've left out words you think would be beneficial to include, I welcome your input!

NEXT UP

SHINY LITTLE THINGS

CHAPTER ONE

"Ooh, shiny."

Emilie placed a hand on Faye's forearm, and Faye followed her friend reluctantly to the jewellery store with a glance at her phone. They didn't have time for window shopping, not really, but there was no point in deterring Emilie. Faye could spare a few moments to humour her friend.

The display windows facing into the mall's main aisle were filled with beautiful things. Faye peered cautiously over Emilie's shoulder. Emilie and her boyfriend hadn't even been together for six months yet, and she was already gushing over engagement rings. Faye had been with Will for over two years, and they avoided the 'm' word as if it were the most dreaded outcome on earth.

"I love that one. Isn't it exquisite?" Emilie pointed to a brilliant diamond with offset sapphires and a white gold band. "But I adore the classic simplicity of that one."

The stones were pretty, sure. And if someone gave Faye one to wear, she'd do so for the pure beauty alone, if not for what it symbolized. Except Faye had stopped wearing her rings a few months into taking over the café she operated. She worried about misplacing them, having to remove them as she worked flour and crumbled butter into scones, so now they stayed safely in her mother's old box on top of her dresser. She had to remind herself to put them on these days, for those rare occasions she went out.

"Which one do you like?" Emilie persisted.

Faye sighed and played along. Who was she to tarnish the joy of a young woman still feeling the glow of new love? It wasn't Emilie's fault that glow of infatuation had worn off her relationship with Will.

She ran her gaze over the various sets wondering how a girl would choose, and couldn't help drifting to the price tag on each one. As much as she admitted before Will she'd dreamed, on occasion, of a man who would lavish her with expensive gifts — who didn't? — she'd never understand why someone would spend that kind of money on a trinket. Some of these rings cost more than her car had, and she'd bet she got a lot more mileage out of the car than these rings would see. Her used Toyota Corolla might be rusting out with a vengeance, but that engine would go on forever.

Nonetheless, one caught her eyes and she couldn't pull them away. It was gorgeous; a simple but flowing design, the rose gold setting accenting a white gold band. The round diamond was modest, but intricately cut so it almost looked like a tiny dahlia.

"That one," she said, pressing her finger to the glass, the heat and oils of the pad leaving a ghost of a print on its smooth surface when she withdrew it. A strange warmth encased her heart; an odd, momentary thing. Did she like the idea? Did some deep part of her long for what it represented, when her head denied it?

She forced the sentiment away and turned to Emilie, letting a smile play on her lips. "Your turn."

Her friend scanned the display, a finger resting on her lips, and Emilie wandered to the next case then back to the first one and tapped her nail against the transparent barrier opposite the simple solitaire she'd commented on earlier.

"That one."

Emilie's boyfriend Tim was a professional hockey player. A rookie, but still, he could probably afford one of the larger stones, and just might be the kind of guy who would go for one — like it would be his introverted way to show how much he loved her — but it didn't surprise Faye that Emilie opted for something more practical. That was Emilie; the only thing she splurged on was expensive coffee and pastry. Even her horse had only cost a dollar.

Speaking of… "I need caffeine and sugar. You in?"

Emilie's head snapped from the rings, back to reality. "Absolutely."

Faye glanced at her phone again as they settled at one of the sticky tables in the food court, but there were no notifications. They were going to run right smack into Toronto rush hour traffic now on the drive home. There was no avoiding it, so they might as well take a moment.

There had been a time, not all that long ago, when a Christmas shopping trip to the city would have been a highlight for Faye, but right now all that flooded her mind, leaving a prickly residue of resentment, was that this would be her last day off from the café until December twenty-fifth, and she could think of better ways of spending it than dealing with crowds of harried parents dragging crying kids, overtired salespeople and tinned holiday music. This is what online shopping was for.

But it was her little tradition with Emilie, and they'd missed last year because last December, Emile's life had been the insanely busy one. And spending time with Emilie was always fun, though Faye could have had just as much fun with her friend without leaving the comfort of the small town of King City where they both lived.

I must be getting old.

"What do we have left to do?" Faye asked as she nibbled a cranberry white chocolate square. She made a copycat for her own shop. It hadn't been hard to figure out the recipe. Her version was better.

Emilie had opted to pack both the sugar and caffeine into her beverage, an industrial-sized gingerbread latte. "I just have one more thing. I'll go back to that little kiosk by the department store for one of those nice toques for Nate. Just to rub it in at Christmas that he hasn't gone to Florida yet." Emilie's sister- and brother-in-law usually headed south for the winter early in December with the racehorses they worked with. This year they'd promised to stay until after the holiday. "What about you?"

"I might grab one for Dean, too — then he'll be done," Faye said, sipping her cappuccino. It also wasn't as good as the ones she made at Triple Shot, but would do its part for her mid-afternoon pick-me-up.

It was a relief when they finally agreed they were finished and trekked to the parking lot laden with their purchases. The mall was so busy, even on a weekday, they'd had to park far from the entrance. What would it be like two weeks from now? Faye shuddered to think. At least they were ahead of the last-minute madness.

Emilie's red Honda Civic was hard to spot — it didn't look very red right now with its layer of brown road slush. Snowflakes falling in slow motion from the grey sky tried to lend a festive atmosphere, a thin layer accumulating on the windshield, but it wasn't quite doing the job for Faye.

As soon as Emilie left the highway forty minutes later, the little Civic decelerating as she took the off-ramp onto King Sideroad — traffic could have been a lot worse — Faye felt her blood pressure drop. There was more snow up here and though the highway had been clear, the ploughs hadn't been out yet. The farm would be pretty with a blanket of white, the vision of it making her eager to get home and take her dog for a walk; decompress.

Yes, I really am getting old.

Emilie pulled up to the café, set in a small strip mall. Faye's Corolla waited loyally under a cosy blanket of white. She'd need more than a swish of the wiper blades to clear her windshield.

"Call me if you need help with anything," Emilie said as Faye transferred her bags from one car to the other.

"Thanks, Em. I will." Faye smiled with a small wave before swinging the door shut and watched as Emilie drove the short jaunt down the road to the physiotherapy clinic for her evening shift.

Emilie's words were merely a nicety. This was one of the busiest times of the year for her friend, as the racing season wound down. When Emilie wasn't at her job or riding, she was helping with the local Thoroughbred retirement group, ensuring all the racehorses had somewhere safe to go. Things would slow down for Emilie in the week leading up to Christmas though, and Faye would gladly call on her then as her own life got a thousand times more hectic.

The "closed" sign was flipped on the door of the Triple Shot Café, but Faye unlocked it and slipped in, just to give it a walk-through and prepare a couple of things to make tomorrow morning easier. Everything was dark, the only sound the hum of the large refrigerator in the kitchen. She flipped on the kitchen lights, finishing her tasks before retracing her steps through the front of the shop in the dim light from the parking lot. Once she'd locked up, she shuffled to the car, letting it warm up while she brushed off the blanket of snow, then headed home.

When she reached the farmhouse Gus waited for her, his fluffy Golden Retriever ears flopping as he bounced on his forepaws. Faye stomped the snow from her boots inside the back door. She wasn't deceiving herself — it wasn't so much her arrival as what came next that made Gus so happy. She changed out of her shopping clothes into sweats and sweaters, dragged on her less-fashionable long, puffy coat, and tugged a knit hat down to cover her ears now that she didn't care what her hair looked like. The crisp air would clear her mind of the building pressure.

It was a beautiful evening. Nights like this she didn't mind winter so much. And Faye was looking forward to a break from the business once the rush was over; a quiet Christmas after working long hours to make the holiday better for others. By then she wouldn't care if she ate takeout, though she wasn't sure how Will and her older brother Dean would feel about that. She was closing for three whole days, a respite before the demands of New Year's Eve and Day, and she couldn't wait to just sit around reading a good book with a glass of wine, letting Dean talk her into a game of Scrabble while Will picked his guitar in the corner. Then, after New Year's, with any luck, January would be relatively quiet. A time for plotting and planning for the months ahead. A time to rejuvenate.

Autumn had been unusually cold; the ground frozen before the first snowfall. The guys were excited because the farm's pond was already solid, planning their own open air hockey game for Boxing Day. Faye wasn't a sports person; never had been, but there was something charming about a group of grown men reliving their childhoods on an outdoor rink. Of course, the women in their ranks — other than Faye — would not be content to cheer and sip hot chocolate on the sidelines like she would. Emilie and her sister, Faye's best friend Liv, were scrambling through old boxes in their garage for skates that hadn't seen action since they'd left Montreal.

A shovel rested against the old willow tree that hung over the pond and Faye picked it up and shimmied down to the frozen surface, two inches of fresh powder giving it a uniform cover. Shuffling carefully, she pushed the sharp edge through the fluff to the firmness of the ice beneath and began clearing. This much she could do. It would be her contribution. Well, that and being in charge of refreshments, as always. Gus the Golden alternated between sniffing rabbit tracks and bounding up to bite the shovel.

Gus didn't mind that they weren't out for long, racing to his food bowl as soon as they were in the house again, looking expectantly from the stainless steel dish to Faye and back again while she removed her outerwear. Dogs were lucky, not needing all the gear to have fun outdoors. Her face flushed and burned as it warmed and she poured herself a glass of water after doling out his dinner.

Other than the sound of Gus snarfing up the last of his kibble, the house was silent. Her brother Dean, with whom she'd shared the old Victorian since he'd returned after their parents' death, was out, and Will was staying in the city tonight. Faye wasn't hungry and carefully contemplated what to do with this precious spare time.

Left with that strange combination of warmth and chill after her walk, she decided on a bath – a rare indulgence these days — and climbed the steps to her room, determined to cherish every moment and every thing: the foaming water, the quiet space, the solitude. A little taste of paradise.

There was nothing fancy about the old bathroom, but one thing she loved most about this old farmhouse was its vintage tub. Cranking the hot water so the room was soon steaming, she poured in bath oil and suds, the mere smell of the combination relaxing. With her hair piled on her head, Faye slowly inched her way into the scalding depths, setting her skin on fire.

Bliss.

She loved the boneless, sleepy feeling it left her with when she climbed out; the knowledge she could pat herself dry, slip into cosy flannel PJs, crawl into bed and give into it. Before she turned off the light, though, the bouquet caught her eye. It always did.

The flowers were dried now, almost a year later, dust clinging to the petals. It wasn't as if she could clean them. And it wasn't as if she could throw them out. She wished the desiccated bunch was only a sweet reminder of her friend Liv's special day: the beautiful beach wedding. Instead, it was a taunt. An insinuation.

But as much as tossing them in the garbage the way Liv had fast-pitched the fresh flowers at her after the ceremony would feel so good, it would also seem disrespectful — both to Liv, and what the flowers stood for.

Faye didn't disapprove of marriage; she'd just never pictured herself in a white dress, standing in front of friends making a public profession of her feelings for someone. That said, she'd never pictured Liv doing it either. To be fair, it hadn't, nor would it ever have been Liv's idea, but she'd gone through with it just the same — and Faye hadn't heard a peep of regret.

Faye would bide her time, and it would pass. The "When are you and Will getting married?" questions would taper off. She loved Will; didn't want to be with anyone else. But she didn't need to wear the white dress or have the big party to prove her commitment. All that money would be better used for something else. Investing in the business. Or a new vehicle, when the day came her faithful old Toyota needed to be retired.

She'd never had a lot of money. She'd learned how to be a smart shopper so she had nice clothes. Nice-ish things, so she could be stylish without going broke. It made no sense to spend that kind of cash on a show any more than it did on the shiny ring. It wasn't as if it guaranteed the success of a relationship. No matter the expense of the wedding, a couple's odds were still fifty-fifty. Most of those folks who put on those lavish events probably would have been better off doing something lower key and investing the rest in a savings account to pay for couples' therapy — or lawyer's fees — when things went sideways.

She could have married rich. Could still, if that's what she wanted. Finding a rich man in the racehorse world was like shooting fish in a barrel. She had the skills and assets. But money could only do so much. Faye had seen it come and go in her life, but one thing endured. Love.

And lack of love wasn't the problem with her and Will. They were happy. They could go on like this indefinitely. And why not? There was nothing wrong with it. Was there?

Expect **Shiny Little Things** *in the fall of 2023. Sign up for my newsletter to be notified when the pre-order goes live:* https://www.lindashantz.com/writes

ACKNOWLEDGMENTS

Thank you, thank you, thank you to my beta readers for taking the time out of your own very busy lives to read.

Beta readers keep me on track with details and readability and help catch stray typos (though some inevitably make it through, so if you see one, don't be shy about emailing me). Allison Litfin, Adeline Halvorson, Bev Harvey, Andrea Harrison, June Monteleone, Ariana Feldberg, and Mary Hatheway — I'm so grateful for all of you.

Thanks to fellow writer Kirsty Davis as well, for the perspective of a non-horse person, and being willing to jump into the story without having read any of the other books. Your input was invaluable!

Thanks to my patrons on Patreon! Your support is so wonderful to have.

And thanks to Sarah LaFrance for proofreading. I insisted on clinging to my Canadian spelling (as I've done throughout the series) and a few other things, so that's all on me and not a reflection of Sarah's proofreading skills. It also bears mentioning that I quizzed my fellow Canadians and we all have the same hybrid spelling, a combination of UK and US English. Canadians are weird! For the record, Sarah is Canadian, so she understands!

I'd also like to thank my friend Lorna Perkins, a former trainer, for answering random texts with questions about different situations. The crazy training stuff is mine though, so please don't blame her!

Thanks as well to Sharon Tomlinson for sharing insight on racing at Ascot.

I'm sure I'm forgetting someone, and I apologize for that! If you're reading this, thank you, too! I hope you'll consider leaving a review to share your thoughts with other readers. You can also email me at the address below.

If you're interested in joining my review team for future books, email me at linda@lindashantz.com

And last but most important, thank you, Lord. You are my only hope.

ABOUT THE AUTHOR

I began working at the racetrack before I finished high school, and after graduating the following January, took a hotwalking job at Payson Park in Florida. Once back at Woodbine, I started grooming and galloping. While the backstretch is exciting, I found I was more at home on the farm – prepping and breaking yearlings, nightwatching and foaling mares. Eventually I started my own small layup/broodmare facility, and in the last few years I've transitioned into retraining and rehoming. Somewhere along the way I did go back to school and get a degree. I should probably dust it off and frame it one day!

I live on a small farm in Ontario, Canada, with my adopted off-track Thoroughbreds and a young Border Collie. If you like my covers, check out my artwork at www.lindashantz.com

Author photo by Kyley Woods Photography, used with permission.

Printed in Great Britain
by Amazon